The Silver Spider

Who will claim the prize?

by N. Slavinski

Rolling Hitch Press

Copyright © 2017 Nadine Slavinski

All rights reserved.

Cover art by Lizaa

ISBN: 978-0982771464

Contents

On Location in Panama		iii
Prologue		1
1	A Taste of Adventure	5
2	A Breath of Possibility	23
3	A Tribe of Sailors	45
4	The Treasure Chest of the Americas	67
5	A River of Riches	87
6	Cowboys and Robbers	107
7	Lotto del Mar	123
8	A Bold New Enterprise	145
9	Out of the Frying Pan	165
10	Shadow and Substance	183
11	The Stuff of Legends	207
12	A Cloud of Reality	225
13	A Change in Plan	247
14	Hunger Drives the Wolf	269
15	New Acquaintances	281

16 A Game of Chess	305
17 Gentlemen and Thieves	319
18 Time to Say Good-bye	335
19 Into the Maelstrom	355
20 Burial at Sea	379
21 Light-years Away	401
22 Pandora's Box	417
23 A Sly Fox	439
24 Into the Sunset	453
A Note from the Author	459
About the Author	461

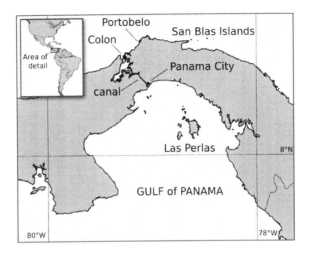

On Location in Panama

This is a work of fiction. Names, characters, and businesses are either the products of the author's imagination or used in a fictitious manner. While many of the characters in this story were inspired by a combination of colorful characters from the sailing world, no single character matches a real person on a one-to-one basis. Locations and sailing details, on the other hand, are all true-to-life based on the author's personal experiences as an archaeologist and as a sailor visiting both coasts of Panama. Every effort has been made to remain true to the history of Panama, although fictional characters have been inserted for narrative purposes.

Prologue

Portobelo, Panama
June 1667

"To hell with the treasure."

Pedro spat the words into the inky Caribbean night. Sixteen miserable months were finally coming to an end. Sixteen months of cursing every sweltering day and every haunted night. Pedro had had his fill of claustrophobic watchtowers and hellish barracks. He never wanted to trudge the jungle trail across the isthmus again, guarding riches in the name of the king. He'd had such high hopes for his posting in the New World but none of it was what he'd been promised. Nothing was what he had imagined.

Today, though, was a day to celebrate. Pedro was on his way home — a day he hadn't been sure he'd live to see. The ship was already weighing anchor, ready to carry him away from purgatory. He could almost taste the civilized soil of Spain, drink the clean air of home.

He swatted a mosquito and contemplated the body before rolling it between his fingers then flicking it aside. His last mosquito in the New World: a minor triumph. He would never lose another drop of blood to this godforsaken land again.

And the treasure? To hell with the treasure. Just getting away was enough. Soon, he would be a free man, still poor but alive and wiser for all the mistakes he had made — including his decision to leave Spain in the first place.

His fingernails dug into the wood of the rail as he pictured his lost treasure. Even as a memory, the silver and gold taunted him. He could still feel the hard edges and hear the heavy clink of precious metal in his pockets. And not just coins but figurines, too. Curved, graceful shapes molded from solid gold and finely worked silver. Some beautiful, some ghoulish, like that awful spider.

He scowled into the night. All that treasure, left behind. Would some poor bastards come along and discover it someday? Would it curse them the way it had cursed him?

The ship creaked as the sails filled, ready to put leagues of ocean between him and the New World. Pedro gave himself a shake. To hell with the treasure. All that mattered was that he was on his way out.

No, he corrected himself, *I am already gone.*

The thought inspired a broad smile, the first since he'd laid his greedy hands on that glittering loot. Ignoring the silver shimmer of the sea, he looked ahead, trying to put the nightmare behind him. With the salt air scouring his skin clean, he could almost pretend none of this had ever happened.

Almost.

He spat again for good measure, but the bitter aftertaste remained.

Chapter One

A Taste of Adventure

San Blas Islands, Panama
December, not too long ago...

The thing about life on a sailboat was that every day brought a new surprise.

Nick wasn't sure that was always a good thing.

He smacked a mosquito, hunched back over his work, and sighed.

Lovely place, Panama. Rain, bugs, pollution. And broken parts, starting with today's first surprise, the anchor windlass. On a good day, it would hoist the anchor on cue. On a bad day, it would groan, wheeze, and grind to a halt. *Aurora* was a home that demanded constant repairs to stay afloat, sometimes literally. Forget palm-lined islands and turquoise water — some days were all about scraped knuckles and greasy parts.

And so far, today was one of those days. He had read more manuals than novels lately — one of the joys of owning a thirty-year-old boat. Maybe that fisherman who cackled at him back in Gloucester was right: *pretty boat — pretty old, har-har!*

But life certainly could be worse. Six months ago, he wasn't just repairing his tired old sailboat, but freezing his tail off. A little lonely, too. Things had taken a turn for the better when Kate had joined him aboard *Aurora*, the little sloop that was now his floating home. It was all quite a change from his apartment in Boston.

"Are you nuts?" his sister had screeched.

Maybe he was. Buying a boat and sailing off into the sunset had definitely been the most impulsive decision of his life. It had all sounded so easy at the time, though the reality was a repair list from here to the equator.

Yeah, definitely a little nuts. But every good sailor was, right?

Anyway, it was hard to beat his cockpit workshop, surrounded by an endless moat of reefy greens and startling blues melting together like watercolors on wet paper. The little island just a coconut's throw away was the perfect pirate hideaway, complete with the requisite palms. Kate, with her orange snorkel, swam past, slicing through the water like a fish. He and she had both quit their jobs and checked out of the rat race, figuring they could stretch their modest savings for a year or maybe even two of the nomadic sailing life.

Kate would grin in satisfaction at the thought. As for him, well... He still hadn't made up his mind.

Sometimes, it really was idyllic. Unrushed days, tropical nights. Quiet anchorages all to themselves. But it was a fleeting kind of peace. Just when he was tempted to give in to the soft comfort of it all, something changed. A subtle shift in wind direction could expose an anchorage to the elements. New places and people disturbed the equilibrium of his world. Small, hidden secrets schemed quietly away until outing themselves as big trouble one fateful day. Today the anchor windlass, tomorrow — who knew?

He sniffed the air uncertainly. If only he shared Kate's wild optimism about surprises that lay over the horizon.

He put down the cylindrical windlass a little too quickly and winced as a line of oil smeared the white cockpit. Yet another blemish on his sleeping beauty of a boat. He averted his eyes and ducked into the cabin, hoping to excavate a miracle tool from one of the lockers hidden in every crevice of the boat. Three steps forward, and he was nearly at the end of the cabin. Two more and he'd be in the forepeak bunk. Thirty-two feet of sailboat wasn't much space to lose things in, but he still managed. Even after six months aboard *Aurora*, he still hadn't gotten through all her mysteries.

"One of these days," he muttered, "I'm getting rid of half this junk."

He rummaged around in the port locker where oversized tools slumbered along with lengths of old cable, unidentified spares, and tubes of sealant — most of it inherited from the boat's previous owner, and the one before that, and the one before that.

"Get rid of half, starting with this."

He picked up a battered cardboard box — the one his aunt Laura had sent for him to keep on a boat that was already bursting at the seams. She was just one of many well-meaning family members who had sent him good-bye gifts completely unsuited for a sailboat — like the wall calendar and electric espresso machine he had left back in Maine. Still, he had to smile. When everyone else had muttered about ruined careers and overreactions, Laura sent him a pair of trashy pirate novels along with a small wooden box and a note about old Grandpa So-and-so's adventures way back when in Panama.

In light of more pressing matters — like keeping the boat afloat — he had never found the time to do more than glance at the contents of that package. Now, he brought it up into the shade of the cockpit along with the puller he needed. He'd have another go at the repair, then sort through that musty old box. Then he could finally get rid of that junk and make space for more useful objects.

* * *

Thirty sweaty minutes later, a splash at *Aurora's* stern pulled him away from the windlass. Kate climbed the swim ladder into the cockpit, water streaming off her skin.

"How's it going?" she chirped.

Half an hour of grunting over various tools and he'd only just cracked the cover of the windlass. Going? It was amazing that he hadn't chucked the entire thing overboard. Yet.

Nick was about to comment about the salt water dripping dangerously close to the toolbox but refrained. The green and blue bikini was a new part of Kate's wardrobe, and she was looking awfully good in it. He was more used to seeing her in a one-piece racing suit, churning the lanes of a pool in a never-ending competition with some undefined adversary. Her lean, lanky body and blue eyes were the same, but the hard edge had grown a little softer. Maybe it was time for a little perspective. How bad was his life when his greatest frustration was a pesky little windlass? And his crew was his ex-ex-girlfriend, now back in his life?

"Could be worse," he decided, resting the windlass motor on his thigh.

She cast a disapproving eye at the toolbox. "I thought we said we'd fix the windlass tomorrow."

He bit his lip. "I guess I thought I'd give it a quick try."

"We said we'd snorkel today and work on the boat tomorrow."

He knew that look clouding her face. The one she used to flash on weekends back home when he'd lapse into work instead of relaxing. Kate was the one hell-bent on living for the present. Hell, it had taken her about two minutes to quit her job and come sailing. The same decision had agonized him for weeks. And here he was, once again giving in to the compulsion to put work before pleasure. A capital offense in Kate's book.

"Old habits die hard," he admitted, quietly sliding the toolbox aside with a foot. "But it would be nice to have a working windlass, don't you think?"

Kate shrugged, then brightened again and gave his knee an encouraging tap. "We can always pull up the anchor by hand."

He had no trouble picturing her doing that, sweating and hauling to prove that she could, even if it meant a torn muscle or two.

"Anyway, I saw these amazing starfish!" she said, launching into a detailed description of her snorkeling adventures that catapulted from grazing sea turtles to offhand suggestions regarding dinner. The words flowed over him in an undulating wave as she stepped below, still dripping and talking. That was the thing about Kate: no shortage of energy or enthusiasm. She reemerged with two glasses of water.

"What's this?" She nudged the cardboard box.

"Remember my aunt, Laura?"

"How could I forget?" Kate grinned and wriggled her wrists, mimicking Laura's jangling bracelets. They were practically a part of his aunt, along with her huge, beaded necklaces. Kate and Laura had immediately hit it off when they'd met. While other people discussed topics like interest rates and politics, the two of them waxed poetic about travel, obscure musical instruments, and endangered species.

"Whoa!" Kate cried as she sifted through the box, holding up the pirate novels. "Two, even!" Then she pulled out a small wooden box and turned it over in her hands. "Nice," she murmured, examining the masterfully pieced cigar box with ornate metal hinges.

She held it up to her nose and then his. He caught the faint scent of tobacco, mingled with something else. A whiff of the past, maybe.

He stretched his legs out under the table until they nuzzled Kate's. "Laura said her grandfather worked in Panama, so she sent some of his things."

"Her grandfather..." Kate worked at the clasp of the cigar box. "So, that's your mother's grandfather, too..."

He nodded. "My great-grandfather. I guess Laura thought his stuff might be interesting."

He couldn't see how, but Kate was sure to discover something in there. Leave it to an archaeologist to find treasure amidst the trash.

Kate lifted a slim batch of letters bound with string, revealing a natty old rabbit's foot and a small notebook with a worn leather cover. She read from the nearly illegible script scrawled over the inside of the box lid. "Charlie Parker." She tilted it toward him, and he saw a crossed-out series of addresses. "Cincinnati. Rapid City. Whitehorse. San Francisco. Ka... Kafue. Where's that?"

He shrugged.

"Cristobal," she finished. "Charlie really lived in all those places?"

He nodded, not half as impressed as Kate seemed to be. "Charlie did all kinds of wild things. One crazy scheme after another. Something in Africa, then gold mining someplace, then Panama. But Laura and my mother never actually met him. He died before they were born. My mother always said the stories were exaggerated."

"Exaggerated? Everything about Panama is exaggerated. And it's all true."

He had to give her that one.

She read a date from the notebook. "1911." Her eyes flickered. "Hey, if he worked in Panama in 1911, did he work on the canal?"

"Depends who you listen to. Laura says yes, but my mom said he was full of tall tales."

"Like what?"

"All kinds of stuff. Crazy adventures."

"*Two* interesting members of your family?" She looked up with a crooked smile. "Hard to believe. What kind of adventures?"

He flapped a hand in the air. "Shipwrecks. Buried treasure. That kind of thing. Mom didn't believe a word of it."

Kate, he could see, was already racing away with the exotic parts of the story and ignoring the cautions. What was that she was muttering?

"Buried treasure? Shipwrecks?"

He glanced up, but Kate was back to studying the notebook, her face inscrutable again.

Cristobal, Panama
April 1910

Charlie Parker pulled the sweaty cotton of his shirt away from his skin and squinted against the afternoon sun. Even Rhodesia hadn't been this hot. Still, it beat April in the Yukon.

Charlie chuckled. His most amusing conversations were usually the ones he had with himself — something that occurred even more often here in Panama, a split-personality country if ever there was one.

He shifted the bag holding his few possessions from one shoulder to the other and scanned the crowd outside the train station. It could have been the rush-hour scene in any North American city if it wasn't for the palm trees, the crushing humidity, and a few incongruous details, like the man carrying a briefcase in one hand and a monkey on his shoulder. Another man wore muddy coveralls and walked with a heavy limp. The woman who met him with a kiss picked a jungle leaf from his hair. Two men with soot-blackened faces but perfectly clean hands were talking baseball. They were all heading home from another day's work on the world's most ambitious engineering project. Charlie couldn't wait to get started himself.

But first, he had to find Douglas Whatshisname.

"Charles Parker?"

Charlie whirled beside the clock tower outside the bustling station and found a trim, neatly pressed man. He drew back just a little bit, searching for an escape route. Just in case.

"I'm Douglass Browning of the Philadelphia Brownings," the man said, extending a hand. "Douglass with two S's," he added with a quick adjustment of his bow tie. "Pleased to meet you."

The new roommate. Oh, boy.

Charlie extended a hand. "Charlie Parker, of the Nosy Parkers. One C, one E."

"Ready to build a canal?"

"Born ready." Charlie nodded firmly, looking forward to hearing more about the project.

But as Douglass ushered him away from the city center, all he did was enthuse about social activities.

"We'll keep you busy here in Panama, don't worry about that. There's so much to do in Cristobal! On Tuesdays, there's bowling." Douglass rubbed his hands in anticipation. "Annual membership at the YMCA is ten dollars and well worth it, mind you me! There's a reading room, even a library. A touch of civilization in the wilderness."

Charlie made a mental note to give the YMCA a wide berth.

"This Wednesday, the art section of the Cristobal Women's Club presents their latest exhibition."

Charlie's mind amused itself with various interpretations of the word *exhibition*.

"On Thursday, there's cooking club, then the IOPK meeting..."

"The IOKK?"

Douglass looked scandalized. "IOPK. You don't know about the Independent Order of Panamanian Kangaroos?" He pointed to the embroidered insignia on his jacket.

Charlie scrutinized it, then Douglass' face. The man looked dead serious.

"I could sponsor you as a new member!" Douglass added, looking awfully pleased with himself.

No kangaroos, Charlie vowed. The annual Lions Club picnic was bad enough, back home when he was a boy. He'd always devoted that afternoon to engineering elaborate toilet pranks. So, no — definitely no kangaroos. And anyway, wasn't Panama supposed to be teeming with crocodiles and snakes? So far, he hadn't seen a single one. On the contrary, if a lone mosquito made an appearance, an entire hit squad of armed men were sent to dispatch it and bring in the body like an exotic trophy. No, Panama was not turning out to be quite what he hoped for.

"On alternate weeks, of course, there's the K of P meeting."

Knights of Panama? Charlie wasn't sure he wanted to know.

"The Knights of Pythias." Douglass gave the haughty nod of an insider.

Charlie pictured a host of tropical knights in rusty armor, lances tangled in jungle vines. A metaphor for the canal builders themselves?

"What's your job here?" he asked.

"Oh, I work in the Department of Social Affairs." Douglass stretched his slight frame and smiled modestly.

"Would never have guessed."

"And what division have you been assigned to?" Douglass asked.

"Engineer," he said, awash in disjointed memories of railroads, bridges, and dams in various corners of the globe.

They reached an open area of identical buildings that could only be the housing area. Douglass Browning's voice dropped as they walked past a three-story building with screened verandas on all sides.

"That's House 47," he noted with a heavy undertone.

A bottle flew out a door and smashed on the walkway, followed by hoots of raucous laughter and shouted obscenities.

"Probably playing cards," Douglass muttered. "And gambling! It's the rough-neck house," he whispered, glaring at the still beside the back door.

Sounds good to me, Charlie nearly said, but Douglass was already prodding him on.

"Now, that" — Douglass' voice rose with anticipation— "is House 46. Welcome home!"

House 46 was, in all respects, identical to House 47 — a three-story building centered amidst a moat of clipped grass, the better to keep disease-bearing mosquitoes away. But as they approached, Charlie noticed small differences. Less laundry cluttering the verandas. More potted plants decorating the corners. Rocking chairs lined up in a neat row.

He cast a longing eye toward House 47.

"Home sweet home!" Douglass announced, swinging the screen door open with a flourish.

He ushered Charlie to a second level that was spanned by four rooms, each shared by two men. Charlie could sense that the rooms were all exactly alike, not only in dimension and furnishings but also in their contents, right down to the residents' membership cards to various social clubs. He looked around, a little forlorn.

Panama. Where was the adventure?

* * *

And it only got worse from there.

The orderly residents of House 46 had a self-imposed curfew of ten p.m. Charlie lay in the dark on a standard-issue bed under a standard-issue sheet, digesting his standard-issue meal.

Chicken.

He'd been hoping for something more exotic. Monkey brains, maybe, or snake steak, even if that, too, reportedly tasted like chicken. He tuned in and out of Douglass Browning's whispered monologue about the dangers of life beyond the Canal Zone.

"The venom of the coral snake will instantly attack the nervous system," Douglass whispered in a voice reserved for ghost stories.

"Would love to see one." Charlie nodded. Better yet, he'd like to hold one. Taste one. Were they edible? He doubted Douglass knew.

Douglass' speech slurred with sleep. "One bite from a ten-foot mapana snake causes internal bleeding and degeneration of the organs."

"In what order?"

The room went quiet except for Douglass' sleepy breaths.

"Browning?" Charlie called into the darkness.

"Hmmm?"

"Is there really an Order of Kangaroos?"

"Yes," Douglass replied a little dreamily. "And you can be one, too."

"Great," Charlie murmured as Douglass began to snore. Not even three days in Panama and he was already beginning to harbor serious doubts.

It wasn't the heat or Douglass' idiosyncrasies. Charlie had weathered far worse. But he'd come to Panama for a taste of adventure. Something different, exotic. Instead, he found himself in a neatly packaged world of ready-made entertainment, familiar food, and comfortable housing, not to mention bowling alleys and art exhibitionists. Why leave the Midwest?

The Canal Zone was threatening to be too reminiscent of the Indiana farm he had once escaped. Six generations of farmers seemed like plenty to him. There was a whole world out there beyond the endless cycle of the corn fields: crop after crop, season after season, all of it the same. His siblings had all gotten hitched early and never left the farm. Well, not him. He wanted to see the world. To be part of something big — something lasting. To leave some mark other than parallel furrows in the earth. It wasn't so much about fame or fortune, but adventure.

He smiled in the dark. Of course, fortune wouldn't be a bad thing, if it came his way. Fame, though, he could do without.

Central America had seemed perfect. He'd see a new part of the world, enjoy a little adventure, and leave his mark. But Panama was turning out to be a little too perfect, a little too orderly.

It wasn't that he was in the wrong place. It was that he might be too late. The days of impossible odds and great obstacles were on the wane. An army of men and machines was taming the landscape. It was only a question of time until the canal was finished — not a question of heroics or even foolhardy deeds. Sure, the pay was good, but the challenges were fading fast.

Beyond the sound of throaty snores and madly chirping crickets, laughter erupted from the fully illuminated bulk of House 47.

Charlie sighed. With any luck, someone in House 47 would be deported, jailed, or killed in a gambling-related altercation. That would free up a space for him.

Adventure?

He could only hope.

Toro Point

April 1910

The good news was, Charlie's job as site engineer of the breakwater on the Caribbean side of the canal turned out to be interesting enough. The bad news was, it wasn't exactly exciting. Still, it had its moments.

He mopped his brow in the punishing midmorning heat and studied the scene. The breakwater that would protect the mouth of the canal was taking its first baby steps into Limón Bay, but they were tottering steps at best. For starters, the crane maneuvering a trestle into place was too jerky, too fast. The trestle threatened to swing out of control as the crew looked on from a safe distance, none of them eager to be the latest casualty of canal construction.

"Whoa there."

Charlie brought his fingers to his mouth and whistled, bringing everything to a halt. The crane operator watched as he made a series of succinct hand motions. *Slow it down, ease it in. You there, stand ready and haul like this.* He mimicked the motion he knew so well. The row of faces nodded and turned back to their task.

The work crew was almost entirely composed of men from the West Indies, most of whom had already worked together on the nearby dam. When they'd been introduced to Charlie that morning, their faces swung to one man, Edgar. He wasn't the biggest or the oldest, but he was clearly the leader. Charlie took it as a good sign that the man wore a thin necklace strung with a single coin, a proud reminder of the first wage he had ever earned, once upon a time.

"Morning, everyone," Charlie had said, eager to get started. "Everyone ready to start?"

Sign language, he quickly concluded, was the best form of communication with this gang. Although he'd been assured that the Jamaicans and Barbadians all spoke English, he couldn't understand a word in the lilting rivers of syllables they emitted. Judging by their blank expressions whenever he spoke, the feeling was mutual. The same went for the two men from some speck in the Caribbean they called Saint Kitten. Now what kind of place was that? As for the two Italians, well, sign language appeared to be their mother tongue anyway.

Edgar spurred everyone into action by announcing something in a jaunty singsong tone. "Susawunnulle monin milads!"

The crew sprang into motion as a fair Caribbean wind propelled a six-foot swell against the rocky shore. The insects were biting, the sun was beating, the men sweating. Somewhere, a few miles into the thick jungle behind, massive locks were being poured from cement — locks that would someday lift entire ships across this narrow limb of the Americas.

Charlie had come to Panama intent on working on those locks, drawn by a boyish wonder for all things gargantuan. Now he was glad he didn't get what he wished for. How often in life had that proven to be the case? The locks were dusty pits of steel and cement, and the teamwork there was a little too prescribed for a person of his mettle. This breakwater assignment was more to his liking, where the sea met the sky with a fresh breath of possibility. Here, he could work with a degree of independence that he would never be granted in the locks.

He took a deep breath. The boy who'd once mixed magic potions from tractor oil and his mother's perfume had found his calling at last.

He watched the men move in ever more coordinated efforts. *Give us a week, and we'll show the Pacific Division how it's done.*

Edgar seemed to share the same sentiment. "Aysa tellya, Mister Charlie, da desboiz debet amonkanget!"

Charlie blinked. Well, whatever Edgar meant, he seemed optimistic, too.

So they were off to a good start, he figured, until Cummings, that nuisance of an inspector from the quartermaster's office came stumbling up the path.

"Mr. Parker," Cummings called, tapping at a clipboard as he approached.

Charlie had been warned about pests in Panama, but he hadn't been expecting this poisonous subspecies of homo sapiens. The man's long mustache tips protruded like antennae. His elbows jutted wide, guarding the space around him. Apparently, that termite of a man had nothing better to do than to follow him all the way out from Cristobal to the work site at Toro Point this morning.

With a curt nod of a hello, Cummings confronted him with an acquisition form Charlie vaguely remembering signing the day before in his first act as an official canal employee. Yep, there was his signature.

"The instructions on form T138 clearly indicate *ticking* the appropriate boxes," Cummings noted. The man sounded like he spoke through his nose. What was it with the guy?

Charlie looked at the X's on the form, then at the diminutive man with the delicate hands. He took the clipboard, turned his X's into deep, dark ticks that gouged the paper, and handed it back in steely silence.

Cummings countered by extracting another form from his folder. "May I bring your attention to the instructions on Yellow Form I-29. They clearly say to submit in *triplicate*." A manicured finger pointed to the top of the sheet.

Charlie took it and studied the form. He slowly folded the sheet into three even sections then unfolded it, ripped along the lines, and resubmitted the form to a red-faced Cummings. The man fumbled with the scraps and stomped off in the direction of the launch.

"Summenduneben no wukfomnunsense," rumbled the baritone at Charlie's side.

It was Edgar, watching Cummings depart. If the inspector was the local storm cloud, Edgar was a ray of sunshine. So what if his speech was an abstract work of art?

Charlie sighed and turned back to the breakwater, feeling small beside the man's muscular mass. "Everybody know what to do?" He waved a hand at the crew.

Edgar's smile grew, a joyous masterpiece in itself. "Jusapuurfitt! Deysa ruddyta lickdacifick lads!"

Right. Well, it sounded good. Better than the news Charlie knew he could expect from the quartermaster's office once Cummings filed his report — in triplicate, no doubt.

He lifted his hat just high enough to wipe his brow, then motioned Edgar back to work. Plain old work, instead of the adventure he craved.

Chapter Two

A Breath of Possibility

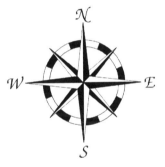

Portobelo
February 1667

The very worst day in the life of Pedro Gonzalo de Ovieto y Martinez came one February in Panama, some months prior to his hasty departure from the New World. A day that would stay in his mind forever.

He'd come with grand visions: making a name for himself, gaining a fortune. Maybe even making his father take notice of him, the forgettable third-born son. The New World beckoned with adventure! Riches! Opportunity! It was all there for the taking. So Pedro had enlisted and shipped out.

How naïve he had been!

The New World turned out to be a deathtrap. Adventure came at the end of a knife point, and gravestones outnumbered opportunities. Luck meant not fame or fortune but getting out alive. Only a fraction of the soldiers posted here ever made it back to Spain. The rest were buried in the dank soil, fallen to disease or any of a thousand violent deaths. Pedro knew — he watched once-crowded barracks grow ominously empty while the graveyard extended row by row in an eerie echo of the ranks they'd once formed. Slowly but steadily, the jungle would creep back in, reclaiming each victim a second time.

Within a day of setting his unsteady feet in Panama, Pedro realized he'd made the worst miscalculation of his life. Now, all he wanted was to get out. But going home empty-handed was almost as bad as going home dead.

By now, he was sick of work. He was sick of adventure. Each day was more miserable than the last, each week a new reason to lose hope.

"Eight? Nine?" He ticked his fingers, counting months as he marched behind the captain along with the rest of his company. The shuffling steps and clinking armor of twenty weary men sounded around him.

"What are you going on about?" Ignacio growled.

Ignacio, the most suspicious soldier in the company — and the most ambitious. Pedro was beginning to think the two went hand in hand.

He squinted at the blinding glare that was Ignacio. The man had the shiniest armor of the entire company — not because he polished it himself, but because he won all his bets. Which meant that Ignacio had the shiniest breastplate, the newest boots, and the softest bed in the barracks. That and a full bowl in the mess hall. Always.

Pedro went back to counting fingers. "How much longer in this hellhole?"

Ignacio let out that barking laugh of his. "Men who will soon die count time. Those who will triumph count opportunities."

Ignacio was full of inspiring wisdom of that sort. No wonder Pedro was losing hope. His boots scuffed the surface of the Camino Real, setting off a cloud of dust.

Only an optimist would call the Camino a road, and Pedro had lost his optimism long before. At the best of times, it was merely a roughly cobbled track. During wet season, rain fell in relentless sheets, submerging it in oozing mud. Armor-clad soldiers could barely move in the knee-deep muck, much less maintain an effective patrol.

His company was tasked with escorting the latest treasure convoy into Portobelo. What romance those convoys had held when Pedro first heard breathless stories of them back in Spain! An entire mountain of silver had been discovered in Peru. Together with gold in the form of bars and native trinkets, unimaginable quantities of silver were transported up the Pacific coast by ship and brought across the isthmus to the Caribbean side by mule train. The treasure was consolidated at the imposing new customs house in Portobelo, then reloaded onto galleons bound for Spain — entire fleets of them, all packed with treasure. That is, whatever hadn't yet been skimmed off along the way by corrupt auditors, ship captains, and the occasional sticky-fingered soldier.

Not that Pedro would get any of it. The treasure convoys that once inspired him to volunteer for the New World were exactly what he now cursed. He could see but not touch. He could die protecting treasure but never obtain any of his own. The convoys meant nothing more than long, sweltering jungle marches. And the only thing Pedro despised more than Portobelo — port of misery, that's what he would have named it — was the seething jungle beyond. A place that stirred images of all kinds of devilry in his mind.

At least he was not assigned to bring the treasure across the entire isthmus. Those poor fools had to endure a month of deprivation, even in the dry season. If the insects or wild beasts — hungry jaguars, blood-sucking bats, venomous snakes — didn't eat you alive, jungle spirits, Indians, or cimarrónes would.

The cimarrónes — bands of escaped slaves taken to the hills — were still a threat these days. In the old days, the greatest danger came from privateering Englishmen, such as the one they called El Dragón, Francis Drake. But those despicable pirates rarely stepped foot ashore these days, preferring to strike from the sea and make a quick escape at the first hint of danger. Miserable cowards, Englishmen!

The greatest threat, as far as Pedro was concerned, was the jungle spirits, who could steal your soul right out of your boots. He crossed himself twice just at the thought of them.

"Damn mosquitos," another soldier grunted, slapping his neck.

"Just another beautiful February day," another muttered bitterly.

"How far now?"

There was no telling, Pedro decided as he trudged along. The mule train they were to rendezvous with and escort safely into town could be leagues away.

The soldiers sweated and cursed as they plodded up the meandering curves of the Camino Real. The trail was dry enough, but Pedro still felt mired in the godforsaken land with its damp, danger, and deprivations. The insect crawling down his collar. He slapped it away. Would he ever see home again?

Next to him, Ignacio was rambling on. As the second son of a Seville merchant, Ignacio always felt that his father's wealth had unfairly passed him by. He spoke in the rushed manner of all Sevillians, primarily about himself, his newest scheme to attain riches, or his latest love interest. Pedro could never keep track of the latter two categories.

"Doña Maria Gonzalez de Alvarez," Ignacio murmured. "Doña Isabela Blanco de Alvarez."

He was at it again: trying out the names of prospective brides combined with his own. All of them rich, beautiful, and back home in Spain. Ignacio deserved nothing less. "Doña Louisa Hernandez de Alvarez..."

Pedro paused at the crest of the hill to catch his breath and gain a little space from the Sevillian's soliloquy. Portobelo stretched out at his feet. He could kick a rock onto the rooftops. Tempting. He'd despised the place from his very first day. Soldiers lived like heathens in their leaky barracks, surrounded by the permanent gloom of the jungle. The stench of death and corruption was everywhere. Nothing ran straight in Portobelo — not the roads, not the roofs, and certainly not the paymasters.

And yet, from this vantage point, the town was almost beautiful. Distance had a way of highlighting the grandiose. Pedro took in the bold lines of the Iglesia de San Felipe — a place he regularly frequented and Ignacio largely avoided. To its left was the angular hulk of the customs house, the treasury of the New World. His dry mouth watered at the very thought of the riches inside. The waterfront beyond bristled with cannons, all of them aimed down the length of the bay. Portobelo was a closely guarded treasure chest, indeed. The town was impenetrable.

The danger, he knew, lay just ahead. In the jungle.

* * *

A miserable hour passed, then two, and the company's silence grew inversely to the din of the jungle. Pedro's breastplate grew heavier and heavier while the leather straps securing it dug into his exposed back. Some good that would do him in a surprise attack from the rear. He kept his eyes on the trail, wishing the shadows away.

As a child of the open plains, he detested the jungle and the narrow trail that was the Camino Real. Ahead, a seething canopy of trees closed off the sky like thick funeral lace. A place for monkeys, snakes, and Englishmen — all closely related species as far as Pedro was concerned — not God-fearing Spaniards such as himself. He gulped a mouthful of air like it might be his last and stepped into the gloom, careful to stay close to the others.

On one side of the trail, a silky stream bubbled along. On the other, his companions crowded him in — Ignacio and Manuel, an amiable if dim-witted Castilian who shared his fear of the woods.

"Santa Maria del Bosce," Manuel murmured, looking up.

A tiny chapel stood upon a small rise beside the path. Pedro doubted that God ever visited this haunted place, if he visited the New World at all. But just in case, he crossed and recrossed himself as he stepped past. Manuel did the same.

Ignacio scoffed.

Just beyond the chapel, the jungle receded, shying back from a clearing where wisps of water tumbled into a shallow stream made of dozens of interlaced arteries. A low bridge arched over the water, leading the soldiers upstream along a soggy grass carpet. Pedro's small company was briefly, gloriously bathed in sunshine as they marched. Beams of light touched their helmets, shoulders, sweaty arms.

"It's like being blessed by an angel," Manuel whispered.

Pedro closed his eyes and tilted his chin up. It was, indeed. But the fleeting feeling was quickly replaced by faint sounds from the path ahead. Scraping footfalls. The snap of a whip. The jingle of mule bells.

"At last," someone muttered as the convoy filed into view.

Swaying Spaniards stumbled along. Sharp-eyed slaves drove mules covered in flies. The leader of Pedro's company exchanged stiff greetings with the head of the convoy, and the two groups merged to cover the final stretch to Portobelo as one.

"Who stinks more, the mules or the men?" Ignacio muttered, squeezing past the single column of men and mules to the rear of the line.

The convoy was so long that it extended the full length of the clearing, and the men at the front approached the chapel before the rearguard had even thumped across the bridge.

"Over a hundred mules!" Ignacio whispered to Pedro as they fell in step at the back. "Each with... What? Two hundred pounds of silver — or gold!"

Even a fraction of that fortune could make a man rich, Pedro knew. But his shoulders slumped at the thought. He could guard the loot — even risk his life for it — but he would never hear the precious metal jingle in his pockets. Even in the New World, Pedro would never be more than the third son of a country don. He'd left home hoping that he might someday return to see heads turn and whisper, *there goes Pedro Gonzalo de Ovieto y Martinez, the one who made his fortune in the New World.* But no. There would be no reward for his toils, no family gathering to rejoice his triumphant return.

A soldier fell into a fit of convulsed coughing. Pedro edged away, snapping back to the present and his goal of surviving one more day. The company had to keep moving if they were to make it back before dark. The only thing worse than being in the jungle was being in the jungle at night. Pedro stepped faster, trying to urge the others along.

"All that treasure..." Ignacio murmured.

Pedro just shrugged. The king could have his treasure. All Pedro wanted was his life.

He trudged along, wishing the minutes away.

Afterward, Pedro would remember it all. The faint creak of leather and armor, the tired snort of a mule. In fact, Pedro would recall the tiniest details of what happened next to the end of his days. The open air of the clearing, the dappled afternoon sunshine. The water humming along the creek. The call of a songbird. Pedro turned his face to the sun, eyes shut for a single moment of respite. Even behind his closed lids, he could see the golden light.

Then, *Pffft!* A huge insect rocketed past Pedro's left ear.

The man ahead of him grunted and stumbled to the ground. Pedro's chuckle was cut off by another soldier knocking into him from behind. Then a clap of thunder split the air, and the clearing erupted in a cacophony of urgent sounds. Shouts rang out above the clang of steel as soldiers drew their blades.

Realization was slower coming to Pedro, still struggling to free himself from the weight of the other man. It was the mules' excited braying that finally communicated the danger to him.

"Ambush! Ambush!"

*East Lemmon Cays,
San Blas Islands
December, present day*

"Heaven," Kate had announced the minute *Aurora's* anchor took hold in the East Lemmon Cays. "No towns, no hotels."

Nick swallowed the view, nodding. The palm-studded islets that protected the anchorage looked to have about three grass huts on them, nothing more. The calm water was a kaleidoscope of pastel greens and smeared blues that shifted and sparkled under the tropical sun.

Everything he'd heard about the San Blas Islands — good weather, natural beauty, and safe anchorages — seemed to be true.

"I'm loving Kuna Yala already," Kate breathed, using the indigenous name of the region. She waved a hand over toward the turquoise water and picture-perfect islets ringed by palms. "And none of it's off-limits!"

"Except the coconuts," he added. Apparently, local custom decreed that every coconut, whether on the ground or still in the tree, had a rightful Kuna owner. So coconuts were strictly hands-off.

It was the perfect place to spend a few days dreaming about new horizons — or battling with a cranky windlass, as the case might be.

"Now all we need is the veggie boat," Kate said, searching the horizon.

A handful of cottage industries had sprung up in the archipelago, with enterprising Kuna locals bringing the market to their sailing guests. Business was conducted from the floating platforms of dugout canoes that came door-to-door — or hull-to-hull — peddling intricate cloth panels with geometric designs called molas. The women, like the molas they wore at the midriff, were a riot of color in their puffy-sleeved blouses, knee-length skirts, and stacks of beaded leg bands. Fishermen made the rounds, too, selling the catch of the day — straight from the ocean to the frying pan.

But the most sought-after vendor of all was an enterprising local who made weekly rounds of the anchorages with fresh produce. His arrival was a major event announced over the radio net by a chorus of excited sailors low in vitamin C. Nick suspected that some crews posted lookouts like greedy whalers: *thar she blows!*

"He's here! He's here!" the radio squawked with the call.

Nick scrambled on deck to signal madly for the skiff. Aurora was nearly out of fresh supplies, and the nearest supermarket was a two-day trip away.

"The good news is..." Kate murmured, watching the skiff motor closer. "He's here."

"And the bad news?"

Kate exchanged a few words with the veggie man as he pulled alongside. "All he has left are *huevos y papas*."

Potatoes and eggs. But beggars couldn't be choosers, so Kate handed five dollars over the rail in exchange for two dozen eggs and a pound of potatoes.

Nick nudged her. "Ask when he'll be back with more."

The wiry man flashed a brown-toothed smile and started his outboard engine with a practiced tug. "Pronto!" He grinned and sped away.

Kate and Nick exchanged looks. He was becoming fluent in plumbing and wiring, while Kate was the language expert. But even Nick knew that *pronto* did not necessarily mean "soon" in the San Blas. His hungry eyes followed the small launch as it powered out of the narrow pass, passing a cluttered catamaran heading in a reciprocal course.

"Another backpacker boat," Kate said with a terse shake of her head.

Even from this distance, he could pick out the rust stains on the hull and count eleven passengers on the crowded deck. It was a common sight in the San Blas: so-called backpacker boats, many of them run by shady individuals who transported adventurous travelers between Panama and Colombia for a tidy profit. Passengers and who knew what else...

"Here today, gone tomorrow."

Nick headed below, already thinking about dinner. Pasta with canned mushrooms was scratched off the menu. Instead, he cooked up a savory meal of *huevos y papas*. The galley was just big enough for him to stand in, left elbow nudging the two-burner stove, right elbow at the sink, which doubled as a work surface when covered with a cutting board. Somehow, it all worked. In fact, meals on board always seemed tastier than back home, which probably had more to do with the setting than his cooking. He was already drooling, and the only thing in the frying pan so far was onions. He caught himself smiling as he stirred. How bad was life when your shopping came to you? Plus, on *Aurora*, waterfront dining was guaranteed.

He glanced up to find Kate sitting cross-legged at the salon table with the century-old cigar box Aunt Laura had sent. Kate wore that dangerous look she got when she passed a museum, pet shop, or pizza parlor. The look of a bloodhound hot on a promising trail.

"Okay, Charlie Parker," she murmured, holding up the cigar box. "What exactly brought you to Panama?"

Nick watched her pause a moment before digging in, her mind calculating. *Trash or treasure?*

Trash. Nick had seen enough of the junk Aunt Laura kept in her attic to know.

He went back to stirring onions as Kate opened the bundle of letters, each smudged with ink stamps.

"To Rosie Ingram, Oswego, New York, United States of America," she read, "from C. Parker, 11th Engineer Regiment, France." She rifled through the stack. "Every one of them is addressed to her. What was Charlie doing in France?"

"After Panama, he joined some kind of engineering corps and got shipped off to World War I."

"And who is Rosie? The one Charlie is writing to."

"I guess you'd say she was his sweetheart. Rosie is my mother's grandmother."

"Your great-grandmother..." Kate murmured, unfolding the first letter carefully. Nick watched her read, more for the fun of reading her expression than for what she might report. Her eyes danced across the page, and her lips moved as if she were making out ancient hieroglyphs. After a few lines, she came to a sudden stop, and her eyes went wide. Kate crinkled her nose, thought a moment, then refolded the letter and moved on to the next.

Nick hid a smile. Definitely trash.

She read a few lines of the second letter and came to another abrupt halt. On the third letter, she snorted out loud.

Nick looked up from sprinkling spices into his concoction. "What?"

"I can't believe this."

"What? What's in the letters?"

Kate sucked in a breath of air and sorted the letters into their original order. Then she presented the top one as if to say *Exhibit A*. Her eyebrows flicked up as she unfolded the sheet and began to read.

"September 7, 1917. My dearest Rosie," Kate quoted, eyes tracing the sloping, loopy script. "Arrived in France two days ago. We're waiting for the equipment before heading out. The talk is all about these new tank machines and if they can win the war, but all I can think of is you. I think of your soft skin, your lush lips, your round..." Kate motioned vaguely with her hand to fill the gap. "Etcetera," she concluded, shooting him an unimpressed look. She thumped the letter down and snatched up the next.

"October 15, 1917. My dearest Rosie. We have moved toward the front, but progress is slow. Don't worry, we engineers are not here to fight, only to supply the troops with these new fighting machines. The nights are cold and lonely until—" Kate licked her lips and read on. "Until I think of you and am overcome by a warm sensation and the longing to..." Kate trailed into a pregnant pause. "Etcetera, etcetera," she finished, giving the letter a dismissive frown.

Nick leaned over the galley partition for a closer look. His cheeks went hot when his eyes found the rest.

Gaining momentum, Kate moved on to the third letter. "November 3, 1917. My dearest Rosie. We are working with British forces now. They mean to keep us engineers well behind front lines, which is fine by me. Still, I can't help but wonder if it will be in heaven or on earth that I am reunited with you and can once again brush your beautiful hair, touch the small of your back, rest my hand on your inviting hips, and..."

Kate stopped, grimacing.

"And what?" Nick demanded. This was getting good.

She flipped the letter around for him to read. He squinted to make out the next lines and whistled.

Kate shook her head. "Lush lips? Inviting hips? What's with this guy?"

"War is hell." He shrugged and made a mental note never to write Kate a love letter enumerating any body parts, attractive though they might be.

Kate made a face. "Can't he find anything to admire other than her body? What about her imagination? Her brains?"

Nick made another mental note. "Maybe she wasn't too smart."

"Can't have been, sticking with a guy like him."

Nick did his best to look apologetic as Kate stacked up the letters and retied the bundle. "You think you find history, but all you get is mush." She sighed, tossing the letters back into the box. "Enough voyeurism. Dinner?"

He nodded. "Three minutes. You pour the wine."

"Chateau du Carton?"

"That's the one."

"Perfect," Kate said a few minutes later when they started to eat.

Nick had to agree. Mealtimes were among his favorite occasions aboard *Aurora*. There was nothing quite as perfect as a candlelight dinner with wine in the cockpit on a calm, tropical night, even if the wine in question arrived from Argentina in an unadorned box and cost less than four dollars. Panama certainly had its pluses and minuses. Still, the journey *Aurora* had undertaken to arrive at this point somehow imparted the cheap wine with extra flavor, and he wouldn't trade it for an award-winning label of the finest vineyard.

The wine level in the box went down, the moon came up, and a profound peace settled over the anchorage. Nick thought they had had enough of Great-Grandpa Charlie for one night, but Kate had other ideas. Once they were tucked into their cabin in the bow, she shuffled closer and curled her arm around him.

"Your lush lips," she chuckled, kissing him. "Your soft skin..."

He couldn't help smiling. Maybe Charlie had a few good ideas, after all.

"The small of your back," Kate continued, tracing the fine topography of his shoulders.

"Your inviting hips..." he mumbled, pulling her in.

"Etcetera..." Kate breathed.

"...etcetera."

Portobelo

March 1911

Women!

Charlie snorted to himself. They could be noisy and persistent, like mosquitoes.

"Meester Charlee!" came a shrill voice in hot pursuit.

Charlie hastened his pace along the cobbled lane. If it wasn't Inspector Cummings, pestering him at all hours, it was this wheezing woman, Angelina.

He had spent the day up in the Portobelo quarry, overseeing the local crew. After dismissing a proposal to mine stones from the ruined forts jumbled around the crumbling old town, his division chief decided to concentrate on the quarry. If only the local workforce were as quick as his Colon crew.

He'd been in Panama for months now, and work at Toro Point was progressing well. Slowly but surely, the breakwater was taking shape. Charlie's crew really was giving the Pacific Division a run for their money — until they hit a snag. The local quarry couldn't yield enough large stones of the right quality, and even the optimistic Edgar failed to find any hope in the local rock.

"Cuddna use nunada rock here!" Edgar had proclaimed, fingering the useless stuff sadly.

Charlie shook his head. Nothing for it but to try Portobelo, twenty miles away.

"Scusamah saying but datsa awffly long way, wuddna say, Mister Charlie?"

"An awfully long way," Charlie agreed. He'd made some inroads into understanding Edgar's speech in the last months. Well, the gist of it, anyway.

Now that Charlie had been in Panama for nearly a year, he had gained a healthy appreciation for Edgar, his right-hand man. Actually, Edgar had become Charlie's right and left hand, plus a bit of his brain. The compact Barbadian might be illiterate, but he was a born engineer and a natural leader who kept work running smoothly in Charlie's absence. If it weren't for Edgar, Charlie would never be able to get to satellite locations like Portobelo. And he had to get away regularly; the breakwater hungered for more material.

Portobelo turned out to have its merits, though, as Charlie discovered over the course of several visits. One was the chance it afforded to escape cookie-cutter living in Cristobal. The Canal Zone was tidy, safe, and predictable. In other words, boring. Even the entertainment was spoon-fed. Portobelo, on the other hand, was wild, fickle, and crooked — in more ways than one. If the Canal Zone was a groomed poodle, Portobelo was a mangy mutt. Charlie loved it.

There was just one catch, and that was the women.

"Meester Charlee!"

Charlie hurried away at a race-walk pace and turned a corner where a pet monkey strained at the end of a chain. His Portobelo boarding house, a place called El Diablo, was a pleasingly ramshackle place, but there was no escaping the vultures there — the women, like Angelina. In Charlie's experience, women were all the same all over the world: shrill, demanding, and possessive. And they could be fiendishly persistent, even when encumbered by skirts, corsets, and ridiculously oversized hats.

Except for the exceptions. Like Mercedes, proprietress of El Diablo. Now there was a woman — a businesswoman! Charlie pictured the steely Spanish eyes that could stare down the likes of Teddy Roosevelt. Mercedes' café served more than just food and drinks to her American clients. But Charlie largely ignored the lovely — and highly willing — ladies of El Diablo, fascinated instead by the formidable Mercedes. The place was aptly named. Mercedes was a she-devil herself. Her beauty was secondary; it was her impenetrable aura that mesmerized Charlie. She could serve up drinks — knocking back a few herself — speed-count her profits, and break up fights without compromising her aloof air. Charlie grinned as he hustled onward. If more women had her sense, he might even be tempted to swear off bachelorhood. Not that Charlie had any designs on Mercedes. He wouldn't dare.

Mercedes aside, the overwhelming majority of the female gender, in his bitter experience, was impossible to deal with. Charlie knew. Oh, he knew. The thought fueled his long legs, carrying his sweating form out past the edge of the town and around another corner.

"Meester Charlee!"

Charlie knew men like him were a way for women like Angelina to move up and out, just like the canal was his way to get ahead in life. Everyone needed a ladder — even him. But Charlie didn't like being used any better than he liked the idea of Angelina being used. Surely she should have gotten the message already and latched on to a more willing victim.

"Meester Charlee!"

And did she have to be so shrill?

The jungle squeezed the road like a boa, constricting it to a narrow lane. Charlie glanced around for some escape. An overgrown archway on the left with a broken gate looked promising, and he dodged into the tangled enclosure half a step before Angelina came around the turn.

Charlie looked around, getting his bearings. At first, he thought it was a high-walled, overgrown pasture of some kind. Then he made out the tombs of an abandoned graveyard. He pushed deeper into the leafy realm of the dead and ducked behind a crumbling tombstone.

"Meester Charlee!" Angelina's voice pierced the air in a last, desperate effort. Her shoes crunched along the gravel road, startling all jungle life into hiding. The woman was loud, but she lacked presence. Not like Mercedes.

Angelina paused outside the archway, calling again in the sharp notes of an off-key cockatoo, then huffed and muttered a dark refrain in Spanish. Charlie had tried his hand at Spanish and quickly committed himself to failure. Bridges, trains, and cranes, he could understand. Women and foreign languages? They defied logic.

"Este hombre," she cursed.

Then it was over. Angelina retreated, heading back to El Diablo and more fertile hunting grounds.

Peace settled over the graveyard, and as Charlie's heart rate settled, he took it all in. The tickle of tiny leaves, the dank jungle smells. So much of his work was in wide-open places like the breezy breakwater on the edge of the sea or the echoing quarry. This place was something altogether different. Shifting shadows in the undergrowth, the shy hop of a bird. He'd spent his childhood dreaming about tangled, overgrown places like this, so exotic and full of mystery. A small place choked with vines that seemed intent on cloaking some mystery.

He leaned against a crumbling tombstone and looked up. There was only one small patch of open sky for orientation, a little like the cornfields he used to hide in as a kid, where he could imagine himself in exotic parts of the world, overcoming great challenges. One day he'd be Livingstone, exploring the heart of Africa, the next, part of the Belgian Antarctic Expedition mushing toward the South Pole. And now he was in Panama — for real.

"Whoa!" he yelped when something thin and alive made him jump.

A lime green snake slithered through the tall grass. Charlie got on all fours and watched it disappear into a gap at the base of a tomb.

He got to his feet, shifting his focus from the reptile to the tomb. Death wasn't the first thing that came to his engineer's mind. The rock was far more interesting. The same type they were working in the quarry: good, hard rock that could withstand the power of the ocean. The tomb itself was little more than an elongated box. Thick slabs of smooth rock stood on edge to form four sides, with a thicker slab across the top. Except for the headstone, no part of the tomb rose higher than his knee. Like all its brooding neighbors in the compound, the grave looked ancient and neglected, one step away from collapse. That a body was interred there only served to make it all the more enticing.

Charlie watched as another snake slithered in through a gap where two slabs met at a corner. He pictured the garter snakes he caught as a kid. A quick grab behind the head and they'd be safe in his hand. He could admire the geometric pattern of their scales and watch their tongues flick before releasing them in the wild — or occasionally, in his sister's bed. Ah, the things he'd done to amuse himself as a kid.

Charlie gave the top slab a long, calculating look. Life had been a little too tame, even in Portobelo. With a good job and a good crew, things were running much too smoothly. Which was satisfying in one way, of course, but frustrating in another. He was turning into just another engineer on just another project. A responsible adult ticking little boxes.

Where had the Huck Finn in him gotten to, anyway? Even as a child, Charlie knew growing up was overrated, and he was right. But right here, right now, he had a chance to play explorer. He could catch that snake and roll back twenty years. No one was looking!

He took hold of the tomb's lid and gave it an exploratory tug. It didn't budge. He knelt and gave it a push. A slight scrape, rock against rock. Picturing the snake, he pushed again, producing a low, grinding sound. He imagined bones, paused a moment, then pushed with new rigor. The lid creaked and shifted, opening a small gap.

He peered into the dark space, flush with the prospect of finding something exciting. Bones, maybe. Reptiles. He searched for a recognizable shape as his eyes adjusted to the dim light.

Huh. The space was filled to the top with... something. Something that called to him as sweetly as a sign that screamed *Keep Out!*

What was in there? An entire cache of skulls? Solid rock? A sarcophagus inside the tomb?

That could be it — a sarcophagus with a mummy inside. Someone important, maybe. The mystery of it was unbearable, an itch he just had to scratch. He stood, listened a moment to be sure no one was near, and pushed the lid again, gaining another half inch.

He got on his knees and looked in. Dark. Dark and creepy.

A mosquito buzzed as Charlie licked his lips and reached straight in.

What was it his mother would have said? Oh, yes. *Think before you act, Charles!* Never his strong point, as the beleaguered woman had so often observed. She'd had four sons, but Charlie kept her busier than the other three put together. Even so, Charlie always refused to accept any blame. It wasn't his fault he had imagination!

His fingers made contact with something mushy and jerked away. A second touch yielded something damp and soft. Charlie pulled his hand out into the half-light of the overgrown graveyard to examine his find. Fibers of some kind.

"Fibers?"

Maybe there really was a mummy in there.

He crumbled the material between his fingers and went fishing in the darkness again.

This time, his fingers clawed past the soft mass until they met something cool and solid. He pictured a human femur and felt a giddy rush. He groped around. No, it was too small for a femur. Charlie tightened his fingers over the edge of the thing and pulled it free.

Much too small for a femur. More like a finger bone. Or not a bone at all.

He rubbed the object on his pants and sat back on his heels. The sun glinted off his find as he contemplated it for a long, long time. He sat barely moving in a ray of diffuse tropical light before allowing himself a broad grin.

Maybe Panama had some promise, after all.

Chapter Three

A Tribe of Sailors

San Blas Islands
December, present day

As far as Nick could tell, the islands of San Blas were only sparsely populated by indigenous Kuna clans, but the archipelago was overrun by a second tribe: sailors. Entire colonies of cruisers hunkered down among those pockets of paradise, season after season, transplanted en masse from their home countries. Popular anchorages had the feeling of content retirement communities. Tidy Germans had taken over entire cays. Proud Canadians displayed massive maple leaf flags, lest anyone mistake them for their lesser North American cousins. The few Italians made up in volume what they lacked in sheer numbers, while the French kept to themselves. The Americans were generally quiet retirees on spacious catamarans with humming generators that powered all the conveniences of home: air conditioning, water makers, refrigerators, even washing machines.

Aurora didn't quite fit in.

Collectively, North Americans dominated the radio waves with amateur morning programs that Nick followed with dubious fascination.

"And that's the weather from *Second Wind*," said a dry male voice.

"Join *Abracadabra* for yoga on the beach at ten!" came a chipper call.

"Book club meeting on *Island Girl* at two!"

"And don't forget cooking club on *Seascape* at four!"

Cooking club? Nick eyed *Aurora's* minuscule galley. How did that work?

The announcements were followed by chitchat that threatened to suck *Aurora's* batteries dry, especially now that the solar panels received only weak input from the cloud-obscured sun. Nick clicked the radio's dial to off.

So far, he and Kate had limited their contact with other sailors to a friendly wave from the dinghy or a quick exchange on the beach. He hadn't felt the need to connect with anyone but Kate, content to remain a cozy twosome and sort out their reforged partnership in a thousand tiny ways throughout each day.

But sooner or later, it was bound to happen. It was unavoidable, like an unforeseen change in weather. It was inevitable, like running aground.

It was the cruiser's potluck.

"See you tonight!" said an older woman after they exchanged pleasantries on the beach.

Tonight?

Their puzzled looks must have given them away because the woman went on the offensive.

"The potluck! Tonight at five! Didn't you hear about it on the radio?" The woman put a reproachful hand on her hip.

"Oh, that potluck!" Kate blurted.

Nick moaned the moment they were back home on *Aurora*. "You could have said I'm sick!"

She turned a deaf ear and chopped their second to last onion into a pasta salad.

"You could have said *Aurora* has a serious leak and we have to pump constantly to stay afloat!"

She gave him a stern look and emptied a can of corn into the bowl.

"You could have said we have too many things to fix! It's not really lying..."

Kate handed the dish down to him in the dinghy and pushed away from *Aurora*. She bailed while he pointed the sputtering outboard in the direction of the beach, wearing a fresh shirt and a glum expression.

The beach was a different place than it had been that quiet afternoon. The sand was awash in picnic blankets, portable barbecues, and beer koozies. Some sailors had even brought real wineglasses with stems — from a catamaran, no doubt.

Kate gave him a horrified nudge, spotting the neatly arranged pots and bowls. Theirs was the tenth pasta salad among twenty or so dishes. All the more proof that they should have stayed aboard *Aurora* where he could seek comfort in the toolbox or fuss over his fishing gear.

But, no. Kate was waved over by the woman they'd met on the beach earlier, who now appeared to be trading recipes with other sailors. Kate shuffled over as if to the gallows.

Someone grabbed Nick's elbow, and before he knew it, he was seated between a talkative couple from Chicago — a former television producer and his decades younger, yoga-instructor wife. They made their professions part of their introductions and looked at him expectantly.

"Nick," he said and left it at that.

The couple sat in matching, low-legged folding chairs, hovering a few inches above Nick's eye level as he sat beneath them in the sand, feeling very much the junior member of the group. Flanking them were a smiling couple from Baltimore in even taller chairs, introduced as Ned the physicist and Amy the nurse. Conversation lurched from subject to subject without forewarning, and Nick could barely follow along. Either the couples knew each other very well, or they didn't listen to one another at all.

"Pass the mustard, honey," said Phil, the television producer.

"I always prefer red," said Sherri, the sinewy yoga instructor, handing Phil a jar while answering an unrelated question from her right.

"I think it's coming this way," Ned noted, removing thick glasses and squinting into the sky.

Nick decided to focus on Ned, whose eyes led to a plane, rapidly approaching at low altitude. The type of plane Nick and Kate had seen in the middle of their week-long passage from Jamaica to Panama: a US Customs drug-enforcement aircraft, sporting an oversized radar dome over the fuselage.

"P3 AEW&C surveillance aircraft!" cried Ned. He chewed on the earpiece of his glasses as the plane roared over their heads, heading east.

Phil, the producer, eyed the sky and spoke in a voice laced with drama. "Something big is up, I can feel it."

Sherri cast an appraising eye at Nick. "Something big made you go cruising. I can feel it." Her bony fingers came to rest on his forearm.

The touch forced him to pull his focus away from Ned and wrestle it around to Sherri. What made him go cruising? A phone call, just a call. He could remember the song that had been playing on the radio when he reached for the phone.

The noise of the plane's engines droned away, then grew louder.

"It's circling back!" Phil nudged Ned. "Must be homing in on a nearby target." Hands cupped over their eyes, the two men studied the sky.

Sherri squeezed Nick's arm, still intent on her interrogation. "Come on, tell me what made you set sail."

"Oh, just the usual... Fed up with work, I guess," Nick offered.

It was only half a lie. The other part, he preferred to leave out. The phone call. The one from his mother, telling him that Cory was dead — a kid he knew from back in elementary school. Sherri would think him crazy.

"Sounds crazy," Ned mumbled as the plane came circling back into view, "but I swear that radar is the new APS-115 prototype!"

Nick could picture Cory at about age eleven, outdribbling everyone on the soccer field. They hadn't seen much of each other after middle school, but somehow, the news of his death hit a nerve. Enough to make Nick quit his job and drive to Maine — in March, definitely crazy — to take over an aging boat. The O in *Aurora* was peeling off the stern when he bought her.

"Probably is crazy," Ned decided, studying the receding airplane.

"What kind of job?" Sherri pried.

"I did network security for an investment company." Nick wiggled his toes in the sand. A meaningless job that was suddenly overshadowed by a nagging, persistent fear that he, too, could fall victim to an early death and have — what? — to show for it all. Countless hours of cubicle time and a modest investment portfolio. He took a bite of extremely dry focaccia and gulped it down.

"Too many hours behind a desk?" Sherri suggested, releasing his arm at last.

Nick nodded. Way too many. He looked at Kate, seated a few places away, and recalled the stress, the constant rush of their old lives. No time to really be together.

Kate had extracted herself from the recipe-trading women and was now entertaining a rapt audience, drawing diagrams in the sand and telling stories about her archaeological excavations. Turkey, Germany, Peru: the woman had flung dirt on three continents before coming to Boston for graduate work. She'd stayed on for a laboratory job afterward, squirreling away for her next grand adventure. Funny that it turned out to be this.

"What do you think they're after?" Ned asked Phil as the plane readied for another approach.

"And what is it you're after in the cruising life?" Sherri echoed.

"Drugs, a major delivery," Phil declared.

"Something different, I guess," Nick mumbled to Sherri. His eyes were on Kate. *I want it to last this time.*

"It's taking forever," Phil commented, watching the plane bank.

For a long, long time.

"They'll never last!" Ned shouted. "Look at that altitude!" He pointed at the wavering aircraft. "Lever her up!" he urged the pilot, as if the man could hear. The plane dipped, then gained altitude, prompting Ned to exhale. "These young guns, I tell you..."

"We were ready for a change, too," Sherri confided in a stage whisper.

So was Kate. That's why she left. Nick stared at his toes in the sand. Just the way he did on too-quiet weekends in Boston, studiously ignoring the empty feeling of the apartment he kept after Kate moved out. Before the phone call, before *Aurora* appeared on his foggy horizon.

"A little adventure," Sherri continued.

A little adventure. Kate's exact words when she left him for the job in Arizona.

"A little Merlot!" Phil called.

Sherri reached across Nick's head to hand Phil a bottle of wine. Phil bumped Ned, who dropped his barbecued chicken in the sand. "So sorry!"

"It's not your fault," Ned replied, recovering his napkin.

Nick pictured Kate the day she left. *It's not your fault,* she'd sniffed, a rare tear glinting along the contours of her face.
Definitely my fault.

Amy the nurse chimed in to the disjointed conversation. "Is it getting cold or is it me?"

Nick thought of his first miserable days aboard *Aurora*. Cold and lonely.

Ned was still focused on the plane. "I bet they're after a drug cartel. Colombia's just over there, you know."

Phil grew distracted, fingering a tear in the canvas armrest of his chair. "Damn thing is falling apart," he muttered.

Me falling apart on my falling-apart boat. Nick remembered that stormy night off New Jersey, when he was ready to call it quits. He had almost dialed a yacht broker to get rid of *Aurora*, but an impulse made him call Kate first. Would she give him one more chance? The words had gone shooting across a continent, impossible to pull back.

"A new start," Sherri declared, continuing her one-sided conversation.

Kate's move on board *Aurora* was unceremonious. She'd simply dumped her duffel bag in *Aurora's* cabin after a pizza dinner at Newark airport. But still, it was a fresh start. Tentative at first, but then progressing to a harmonious blend of old and new ways. They left a lot unsaid, but somehow everything eased into place, like the way she slipped into her old spot beside him on the right side of the bed.

"And this time," Sherri stressed, "we're going to live it up!"

And this time, I'm not going to mess it up.

"So far, so good," commented Ned, giving the plane's flight path an approving nod.

"So far, so good," chuckled Sherri, leaning to clink glasses with Phil.

Nick ducked out of their way. *So far, so good.* He, Kate, and *Aurora* made it down the East Coast and across the Caribbean without further breakdowns, mental or mechanical. Since then, most of their mistakes were in the realm of sailing and not in arranging their re-formed partnership. In fact, they'd become a surprisingly good team.

He found Kate's eyes trained on his, her face glowing with the first hues of sunset. His mind skimmed over the past months in a rushed fly-by, then slowed down to soak in the now: the warm sand, the whispering palms, his very own sailboat riding at anchor, just over there. And behind *Aurora*, a wide-open horizon.

Except for one rapidly growing shape in the sky. With a whir and a roar, the surveillance airplane zoomed over the beach, heading for its unseen objective somewhere not far to the east.

Ned murmured at his side. "I wonder what's going on over there?"

San Blas Islands

present day

The morning after the potluck, Nick fiddled with knots while he tuned in to the radio waves, now thick with rumor and intrigue. A sailboat had gone up on a nearby reef, the subject of the plane investigation the previous day. First to reach the scene were two fishermen in a dugout canoe, and word of their startling discovery electrified the coconut grapevine.

"A dead body?" Kate yelped at the radio.

A dead body aboard the unidentified sailboat, as it turned out.

Who was it? What happened? An accident? Suicide? Murder? Anything was possible!

"Might have been that Colombian guy..." someone offered.

"Has anyone seen *Runaway*? What if it's them?"

"I bet it's one of those backpacker boats! Maybe the passengers drowned!"

As speculation grew out of control, Nick clicked the radio off and tucked himself next to Kate as rain tap-tap-tapped on the deck overhead.

All of *Aurora's* interior would have fit into the single bedroom of the apartment they had rented back in Boston. The chart table with a built-in seat, the one-man galley, the salon with its wraparound sofa and table, and forward, their den of a bunk. *Aurora* wasn't new or fancy. In fact, she was pretty worn around the edges. But *Aurora* was practical, snug, and she was theirs. Home.

Even more so since Kate had joined him on board. She'd started decorating the walls with trophies of all the places they'd visited: vibrant postcards from the East Coast, the Bahamas, and Jamaica. It was not lost on him that the way she hung them left space for many more. The question was whether one lifetime would suffice to satisfy her wanderlust.

It was a cozy space, and a good thing, too. A deluge worthy of Noah had set in and was forecast to pour through the entire week. They made the best of it, catching rain to fill *Aurora's* tanks and indulging in luxurious — if chilly — freshwater baths in the overflowing dinghy. Then they retreated to the cabin, where the smell of baking bread filled the air. Kate's latest attempt at three-grain bread was looking like a winner this time.

"God of fickle propane ovens willing," she muttered as she set the timer.

Yes, every day on a sailboat was full of surprises, right down to the consistency of the bread.

Being cooped up in rainy weather proved surprisingly bearable. He was amazed to see Kate was handling it so well, given where inaction ranked on her list of cardinal sins, right up there with frailty or cowardice. They had the hatches open, thanks to the rain tarps she had made from an old sail they found back in Virginia. Fresh air and good company made a winning combination. Kate was leaning intently over a thriller while he thumbed through the owner's manual for *Aurora's* diesel engine. But it was dull reading, and he eventually turned to something more inspiring: *The Cruiser's Handbook of Fishing*.

Kate looked over and laughed. "You know you've got it good if fishing is your biggest preoccupation."

Nick couldn't agree more. Compared to life in Boston, life on *Aurora* was good, indeed.

* * *

"Good book?"

"Good enough," Kate said, turning the last page, then reading the back cover one last time.

It was evening, and she'd just finished the espionage novel she had picked up in a musty book swap back in Jamaica. As her heart rate recovered from the action-packed ending, she popped her head into the cockpit to check back in with reality. A drizzle filled the space between *Aurora* and her neighbors as every crew hunkered down in their own private worlds. From the outside, *Aurora* was just one more yellow glow.

Panama. She could spend one day snorkeling over a rainbow of starfish and the next cuddled in *Aurora's* cabin. It was the sheer antithesis of her world back home because neither Nick, starfish, nor rain had featured in her unhappy stint in Arizona. The job in Tucson that had lured her away from Boston with the promise of independent fieldwork had fallen prey to budget cuts and come to a sudden dead-end in a lab. She'd always pictured herself slashing dense undergrowth from tangled jungle ruins, not punching computer keys in a windowless lab.

Then the phone call. Nick, huddled in a phone booth on the East Coast, wind and rain in the background conspiring to steal his faltering voice. Would she give them another chance? Him — and *Aurora*?

It was supposed to be the other way around. She was the one who schemed about trading the rat race for a different lifestyle. Independence! Adventure! That's what she wanted. Nick, on the other hand, was the practical one. He always had a list of reasons why her latest, greatest scheme would never work. Too expensive. Too risky. Unfavorable exchange rates. Whenever she brought up the dream of sailing, he'd whittle it down to something "more reasonable," like a weekend rental on a lake.

Compromise, he called it.

She didn't mind compromising some things — but compromising her dreams? Once you let those go, you let go of your soul.

And yet it was Nick, of all people, who had bought a boat. Nick, who had called, asking her to come back to him and sail away on *Aurora*.

"We were good together," he had mumbled through the phone. He trailed off without articulating the next part: they'd been good together before she left. Kate winced at the memory. She always believed that Nick was perfect for her: sweet, patient, and sincere. Perfect in all ways but failing to dream big.

Aurora was more than a tempting option — she was a dream come true. That and... Well, Kate had missed Nick. A thousand little things she never noticed until they were apart. Jogging with him in the mornings, when the river path was wispy with mist.

Watching him tinker with broken appliances with the enthusiasm of a little boy or cook with the intellectual curiosity of a chemist. Nick, reading out interesting passages from whatever book he was reading in bed at night. She missed him more than she ever admitted in the bolder moments of her move, leaving him and Boston behind.

But now, four months and two thousand miles later, they were together again, bobbing on the pulse of the ocean. She stole a glance at him reading, his legs stretched across the cabin, and shuffled her toes over to join his. Nick's boat, her dream — the perfect combination.

They really were here, in the tropics, living an adventure. All thanks to *Aurora* and Nick.

She peeked over again. He had a little smudge of grease on his chin, along with the two-day stubble. Caramel eyes, fringed with green. The man was getting more handsome all the time. Back in Boston, his daily uniform had been a dark suit, tie, and furrowed brow. Here, it was ragged shorts and a faded baseball cap.

She hid a happy sigh, then stretched and stood. A good time to dig into one of Aunt Laura's pirate novels.

She rummaged around the starboard bookshelves until she found the cardboard box. When she reached in, her fingers slipped right over the glossy paperbacks and stopped on the rich grain of Charlie's notebook. Running her fingers over the uneven cover, she considered the possibilities. What adventures might be recounted in there?

The faint scent of leather and wax tickled her nose. Maybe it was time to give Charlie Parker a second chance.

She sat down with the time-worn notebook, opened the clasp, and turned to the first page.

The first section was devoted to cranes, cubic yards of spoil, and sketches of various mechanical objects, dated from 1910 to 1914. Then came rough maps of a harbor entrance. No, two harbor entrances — shapes she recognized from their cruising guide. She pulled it out to compare and found a perfect match: the breakwaters protecting each end of the waterway.

"The breakwaters?" she murmured.

Had Charlie been involved in breakwater construction on the Panama Canal? She shot Nick a look. Why hadn't anyone mentioned Charlie before?

She went back to leafing through the thick pages of Charlie's notebook. Equipment lists alternated with scribbled reminders such as *Edgar: ham + cigarettes* circled and underlined for emphasis. Several pages were devoted to jotted maps, none with any identifying headers. Kate cocked her head, trying to place them. Apparently, the notebook served as half of Charlie's brain, not an encyclopedia. He knew what they meant, but anyone else? Good luck.

Turning the page, she found more sketches — circles subdivided by X's. One page simply noted: *Yolanta — Friday 5:00*. Another had a list: *Mercedes — whitewash, 20 bottles red wine, 6 parasols*. She couldn't make any sense of it. Some of the pages were folded over, while others were torn out.

She ran her finger over one jagged edge in the binding. It was more than interesting. It was mysterious.

Such as a sequence of drawings that appeared intermittently throughout the notebook. The image each time was a human face, gaining detail with each successive rendering. The first face was just a disembodied oval set within concentric circles. The second was drawn with more deliberate strokes; eight lines radiated from the face into the outer rings. Several pages later, a third rendering took up a secretive position on an inside corner of the sheet. This face was drawn carefully, the details rotated into focus.

A staring human face with bulging eyes. An aquiline nose. A cap-like headdress. The face filled the center of a stylized spider's body, clinging to a radiating web.

Rain drummed on the cabin roof like muffled applause as she flicked her eyes across the pages. A spider with a human face for a body, sitting in its web, waiting for its prey.

"Impossible," she whispered to herself.

She knew that spider. She'd even held it in her hand. But for it to appear in Charlie's notebook?

Impossible.

Absolutely impossible.

Camino Real, near Portobelo
February 1667

Booted feet hammered over the bridge. Light flickered as the air hissed with the blur of poison darts. The wet thump of falling bodies filled Pedro's ears. Voices rose: panicked Spanish voices, deep-voiced African shouts, and, from somewhere in the shadows of the forest, garbled, ghoulish voices.

"Wait! Wait!"

"No!"

"Madre mía—"

Pedro scrambled to his feet and raced for the chapel, cursing the weight of his breastplate. An arrow whistled past, convincing him to pivot left and make for the woods instead. A second later, he crashed through a wall of vines into the tangled darkness he so despised.

The effect was immediate — the jungle muffled the clamor to a distant confusion, the way the roar of the sea recedes to a gentle murmur away from the shore. Pedro cowered in the damp shadow of a tree, gasping. A minute ticked by, or possibly an hour, as he fidgeted, wrought by cowardice and a dreaded sense of obligation. A curtain of roots dangled from above like strands of a giant web. Any minute now, he'd find himself ensnared.

Finally, Pedro gritted back his fear and crawled forward, wiggling on his stomach like a poorly armored insect. The first thing he saw when he peered out into the open was the motionless body of a Spaniard, felled by the dart protruding from his unprotected back. Beyond was the wreckage of the convoy — human wreckage, with soldiers strewn across the ground in lifeless heaps. A few moaned, waving in feeble attempts to escape. Braying mules trotted in confusion. One's pack had slipped and was hanging sideways, sprinkling silver coins across the grass like magical dewdrops.

Dark figures emerged from the far side of the woods. They skipped down the steep slope and into the clearing, fanning out among the remnants of the convoy. Pedro's gut jolted as he watched one lean over a fallen soldier, raise a dull blade, and hammer down with it.

"Cimarrones!" a voice hissed next to Pedro's ear.

He jumped halfway out of his skin then cursed. "Damn you, Ignacio!" The man loved a dramatic entrance.

"Cimarrones — Maroons!" Ignacio repeated, pointing at the dark-skinned figures in the clearing.

So the stories were true. Pedro eyed the wild-looking Maroons. Bloodthirsty Africans — escaped slaves — living unfettered in the wilds of the New World. He watched, fascinated, as one approached a pair of kneeling slaves and pulled them to their feet. The Spaniards might have lost an entire company, but the Maroons seemed to have gained several new recruits.

The clearing fell into an unnatural silence. Even the jungle birds seemed to strain quietly, listening. Pedro could hear his heart hammer in his chest. Surely the Maroons would hear it, too.

He flinched as more shapes separated themselves from the trees. But they were different: tall, pale, fully clothed. Jungle spirits?

"English!" Ignacio hissed through clenched teeth.

Their armor was tarnished, their beards thick, and their swords glinting like water in the stream. A few carried rifles; others, bristling pikes. They picked their way among the Maroons, finishing off fallen Spaniards and rounding up the treasure.

"The treasure," Ignacio breathed.

He pulled on Pedro's leg, and they crawled backward into the jungle. Manuel was there, shaking and mumbling. They were three against countless attackers. Impossible odds, even if courage happened to have been on their side.

Ignacio's eyes, however, shone with the gleam of a calculating mind. "All that treasure..."

* * *

Shadows lengthened, throwing the clearing into sharp relief. Contrasting streaks of dark and light pierced the thick air. The ambushers rounded up the convoy's treasures in one impressive heap. The English let out a staccato cheer, while their Maroon allies howled a guttural cry. Pedro's skin crawled.

He turned away, not wishing to watch his enemies rake their dirty fingers through bag upon bag of hard-earned Spanish gold and silver — all lost to the devil now.

Ignacio, on the other hand, was watching like a hawk.

"Something is wrong," he commented at length.

That seemed eminently clear to Pedro, so he ignored the Sevillian, nodding instead to Manuel's pleading looks in the direction of Portobelo. But Ignacio was so intent on the scene across the clearing that Pedro had to follow his gaze. Despite the rapidly dimming light, they could see the attackers engaged in an animated discussion.

Ignacio smiled, triumph creasing his face. "They've made the same mistake!"

Mistake?

Ignacio gave an exaggerated sigh, regarding Pedro the way one regards a thick-headed mule. "El Dragón — that pirate, Drake — ambushed a convoy many years ago. But the stupid bastards didn't have a way to carry thirty tons of silver and gold!"

Surely as legendary a pirate as Drake would have a plan for such an eventuality?

"What did El Dragón do?"

"They took the gold and buried the silver to come back for later. But someone saw, and the garrison dug it up before the pirates returned. We Spaniards got the silver back!" Ignacio smiled in delight at the minor victory snatched from the jaws of disaster — the type that seemed to befall Spain ever more frequently these days.

In the clearing, the allies muttered in discord. The Maroons seemed content to operate by day or night and moved with corresponding leisure, but the Englishmen were clearly eager to move on. They organized the loot, taking the most valuable items while relegating others — entire sacks — to another pile, each man stuffing his pockets along the way. The Maroons cleared a shallow pit among a mass of tree roots in higher ground and transferred the secondary pile into it. When the cache was covered, the Englishmen retreated into the jungle, their voices merry, their swords jangling — all insults to Pedro's ears. The Maroons simply vanished into the dark shadows, most of them unburdened. A dangerous foe, Pedro noted — motivated by revenge, not riches.

The clearing fell into an uneasy silence. Only the mules were left behind, sullen and disorderly.

Pedro, Ignacio, and Manuel inched to the edge of the woods with the halting steps of men on thin ice. Pedro could barely make out the clearing in the muted glow of twilight. Mules moved among the bodies of fallen soldiers, and Pedro swore he saw ghosts among them. Jungle creatures voiced their bold calls as if nothing unusual had occurred, nothing unusual at all.

Pedro took a resigned step toward Portobelo with Manuel on his heels. A moment later, they both spun to face Ignacio's cackle of delight.

"The silver!" he cried.

Pedro and Manuel stared at him, uncomprehending.

"The silver is ours!"

It took Pedro a moment to catch on. "But we have to report the ambush..."

Ignacio sneered. "Naturally, we will do our duty and report the attack."

"Naturally." Pedro nodded even as his eyes slipped toward to the treasure cache.

"But who's to know we kept a small percentage for ourselves?" Ignacio finished with a triumphant flick of the eyebrows.

Pedro looked from him to a blank-faced Manuel, and then to the treasure cache. All that silver, all his toil. Surely he deserved some reward.

Something flitted overhead — a bat? Pedro shivered and cast an unsure glance in the direction of the chapel. Though the dim light hid it from him, he knew the cross was there, hanging in silent judgment. But then again, he reasoned, the shadows worked both ways, hiding him from the chapel. They shifted and blended anew, forming an entirely new image in his mind. An image of the townsfolk back home, turning their heads. He pictured the weight and the sound of coins clinking in his pockets. Ignacio's words echoed in his mind. *Who's to know?*

Pedro felt his own lips curl up. Who, indeed?

San Blas Islands
December, present day

Impossible. All of it was impossible.

A rainy night had settled over *Aurora,* and Kate had moved into the forepeak bunk along with Nick. Her heart was thumping like she'd just slapped the timing board at the end of a race, but all she'd done was think about Charlie and his spider.

Impossible.

Somehow, though, it had to be possible. But how?

She leaned into Nick's space and found him engrossed in a fishing book. *Chapter 9, Processing Your Catch*, she read, eyeing the step-by-step guide to gutting fish. Bedtime reading for the idle engineer.

"Nick," she said.

He didn't respond. How could anyone be interested in fish when a historical mystery was running away with the other end of their line?

"Nick." She tapped his hand with Charlie's notebook.

His head barely turned. "Hmm?"

She nudged until he lowered the fishing guide to his chest and looked her way. Then she held up Charlie's notebook and waited for his reaction.

"A spider," he said. "A spider with a human face for a body."

"An anthropomorphic spider," she agreed, wanting — willing — him to recognize it. Surely he read National Geographic Magazine? Didn't everybody?

Apparently not.

"Aha." He paused. "I wonder why Charlie was drawing spiders." A rhetorical question, it seemed, because he raised his fishing guide as he said it.

She pressed his book down and sat up to face him. "I know that spider, Nick."

He blinked. "You know Charlie's spider?"

She nodded.

"So... what is it?" He looked expectant, as if she'd be able to provide a clear, logical answer. If only she could.

"It's impossible, that's what it is."

"What's impossible?"

"Remember I told you I worked on an excavation in Peru one summer? There was another dig close to ours called Sipán." She waited for a flicker of recognition in his eyes. For him to shout, *Sipán? Of course, I remember. That was a great issue of National Geographic!*

But no. No flicker of recognition, so she went on.

"They found a very important tomb in Sipán, loaded with grave goods. Gold. Silver." She caught her own voice rising. "I was loaned to their team for a week to train their student help, so I got a good look. The tomb had several burials: lords and priests with all sorts of jewelry — including spider medallions, just like what Charlie drew." She tapped the notebook.

Nick's eyes flickered uncertainly to the leather cover, then back to her.

"The spiders hung from a necklace, like this—" She traced a line well below her collarbone, then held a fist up to it. "Big spider medallions — six or seven of them, all hanging from the same chain." She moved her fist along the imaginary necklace — there, there, and there. "Each of them baseball size, more or less. And thick." She held out an imaginary medallion, fingers miming a wide gap. "Like a hockey puck. I held one, Nick."

Nick closed his fishing book and put it aside. "You held a spider like Charlie's?"

"Exactly." She tapped Charlie's notebook.

"Exactly?"

"Exactly."

"Okay... so what's impossible?"

"For Charlie to draw a spider medallion, he had to have seen one, right?"

"Right."

She shook her head. *"*Well, the tomb with these medallions was only discovered in the 1980s." She paused, watching the gears turn behind Nick's eyes. "How could Charlie have seen a Sipán spider — or a Sipán-like spider — in, what? 1910? 1914? That's decades before the tomb was discovered. It's impossible."

Nick arched an eyebrow at her.

"Impossible," she assured him.

"Maybe he saw a different spider."

She shook her head. "The Sipán spiders were the first of their kind. Nothing like them has ever been found anywhere else. None. Nowhere." She let her eyes examine the cabin roof. Blank. No clues there.

"There has to be another spider if he drew one."

"Theoretically, there could be other spider medallions that no one knows about. Never discovered. But that would be huge! The find of the century!" She stabbed at the notebook because, wow, *that* might be the find of the century. "And Charlie saw one? How? Where? When?"

Nick opened his mouth, reconsidered, and closed it again. Her cue to continue.

"Not only that, but we're talking about a Peruvian artifact from roughly 300 AD. Peru," she emphasized. "What's a Sipán spider — or a Sipán-like spider, from Peru — doing in Charlie's notebook?"

"Charlie went to South America?" Nick ventured.

"You tell me."

Nick closed his eyes, searching his memory. "No. At least, I don't think so." He shook his head with more certainty. "No, none of the stories about Charlie mention Peru."

She pressed on, half expecting this. "The sketches in Charlie's notebook come from his time in Panama. I'm sure of it."

Nick sat up to face her. "What would a spider necklace from Peru be doing in Panama?"

Kate stabbed her finger in the air, as if to say *therein lies the problem*. "How does a fourth-century necklace from Peru turn up in Panama in the 1910s?" she asked. "And what does it have to do with Charlie Parker?"

Chapter Four

The Treasure Chest of the Americas

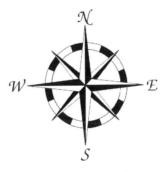

San Blas Islands
December, present day

The questions teased and taunted them throughout the night and the next day. But Charlie Parker was only one concern. After six weeks among the sleepy cays of Kuna Yala, *Aurora's* food lockers were nearly empty. It was time to stock up on supplies — and time to make some decisions.

Nick had started his trip in Maine with rather vague notions of heading south. Through some strange process he could hardly recall, he and Kate had settled on the idea of sailing as far as Panama. The islands of Kuna Yala were idyllic — a taste of the South Pacific, some said. Many sailors spent happy months, even years, there. And that was the very problem.

"I love it here, but it's time to pry ourselves away before *Aurora's* anchor sprouts its own coral reef," Kate said.

But where next?

He, for one, would be perfectly happy to cruise the Caribbean coast of Panama for the rest of the season. He equated warm weather with slow motion and liked it that way. Kate, on the other hand, was of a more restless mettle. She had her eye on transiting the Panama Canal and exploring the Pacific side of the isthmus — and beyond, far beyond, if the budget, boat, and relationship proved up to it.

"Portobelo," Kate said, putting her finger on the chart. "A historic town with a safe anchorage."

Nick measured the distance. "Fifty-five miles west."

He figured if they liked it enough, they would stay for the coming holidays. And then they would see.

Rising early the next morning, they readied *Aurora* and weighed anchor. It was a moment of truth, and Nick only exhaled when the anchor windlass rotated on cue, steadily raising one hundred feet of chain and the anchor. He'd done it! All those parts, painstakingly greased and reassembled. He'd had to crawl into the coffin-like locker at the bow and fiddle the motor into an impossibly tight space. Now, he watched and celebrated each link of anchor chain that rattled on board, then, with a heavy clunk, the anchor itself. A great moment for mankind!

"Did you see that?" he called back to Kate.

"See what?" She steered *Aurora* between the fringing reefs, paying no attention whatsoever to his amazing deed.

"The windlass worked!"

"Of course, it worked. You fixed it." She gave him an easy smile, like she'd known it all along.

Part of him was disappointed at the lack of fanfare, but the other part glowed just a little at her trust. The question was whether that trust was misplaced...

The sails filled with a brisk easterly, and *Aurora* cantered away on what promised to be a beautiful day at sea. As the morning wore on, the coast sliding past on the port side grew more and more dramatic. Dense forest tumbled straight off verdant hills into the sea.

"Costa Arriba," Kate said, reading from the chart.

She stood at the wheel, guiding *Aurora* like a horse over uneven terrain, her left leg propped against the boat's angle of heel. Nick stood one step ahead, tweaking the sheets for optimal performance. It was an occupation that could mesmerize him for hours. A full-time job, too, as the boat progressed along the curve of the coast and the wind angle shifted. Winching the genoa a little tighter, playing with the curve of the mainsail, watching the flapping telltales to judge how smoothly air was flowing over the sails. There was a magic to seeing the wind, harnessing it. Sailing solo, he had never found the time to appreciate it all. With Kate's help, though, tasks that once seemed like chores had become real pleasures.

"Nice, huh?" he grinned.

"Nice," she agreed.

He loved trimming, while she preferred steering in a more Zen-like approach. She rarely bothered with details like optimal sail shape. In her book, peak performance was measured in how enjoyable the day was rather than speed over ground — unless, of course, another sail appeared on the horizon and her competitive edge kicked in.

Men are from Mars, women are from Venus. But all in all, they made a surprisingly complementary team. He downloaded weather faxes, while Kate monitored the water supply. He cooked; she did the dishes. He repaired the bilge pump when it failed; she mended the torn mainsail. They alternated worrying about details and fretting over the big picture. By the time they had arrived in Panama, each had evolved into their own niche.

Just like Darwin's finches, Kate once commented with a satisfied glow.

Without her, he'd never have made it past New Jersey. Hell, he might never have left his job. She was the one who planted the idea in his mind, even if it had taken a while to digest.

A tiny rainbow formed in the spray at *Aurora's* bow, and in it, he saw everything that had brought them to this place and time. Sure, it was his boat, but Kate had provided the initial drive. If he were the hull, she'd be the sail. Together, they made a winning team.

Which wasn't to say they didn't experience the odd moment of friction. Such as when he found himself waging an inner battle between reminding Kate to steer a more optimal line and the knowledge that correcting her was likely to unleash her wrath. That was the problem with smart, independent types. They didn't like to be wrong.

"You're pinching a little," he murmured, trying to muster a casual tone.

Kate tightened her grip on the wheel and stared straight ahead. "Do you want to steer?"

"No, but I think you should fall off a tiny..." His voice faltered as he watched her eyes flicker and toss like the wave tops. "It's just... if you go too close to the wind, the boat loses speed."

"I know." Kate's voice could have chiseled a statue of an angry Neptune.

"Maybe if you fall off a few degrees..."

She stared straight ahead, lips squeezed in a thin line.

Nick reflected on the trade-off between boat speed and harmony with one's partner for a few moments. He let a stiff silence pass, then spoke again. "I think it's cookie time," he observed, waving the figurative white flag.

Kate's frozen visage thawed just a crack. "I'll have one."

He brought her three.

Peace thus restored, they enjoyed a period of wary silence before Kate turned the wheel over to him so she could photograph the landscape. He did as he was told and held back a comment on her aperture setting. Maybe now was not a good time.

Kate waved her hand at the untamed coastline, its green hues tending toward blue in the distance. "You know, this wouldn't have been much different in Columbus' day. Or Charlie's."

He followed her gesture to the wild coast, thinking of Charlie. What to make of the man and his notes? "What do you think Charlie was up to with those spiders?"

Kate scowled. "What wasn't Charlie up to?"

"What do you mean?"

In reply, she fetched Charlie's notebook. "Well, other than buttering up the local beauties..." She pointed to the page that read *Mercedes — whitewash, 20 bottles red wine, 6 parasols.* "What woman needs six parasols? And why was Charlie buying them?"

He shrugged. He glanced to the open sea on their right where a freighter steamed westward, just like *Aurora*. Heading to the canal, probably. *Aurora,* too? The question was an open one.

Kate turned more pages of the notebook. "Charlie seems to have been a bit of a procurement officer for a lot of people: wine for Mercedes, ham for Edgar. Then there's this Yolanta woman..."

"Who's that?"

"No idea."

Mercedes *and* Yolanta?

"Anyway—" Kate rifled the pages "—Charlie was up to something. Look at these circle things," she continued, giving Nick a quick glimpse of Charlie's sketches. "Why the X's in them?"

"X's? Or T's?" he asked, cocking his head.

In the pensive pause that ensued, he glanced at the fishing lines trawling off the stern. A small fan of spray rose from the leeward line. A strike!

"Whoa!"

Nowhere along the 3000-plus miles from Maine to Panama had he managed to catch a fish. On the contrary, fish had stolen a number of hooks from him, mocking his efforts with dangling monofilament and snapped-off lures.

Charlie flew out of his mind as Kate grabbed for the wheel, freeing his hands to pull in the line in a lopsided tug-of-war. The fish cut right, then left. The silver flash came nearer. A tuna! His heart rate jumped at the prospect. Taking careful aim with the gaff hook, he concentrated on landing his struggling catch without scratching *Aurora's* hull. With a grunt, he heaved the flapping fish into the cockpit.

He felt something gratifyingly primitive in finishing off the fish, the image of fresh sashimi at the forefront of his mind. Kate snapped a commemorative photo as he scurried about, eager to put his research into action: Bleed fish! Identify species! Gut! Then he filleted his catch, referring to the diagrams in his book.

"Hey, I caught a fish!"

In no time, the two of them were dipping their fingers into a bowl of soy marinade, sucking succulent bits of skipjack sashimi into their mouths and groaning with pleasure. The last ten miles to Portobelo saw an especially content sailor gaze along the length of his vessel.

My boat, Nick marveled as they edged between reefs and rocks lying off the entrance to the bay. *My beautiful boat.*

Life seemed good indeed. So good that Nick was not only distracted from thoughts of anthropomorphic spiders — he even pictured himself and Kate crossing the Pacific in *Aurora*, weighing anchor with a working windlass and catching fish as they sailed from one exotic landfall to another. Suddenly, the prospect of unexpected adventure didn't seem so bad, after all.

Portobelo

December, present day

"Wow," Nick murmured the next morning when they went ashore.

Upon closeup inspection, he concluded that Portobelo was considerably more "bello" from afar. The town was swimming in litter strewn across streets and gutters like faded confetti. Strips of dusty plastic, flapping silver foil, and shattered glass all clamored for attention, stealing the show from what should have been a strikingly beautiful old town. Somewhere, a trash pile was burning, and Nick could taste everything in it.

Kate shot him a dubious look that said, *What a dump.*

Historic buildings from the colonial era were streaked and mottled with age. Tiled roofs sprouted blankets of weeds. Signs acknowledged recent UNESCO-sponsored restoration work, but even those efforts were tarnished by the patina of time and indifference.

"It's like a different Panama," Kate murmured.

Gone were the gentle, wiry Kuna people, their dugout canoes, their quiet industriousness. This Panama was stocked with West Indians whose forefathers built the canal. Nick remembered that much from his guidebook. Their ancestors had left Jamaica and Barbados in droves to work on the most ambitious engineering project ever attempted. But times had changed. Idle inhabitants with inscrutable faces watched them pass. Kate edged closer to his side as they walked the cobbled lanes.

Nick hesitated at the next crossing, wondering which trashed street looked better.

Neither.

He and Kate had come to Portobelo with a vague notion of spending Christmas in a place so highly lauded by their guidebook. Now, he wasn't so sure.

"How about we just hit the ATM and the stores, then get out of Dodge?"

Kate scuffed something sticky off the sole of her sandal. A man sitting on a stoop to the right kicked a dog that yelped and scurried out of range. Nick was ready to write Portobelo off completely when he spotted a store: a Chinese-run "Mini-Super" near the central plaza. It was small but packed with exotic treats. The place was run by three generations of the same family, from the gap-toothed grandmother stocking the shelves to the chubby toddler cooing behind the counter.

Nick homed in on the cooler, already salivating. "Cold drinks!"

"Yogurt!" Kate called in delight. "Vegetables!"

The Mini-Super was an oasis of edible delights after weeks of a monotonous diet and no refrigeration. For starters, they treated themselves to a couple of orange Fantas and toasted each other on a rickety park bench — the only one that still had any slats. Nick let the cold drink slide down his throat and cool him from the inside as he slowly took in the scene from a different perspective.

Barefoot youngsters chased a soccer ball around the dirt plaza, laughing and scattering dust as they ran. A bus — a classic American school bus — passed in a riot of color, bass notes, and exhaust fumes, bringing a cheerful touch of Disney to town with airbrushed images from *The Lion King*.

"Rated G," Kate noted, "if you ignore the mudguards."

Nick glanced at the flaps of rubber, decorated with silhouettes of impossibly curvy women leaning back in suggestive poses.

"I guess they're aiming at a broad market."

He half expected her to make a face, but Kate just broke into chuckles. A minute later, they were laughing themselves silly over nothing but themselves.

"Hey, you know what day it is?" Kate nudged him.

"Uh... Tuesday?"

"Wednesday. And you know where you'd be on Wednesday at..." She checked her watch. "...eleven o'clock if you were still working in Boston?"

Nick smiled. It was their favorite game, comparing the sailing life to life back home. "I'd be behind a computer, completely stressed."

"Wearing a suit and tie," she added, giving his faded T-shirt an approving poke.

He dredged up the image from the depths of his memory. Maybe Portobelo wasn't so bad, after all.

Then Kate was up and off, heading for the largest building in town, the customs house. He formulated a quick plan as they ducked under a row of stone arches of the historic building. They'd snap a few pictures and skim the sites Kate was so eager to see. Do a little speed shopping and then weigh anchor — if it wasn't caught on some junk at the bottom of the harbor — and then hightail it back to the islands. That's what they'd do.

But each step up the creaking wooden staircase to the upper story nudged them back in time. Even Nick could hear the whispers behind the massive beams, imagine ghosts haunting the shadows. He found himself pausing to soak it all in. When he followed Kate onto the second-story porch, he squinted against the intense sunlight.

"Beautiful," Kate breathed, leaning over the railing toward the deep, protected bay.

Even he was inclined to agree. If you zoomed out, the town wasn't bad at all. Porto Bello, indeed. He aimed his camera at the green hills hemming in the anchorage, all of them lined with tiered fortresses. Then he turned the camera around and squeezed in close to Kate to snap a selfie.

"Smile!" He threw in a smooch for good measure, and their mood lightened considerably. The place had a certain appeal, after all.

"Can't you just see it?" Kate breathed, eyes roaming over the scene.

"What?" A bead of sweat rolled down his brow.

She motioned vaguely. "It." Her fingers drew in the air, resurrecting crumbling buildings. "Them." Nick figured her imagination was populating the cobblestone streets with colonial figures. "Those guys are counting their pieces of eight," she said, turning a trio of locals into Spanish soldiers. "And that one—" she pointed to a man fanning himself "—is counting down the days until he can get home."

He smiled. Kate was good at that kind of thing: Imagining. Dreaming. Bringing the past to life.

He indulged her for another minute of inhaling history before pulling her back to street level and sniffing the air. Somewhere in Portobelo, a coffee was brewing just for him, and he was determined to track it down.

"Come on, Kate." He coaxed her past a one-room museum tucked into an alcove.

"Oooh, look at the—"

"Later, okay?"

He tugged her along, but she dug in her heels at a sun-bleached information plaque at a street corner.

"Wow. Over the course of one century, one-third of all the world's silver passed through the doors of the customs house."

"Wow." He pulled her onward.

"One-third of all the silver in the world!"

He'd give about that much for a decent coffee right now. "This way."

He led her along the main road, then up a winding side street, following signs to an internet café. Kate slalomed around a series of potholes, then pointed to where a woman bustled around a rough cinder block home.

"Check out Santa," Kate said. The house was run-down but tidy and made festive with garish Christmas decorations like the rest of the buildings on the street. "And look." She pointed the other way. "See Frosty the Snowman? He's adoring baby Jesus in the manger."

The woman stretched a *Feliz Navidad* sign over her door and waved. Nick waved back. Maybe Portobelo was friendlier than it first seemed. The wintry decorations seemed out of place in this tropical climate, but Christmas was Christmas, and — oh, a good reminder that he'd have to get Kate a present soon.

Two blocks later, the street dead-ended at the foot of a whitewashed building. *El Diablo,* the sign proclaimed in large, flaming letters, with *Internet Café / Backpacker Lodge / Hardware* in smaller font beneath. Nick perked up. Coffee, internet, and the chance to stock up on duct tape? This, he had to see.

The lower floor and the annex behind it seemed to be the lodgings. He led the way up a set of exterior stairs, following the smell of damp rain forest, frying hamburgers, and a faint hint of rum. In the shaded rooftop bar, the temperature promptly dropped ten degrees. His sweat-drenched shirt practically sighed in relief.

"If we can cool off when we step into El Diablo," he whispered, "what does that say about Portobelo?"

"Panama: heaven or hell?" Kate grinned.

They slid in across both sides of a wide table and glanced around. Aside from the shade, El Diablo offered an airy vista over the old town, where the customs house and church tower punctuated a lumpy carpet of red roofs.

Nick scanned the menu and nodded. "I think I could spend some time in Portobelo after all. As long as it's up here," he emphasized. "If the coffee's any good."

"Coffee's good," came a merry voice, "But the beer's better!"

El Diablo, Portobelo

present day

Nick glanced left to find two young men sporting spectacularly unkempt beards and tangled mops of hair, holding frosty bottles up in a toast. Sailors, no doubt about it. One wore a T-shirt advertising the very drink in his hand.

"A nice cold Balboa?" Nick asked. The local label wasn't much to write home about, but after a few weeks without — well, he could see the appeal.

"Na, mate, it's a Panama," said the twenty-something man on the left. His beard seemed to be saving a fleck of foam for later. "Just as good!" Something in his tone suggested thorough research.

"G'day," said his smiling sidekick, "I'm Trevor." *Trevah,* his Australian accent sang.

"I'm Tyler!" called out the first, also dropping the r. "We're your neighbors from *Free Willy*."

The sloop next to *Aurora*? Until now, Nick had only seen the boat, but the scraggly crew matched the vessel perfectly. *Free Willy* was about as poorly groomed as her crew but exuded the same kind of impish charm in spite of the rust marks dripping down her sides.

The young men's attention was abruptly diverted as a Latina waitress in a frilly top strutted over to tend to the new arrivals. When she leaned in to wipe the table, the Australians swayed closer in enthralled unison. Kate ordered a Fanta while Nick asked for coffee and the Wi-Fi password. By the time the waitress disappeared into the kitchen and Trevor and Tyler recovered their senses, Kate had unfolded the laptop for a quick email check, leaving him to make conversation.

Nick started where all sailors started — by asking about their boat.

"*Free Willy*? Bought her in Florida!"

"Gonna sell her back home," Tyler's eyes shone. "Make a profit!"

Trevor winked. "And if the boat doesn't fetch a good price, the rum will!"

Tyler giggled, letting Nick in on their brilliant plan. They had packed their forty-two-footer with cases of Jamaican rum to sell in Tahiti. He related the details in a hushed tone which came out between a shout and a quiet roar.

"But don't tell anyone!"

Nick made an appropriately sober face. "Have you done much sailing before?"

"None!" Tyler blurted.

"We did find Panama, though."

"Yeah, after a wrong turn to Cuba."

"I still don't know how we missed the Caymans," Trevor conceded, suddenly morose.

A brief, muted cloud fell over the pair. Then Tyler shrugged and clinked his bottle against his friend's, restoring the world to order.

Trevor was the louder and shaggier of the pair. Tyler was a restless soul, constantly shifting salt and pepper shakers around the table in a frenetic two-piece chess game that followed its own set of rules. They regaled Nick with tales of their fabulous misadventures to date until the waitress reappeared with their drinks — at which point the conversation hit a lull. Nick barely looked up other than to give the coffee an approving nod, but the boys were transfixed. When the waitress left, their eyes trailed longingly after her.

Eventually, Trevor and Tyler widened their conversational circle to include the other customers in the place, a couple of taciturn Swedish sailors and two English backpackers. The subject quickly turned to the wrecked sailboat back in San Blas.

"The *Persyphonic*," Trevor started.

"*Perphylactic*," Tyler tried.

"*Percypholic*?"

"Percy-bloody-something."

One of the Swedes weighed in with a note of authority. *"Persephone*."

"Whatever." Tyler waved a hand and carried on.

A thrilling new development, according to the Australian duo, was that the body aboard the wrecked boat was not just dead but decomposing — a condition imagined in full, gory detail by an enthralled Trevor — which suggested a long-past accident or foul play.

Nick found his attention wandering, and it wasn't long before he nudged Kate for a turn on the laptop. That was one of the things about sailing: he sure didn't miss the sensationalism of the press. But a spoonful of email — that would go perfectly with his coffee.

* * *

Kate felt Nick's tap on her shoulder and nodded while speed-typing a reply to her friend's message.

"Almost done," she murmured, hurrying to reread another email — the one with *Get this* in the subject line. Then she logged off and ceded the computer to Nick, who promptly slipped off into the ether.

Kate pulled Charlie's notebook out of Nick's backpack and stood. Her feet took her on a loop of the rooftop cafe, but her mind was on that email. *Get this.* A message from Susan, a former colleague, reporting on her latest excavation in Cyprus and filling Kate in on the news.

Richard Brewster Lewis is at it again, Susan wrote.

Kate recognized the name immediately. The sensationalist author of several books had a knack for arousing public interest in history — the wrong kind of public interest. His best-selling book to date — *Treasures of Troy!* — was a controversial tale of artifacts unearthed in the 1870 Schliemann excavation — treasures later lost, never to be seen again. The author's suggestive tone and free-ranging conjecture spurred an epidemic of tomb robbing throughout Turkey as amateurs hoped to cash in big. Archaeologists and legitimate historians decried Lewis for inspiring illegal exploits, declaring his books fit only for fiction shelves. Lewis countered that archaeologists were simply jealous of his success in capturing the public imagination.

Imagination is right, Kate thought.

According to Susan, Lewis had just published a new book called *Pirate Gold!* that focused on the colonial-era Caribbean. His account included several anecdotes set in Panama, pipeline between the riches of South America and Spain. When Kate looked up the book, she'd immediately scowled. The breathless description echoed through her mind as she paced between tables.

In another blockbuster tale, bestselling author Richard Brewster Lewis shares the electrifying true tale of lost treasures in the Caribbean! Startling and incredible revelations expose countless riches just waiting to be unearthed in this tropical paradise! Pieces of eight! Gold doubloons!

Four exclamation marks in four sentences. Kate cringed.

A work of monumental importance! A must for every armchair historian!

Kate snorted. A must for every aspiring grave robber, that's what it was.

Susan reported that rumors were already circulating of black market bounties on these purported treasures. Illicit traders couldn't wait to cash in.

She sighed. Now every moron with a machete and shovel would be tearing up Panama looking for artifacts that probably didn't exist.

Her mind snagged on her thought. Probably?

She fingered Charlie's notebook.

* * *

The back section of El Diablo's upper story was a common room with a lumpy couch, an outdated desktop computer, and shelves of books labeled *Leave One — Take One*. Kate glanced into the open-air bar where the shaggy Australians had burst into fits of uncontrollable laughter. One of them delivered a punchline — something about beer and balls. The Swedes blinked in confusion. Nick flashed a smile and went back to his screen as the English backpackers steamrolled right into another off-color joke.

"A retired sailor goes to a brothel..."

Kate tuned them out and continued her explorations, turning to the photographs decorating the wall between the bar area and the rear room. Black-and-white images in thick frames hung in irregular rows, each at its own unique angle off the perpendicular. Most were stiff, grainy shots from a bygone era. A young, regal-looking Spanish woman looked out from one photograph, standing with timeless confidence. One hand was folded precisely over the other, and she held the parasol thrust before her like a scepter. Dark eyes burned into the camera, coolly considering her latest visitor.

I bet she didn't make many compromises. Kate looked past her own reflection in the glass. *Didn't arrange her life to suit a man. Didn't let society keep her from being her own person.*

Kate looked long and hard, then proceeded to the next frame. In it, a small group of young women in high-collared dresses stood under dark parasols in a neat line. The women represented the full range of Central American ethnicities, from white to black with every shade in between. A figure at the left dominated the group portrait — the same woman from the first photo, decades older but showing the same regal bearing. There were several more photos of the same person alone or with a supporting cast of younger women. In one photo, she stood with a swarm of young Caucasian admirers in khakis. Kate lingered on it for a moment before stepping over to a different image. It was a sketch rather than a photograph, but equally old, judging by the faded paper. In it, a small sailboat with tightly sheeted sails raced over spraying waves. Kate admired it for a minute then worked her way back to the first picture.

"*Mi bisabuela.*"

Kate looked over and squinted at a blinding Hawaiian shirt. Somewhere behind the orange flowers and pink swirls, she made out a deeply tanned, fifty-something man with dark, curly hair. Either he had neglected to shave for several days or the scruffy shadow across his face was a cultivated effect. She wasn't sure which.

"Juan." The man nodded and switched into fluent English delivered in machine-gun Spanish style. "She started El Diablo," he said, gesturing at the photograph. "Now it's my place. Fourth generation!"

"Your great-grandmother ran a café here?"

"Well, ah... It was sort of a...a..." Juan stammered. "She ran a café and... other business interests."

Kate was all ears, eager for an example of female success in a male-dominated world. "What kind of business?"

Juan hemmed, hawed, and changed the subject. "You on a boat? Need parts? Bottom paint? Shackles? New hose pipe?"

She shook her head. *No thank you.*

"I do imports, you know," Juan continued to pitch his business in staccato bursts. "I can get anything you need! Tax free!"

The Lone Ranger tune burst out of his pocket, and Juan dug out a cell phone.

Kate nodded. "Great. If we need something, we'll let you know."

Juan kept speaking as he raised the phone to his ear. "I put in the orders, my cousin Juanito in Panama City delivers. Very reliable! You going through the canal?" Juan asked, already nodding for her to say yes.

"Maybe," she answered, glancing over at Nick.

Juan left it at that, firing words into his phone while striding over to two travel-weary backpackers who'd just stepped in. He led them downstairs, plugging his services while putting his device on hold and fishing a second ringing cell phone out of a different pocket.

"We have laundry service! Internet! Boat trips to Colombia! Hang on... *Sí? No! Juanito, te dije que...*"

Kate returned to the back room and sat down a little hesitantly at the computer marked, *Strict ten-minute limit!* She opened Charlie's notebook, clicked on the guest internet portal, and initiated a search. After glancing around the empty room one more time, she turned back to the screen and began to read.

She clicked from one lead to another, getting more intent with each hit, glancing frequently at Charlie's notebook and the door. She was on her seventh or eighth site when a shadow appeared behind her.

"I'll just be a second," she called, scribbling a note on a scrap of paper.

The figure gestured. "Please, take your time."

Kate couldn't resist glancing up in the direction of the smooth, accented tenor. But whoever it was, he had already retreated out of view. She closed the browsing window, collected her things, and gave the area a last check to make sure nothing was left behind. When she stepped back out into the restaurant, she spotted the olive-toned man at a nearby table, gazing over the undulating rooftops.

"How's the coffee?" she called to Nick.

She was so engrossed in her own thoughts, though, that she barely heard Nick's reply. Neither did she notice the man whose eyes followed her with a long, appraising look before he moved to the rear room with the silent step of a cat. He slid into the creaking desk chair at the computer and glanced back through the open doorway. Then he rolled the mouse over the toolbar, clicked on *View Browsing History*, and proceeded most attentively.

Chapter Five

A River of Riches

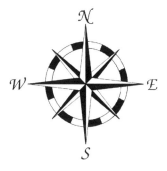

Camino Real, near Portobelo
February 1667

"It's brilliant, I tell you! Brilliant!"

Ignacio stood at the scene of the massacre, outlining his plan.

"We'll report the ambush, of course."

Of course. Pedro nodded, ready to go.

Ignacio held up a finger to halt him. "But not before stashing away some of the silver for ourselves." His eyes flicked back and forth, and he poked Pedro in the chest. "For you. For you." He poked Manuel, too, then turned his thumb to tag himself. "For me. All that treasure!" He grinned, flashing his white teeth in the dim light.

Pedro had started out leaning away from Ignacio, but now he was hanging on every word, feeling the glow of possibility in a way he hadn't in a long, long time.

"I'll be rich!" Ignacio concluded, then quickly corrected himself. "Er — all of us will be rich! You, Pedro. You'll be rich! You too, Manuel." He smiled his winning smile again, then shooed them off. "So get to work!"

The three comrades — now accomplices — set to work. First hugging the tree line, then more boldly, they stole over to the buried cache. Ignacio stood to one side, keeping his hands clean while Pedro and Manuel dug in the damp soil to expose the loot.

"I'm keeping a lookout," Ignacio said at Manuel's protest.

Pedro's fingers scratched at the damp soil until they unearthed the first canvas sacks. Even the moon seemed to lean in for a curious look over his shoulder as he excavated sacks full of coins that glinted seductively in the silvery light.

"Look at it all!"

Ignacio ran ten greedy fingers through a sack then held two dripping handfuls up to eye level. They fell with a heavy, cascading sound, a river of riches. As Pedro and Manuel toiled, more and more sacks poked up above the earth. Ten minutes later, Pedro sat back on his heels and wiped his brow.

All mine, he thought, staring at it all.

All mine. Ignacio's eyes glinted in the dark.

Most of the sacks were lumpy with coins, but not all. Pedro rooted around in one that held more blocky, irregular shapes and pulled out a large, round object.

A giant coin?

He fumbled with the leather strap then pulled out a chunky piece of solid silver. Far too big and fat for a coin, it took up most of his fleshy palm. He turned it over. Thin silver strands lay over a solid base, forming a hollow dome. Concentric circles of silver drew his eye to the center, where a crudely fashioned human face stared out. When he tilted it in the moonlight, he immediately recoiled.

"*Madre de Dios!*"

It was a hideous, heathen creation. The human face formed the body of an eight-legged spider. Pedro thrust the abomination back into the sack and pushed it away. He cursed, crossed himself, and rubbed his hands on his pants. Anything to erase the feel of it in his hand.

"Enough!" he cried, pushing himself to his feet. He scooped up as many sacks as he could carry, avoiding the one with the silver spider. He'd had enough of this evil night.

Manuel managed to grasp several heavy sacks and maneuver yet another under one elbow, while Ignacio tied sacks in pairs to sling over his shoulders. The trio struggled off in the direction of Portobelo, their burdens complaining in dark, metallic tones. Within a few lumbering steps, however, Pedro cursed and dropped his load beside the chapel gates.

"We'll never make it to Portobelo like this!"

Even that petty amount — a mere drop in a sea of silver — was too much to carry. Pedro was already sweating from every pore. Manuel dropped on his knees and began to pray. Pedro joined him, feeling the damp soil press through the worn cloth at his knees. He prayed like he'd never prayed before, not in all his miserable days and nights in Portobelo. Surely their lives had been spared and all that treasure granted to him — him, Pedro! — for some higher purpose.

Ignacio looked around and finally cried in triumph. "A solution! A holy solution!"

Pedro looked up. Was the Virgin Mary coming to their aid?

Nothing stirred except Ignacio, who leaped to the chapel gate and studied the interior.

"We can hide our silver here and return for it later!"

Pedro couldn't help but admire the man's tenacity. Ignacio pulled the gate open, ripping out weeds tangled in the bars like emaciated sentries at a long-forgotten post. They cried in protest, then went deathly still as Ignacio forced his way inside.

Pedro followed, crossing himself. A figure flew out at them, attacking in a flurry of claws and fangs. He jumped aside in blind terror. Ignacio whooped in surprise, then laughed at Pedro.

"Only a bat, you fool!"

Pedro picked himself up off the ground, trying to calm his thumping heart. One way or another, the New World seemed determined to kill him.

Inside, the chapel was cool and damp. One arched window admitted a single shaft of moonlight as if the devil himself held a torch to their unholy escapade.

Ignacio seemed completely at home. "It's perfect!" he declared, spinning around the small space.

Pedro wasn't so sure. The chapel was too obvious a hiding place, and it was barely five strides across.

"Where can we hide the treasure?"

They fumbled for a place to conceal the loot, sending Manuel back for more sacks from the cache. Surely there was a corner somewhere that would do...

A wooden statue of the Madonna stood at the head of the chapel, draped in a moldy red shawl. Her sad, downward gaze fixed on a spot on the floor. Pedro studied the angle for a time then dragged a heel across the floor.

He glanced back up at the Virgin Mary, then dropped to his knees and worked the blade of his dagger between the uneven flagstones.

"What are you doing?" Ignacio demanded.

Pedro motioned for Ignacio to help, and to his surprise, the man actually did, working in the opposite direction. When the flagstone gave way with a groan, Pedro shifted it aside, revealing a thin layer of pebbles that made up the chapel's foundation. He dug a little more and found nothing but moist earth.

Ignacio grinned in a way that said he'd known it all along. "Perfect!"

They scraped out a pit deep enough to contain two layers of sacks. Pedro lost count after sixteen canvas bags, though he was sure Ignacio made an exact tally. Among them was the sack that had so repulsed Pedro, brought by that stupid Manuel on his third load.

"Enough," Pedro finally declared, fixing Ignacio with his most determined look.

Ignacio's eyes blazed with visions of grandeur as he cast a longing gaze in the direction of the treasure heap in the clearing. The fire in his eyes flickered, burned high, and finally dimmed.

"Enough." He sighed.

Hefting two smaller sacks each, they started down the Camino. Another eternity passed, and after much stumbling and cursing, the sweat-soaked trio arrived on the outskirts of town at the first light of dawn.

"What do we do with this?" Pedro whispered, swinging his silver sacks. They couldn't march into Portobelo with their pockets bulging, clinking, and clanking.

"There!" Ignacio pushed past Pedro and stepped under the archway of the cemetery on the outskirts of town.

Pedro had had enough of death for one day. Still, they needed to stash the loot somewhere, and the cemetery would have to do for now. He threw his sacks in one corner of the enclosure and brushed his hands clean all the way back into town. The dirt rubbed off, but the guilt didn't. What if they were caught? Theft was theft, even if it was for a noble cause. They could be jailed. Court-martialed. Maybe even hung.

"Alert! Alert!"

"Quickly. Quickly!"

The town was alive with urgent voices. Hasty steps heralded the troops beginning to muster.

Pedro hurried onward.

"Just in time," Ignacio murmured.

Concern over the overdue convoy had spread through the town, and two companies were already collecting their arms. No sooner had the three ambush survivors stumbled into town than they were whisked to the garrison's commander.

"Allow me to explain, sir." Ignacio bowed deeply and went on to outdo himself with tales of his valiant defense of the king's treasure, leaving Pedro and Manuel to minor supporting roles.

Pedro didn't care. He'd never been so weary or so desperately in need of a bed. But before he could so much as swallow a bite of food, he was forced to trudge back up the Camino. Ignacio led the way, his face drawn in a feigned look of despair. His step, however, was light and energetic as ever. Manuel was left behind, too big and too soundly asleep to budge.

When the company passed the chapel of Santa Maria del Bosce, Pedro's flagging reserves revived with the edgy taste of adrenaline. Neither he nor Ignacio dared cast so much as a sideways glance at the chapel where their buried treasure lay. All was quiet. Quiet, that is, but for the disembodied screeches echoing from the jungle.

How far were the Maroons now? His eyes vaulted from shadow to shadow. What was that movement over there?

Soldiers fanned out across the clearing. Ignacio led the officers to the cache among the tree roots. Distressed calls went out as the new arrivals found fallen comrades, but dismay quickly turned to a subdued cheer.

"Here! The treasure is still here!"

Well, most of it, Ignacio's dancing eyes said.

"Get the mules!"

A fraction of the loot had been spirited away by the English, but the majority remained. Because the mules hadn't strayed far, the ill-fated convoy — or what was left of it — was reassembled by noon, ready to finish its trek into Portobelo. The fallen were buried in shallow graves behind the chapel, where the commanding officer called the company together.

"Let us pray," he announced, lowering his head.

"Yes, let's," Ignacio murmured, casting a concerned eye toward the chapel interior.

A hush fell over the clearing as men solemnly followed suit. Jungle birds mocked them from a safe distance, and a monkey screeched.

A minute later, the captain raised his head. "Amen," he said, replacing his helmet.

"Amen," the rest of the company echoed in low voices.

"Amen," Pedro and Ignacio mumbled, shooting each other sly looks.

Portobelo

December, present day

Nick had been listening to Trevor and Tyler with one ear, more occupied with his email backlog than anything else. The next time he looked up, the Australians had shifted closer to the bar and Kate had reappeared from her explorations. He patted the seat next to him and shared all the minor news from home.

"My mom's dog got skunked. My niece got a new tooth. Mark's business is booming, and he put in a new kitchen."

"Haven't missed much, have we?"

"Nope." One more confirmation that they'd done the right thing by sailing away. "Want to stay for lunch?"

For once, Kate didn't take much convincing. After they ordered, she took the computer back, motioning for him to sit on her side of the table.

"I need to show you something."

The way her eyes shone warned him that a wave of breathless excitement was heading his way. Maybe she'd learned about an endangered animal endemic to Panama. Maybe she'd uncovered some obscure historical fact. It was sometimes hard to relate to Kate's enthusiasm for her pet topics, but he loved the way she lit up about them. So many people lacked passion for life, but not Kate. A characteristic that could be maddening at times, endearing at others.

While the computer searched, Kate opened Charlie's notebook to a page filled with ovals and strange marks.

"Remember these?"

Nick peered closer. Right, the circles with Ts. And she made fun of him for reading about fishing?

"Over the course of one century, one-third of the world's silver passed through the doors of the customs house," Kate started.

Here she goes again. Nick glanced at his watch and squeezed his lips. *And?*

She scrolled through her search results, selected one, and angled the laptop toward him. Her finger pointed at a photograph of historic coins on the laptop then moved to the circular illustrations in Charlie's notebook.

"They're Spanish coins. Pieces of eight," she whispered. "Old. Very old."

Nick studied her face to see if she was kidding. Apparently not. He stared down at Charlie's notebook. "Pieces of eight... Like from pirate stories?"

Kate nodded.

He looked more closely at the sketches. Wow. They really did look like coins.

"But wait — I thought pirates had... What are they called? Doubloons?"

"Doubloons are gold coins. Pieces of eight are silver."

"Eight what?" Nick asked, stalling while his mind whirred. *Jesus, Charlie, what were you up to?*

"Eight *reales*. A *real* is a denomination, like a dollar. The 'pieces' part comes from how the coins could be subdivided into fourths and eighths. See the cross-lines?"

He scratched his brow. Where was all this going? And did he really want to find out?

"They're silver coins. Pirate stories are full of them, right?" Kate tapped Charlie's drawings. "These are the same. Pieces of eight."

An image of pirates huddled around a glittering treasure chest on a palm-studded beach jumped into Nick's mind.

"I thought Charlie was working on the canal."

"Looks like he had some extracurricular activities."

Nick gaped at her. Was it really possible?

A second later, he shook his head. There had to be some other explanation, right?

Kate tapped the notebook. "Let's back up. After Columbus 'discovered' America..." she said, putting air quotes around *discovered*

"... the Spanish claimed most of Central and South America, where they more or less wiped out the Aztecs and Incas. Right?"

"Right." That much history, he knew.

"The Aztecs and Incas had unbelievable riches. Gold and silver — heaps of it. Either in raw lumps or worked pieces, like jewelry and figurines. The Spanish took everything they could get their hands on and shipped it back home. Pieces from older cultures, too. Moche, Lambeyeque, Nazca." Kate rattled them off like the names of old friends. "Anything of value. The Spanish forced the locals — the few who didn't die of introduced diseases, that is — to work the mines for raw silver and gold. Still with me?"

Nick wasn't sure he was, but heck, she was on a roll.

"One of the mines was in Bolivia — a place called Potosí. Loads and loads of silver came out of there. Eventually, the Spanish established a mint in South America, making the silver into coins before it was shipped to Spain — via Panama. It was all funneled through a trail from the Pacific side to here. To Portobelo." She gestured at the roofs of the old town. "The trail was the colonial equivalent of the canal — a foot trail with mules instead of water and ships."

Nick followed her eyes. A breeze stirred life into the dusty lanes below.

"So these coins...?" He pointed at Charlie's notebook.

"They're pieces of eight minted in the New World. You can date them by looking at how well made they are. Look at this." She pointed at the computer screen. "The early coins were made at a mint subcontracted out by the king. They were handmade and pretty crude. See? As long as the coins had the right weight, twenty-eight grams, they were considered okay. But apart from that, they were pretty messy. No exact thickness or diameter."

Nick could see what she meant. The coins on the screen were more oval than round. The inscriptions were off-center and smudged. Charlie's careful drawings reproduced the blurred effect with thick pencil strokes.

"In the seventeen hundreds, they started making coins to tighter specifications which made the coins more uniform. The inscriptions were neat and crisp, and the edges were milled. So we know the crude coins that Charlie drew must be from between 1570 and 1731."

What a mind. Kate didn't know current interest rates, but ask her about a date...

"You with me?" She gave him a hard look.

Keep a happy crew mate. Nick nodded. "Sloppy coins, neat coins. Old and new." He focused on the image of a cleanly minted coin, the intricate coat of arms sharp and centered. None of Charlie's sketches had clear inscriptions. "So... Charlie was sketching old coins?"

Kate nodded and raised her eyebrows.

"So... Charlie had to have seen old coins?"

A tilt of the head.

"Charlie *found* old coins?"

Kate made a noncommittal sound. "He sure had a lot of time to sketch them." Her voice was even, but her eyes were full of speculation.

"Whoa, wait. What about the spider things?"

"Charlie sure did spend a lot of time with some pretty valuable stuff."

Just then, the waitress intruded with their forgotten lunch orders, and Nick slipped back to the opposite side of the table.

What was Charlie Parker, canal engineer, doing with Spanish treasure dating hundreds of years before his time?

He looked out over the tiled rooftops, trying to make sense of it all. First the spider medallion. Now pieces of eight. Nick shook his head. What was Charlie doing, sketching such things? How did they fit together?

He chewed the questions along with every bite of his greasy burger lunch. Beside him, Kate leafed through Charlie's notebook and continued her online search while taking wolf-sized bites out of a sandwich.

Her brow furrowed in concentration. She bit her lower lip and twisted her sandy brown hair. He had once watched her spend three rainy days on an intricate puzzle of an Egyptian tomb, and the effect was similar. That dogged determination, comparing countless pieces until the right match was made.

He smiled. God, it was good to be together again. The question was how long the good times would last. Nick was fully aware he currently possessed two things that Kate found completely irresistible: a sailboat and the utter lack of a plan. Some women had a thing for men with fancy cars or tailored suits. For Kate, it was anything that hinted of adventure and travel. When the money ran out and they went back to real life, what then?

He studied her intent face. Would the relationship itself suffice without the sailing lifestyle?

Kate made a triumphant sound and looked up, gripped by some new discovery, then did a double take at his expression. "What are you thinking about?"

You.

"Charlie," he said.

She smiled, and he almost wished he'd told her the truth. But Kate was already plowing on. "So, Charlie was drawing coins."

Nick nodded, eager to show off what he'd learned. "Pieces of eight. Old ones."

Kate leaned in close. "It gets better."

Better seemed like a dubious distinction, but he kept his mouth shut.

"Charlie was drawing lots of things, remember?" She turned the notebook around so he could see it. "Remember this?"

Nick followed her finger. "The weird spider face? The impossible one?"

"The Sipán spider."

That would be it. *What had Charlie gotten himself into?*

Kate beckoned him over so they were both sitting with their backs to the hip-high outer wall of the rooftop bar, keeping the computer screen out of view of other guests. She tapped the picture that came up on the screen, first as a small thumbnail, then a full-screen image.

Nick leaned closer. "Charlie's spider?"

Kate nudged him in the ribs, miming for him to drop his voice. "The Sipán spider," she whispered. "I was right!"

King Tut of the Americas, roared the web page headline. Maybe Kate wasn't kidding when she called it the find of the century.

"But how could Charlie have—"

A chorus of excited voices erupted from the far side of the rooftop bar. Trevor, Tyler, and the backpackers had just discovered the dart board — a circle decorated with the pocked image of former US President George W. Bush. They were already licking the ends of their darts.

"Nah, mate, I get to go first."

"No, I do."

"No, me!"

Kate ignored them and scrolled down to another image of the Sipán tomb. A human skeleton stretched out in the dirt. Ceramic pots and other grave goods circled a laid out body, its chest studded with spider medallions just like the one in Charlie's sketches. From the look of a ruler in the photo, one spider was a good three inches across, and the thick gold bulk cast a heavy shadow. Each was much bigger than what Nick had been imagining. Two empty eye sockets stared out in silent challenge.

Charlie's sketches and Kate's recollections were one thing, but photographic evidence was another. Nick's heart slowed down a little, then revved into high gear. It was exactly like Charlie's spider, made of solid gold. Except that the spiders weren't discovered until the 1980s.

Impossible.

Nick shook his head. Maybe that would rattle a piece of the puzzle into place. There had to be another spider. What had Kate said? *The find of the century.* Jesus.

They looked at each other wordlessly, shaking their heads.

"First coins, now spider medallions?"

Kate nodded. "But how did Charlie see these things?"

"You're asking me?"

"He's your grandfather."

"Great-grandfather," Nick corrected. One who died before his only child was born, leaving no clues except those in the notebook lying before them now.

Guffaws drew his attention across the room. A sheepish Tyler looked out over the edge of the railing and into the lush foliage, where his dart had gone wide. Very wide.

Nick turned back to Kate and leaned over his elbows, close to her face. "Okay, Madame Archaeologist, let's back up. What would medallions from Peru be doing in Panama? With silver coins from, what, Bolivia?"

Kate motioned outside, at the dilapidated roof of the customs house. The gesture said *There, there is your answer.*

"The Spanish funneled the treasures of the New World through Portobelo. Silver and gold from Bolivia, Peru... all over." She grasped at an imaginary map and scooped the pieces together. "All kinds of valuables — raw metal and worked artifacts — were sent to Spain by ship. Who knows what got mixed with what?"

Nick struggled to keep it all straight. Logic, consistency: that's what he needed. A nice, orderly list.

He extended a finger. "The Spanish collected all kinds of treasure in South America and consolidated it in Panama."

Kate nodded.

A second finger. "They collected the treasure here in Portobelo and shipped it back to Spain."

Check, her eyes said.

Three. "Except... some of it never made it out?"

Kate held her tongue, but her eyes shone.

Nick searched his list for some logical connection, but nothing clicked. On to point four. "A couple of centuries later, Charlie comes along and... finds lost treasure?"

"Finds... gets... buys... Who knows?"

Nick leaned back, distancing himself from the whole crazy idea. "So what was Charlie up to?"

Kate nodded quietly, then spoke. "One thing's for sure. He wasn't just building breakwaters for the canal."

Portobelo
June 1667

Three months after the ambush, Pedro stood on the deck of his departing ship and turned his back on Portobelo. The fermenting scent of the New World followed him into the open sea, but he shrugged it away, resolute.

How grand our plans were. He shook his head. *And how quickly they fell apart.*

All his anxiety about being caught and executed for treason had been for nothing. As fate would have it, the garrison commander was as eager as everyone else to cover up the disaster of the ambushed convoy and quickly concluded his perfunctory investigation. The accountants were ordered to credit some of the last convoy's silver to this reduced shipment, together with a small portion from the next.

"By the time anyone can compare the ledgers—" the commander had winked "—we'll all be enjoying our pensions back in Spain."

Truly a man after Ignacio's heart.

"As if we'll ever get a pension," one of the guards at the door muttered.

Pedro held his tongue and looked at Ignacio, whose smug look said, *Not likely. But we have our own special savings plans.*

That they did. Or rather, they had. Pedro closed his eyes, thinking back over it all.

Through clandestine efforts over a period of weeks, he, Ignacio, and Manuel managed to transfer their private cache from the chapel of Santa Maria del Bosce to the graveyard on the edge of Portobelo. They concealed the loot in a stone tomb so worn by the elements that the inscription was an illegible series of faint scratches. Ignacio had pushed the capstone aside with a grunt and unceremoniously raked the few moldy bones to one end of the grave.

Pedro mourned, thinking more of himself than the anonymous soul whose final resting place they were desecrating. *Only a few decades and already the memory of our existence is extinguished.*

With the silver so near at hand, he was sure they were nearly finished with their ordeal. Soon, they would reap their reward.

But how to capitalize on sudden riches in a tiny New World outpost? How to avoid discovery?

Alone and in small amounts, the coins were unlikely to raise suspicion. Pieces of eight were common currency throughout the king's realm and around the world. But too many coins appearing at once would be noticed, as would repeat trips to the cemetery. So Pedro, Ignacio, and Manuel agreed to leave the tomb stash untouched but for the few handfuls they could fit in their pockets. The rest would have to wait until they had a safe plan for extracting it all. Surely, there had to be a way.

Pedro lamented, holding on as the galleon lurched in a growing swell. *How naïve we all were!*

Bit by bit, everything had come unraveled. It started when Ignacio let his ego and ambition inflate to the point that he decided to vie for the hand of the lovely Doña Louisa back in Seville. He was promptly challenged to a duel by Rodrigo de la Verramilla y Hernandez, who claimed her for himself. That neither of the combatants had laid eyes on Doña Louisa in over two years and had no confirmation of her interest in either of them didn't sway them one bit. No, a man's honor was a man's honor. As it was, the duel turned out to be more a matter of deadly looks and lethal postures than a marvel of swordplay. Both combatants wielded heavy swords yet failed to inflict anything more than a few minor scrapes before friends intervened to end the madness. Sadly, both men died soon after of infection. Whether word of this tragedy ever reached the distant ears of Doña Louisa, Pedro didn't know. Only that the world was now one cunning fox poorer.

The garrison mourned the cunning Sevillian in its own soulless way. Who would organize the weekly card games now that he was gone? Who would petition the commander for better wine? The local girls all went into mourning, while their mothers released heavy sighs of relief and crossed themselves.

Try as he would, Pedro couldn't quite produce a tear of genuine sorrow at the untimely demise of his fellow conspirator. His principal regret was that Ignacio had not yet devised a plan for transporting the silver home.

Damn the man. Damn it all.

After a few weeks, Ignacio's name came up less and less often. The ladies found new suitors. The soldiers appointed a new spokesman — if one with less flair. The card games went on. It was as if Ignacio had never even visited this accursed corner of the world. That thought made Pedro shiver as much as the tortured cries of ghosts in the night.

And when poor, stupid Manuel died a month later of fever, Pedro truly did grieve. Well, for a little while. Then his mind wandered back to the graveyard, and he brightened. Divided into thirds, the silver concealed there would have made a modest sum. As a whole, it would make Pedro a rich man, indeed. If only he could get it out and away!

But how?

He spent the next weeks deliberating how to extract the treasure from its hiding place and move it not just into Portobelo, but back to Spain. A pity that inspiration refused to visit, no matter how hard he prayed. Then he, too, fell ill with the fever, just like Manuel. In the throes of his delirium, Pedro heard voices arguing over who would get his blanket, who would claim his boots.

"I get his spot by the window when he's gone," one soldier declared.

"I get his sword," another proclaimed.

Pedro wanted to protest, but he couldn't produce a peep.

Day merged into night. Everything felt too bright or too dark, then only dark. Pedro knew he was slipping away, one foot already in a muddy grave.

Somehow, he eluded the death that had seemed so near in the sweaty throes of his fever. Darkness gave way to light; light took on shape and substance until his mind could sustain coherent thought. His body felt shattered, but he was alive.

Alive and bitter and alone.

It was weeks before he recovered the strength to stand or walk. When he did, Pedro wobbled to the cemetery and stood swaying at the foot of Manuel's grave. It looked ancient already. The stone was only marked with Manuel's initials — a few lonely letters the sole reminder of the man's time on earth. Pedro considered the graves all around, feeling hollow. Fully three-quarters of the men he'd arrived in the New World with lay in that cemetery now. Men who left Spain with high hopes — to make something of themselves, to earn some recognition, to find their fortunes. Just like him.

Finding a fortune. He scowled. That alone was not enough. He had his own loot — it lay just over there, secreted away in the oldest section of the cemetery. But what good did that do him?

He had forced his creaking limbs into the church and lowered himself to a pew like an old man. Above him, the ceiling stretched away into a vast nothingness devoid of light, of hope, of inspiration. Candles flickered, teased by a draft that snuffed out the weaklings, one by one. Already, half a dozen wafted pathetic plumes of smoke that drifted aimlessly in the dusty air. Each one of them represented a soul lost, a dream destroyed. Pedro turned to the statue of the Madonna for some solace, but her face was as impassive as ever.

The draft brought a whiff of the candles to Pedro, and he was overwhelmed by the image of home. Home! What he would give to breathe the clean air of Extremadura again! Here, the stink of the jungle permeated everything, even the wax and incense of this sacred place.

"Enough."

A gaunt, heavily lined Pedro concluded that getting out of the New World alive and rich was too much to ask of either the Father, the Son, or the Holy Ghost. After one more night of haunted sleep, he greased the harbormaster's sweaty palm with the last few coins in his pocket and secured a berth on a ship departing immediately for Havana, then on to Spain. He left without any good-byes, without collecting his belongings, without so much as a final hurried visit to his secret cache. There was no time. It was the treasure or the ship.

Pedro chose the latter. Wisely, he decided, as the sails filled with a cleansing breeze.

Did he feel regret? Frustration? Relief? Pedro wasn't sure. All he knew was that he was leaving the hellhole of the New World forever. He was poor and broken but alive.

He imagined the sun rising before him. East, that's where he was going. Spain. His father's second cousin had a large estate where he could find work. The estate was plain, like the man's daughter, but they would both do for Pedro. He'd long lost the ambition for anything more.

Behind him, the deep-cut bay of Portobelo was a mere shadow in the night, another dream lost to the jungle.

And as for the treasure?

Pedro snorted. *To hell with the treasure.*

Chapter Six

Cowboys and Robbers

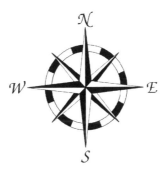

Portobelo

December, present day

Apparently, his great-grandfather really did have a few wild adventures. Nick wished he could beg his mother or aunt for more information. But how could he even pose such a crazy question?

Hey, about Charlie... Did he really find a lost treasure?

In any case, it was time to leave El Diablo and head back to *Aurora*. Nick gathered his things while Kate came around the table, about to shut the computer. Then she hesitated and referred back to the page about early Spanish coins, jotting a note on a scrap of paper.

"Interested in Spanish treasure?"

Nick looked up to see an olive-toned sailor. The kind of man who looked twenty after a shave, but forty with a two-day shadow, as he sported now. The man who'd wandered into the back room after Kate came out.

A man who leaned toward Kate and flashed a row of teeth as impossibly white as his polo shirt.

"They say one-third of the world's silver passed through Portobelo at one time in history."

Kate glowed. Nick glowered, going instantly to red alert. So the guy read the information board. Big deal.

"They say there is still treasure hidden in Panama." The stranger dropped his voice to a whisper and raised his eyebrows dramatically. "Silver. Mountains of Spanish silver." He pointed at the images on the screen.

Nick folded the laptop with a sharp click.

The olive-skinned stranger straightened, unfazed. "I am Alejandro," he announced with a slight bow. "From Venezuela." He spoke with just enough of an accent to sound exotic and interesting. The kind of voice women swooned over and their partners despised.

Kate was all ears. "I'm Kate."

Nick mumbled his name and scooped up their things. Time to escape unwanted company — pronto.

"I'm from *Carmela*," Alejandro announced with an air of self-importance.

Kate's eyes went wide. "The yawl anchored on the far side of the bay? The one with the gold stripe?"

Nick had seen it, too — a sleek wooden classic with virginal white sides and a blindingly glossy deck house that sported at least seven perfect coats of varnish, if not more. *Carmela* was twice the size of *Aurora* and twice the age, qualifying her as classic and not simply old.

Alejandro nodded, eyes fixed on Kate's. Eyes that teased and danced, promising much too much. Not just a steady waltz or an innocent polka but a full-contact tango. Steamy, sultry, with dazzling dips and tight turns.

Kate might have missed a breath there; Nick wasn't sure. He cleared his throat in the coarsest possible way.

"I am a singlehander," Alejandro continued.

"Wow!" Kate gushed.

Big wow. Nick inserted himself between Kate and the Venezuelan, shoving things in his backpack, elbows wide. He handed Kate her wallet and motioned to the bar. "I'll clean up — you go pay."

Nick saw Alejandro following her every move. He knew that poaching look.

"So—" he pushed a chair with an ear-scraping screech "—how long are you in town?"

The Venezuelan's eyes slid back to Nick, studying the grease stains on his shirt.

"I sail with the wind, the seasons," he said at last. "I see what opportunities arise, then decide."

Nick didn't like the sound of that.

"Which boat are you on?" Alejandro asked.

Nick's hackles rose a notch higher. The man said it like maybe Nick didn't own his own boat. Well, he did, damn it. *"Aurora*. A Valiant 32, over by the green fishing boat."

"Nice," the Venezuelan said in the flat tone of a diplomat.

So what if *Aurora* was a little old? Not everyone owned a classic yacht.

Kate returned, bringing warmth back into Alejandro's smile.

"I see you have an interest in history," he said, half question, half statement.

"Actually, I'm an archaeologist."

Alejandro eyed her in approval. "Then you're in the right place."

Nick had in mind a very different place. Like far away from this guy. He took Kate by the elbow, ready to maneuver her toward the exit.

"Have you visited the Aztec ruins in Guatemala?" Alejandro lifted a set of perfect eyebrows.

Kate winced. "Mayan ruins, you mean. Aztecs came later and were farther north."

Nick gave an inner cheer. Point for Team Aurora! He'd better get Kate moving, though, before the Venezuelan regained his stride. Not that Alejandro looked at all flustered. In fact, he winked and nodded sagely, as if he had just been testing Kate's knowledge. Maybe he really had. Nick couldn't tell. Either way, he started pulling Kate toward the stairs — but by then, another guest had rambled up, blocking his escape.

"So let me guess," mumbled the slightly inebriated, very sunburned sailor with a bloodshot nose. American. "Lemme guess," the man repeated in a wheeze. "You're after the treas—" The last words were cut off by a triumphant roar from the dart players.

"Bull's-eye!" Trevor cried, cheering at the dart that had landed a bull's eye in the nose of the smiling ex-president.

The sunburned American pointed a tobacco-stained finger at Kate. "You're after a lost treasure of Spanish gold!" The man wheezed and laughed a hearty *har-har-har* as Nick towed Kate along.

"Don't be ridiculous," Kate retorted in her most dismissive tone. She waved a cheery good-bye to Alejandro, who waggled his fingers in response and turned — slowly — back to the bar.

"We're after a lost treasure of Spanish *silver*," she whispered once they were out the door.

Nick wrapped his arm firmly around her shoulders. "Idiots," he agreed, blinking in the sharp light of day.

When they were halfway down the street, he groaned at himself. Wait. Had he just agreed to another one of Kate's crazy ideas?

Portobelo

present day

Two days later, Kate stood at the bus stop along Portobelo's main road, opposite the litter-strewn plaza. The sidewalk was gritty under her feet, and the air smelled of yet another garbage heap. She let out a small sigh. Centuries of history, neglected like the mangy mutt sniffing in the gutter just over there. The place deserved better.

Beside her, Nick checked his watch for the fourth time.

"It's not like the buses run to a schedule, you know," she said.

"That much, I got." Nick nodded and went back to the copy of *The Economist* he'd picked up in El Diablo. *Only six weeks old!* he'd exclaimed in delight.

She patted his arm. It was going to be a long day. Since the novelty of the Chinese "Mini-Supers" in Portobelo had worn thin, they'd decided on an expedition to a large supermarket in the crossroads town of Sabanitas, and their shopping list was a mile long.

Morning humidity pressed over the town like a thick blanket, and everything moved slowly. Like the man ambling by, eyeing her a little too openly. Make that leering. Kate switched on her most scathing look and watched with satisfaction as he hurried away. The people of Portobelo were as varied as the buildings, it seemed. Some noble, others crooked and decayed. She'd leave that part out of her report to her mother.

She leaned against Nick's shoulder, just because she could. Traveling solo had its merits — no need to constantly negotiate when and where and how, for starters — but this was awfully nice, too. Even with his nose in a magazine, Nick was good company. He saw things differently, picked up on things that she missed. A two-way street, because he listened to her observations, laughed at her jokes, and endured her occasional rants. She closed her eyes and let herself bask in the quiet of the moment.

That is, until the quiet street exploded in noise and color. Her eyes snapped open.

A bus labeled TERMINATOR rolled up with screaming brakes. The hood was decorated with snarling teeth. Painted flames encircled the wheels. All in all, the bus was about as inviting as a one-way shuttle to the netherworld. But there was something reassuringly familiar to it, too.

"Check it out. It's an old school bus," Nick said, boarding behind her.

That's what is was, exactly: a retired, North American school bus. A blast from Kate's past from the *Bluebird* plaque to the green vinyl seats. They took the row behind the driver, who sped off with the passenger door ajar.

"Hang on," Nick muttered, grabbing the side of the seat.

Kate, at the window, folded her legs over the wheel well. She peered over the driver's shoulder. "How does he even see the road?"

The windshield spanned the entire width of the bus, but decorations reduced the driver's vision to a twelve-by-twenty-inch rectangle. The rest was plastered in red and blue FC Barcelona stickers, film stills of a machine-gun toting Arnold Schwarzenegger in dark sunglasses, and pastel images of the Virgin Mary. The perimeter of the windshield was framed by a fluffy pink boa that flapped like a hysterical bird in the breeze generated by the open windows and door.

Just another day on public transportation in Central America, in other words.

"I wonder what the vehicle safety laws in Panama are," Nick said under his breath.

"We're in her hands now." Kate pointed to the dejected-looking Madonna figurine on the dashboard. The tinsel surrounding it drooped over the speedometer, making it impossible to tell if the bus was going fifty or Mach 1. Nick, she saw, had his foot clamped over an imaginary brake pedal.

Stop by stop, the entire spectrum of humanity took their places aboard the Terminator like so many passengers aboard Noah's Ark. A human rainbow in which races were shaken and stirred into a wondrous potpourri. There were Asians, whites, copper-skinned *Indigenos*, Afro-Caribbeans, and every possible combination thereof. It was an hour of enlightenment costing a mere $1.70 per person, one way, right up to the point when a woman tapped Kate's arm and indicated the supermarket ahead.

They stepped off the bus and into the blazing sun, then hurried into the cool air of the supermarket.

"Whoa," she murmured.

"Wow." Nick nodded.

It took her a minute to recover from the initial culture shock. At last, a store with shelves that extended over her head — and fully stocked shelves at that.

"Look — an entire wall of dairy products!" she gushed. "A whole aisle of baking goods!"

"Juice!" Nick pointed.

"And cookies!" Lots and lots of cookies.

Kate felt like a parched explorer stumbling into an oasis. She went straight for the chocolate, while Nick practically ran to the hardware aisle. When she found him twenty minutes later, she caught him ogling ratchet sets and caressing sheets of sandpaper.

"Come on, Captain," she coaxed, pressing the handle of a shopping cart into his hands. It was time to start whittling away at their shopping list — and the ever-present mystery of Charlie Parker.

"What if Charlie found something somewhere?" she wondered out loud as they hunted through the cereal aisle.

"What if Charlie met someone from Peru?" Nick suggested, assembling their purchases into neat, balanced bags.

"What if Charlie got involved in the antiquities trade?" Kate tried as they bumped back along the road to Portobelo in a *Little Mermaid*-themed bus.

The jagged profile of Isla Drake, a craggy rock named for the English privateer, came into view just outside the entrance to Portobelo harbor. Somehow the view plucked a chord in Kate's mind. Sir Francis Drake. The man had prowled the seas for Spanish treasure. Which served the Spanish right since their wealth came from plundering the Americas.

Kate halted the thought there, looking for *Aurora* as the bus circled the bay. It was always a special thrill to see the little craft waiting obediently at anchor in each exotic location. She counted down the sailboats one by one. There was a fancy vintage yacht — *Carmela* — farther out in the bay, along with the hulk of a green fishing boat. Next was *Free Willy* with her drooping boom, and yes, little *Aurora*, right where they had left her. She and Nick exchanged smiles like proud parents at the sight of their child, busy with her buddies on the playground.

Sir Francis Drake.

Treasure.

Portobelo.

Her mind bounced over each thought as the bus lurched into town. Vast treasures from all over the New World had been funneled through Portobelo, much of it via a cobbled trail over the isthmus. She imagined the excited bustle as convoys laden with great masses of silver paraded into town and passed under the archways of the customs house, eventually to be loaded onto treasure fleets. But not all the treasure made it to Portobelo, much less Spain. One convoy fell victim to Sir Francis Drake in 1573. She'd read about that in her guidebook. Henry Morgan had been through, too, sacking Portobelo in 1668. Who knew what circumstances might have led to treasures being secreted away, only to be unearthed centuries later?

Nick nudged her, indicating their stop.

Charlie. What did he stumble across? Where?

The bus hissed to a halt.

What had Charlie been up to, damn it?

Portobelo

March 1911

Charlie reached into the dank tomb a second time, letting his fingers swim in a mass of clinking, glinting material. He pulled out a piece that matched the first he'd extracted, then another, and another. A little spit and polish and the inscriptions on them came to light.

"Holy...."

Charlie shot a wild-eyed glance at the archway. A small bird cocked its head at the shiny metal, and insects telegraphed the news, but that was all.

He looked at the objects one more time and whistled. He'd read his share of pirate stories.

"Pieces of eight..."

He reached back into the grave and excavated a little more, pulling out more. There were hundreds of coins in there. Coins and other things, too, like amulets and strange figurines. He found a chain link bracelet in the form of a snake and an eagle-headed necklace, too. Mostly silver, some gold.

He brushed through most of them quickly but stopped at a strange, staring face sculpted upon an oval.

"What the..."

The face was etched into the body of a spider made of solid silver. Charlie wasn't much of an art connoisseur, but even he knew a masterpiece when he saw one. The bulging eyes bored into his own, and everything else faded away. A bead of sweat dropped from his brow. Then the grass rustled, calling him back into real time. He put the spider down and sat back on his heels, gaping at his find. How the pieces of eight got here, or what the other pieces were, he didn't know. He didn't care.

One thing Charlie did know. He was rich! Filthy rich!

He stayed in the cemetery for as long as the mosquitoes and dimming light allowed, hiding all outward traces of his find. Then he headed out, hoping the evening would disguise his giddy mood. He walked down the road, past the church, and turned left up the track to El Diablo, quietly fingering the coin he'd slipped into his pocket. Wondering who had put it in the graveyard and why.

"*Buenos tardes, Señor Charlie.*" One of the women winked as he approached.

He flapped a hand and headed for the front door, pretending his heart wasn't hammering at two hundred beats per minute.

The bar was in the front section of El Diablo. Behind it was a clutch of tiny rooms — a ramshackle arrangement that hadn't seen a fresh coat of whitewash in years. He took care to climb the stairs quietly, bringing back vivid memories of sneaking a bottle of whiskey past his father. What a fifteenth birthday *that* had been!

He barely reached the landing when a man came tumbling out, chased into the street by a hurtling rum bottle and Mercedes' strident voice.

"Not in my beezniss! You out!"

Charlie flattened himself to one side just in time to avoid a second hurled bottle. It shattered on a step, and the bar patrons erupted into applause.

Yep, it looked like business as usual at El Diablo. And Mercedes was clearly at her best tonight.

Charlie smoothed his shirt, readjusted the brim of his hat, and stepped inside as casually as he could. He rubbed the coin in his pocket along with his lucky rabbit's foot. He'd need all the luck he could get to slip by Mercedes unnoticed.

She was wiping shot glasses behind the bar as if nothing had happened, with her usual group of admirers adoring her from a safe distance. Mercedes was unapproachable, and all the men knew it — or found out the hard way.

"Carlito!" When she smiled in his direction, he tipped his hat.

By some small miracle, Mercedes had taken a shine to him from the very beginning. When he'd first arrived in Portobelo, he'd been sweaty and tired, wanting only to wash up at the end of a long day. But the water pump out back had been out of commission, disassembled and left in hopeless disarray. The parts had called to him like a puzzle begging for its last pieces, so he had a quick look. Half an hour later, the pump was working again. Mercedes had walked in just as he was shaving, her face the picture of surprise.

So without even trying, he'd earned her eternal gratitude. Mercedes even went as far as stroking his cheek and mumbling something about being reminded of someone named Herman. Only later did he find out that *hermano* meant brother. Ever since then, she'd received Charlie on each successive visit with a greeting like, "Carlito! You come to fix my keetchen!" or, "Carlito! You come to fix my phonygraph!"

And he did, every time.

She didn't shower him with praise or favors. The reward was always a single, short look of approval that felt better than all the fake kisses in the world. Then she'd be off checking on the girls or upbraiding a client behind on a tab. That about summed up their relationship since then. Friends.

Charlie enjoyed the novelty of it.

He scanned the room to find the usual clusters of canal workers and girls. A moody tune played on the phonograph — familiar because it was one of the dozen singles that made up Mercedes' entire collection. Angelina, his shrill pursuer from earlier that day, was draped across another man's lap. When she spotted Charlie, her face radiated through various hues of red, much like the evening sky. She punished Charlie with a sloppy kiss for her new man.

Charlie cheered inside. He was off the hook! Well, at least as far as Angelina was concerned.

Then he spotted Mercedes, studying him from across the room. Not off the hook. Not yet, he wasn't.

He scratched his nose, hiding behind the gesture. He slunk to his usual corner table and took out his notebook on the premise of working out some calculations. His pencil stroked idly in one corner while his eyes studied the sketches he had drawn in the graveyard. Except for the one coin in his pocket, the loot was still in the closed tomb, a few leaves scattered over the top to hide evidence of a recent visit.

The coins were pieces of eight. He was sure about that. But the other objects? What were they? What was that unforgettable spider? He flipped to another hastily drawn sketch. That spider was solid silver, he was sure of it. He glanced up at the evening sky just in time to see the hunched form of a vulture fly over the church. The damn things watched over everything in Portobelo.

Never mind. Charlie had other things on his mind.

All that silver. Surely it was worth a lot. A fortune. A comfortable future.

But it posed a problem, too.

Charlie scratched his head and contemplated the very dilemma that had so vexed the previous custodians of the treasure, centuries before. The loot had no value where it was. No value to him, anyway. How to cash in on it? That much precious metal — an entire grave full — had to be worth a lot. But how to transport it? How to escape notice?

He had already failed in the third point, because Mercedes was on her way over to his table. Clearly, she was not coming over to take an order. Mercedes did not do the waitressing at El Diablo. No, she knew he was up to something, all right.

Charlie closed the notebook with a subtle flick and straightened quickly, the better to meet the onslaught.

She wasn't an especially tall woman, but she seemed like one as Charlie looked a long, long way into her bottomless eyes.

"You have a worry, Carlito." A statement.

Charlie tried an innocent smile. *Worry? What worry?*

Mercedes mocked him by fluttering her eyelashes. *As if I would fall for that, Carlito!*

"Just a little problem at work," he explained to the tabletop.

But it was no use; the fabric of her lacy black dress shifted at the periphery of his vision. Even a square inch of Mercedes had more substance than most people. His eyes were drawn back up like a moth to a burning candle.

"You tell me problem," Mercedes said in her Spanish-laced contralto, "I give you solution."

Her eyes blazed, and Charlie had to fight off the urge to lean forward and confess all. He glanced around and found that several of the guests were jealous of his audience with the queen. Not good, attracting interest. He played nonchalant. Even if Mercedes would never buy his charade, the others might.

He gestured Mercedes into the empty chair opposite him. She humored him, radiating authority in a not-so-subtle reminder of who owned the joint. Without breaking her gaze, she waved two lazy fingers in the air, signaling for drinks.

Mercedes didn't demand that he reveal anything. Instead, she bored into his eyes for an answer, scolding, teasing, and unraveling him with her fiery gaze. If she'd lived in North America, Charlie decided, she'd be a school principal, and he'd be the kid banished to the office — again.

He attempted to lose himself in details: the thick, black hair falling in waves. The shadows formed by her aristocratic cheekbones. Her ramrod back. If only he could avoid those eyes... but that was hopeless. Partial disclosure, he decided, was the way to go. Just enough of the truth to cover up the lie.

"I have something valuable," he started. Mercedes didn't shift, but he could feel her aura swoop in. "And I'm not sure how to keep it safe."

Mercedes studied him closely, trying to decipher the riddle. A lesser woman would try to tease and cajole information out of him, but Mercedes just let her eyes probe. How anyone with eyes so dark and deep could still see, Charlie didn't know.

She stared and stared and finally backed off. Charlie felt the pressure ease as surely as he would have felt a tight grip being released. He sent a silent thanks to Fortuna, the only spiritual being he was on speaking terms with. If it hadn't been for that broken water pump, he wouldn't have gotten off so lightly.

"This ees very simple thing, Carlito." The words skipped off Mercedes' tongue.

He was all ears.

"You trust the close friend." She fluttered her eyelashes like a woman half her age.

He laughed out loud. Friend? He twisted and turned the word in his mind and found to his utter surprise that, yes, Mercedes really was a friend. If he could trust anyone, it would be her.

But he couldn't, and his eyes admitted as much.

They both pondered that betrayal while a waitress set down two drinks and scurried off to a safe distance. Mercedes contemplated him through the amber liquid in her glass, then took a heavy swig that left her lips shiny. She looked into the candle and seemed to make up her mind.

"The best place for hiding is where every man can see."

Charlie chewed on this a minute before picking up his glass in a silent toast. Mercedes' eyes dragged a promise out of him — a promise to divulge more. If not now, then at some point in the future.

As if in a trance, Charlie's eyes promised. They had no choice.

He drank his rum and sniffed the evening scent of the surrounding jungle. Then he started to do what he did best: engineer a solution. How to hide — and better yet — to move a few hundred pounds of treasure in plain sight?

Chapter Seven

Lotto del Mar

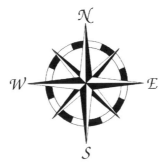

Portobelo

December, present day

"So who is Yolanta?" Nick demanded.

Kate hid a smile by scratching her nose. Nick's face was flushed, his eyebrows intent. Yep, he showed all the signs of getting hooked on the quest for illumination in the Mystery of Charlie Parker. Maybe the man was developing an imagination, after all.

They were rewarding themselves for a morning of long-procrastinated boat work with an afternoon pilgrimage to the bakery, ready to judge Portobelo on the basis of its culinary merits. The verdict thus far was encouraging, at least as far as cinnamon rolls were concerned.

Nick leafed through the entries in Charlie's notebook for the thousandth time. His finger poked a name: Yolanta.

Kate shrugged. "A girlfriend?"

"What about Rosie and her lush lips?"

"Don't remind me." She rolled her eyes. "But those letters were from 1917. Charlie was in Panama before that."

"And Mercedes?"

Kate shrugged. "Another girlfriend?"

"One who needs six parasols? And twenty bottles of wine?"

"Sounds like a heck of a party."

A mocha-colored arm pushed into their field of vision, delivering another round of mango smoothies. The proprietress of the tiny bakery-cum-café was a stout West Indian who whirled between the kitchen and her customers, periodically checking in on a cooing baby in a corner playpen. When business peaked, as it did now, she was assisted by a young girl and an old woman. It was amazing how much she juggled while maintaining a broad smile.

"And who's Edgar?" Nick demanded, tapping another entry in the notebook.

"Roommate? Colleague?"

Nick sighed. "Why couldn't Charlie have left behind a stack of letters describing his time in Panama instead of love letters from the front?"

"Wait. The letters..."

"What about them?"

"We didn't actually get past the second or third one. Maybe we should read more." She grimaced, thinking of Charlie's lusty prose. Still, they could use any clue they could get — and maybe learn something about Charlie in the process.

Letters are a window to the soul, an archivist friend once said.

"I think you're harboring a secret passion for trashy literature," Nick joked.

She opened her mouth to vehemently deny any interest exceeding a strictly academic one when a small group of dejected-looking backpackers filed into the café. They dumped their oversized bags to the ground, setting off a wave of dust, and dropped into plastic chairs.

"Rough ride?" she asked.

A young woman nodded wearily and peeled off the yellow bandana covering her hair. She shook it sharply, whipping some memory away.

The backpackers descended over the place like a swarm of locusts, and one replied.

"The worst," he said, piquing Kate's curiosity.

The backpackers looked wary. Defeated. They eyed her drink like thirsty gazelles drooling over a watering hole where a single lion lapped away. Nick slid his smoothie to the exhausted young woman, who knocked it back in one long, despondent gulp.

"Thanks," she said, voice hollow.

"We had the trip from hell," the man at her side sighed.

If Kate hadn't been hooked before, she sure was now.

"It started in Colombia..."

The man related their sorry tale. Ten travelers had all signed on, individually or in pairs, for a backpacker boat from Colombia to Panama. Other than expensive air travel, this cowboy industry was the only way to bridge Panama's wild Darien Gap, where even the Pan-American highway came to a dead end. Unfortunately, adventure often turned to misadventure, as the backpackers confirmed. They had been promised a $400 trip with a maximum of five passengers, only to find themselves crammed in a boat with ten.

She could picture it all too easily. She'd seen plenty of overloaded backpacker boats in the San Blas.

"Four miserable days..." one started.

"A nightmare," another backpacker added.

"It was so rough, we were all seasick..."

"When we were offshore, the captain hiked the price up to $500 per person and held our passports as ransom."

"What option did we have but to pay up?" The backpackers shook their heads at the ugly memory.

"The worst thing of all," lamented a young woman, "was how mean that captain was!"

Her boyfriend nodded. "He was a real jerk, that Vadz."

The woman continued, "The other one, Gregor, was nicer, but still, he was part of the crew. They cheated us!" She frowned. "I don't want to say that you can't trust Polish people, but at least I can say you can't trust those two."

A bell rang in Kate's head. A couple of Poles named Gregor and Vadz? "Was the boat named *Odysseus*?" she asked.

The backpackers nodded.

"Wow. We've met them." *Aurora* had been getting ready to depart the San Blas when *Odysseus* had pulled into the anchorage. "We saw that boat in the San Blas! I never talked to Vadz but Gregor seemed decent enough..."

She pictured the Polish crew. Vadz was a bulky, brutish man with a shaved head who looked angry about something — or maybe everything. The other, Gregor, was a trim, polite man who left a good impression when he rowed over to *Aurora* for information on clearing in to Panama. They wanted to take *Odysseus* through the canal, Gregor had said, if they could get the money.

Apparently, they found a way. But cheating young backpackers was hardly a fair means of financing a canal transit. The victims were now huddled in the bakery, waiting — hoping — that the

Poles would return their passports once they finished at the immigration office.

"That's terrible," Kate said.

Three more backpackers arrived, shaking their heads sadly at the others.

"Still nothing?" the first woman asked.

"Still nothing," one replied, looking around for an empty seat in the overfull café.

Nick nudged Kate's elbow and nodded toward the street. It was time to move on and make space for the others — and high time to start the hike she had planned.

They wished the others good luck, picked their way past the backpacks, and headed out.

"I think I see the way up." She pointed.

"Up?" Nick's voice rose in alarm.

"To the viewpoint, remember?"

The look on his face told her he'd forgotten, but he soldiered on. Good old Nick. Why had she ever thought splitting up with him was a good idea?

The crooked path she'd spotted led them over hill and dale as they picked their way to the Mirador Peru, a crumbling watchtower perched high over the town.

"Are you sure this is the right way?" he asked.

"Pretty sure."

Nick sighed. "Why was it that so many of your adventures led off the beaten path?"

She grinned ear to ear. Now that was a compliment. She led him up a weedy expanse, scaling the steep slope with hands and feet.

"We're almost there!"

A few steps later, she crested a rise and pulled up short, panting as much from the view as the exertion. She turned as Nick stepped clear of the bush and emerged upon the ruins of a square stone platform.

"Nice, huh?" She swept her arm over the view.

Portobelo nestled under their feet — a meandering row of stone buildings along the main road, no two roofs pitched at the same angle. She could picture it bustling with Spanish soldiers, centuries ago.

"Definitely worth the hike," Nick agreed, already fishing for his camera.

The wake of a moving fishing boat sliced a white line across the bay, and Kate instinctively picked out *Aurora*. Home.

Click-click-click! The shutter of Nick's camera snapped in quick succession as she pointed out landmarks.

"The customs house... There's the park... And I think that's the café over there."

Nick made a long face.

"What? You didn't like the smoothies?"

He shook his head. "The smoothies were great. I just can't believe what happened to those backpackers. There's definitely a thin line between adventure and misadventure."

She patted him on the arm. "Thank goodness we have *Aurora*. Thank goodness for you."

He smiled at that one and slung an arm around her shoulder as they pondered it all, together with the view.

She took a deep breath, counting her luck. She had Nick and *Aurora*, which meant she could have adventure, a comfortable home, and fine company. And people said you can't have it all — Pah!

Then she chided herself. It's not that she couldn't live without Nick — because, of course, it wasn't that she *needed* him. It's just that she wanted him. His steady nature, that special blend of brains and good humor. The man was so genuine. So reliable. And a lot of fun, especially now that he was away from the evil influences of work and a thoroughly unadventurous family. She leaned into his solid frame, feeling his warmth. It was easy to imagine being with Nick for a long, long time, throughout many adventures.

But what would the next one be? The question teased her. They were getting rapidly sucked into the mysterious vortex of Charlie Parker's trail. A very faint trail, but one with promise. She was sure of it.

Then there was the more practical question of where to sail next. Portobelo had grown on them, but the place had its limits. Soon it would be time to push on. Where to?

One choice was obvious: to continue up the coast to Colon, gateway to the Panama Canal and a new ocean full of exciting possibilities. Her pulse quickened just thinking about it.

"Hey, what do you think about heading for the canal next?" She tried to make it sound casual, like the thought had just occurred to her for the first time — when in fact, she was trying really, really hard not to mentally connect the dots that led from Panama all the way across the Pacific. *Aurora's* next adventure?

"The canal? I'd love to see the locks," Nick gushed.

Not quite what she'd meant, interesting as they might be.

"I was thinking we could take *Aurora* through the canal," she said. "We could get away from the crowds over here and see the Pacific side. I've heard the islands there have hardly any visitors."

"Why rush? Staying in the Caribbean keeps our options open."

As so often happened, Kate followed the same logic Nick used to reach a different conclusion. The Pacific called like an enchanting siren. Another fascinating part of the world was waiting to be explored, just over there!

We've got some momentum now, so why not use it? She almost said it out loud. But it would be much easier to coax Nick into a Pacific crossing once they were on the west coast of Panama. Not that they had to leave the country soon, not with so much still to see and do — and certainly not without discovering what Charlie had been up to. But when the time came, there would be one less obstacle between *Aurora* and the fairy-tale islands of the Pacific. The Galapagos! Fatu Hiva! Tahiti!

Kate slammed the brakes on the runaway images and gave herself a stern lecture on the virtue of compromise, during which time she developed a severe itch on her left ankle. She scolded herself. Could it be that she'd spent too long on her own and become too set in her ways? That she'd inherited a couple of chips on her shoulder when it came to compromise?

Nah.

The big issues still hovered over them, unresolved. Where would they end up? How would they ever reconcile their differences? Whose dreams would they follow — his or hers? *Aurora* had brought them even closer than they'd been before, but would the boat help them launch dreams that weren't his *or* hers but his *and* hers?

She sighed, listening to her own skipping record. One thing she did know: it was too early to bring up a Pacific crossing. So she kept the conversation limited to the Pacific side of the Panama Canal and its immediate cruising grounds — for now.

They talked until the narrowing gap between the sun and the shimmering horizon reminded them of more practical matters, like dinner and drinks, not to mention the private love letters of Charlie Parker.

Inspired, she grabbed her backpack and pulled Nick along. "To the boat!"

* * *

"My dearest Rosie," she read aloud. "Not a day goes by without me thinking of you."

There they were, hours later, lying in the forepeak bunk together. Nick rested on his side, facing her. The boat shifted on a ripple of water. Outside the cozy cabin, the night was silent but for a distant choir of crickets.

Kate studied the next lines, imagining Charlie's pen scratching across paper under a flickering lantern.

> *My dearest Rosie,*
>
> *Not a day goes by without me thinking of you and wishing I could see you, hold you, kiss you. How I wish we could have had more time together! If I hadn't already enlisted when I met you, I never would have left. Fortuna gives, she takes away. Why?*
>
> *I remember our short time together in the summer sun, warm like your body next to mine. Here, I am shivering and alone. But dreams let me escape. Last night, I dreamed I was back in Panama. You were there, too. We were on a beautiful tropical island. No fighting, no politics. Just the sun warming the sand and your smile warming my heart.*

Panama. One day I will tell you of the incredible things I found in a beautiful port. Some of the strangest things I ever held. But I had to leave them all behind, all but that one. There was more, much more. Enough for a silver-lined future for us both. How I wish to go back there and bring it all home to you. We'd put it to good use, start a new life together.

Her pulse skipped. Her cheeks felt hot. Strange things?

Nick pushed himself up on an elbow and leaned in to echo the lines. "A beautiful port?"

"Portobelo!" She sat up straight.

"But I had to leave it all behind..."

They stared at each other, then back at the letter.

"A silver-lined future for us both..."

"I wish so much to go back there and bring it all home to you..."

"My love, wait for me. Please keep my letters so I know part of me is with you. Yours forever, Charlie."

Kate looked at Nick and let a long, quiet moment tick by. "He never did get home, did he?"

Nick shook his head, and she exhaled slowly. Sadly.

"He died in France in World War I." Nick straightened the top of the letter with one finger and pointed at the date. November 12, 1917.

She leaned into Nick without realizing it, seeking his warmth, silent in thoughts. Then she reached for another letter that was folded and brittle with time. The last one, dated November 29 of the same year. The script matched Charlie's earlier letters but gave a rushed impression. The ink was smudged, blurring one word into the next. The corner of the sheet was soiled, perhaps from the mud of a trench. Kate pierced her lips, imagining Charlie in a whole different light.

She angled the letter so that Nick could follow as she read aloud. "My dearest Rosie..."

My dearest Rosie,

I could write a hundred pages explaining all the ways I love and miss you, but there is no time. They're collecting the mail right now, and then we're off to the front. We weren't supposed to go, but now they need us... A real mess.

I know I've lived nine lives already, and all of them good — but none like the one we could share. I wish... Well, I wish a lot of things. And God, have I learned a lot the hard way.

I love you more than I can say. Please forgive me all my faults and know that I am yours forever.

Love, Charlie.

She finished reading and slowly turned the letter over. There was nothing on the back save a few stray marks. She stared at Charlie's handwriting for a long time, wavering over words written so long ago, so far away, from one lover to another. The gentle looping script, the rushed, blurred passages. It was easy to imagine Charlie hunched in a uniform, composing the letters. Easy to imagine Rosie holding them with shaking hands. Kate could feel it as clearly as she felt the lump in her own throat. Emotions stirred by love, war, and loss collided with the excitement of a mystery that fascinated and frustrated.

A few quiet minutes later, Nick shifted and climbed out of the bunk. He rooted around in the salon then returned, handing her something before crawling back into bed beside her.

"Charlie's cigar box," she said, touching it gingerly. The box that contained Charlie's notebook and lucky rabbit's foot. She held it gingerly in her lap, running her fingers over one edge. Just a box? Or the hint of a soul?

Her eyes met Nick's, and then, with a mute nod, they explored the contents anew.

Cristobal

April 1912

Charlie knew life was full of ups and downs. That was a given. If only they didn't come in such quick succession.

Discovering the treasure in Portobelo was high on the "up" end of the scale. Not only that, but he had returned to Cristobal to find that House 47 had a vacancy. Charlie practically pranced through the room he shared with Douglass Browning, collecting his things. Since it was Thursday evening, everyone was out at the meeting of The Benevolent and Protective Order of Elks. Everyone from House 46, that was.

Over in House 47, it was craps night, and the joint was packed. Charlie settled into his new room, leaned back in a rocking chair on the veranda, and took a deep, satisfied breath of the cigar smoke wafting from the center of the action one story down. A bottle smashed. Voices rose. A fight broke out. Things were looking up!

He should have known it wouldn't last.

After months of repeated run-ins with Inspector Cummings, Charlie came home one evening to find out that word had reached higher levels, and they were not amused. He was summoned to the chief quartermaster for a lecture with Inspector Cummings in smug attendance.

"Charlie Parker, as one of our top engineers, *blah blah blah,* you must understand that the Panama Canal Company has its procedures and procedure must be followed, *blah blah blah...*"

The Chief droned on and on. Charlie tuned out most of it.

"An enterprise of these proportions, *blah blah blah...*"

It was a lecture he'd heard with minor variations in all every job he'd ever held. Was it his fault he was an engineer and not a secretary?

He drifted away on his own thoughts until he heard a concluding note in the quartermaster's voice, commanding him to fill out a three-foot stack of documents — some in triplicate, for Christ's sake! — and to submit to a thorough audit of the tiny office he avoided like the plague.

He'd been in the stuffy office in town for less than two hours and already ached for the open sky and a fresh breeze. A tiny window opened on a twisting alley that even the strongest trade wind couldn't penetrate. The cramped desk brought back unwelcome memories of elementary school. Charlie fidgeted. Give him scorching heat, pounding rain, droves of mosquitoes — all better than this cell.

He pushed his chair back with a screech and propped his feet on his desk when Cummings arrived for the audit.

"What exactly are you looking for, Cunnings?" Charlie asked, watching him rifle through filing cabinets.

The man's eyes reminded him of Douglass' lecture on poisonous snakes. "My name is Cummings. And I am looking for evidence of work. Or lack thereof." He slammed the drawer shut and snatched at the next.

Charlie waved the remark aside like an annoying bug. He rolled a cigarette a little too tightly. "You should visit the breakwater, Bunnings. Lotsa work there."

Watching Cummings whisk self-importantly through his files extinguished Charlie's hopes of bringing the silver to the office for safekeeping. Too risky. Where else, then?

House 47 was out of the question. So, too, was its tidy alter ego, House 46. None of the doors had locks, and dozens of people trooped through on any given day. Not just the residents, but their guests, a few enemies, as well as laundry men, janitors, tailors, and the like.

He half-heartedly considered a blank report form as Cummings took his leave.

"Well," the inspector crowed, "I hope you'll appreciate the need to follow procedure from now on." He left, humming.

Charlie contemplated all the procedures he'd like to subject Cummings to, given the chance. When the sound of those self-important footsteps faded down the hall, he held his cigarette to the blank report and watched pink blaze into orange, then collapse into ash. Small consolation, because another few hundred forms waited on his desk. Charlie's foot slipped — oops — and the pile scattered across the floor.

"Now what?" he murmured aloud.

The walls of the tiny office were covered with plans for the breakwater and a map of the isthmus showing the proposed canal route. Charlie stared at the latter, longing to get back to real work.

His green-brown eyes traveled the Canal Zone, all the way across the isthmus of Panama and back. How could he get the silver out? Portobelo lay twenty miles to the east through thick jungle tracks. His office and bachelor's quarters were here in Colon, a place rife with corruption. Perfect for his purpose, in a way. There had to be someone he could pawn the treasure to for hard cash.

Starting with that spider.

Charlie took out his notebook and studied his sketches. Before leaving Portobelo, he'd made a second visit to the graveyard and sketched the startling piece in greater detail, paying more attention to the bug-eyed face and spindly legs. He couldn't quite decide if that face was sneering at him or promising good fortune.

Whatever it was, it would fetch a pretty price. That was solid silver, sure as mud was mud. But how? His eyes drifted back to the map. The treasure was trapped in the cemetery just as Charlie was trapped in his office.

He shifted in his creaking chair. A stash of money would make him his own boss. No more filling in paperwork, paying lip service to senseless regulations. He could run his own show. It wouldn't have to be a big operation. Something modest would be fine, as long as it was his. Now *that* was an enticing prospect.

He bent to collect the papers littering the floor, already cursing all the boxes he'd have to tick, all the blanks to fill in. He put the first form in his typewriter and began to type. They wanted reports? He'd give them reports. So many and in such detail they'd be sorry they asked.

Clack-clackity-clack, the typewriter went as he stabbed at the keys.

5514 lineal feet of double-track and 48 lineal feet of single-track trestle completed, making total length of trestle 10,927'. Fill dumped from trestle, 460,040 c.y. Porto Bello rock for exterior of breakwater delivered March 1912. 65,133 c.y. unloaded and plowed off on the north side of the trestle...

He looked out the window and heaved another sigh. For now, Operation Get Rich Quick was grounded. But someday...

Portobelo
December, present day

"Merry Christmas!"

Nick lifted this head from the pillow and looked through the companionway to find Kate smiling from the chart table.

"Merry Christmas," he called, flopping back down.

It took him a minute to get oriented. On any other morning, he and Kate might have woken to continue their collective head-scratching over Charlie's riddles, but it was Christmas day in Portobelo, and he was sure it would prove to be whole new experience — and a welcome distraction.

"Doesn't quite feel like Christmas," he murmured.

He'd "missed out" on the pre-holiday rush and stress and was therefore in a completely different frame of mind going into the holiday. Then there was the fact that he was aboard his own boat in the tropics, living a lifestyle in which he woke up feeling as though it were Christmas every day or he'd hit the lottery — if the boat systems appeared to be cooperating that day, of course. Instead of organizing himself for visits to various relatives, all he awoke to was another gloriously sunny morning in the tropics.

"Well, Santa found us," Kate called from the chart table.

"Really?" He faked surprise.

"Yep." She flicked off the anchor light and bounced back into the forepeak with the presents he'd left out for her. "I love Santa," she said, kissing him.

"I love Santa, too."

A good start to the day. A great start, even.

Kate pulled out the presents she had stashed for him, and they both dug in.

"Wow, this is great," he said, examining his new fishing lure.

"The king of lures, or so Juan called it." She grinned.

He got a diver's knife, too, while Kate got two books on the building of the Panama Canal. One was a straightforward history tome, and the other, a 1912 eyewitness account written by a canal worker.

"This is great!" she said, already studying the table of contents. "Santa did good."

Operation Keep Crewmate Happy was running smoothly, Nick decided.

They lingered over a decadent brunch on *Aurora* and toyed with their presents, then prepared for Juan's Christmas party at El Diablo. The occasion called for clean T-shirts, the very best they had. Kate pulled on her nicest running shorts, too, while Nick donned the last shorts he owned that were free of grease stains. Spiffed up and ready to hit the town, they climbed into their dinghy with a bowl of potato salad and made for the shore where a gaggle of inflatable dinghies were already docked.

"Feliz Navidad!" called a cheery voice. It was the man who always sat on the third stoop on the right, every time they came ashore.

"Merry Chreestmas!" said the lady from the bakery as they passed by.

Funny, Nick thought, how Portobelo had grown on him in the past week.

Cruisers of all nationalities crowded the rooftop bar at El Diablo. They marveled at the roast pig that Juan had provided, as well as the huge spread created by their potluck. Everyone was there, from youngsters like Trevor and Tyler to the stoic Swedes and a number of retired couples Nick recognized from the San Blas. Phil and Sherri, the television producer and the yoga instructor. Amy and her husband, Ned, the physicist/plane enthusiast, and many others. A pair of Dutch children scampered around the place and were immediately adopted as surrogate grandchildren by the older women in attendance. The sunburned American expat with the bloodshot nose was there, too. Arty was his name — the one who'd joked about a search for lost treasure.

"I think he's been in the tropics a little too long," Kate murmured upon seeing him.

Nick nodded in agreement. The man's boat, *The Artful Dodger*, had sprouted a bushy beard of weeds, and he had just run off a Panamanian girlfriend, his junior by decades.

"God, this looks great," someone said, eyeing the potluck spread. "Dig in!"

Food wasn't the only thing to be consumed at the party. Gossip was generously passed around, too. Conversation centered on the latest news about the mysterious sailboat that had washed up on a reef in the San Blas.

"The *Persephone*," said Phil, who was full of juicy facts on the case. According to him, the unidentified dead body was not the registered owner, a Frenchman known to have dabbled on the shady side of the "transportation" industry along the coasts of Panama and Colombia. The Frenchman was missing, gone without a trace.

"But it gets better!" Phil announced to a growing audience. "They found a lot more than just a dead body!"

Nick couldn't help leaning in to listen.

Apparently, the boat not only carried a body — cause of death undetermined — but also plastic-wrapped bricks of cocaine. Hundreds of kilograms' worth.

"A street value in the millions!" Phil threw his arms wide.

"What about the dugout value?" quipped Ned, the physicist.

Ten heads swiveled in his direction.

"Haven't you heard of Lotto del Mar?"

Nine out of ten heads shook no.

"That's what the Kuna call it. Whatever the wind and tide bring to them, that's Lotto del Mar — the lottery of the sea. Sometimes it's a shipment of shoes, fallen off a container ship..."

"And sometimes it's two hundred kilos of cocaine!" Phil chimed in.

Ned nodded. "There are some sharp businessmen among the Kuna. They'll have long passed the odd bundle of cocaine on to the cartel at a nice profit to themselves."

"Tradition meets innovation!" The producer grinned, wrapping up the show.

A joint Panamanian-US investigation was underway. Meanwhile, speculation ran unfettered through the radio sets of the Caribbean cruising fleet.

Another sailor started to lecture on cartels: something about keen business strategy, branching into new ventures, and even providing civic services to win over locals. Nick tuned out and listened to cruising talk instead. Repair tips, engine maintenance, weather forecasts. That was his world.

Kate, for her part, was playing sheriff by the dessert table with a Canadian named Cheryl, making sure no one hogged. A grizzled old salt who'd tried to make off with an entire plate of cookies was getting a stern lecture right now. Nick smiled, watching them. That was Kate: serving justice, one bite of chocolate at a time.

Plates were scraped and stacked as the Christmas spread was reduced to mere scraps. Nick and Kate joined other guests in rolling up their sleeves and cleaning the aftermath. Then the gift-giving began, an uproarious white elephant affair in which each crew drew a number and chose a gift from the selection that had been heaped on a central table, one gift from every crew.

"Great! A bottle of Abuelo rum," the lucky winner said, holding his gift high.

"A CD of Christmas music!"

"A pink memory stick?" Trevor gaped, holding it at arm's length.

"Suits you, mate." Tyler laughed.

No gift was safe in its owner's hands for long, however. According to the rules of the white elephant party, the next crew could choose to appropriate an already opened gift from its recipient instead of drawing a new one from the pile.

"Hey, that's mine!" the owner of the rum bottle cried.

"Not anymore, it's not!" Tyler crowed.

The rum bottle exchanged hands several times, as did a garish Bob Marley-print tie-dye shirt.

On *Aurora's* turn, Nick watched as Kate slowly unwrapped a small bundle.

"A pornographic coffee mug?" She blinked.

That one drew hoots of laughter and a few jealous looks.

"I'll trade you," Trevor tried, holding up the memory stick.

The mug was immediately claimed by the next person in line, much to Kate's relief and Nick's quiet dismay. When Kate drew again, they ended up with a prepaid phone voucher.

"Much better," she breathed.

All in all, everyone agreed it was a wonderful and wacky way to spend the holiday far from home. The party was also a vehicle for forging new friendships, with crews breaking off into small clusters delineated more by cruising plans than age cohorts. Crews with big plans to venture into the Pacific found themselves drawn to each other like a flock of birds guided by some mysterious magnetic force. Those with a laid-back, we-might-just-spend-another-decade-in-the-Caribbean outlook migrated to a different table and discussed the relative merits of Colombia and Panama as homes-away-from-home. Kate listened in to the Pacific-bound gang, shooting Nick daring looks the whole time.

"Yeah, we're going through the canal," Tyler announced. He was already wearing the gift he'd ended up with: a pirate eye patch and skull and bones headscarf.

"When?"

The Australians shrugged in tandem. "Whenever we get there."

A grizzled old sailor — the one from *Lucky Stars* — piped up. "You know about the procedure?"

Tyler looked like he didn't like the sound of the word *procedure*.

"You don't just show up and get in line, you know. You have to get officially measured. Then you have to pay the fee."

"Fee?"

"$600."

The Australians' eyes just about popped out of their heads as Lucky went on. "Then you need line handlers, hundred foot lines, and tires."

"Tires?"

"As fenders."

"Got plenty of fenders, mate."

The sailor shook his head. "The walls of the locks are raw cement. You're required to have tires. And four line handlers, one for every corner of the boat."

Tyler scratched his beard and ordered another beer.

"It can take anywhere from three days to three weeks to get a transit date."

"Three *weeks*?"

"And you only get a date if your boat passes inspection."

Trevor wiped his brow. "Inspection? Then what?"

Lucky shrugged. "Then you're ready. They bring you an advisor, and you're off. Three locks up, and you're in Gatun Lake. Three locks down, and you're at the Pacific."

"How long does that take? About two hours?"

A host of sailors broke out in laughter. "Two days," said Lucky, slapping Tyler on the back as he choked on his beer.

"Two *days*?"

"You start one afternoon, and by nighttime, you're up in the lake. You anchor there, and the next morning you continue across the lake and down three more locks."

Ned had wandered over, shaking his head at the clueless boys. "The canal is huge. It's incredible! One of the engineering wonders of the world. A once-in-a-lifetime experience!"

Tyler leaned back and fanned himself.

"And where are all the freighters while this is happening?" someone from the crowd asked.

Lucky smiled. "Right in the lock with you. Little guys like us get squeezed in behind them."

Tyler's hand went to his chest. "Squeezed?"

"And this is easier than going around Cape Horn?" Trevor said.

Lucky patted his shoulder. "But then you're through. A major experience for any sailor. The whole Pacific is ahead of you."

Kate kept shooting Nick probing glances.

We could do it! her wildly hopeful look insisted.

Nick responded more warily. *We'd have to fix about a hundred things first.* Still, he found himself slipping down the path to temptation. A trip through one of the engineering wonders of the world. Pacific sunsets. And a very happy crewmate.

Tempting. Very tempting, indeed.

Chapter Eight

A Bold New Enterprise

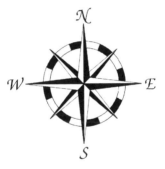

Portobelo

December, present day

While the rest of the world busied itself in holiday revelry, one brooding figure cast a long shadow over the main street of Portobelo. Veins bulged in his bullish neck as he paced at the deserted bus stop, ignoring distant sounds of merriment.

A single refrain echoed through his mind. *A businessman never rests.* Christmas was a holiday for children, not for him.

Vadz cracked his knuckles and admired his broad, powerful hands before scanning the empty street. *Let them party*, he scoffed, thinking of the lesser sailors now gathered at El Diablo. *I launch a bold new enterprise.*

He threw out his chest another half inch. That expanded his shadow, so Vadz did it a few more times, experimenting to find the best angle for maximum effect. And all the time, he schemed. The world was full of opportunities for aggressive, capable, multitalents such as himself. And he was on his way to the big time — all the way from humble beginnings on a Polish farm to the world of international business. He smiled and crushed his right fist into his left, squeezing until the joints cracked and groaned. Then he repeated the motion, letting the right hand exact revenge on the left.

Satisfying. Such a satisfying sound.

A bell rang, and a child pedaled by on a purple bicycle with training wheels. Colorful streamers trailed from the handlebars. Two friends followed in hot pursuit, all of them giddy with joy at their wonderful Christmas surprise.

"*Feliz Navidad!*" called a little girl.

Vadz scowled.

Finally, the faded red Nissan he'd been waiting for swung around the corner and approached. Vadz smoothed a hand over his clean-shaved head and squared his shoulders for confrontation. He squinted at the immaculately dressed driver as the car pulled up. A weasel of a man — obviously not a man of action like himself. The only thing Vadz admired about his business contact was his oversized cuff links. Solid gold, from the looks of them.

"Merry Christmas," the weasel said in a flat, disinterested tone.

Vadz grunted a greeting and folded his boxy frame into the vehicle. His head brushed the ceiling. His knees folded tightly in the Japanese deathtrap. Someday, when he made his fortune and settled down on a beach somewhere, he would buy himself a vehicle that reflected his success in life. Something worthy. Something engineered in Germany. Expensive, eye-catching, and roomy. With a sunroof. His fingers flexed over an imaginary control panel.

He reminded himself to be patient. He had just earned a tidy profit with his last run from Colombia, but that was just the beginning. With his new business connections, he would make more. Much more.

Portobelo

One week later

Vultures stared like dark sentinels, stooped from centuries at their posts. There seemed to be one on every watchtower of Fort San Jeronimo, low at the head of the bay. All with the same hungry look in their eyes. Kate watched them, wondering what they were hoping for. The dead should be long gone from this place.

She shrugged. Even on this oppressively humid day, it felt good to be out at last. After a week of post-Christmas boat projects, she felt released.

She scrambled up a ramp to the parapet and sighted down the barrel of a cannon, imagining a pirate attack. First, there'd be the deafening sound of cannon fire, followed by eruptions of water, then shouts of alarm and clattering footsteps. The acrid smell of smoke and—

A clicking sound fired at her shoulder. She whirled to find Nick, shooting away with his camera.

"You don't need a time machine in a place like this," she said, sweeping a hand over the scene.

Forts ringed the bay, and the sailboats at anchor were place-holders for Spanish galleons. Over to one side, the roof of the customs house rose above the rest of Portobelo — the vault of the Americas. It had once glittered with silver. Gold. Riches to die for. She could see it in the glint of sun playing over the water.

A tour guide walked past with a gaggle of North American tourists. "Over the course of one century, one-third of the world's silver..."

Nick fiddled with the manual settings on his digital camera. For her, the place was about centuries and secrets hidden in every stone of the massive walls. For Nick, it was all about f-stops and

ISO. She knew he had been more inclined to spend the afternoon rewiring their erratic solar panels. But even budding electricians needed a break, right?

"Do you want to get a coffee while I check out the last sights on my list?"

He perked up at the mention of coffee. "Well, if you don't mind... I mean, it's not that I'm not interested," he tried.

Of course, he wasn't interested. But she knew better than to drag him to every obscure sight in town. She nudged him in the direction of the exit. "You've earned it."

"See you at El Diablo!" he called, moving with the joyful step of a child leaving school grounds.

Kate set off in the opposite direction, to the last section of the old town she wanted to explore. Having spent nearly every minute of the past months with Nick, it felt strange to be alone. A reminder, she decided, not to get so swept up in togetherness that she lost the knack for heading out on her own.

A soccer ball came flying out from between two houses. She chipped it back over the fence and waved to the kids, each of them dusty from head to foot but smiling all over.

"El cementerio?" she asked, checking if she was on the right path.

The kids waved her down the street. *"Por allá!"*

She nearly missed the graveyard, tucked as it was at an edge of town where the buildings petered out among nondescript walls leading nowhere in particular. It proved to be a derelict affair.

"In other words, typical of Portobelo," she joked to Nick, only to remember he wasn't there.

The place looked more like the scrappy mule pen it had been converted to at some point than a significant historic site. The stone Madonna overlooking the walled compound seemed sad and tired, an effect heightened by the faded plastic flowers arranged at her feet. Kate made a cursory round of the cracked tombs and quickly left, thinking about the futility of marking a final "resting" place.

But the cracked and tumbled-down tombs stuck a chord in her mind and occupied her thoughts as she walked on. She'd seen a crater-filled graveyard in Peru, a place raided by greedy treasure hunters. The place where people had once been laid to rest had been ransacked, all for the few trinkets once tucked tenderly alongside loved ones. She shook her head. What people did for money...

And just like that, her thoughts bounced over to Charlie. How had he stumbled across his strange things? What had become of them?

Charlie Parker. Was he an adventurer? A thief? Or a chance discoverer, acting innocently? Which category did Charlie fall into?

Which category did she fit into?

Images of silver coins and golden spiders danced in her head in a manner very unbecoming of a professional archaeologist. She shook her head and crossed the plaza, briefly eclipsed by the shadow of the twin church towers: shadow, daylight, shadow, and daylight again, where she tugged the brim of her sun hat firmly down. She kicked at the dirt road, sending pebbles skipping.

It was probably just crazy, anyway.

She scuffed along and eventually paused at El Merced Bridge, one of the oldest structures in a very old town. The graceful arch straddled a polluted stream, maintaining an air of serene dignity even when a bus rumbled past on the modern bridge paralleling it. She lingered there, feeling a faint but steady pulse, a breath of a bygone era. But the past was fading away. Soon it would be nothing but legend. Stories, undecipherable notes in a leather notebook, tumbled-down tombs. What to make of it all?

A mangy mutt wandered past, and Kate found herself stroking its matted fur until Nick came trotting across the cobblestones.

"You have to see this!" He grabbed her hand as the dog scampered away.

"What?" she yelped. It wasn't often that Nick got worked up about something. He was supposed to be the even-keeled one. "Wait!" She struggled to don her backpack with her free arm while trotting behind him.

Nick plowed on, glancing up and down the main road. He crossed and headed for the center of town, ignoring her questions. At last, he came to a stop at the far side of the littered town plaza and pointed triumphantly at an information board there.

Kate squinted at it. Just another informative plaque — the type Nick avoided whenever possible. Was he suffering from heat stroke? She studied his flushed cheeks.

"Look!" he insisted, holding Charlie's notebook open to a sketched map.

"So, Charlie drew a map?"

"No," Nick drew out the word. "Charlie drew *this* map!" He jabbed a finger at the information board and rotated the notebook so that the sketch aligned with the map of eighteenth-century Portobelo on display.

The breath caught in her throat. When she recovered, she whistled a low, drawn-out note. "Portobelo!"

"Portobelo," Nick echoed.

She took Charlie's notebook and compared the maps. They really were the same.

"Wow. I owe you a beer."

"You owe me many beers," Nick said, looking awfully pleased with himself.

She traced the lines of the map. Thanks to the information board, Charlie's unlabeled sketch took on meaning. The boxy shape of the bay was clear, as were the fortifications ringing it. The bold line that dominated his drawing had to be the main road, its path unchanged from historic times to the present day. Among the boxes that represented buildings was a large block that must have been the customs house, and another, the church. Several streets beyond that was a wide, open rectangle that corresponded to the old graveyard. Even the side road leading to El Diablo was on Charlie's map, an area labeled "colonial slave quarters" on the information board.

"Hey! Look at this." Nick pointed at the dashed marks on Charlie's sketch.

"The street to El Diablo?"

"Exactly! The road to El Diablo!" Nick said. "Look at the marks at the top of the road!"

At the top of the dashed line, Charlie had drawn a square with some squiggles inside. Kate squinted at them. "E.D.?"

"E.D!" Nick exclaimed. "El Diablo!"

Kate stared at him. With a joint nod, they rushed off.

* * *

Nick's backpack jostled as he speed-walked across town, and he immediately broke into a sweat. But he had to smile in spite of himself. For once, he was the one leading the charge on some quixotic quest.

Without warning, Kate pulled up short, and he nearly ran into her from behind.

"What?"

"Juan!" she started in a jumble of words. "Juan said El Diablo belonged to his great-grandmother! He said he's the third generation there."

Nick cocked his head at her. "Juan's El Diablo is Charlie's E.D.?"

"He's even got pictures on the wall..." Kate started to say.

Nick nudged her and they continued, quickening their pace with each step. Past the puzzled grandmother stationed at the door to the mini-super. Past the giggling children in the park. Past the woman fussing over flowerpots along the winding lane to El Diablo. They burst on to the rooftop bar and found Juan with a phone at each ear. After an eternity, he wrapped up the conversation at his right ear and signed off with cousin Juanito on his left ear. No sooner had he lowered both phones than one start ringing again.

"What can I do for you?" Juan asked, raising the left phone and clicking *receive*.

"I wanted to ask about your great-grandmother," Kate said. "The one who started this place."

Juan cursed at the phone; it was the other one ringing.

"Mercedes." He jabbed a finger toward the photo wall. "Mercedes de la Costa."

Then he turned away and began rattling away to the caller. A good thing, too, because he missed the widening of Kate's eyes, the sharp intake of Nick's breath that had nothing to do with his run across town.

Kate pulled him to the photo wall and pointed at the aristocratic-looking woman in the first portrait.

"Mercedes," she said in a hushed, almost reverent whisper.

"Charlie bought... What did he buy for her?" Nick's mind spun with images from the leather notebook.

"Wine... parasols..." Kate murmured, then pulled him over to the photo of a young Mercedes surrounded by Anglo admirers. "Would you recognize Charlie?"

He examined the faces closely. All seemed to fit the same mold — healthy, happy twenty- and thirty-year-olds out on the adventure of their lives, smiling courtiers surrounding their exotic goddess. None, however, resembled the face in a photo Nick recalled seeing at his aunt's house. Charlie was tall, lanky, and fair, like some of the men in the photo, but in every picture Nick had ever seen of him, he wore the crooked smile of a little boy planning his next prank.

Nick shook his head. "No Charlie here."

More riddles. Nick tried forming connections between them, setting them off like a row of dominoes — but all dead-ended after a few clicks. Were they pieces of a single puzzle or just unrelated facts?

Kate began examining each photo on the wall, and he followed suit, starting with the sailboat sketch. He almost moved away but stayed riveted a moment longer. Something about it...

Then he spotted it and muttered out loud.

"What?" Kate asked.

He pointed, running a finger beneath the tiny letters written on the cutter's upswept bow. Y-O-L-A-N-T-A.

Kate went very still. "Not a girlfriend."

"A boat," Nick whispered.

"Charlie's boat?" Kate breathed.

Nick gulped. *Go, Charlie.*

He hadn't heard anything about a boat in any of the stories, but then again, he hadn't always listened that closely. Charlie, the sailor? It certainly fit. If so, that meant Charlie knew the feeling of the wind in his hair, the sun on his cheeks. The sound of water gurgling along the hull, the sheer freedom — and sometimes, the sheer terror — of the sea. Charlie must have had dreams, hobbies, pursuits. And he had a boat. A boat memorialized on the wall of El Diablo.

Nick stood there, shaking his head at the sketch. *What were you up to, Charlie?*

A little at a loss as to what to make of it all, he pulled out Charlie's notebook to the Yolanta entry. Kate pointed, speculating, and their conversation became more animated. But then the hair on Nick's neck prickled. He turned to see Alejandro at the threshold of the rooftop bar, his dark eyes so piercing that he seemed much closer. The instant Nick turned, Alejandro whipped his attention to the bar and sauntered toward the waitress with a cheery smile.

Sucking back a curse, Nick hustled Kate over to a table in a far corner. She waved at the Venezuelan but followed without comment.

"Okay, let's get this straight."

He sat with his back to the restaurant, leaning over the tabletop to shield the notebook from view. Flipping through Charlie's notes, he tried to establish some context among the disjointed phrases. There was the entry listing *Mercedes — 20 bottles red wine, 6 parasols* and the choppy notes of another page, *Yolanta. Friday 5:00.*

The first part was clear. "Mercedes needed the wine for her café and the parasols for her friends," he deduced.

Kate raised her eyebrows at the word *friends*. "Juan said Mercedes had 'business interests,'" she said, using air quotes.

"So?"

She leaned closer. "You tell me what kind of business interests involve a cadre of attractive young women?"

Nick looked up at the photo display, a little scandalized. But he couldn't think of any plausible alternative to a brothel, either.

"So I guess we know what Charlie was 'up to' in Portobelo."

Kate turned to another page. "So what's this with Yolanta at 5:00?"

A breeze ruffled the pages past sketches of coins and spider medallions.

Nick couldn't make sense of it all. Even a cold drink didn't seem to jar any new connections. The best he could do was to email his aunt, asking if she could shed any light on the matter.

He stared at the keyboard for a while, choosing his words carefully.

"Just write it, already," Kate urged.

"I don't want to sound totally loco." Because how exactly did you ask something like, *What the hell was Charlie doing with pieces of eight, a Peruvian spider, and a boat named Yolanta?*

PS, he'd write if he could. *Did Charlie get rich?*

El Diablo, Portobelo
present day

It was Thursday — billiards night at El Diablo, an event that seemed to commence earlier and earlier each week. Juan pushed aside two tables and replaced them with a wobbly pool table that delighted the likes of Trevor and Tyler, who somehow managed to keep their beers upright while aligning their shots and entertaining two young and far too impressionable female backpackers. Maria the waitress worked alongside her sister, each vying with the other in daring necklines.

Nick ignored the increasingly bustling scene, concentrating on the disjointed pieces of Charlie's puzzle. He kept waiting for Kate to voice the conclusion he couldn't quite utter himself.

"So... Charlie was here in Portobelo," she ventured, speaking slowly as if wary of her own words.

Nick nodded. "Here in El Diablo. He knew Mercedes."

"He found something strange in Portobelo. Something he had to leave behind. He told your great-grandmother Rosie so in that letter."

Nick raised his eyebrows at her, daring her to say it.

"Somehow, he found Spanish coins and a Peruvian spider..."

Nick was thinking that *strange* didn't begin to describe it.

Kate's tone was carefully neutral, but her eyes were on fire. "And he wanted to take it home. How?"

He filled in his own conclusion. "In Yolanta." He felt a touch of pride at Kate's surprised look. She hadn't thought of that.

"Only he never did get it home."

"So whatever he found is still in Panama."

"If no one else got to it in the meantime," Kate countered. She told him about Richard Brewster Lewis' latest book. The sensationalist tale of priceless treasure in *Pirate Gold!* was giving new impetus to amateur treasure hunters throughout the Caribbean and the Americas.

Nick knew he shouldn't let Richard Brewster Lewis' inspirational magic work on him, but he couldn't help it. Charlie's notebook was looking more and more interesting all the time.

"How much would pieces of eight be worth?"

Kate looked at him suspiciously, but he nudged her. "Come on. How much would a piece of eight be worth?"

"You mean if you wanted to buy one?"

"Or sell one."

Both her eyebrows shot up. "A single coin might not be worth a huge amount. A hundred dollars, maybe?"

But Nick was already ahead of her, looking it up on a coin dealer's website. "Seventy dollars."

"That's it?"

"Wait — here's another one for two hundred and another for three hundred. Boy, they do look smudged." He leaned close in to the screen. "But even seventy times..."

"Seventy times a lot would be a lot," Kate finished.

Behind him, billiard balls clicked together, and Tyler cursed.

Nick couldn't help but do the math. Ten coins would be worth seven hundred dollars. A hundred coins, seven thousand dollars. Maybe more. Much more. "Too bad Charlie wasn't a little more specific."

Kate chortled. "My dearest Rosie, I have discovered 237 pieces of eight..." She broke off as Nick shushed her. El Diablo had gained a half-dozen additional guests. The afternoon shadows were lengthening, giving the air a mystical glow.

"It had to have been a lot," he whispered. "He mentioned 'a silver-lined future for us both.' Remember?"

A heavy silence fell between them.

"What about the spider?" he continued.

"What about it?"

He rubbed two fingers against his thumb. Money.

Kate's face took on a whole new expression. "That's totally different. You couldn't put a value on something like that. It's unique. The find of the century."

He stirred the air with his hand, prompting her along.

"Any museum would kill for it," Kate continued. "Not just for historic value. It would be a major drawing card."

"How much if a collector or museum wanted to buy it?"

"Something like that would never be for sale," she said, but then her voice fell. "Except on the black market."

"How much?"

"How would I know about the black market?"

"Just guess!"

She made a face. "Half a million, easily. Maybe even a million."

Nick started to warm to the idea of pursuing Great-Grandpa Charlie's crazy notes.

Kate leaned in closer. "It's totally illegal. As in jail time. Jail in Central America, not some white-collar prison in Florida."

Nick's enthusiasm waned. Probably the entire venture was a wild-goose chase, though he couldn't quite shake the notion. "Same with the coins?"

"Still must be illegal, but hell, if they're on the internet, there's got to be a way." Then she shook her head.

"What?"

"I'm an archaeologist, not a tomb robber."

"But there's no tomb."

She made a face. "It's the principle of the thing."

A cheer went up behind them, then faded into a chorus of groans as Trevor came close to sinking an impossible three-ball shot.

Nick looked up at the distraction and found himself laughing out loud when he turned back to Kate.

"What?" she asked.

"Can you believe we're even having this conversation?"

Kate caught the smile, too. "A little crazy," she agreed.

"Very crazy."

"And anyway, we have zero clue as to where Charlie left his 236 pieces of eight," she joked.

"237," Nick murmured, flicking through the pages of Charlie's notebook.

"What are you looking for?"

"A big X marking the spot," he replied in an absent mumble.

It was a joke, of course. He reminded himself that it was only a joke.

Portobelo

New Year's Eve, present day

"Oars?"

"Check."

"Insect repellant?"

"Check."

"Champagne?" Kate asked.

"Got it," Nick replied.

"Well, then. I guess we're ready."

Having spent an enjoyable Christmas in the company of strangers, Nick and Kate had agreed to reverse tradition and spend New Year's alone. Just as well, Nick decided, with the likes of Alejandro hanging around the bar.

It had been a year of sudden changes and new beginnings. Now they stood poised between two oceans, the two of them together, with a sailboat as their home. A New Year like none Nick had ever celebrated. Alluring possibilities beckoned, and the horizon stretched wider than ever before.

As other sailors headed to El Diablo for Juan's pirate party, Nick pointed the dinghy's bow in the opposite direction and puttered away with Kate. They headed to the uninhabited side of the bay and hiked the hill to the upper level of Fort San Fernando. As dusk captured the raw contours of the surrounding landscape, lights from the town and anchored boats dotted the scene like so many flickering fireflies. From a distance, Portobelo looked serene, even enchanted, but Nick knew better. There were secrets in there amidst the litter and decay, secrets that might lead... Where? The lights were tiny pinpoints in a vast darkness.

"This is perfect," Kate sighed.

They sat in an opening in the stone battlement alongside a rusty Spanish cannon. Behind them, the sweet aroma of a citronella candle held mosquitoes at bay as the night deepened and ushered the constellations to their places on the wide stage of the sky.

She nudged him. "Hey, maybe the conquistadors celebrated their New Year's up here, too." Her voice was hushed, as if maybe their spirits could overhear.

His mind was on a different sort of ghost. Charlie. That specter, he couldn't quite shake. Charlie, the coins, and the spider. What if he and Kate managed to locate the valuables that his great-grandfather had left behind? Now *that* would be something.

There had to be a way to bring a few old coins to a market. Given the number of coins in circulation, that didn't seem to be a big problem. Surely there was a finders-keepers rule, at least for small-scale items like coins. As for the spider... Nick felt his gut clench in warning. Trouble there. Best to steer clear.

But the coins weren't quite so intimidating. And if they actually amounted to something, then he'd have a tidy sum with which to extend *Aurora's* cruise for a while. He and Kate could probably squeeze enough out of their savings to eke out a year. Longer would be nice, and he knew Kate wanted nothing better than to sail off into the sunset. The way he saw it, after a few years together on a boat, they would be ready to move on to the next stage of life together. Of course, he couldn't quite voice these thoughts to the great adventuress herself. Not yet.

Kate sighed a little at his side, lost in her own thoughts.

They spent much of the night cocooned within long, contemplative silences. When they spoke, it was to appreciate all that had gone well thus far: their reunion on *Aurora*, a safe passage from the eastern seaboard to Central America, and adapting to shipboard life.

"Remember in the Chesapeake Bay..."

"...all that bashing into the wind on the way to the Bahamas..."

"...and that amazing man we met in Jamaica..."

Looking back, Nick was amazed to find that things had just...fallen into place. That was a foreign concept for a person used to meticulously engineering projects as small as cooking a meal or as complex as a challenging software project. Always following through, leaving nothing to chance. Well, he had left plenty to chance since buying *Aurora*, and somehow, things had worked out.

Kate smiled. "Trust me. It always works out."

When the topic of their next step came up on this New Year's Eve, Nick found himself agreeing to what he knew Kate wanted so badly: they would transit the canal. *Aurora* would taste the Pacific, and they would explore that side of the isthmus.

"Seriously?" she cried. "You'll go through the canal?"

"Seriously," he nodded as she trapped him in a bear hug.

Once they got there, they could tackle the issue of where to go next.

Kate didn't say it, but he was sure she was thinking it. *We might even uncover more about the curious Panamanian sojourn of Charlie Parker.*

He sighed, looking down on the town lights. Portobelo had grown on him, but Kate was right. It was time to move on. Even if Charlie had found his strange things here, hanging around didn't seem to promise much.

Of course, he had some misgivings about both enterprises: transiting the canal and pursuing Charlie's treasure trail. He'd surprised himself by agreeing to transit at all, but then again, he was getting used to surprising himself. Besides, who could resist when so many stars pledged to see *Aurora* safely on her way?

"What time is it?" Kate asked, rubbing her eyes.

"Still an hour to go."

She fidgeted quietly, then nodded toward her backpack. "Would you mind moving things along a little?"

No, he didn't mind. Not in the least. Kate pulled a miniature bottle of champagne out of the backpack, and he popped the cork.

"Happy old year," Kate said, clinking her plastic cup against his.

"Happy new year, too."

Kate raised her cup in a toast. "To the Atlantic!"

"To the Caribbean," he added.

"And the Pacific," Kate said with a twinkle in her eye.

"To Charlie," Nick said, changing the subject.

"To Mercedes, and that mysterious spider..."

"... whatever they have to do with each other," Nick finished.

Then, with a lingering kiss, they toasted *Aurora* and themselves.

"Hey," she whispered into the kiss. "Thanks for everything."

"Thanks to you, too," he whispered back.

Pretty much the best New Year's ever, Nick decided, taking it all in. The place. The company. The past, present, and future, all woven together like a multicolored ball of yarn.

Eventually, they stumbled down the hillside, picking their way across dark ruins to the dinghy, then headed off, aiming for *Aurora's* faint masthead light. They climbed aboard just as small-scale fireworks flared over the tiled rooftops of Portobelo in a wonderfully haphazard display.

"Happy New Year," Kate whispered, one hand on Nick's shoulder, one on the coach roof.

"Happy New Year," he echoed, wondering what adventures it would bring.

Chapter Nine

Out of the Frying Pan

Portobelo

January, present day

"It's not like we're stealing," Kate whispered. "We're just borrowing!"

Nick had to wonder if she was trying to convince him or herself. They had one more errand to run before leaving Portobelo, and that lay at the top of the stairs to El Diablo.

The rooftop bar was still cluttered with the debris of the New Year's party, including Arty of *The Artful Dodger*, who was slumped over a table in a disheveled heap. The expat was surrounded by empty bottles lit by the morning sun like votive offerings to the god of hard drinking.

Nick's eyes darted around the bar. "Maybe we should just ask."

"Then Juan would wonder why." Kate peered at the pictures hanging across the room. One in particular.

Nick had to concede she had a point. Juan would definitely want to know what they were up to. But that didn't mean he liked this plan. It was just that he didn't have a better one. So they waited, fidgeting on the rooftop bar until Juan appeared in just the right state of distraction. As it was, the man was looking rather worn after a night of New Year's celebrations. The moment he clicked off his phone, Kate pounced.

"Juan, could you help us order some LED lights?"

Juan looked like he was the one who needed help ordering — aspirin, that is. But the businessman in him took over.

"What type? What color?" he rasped. "Color temperature? Current draw? How many?" He put a hand on his forehead and winced.

"Well, we're looking for a replacement for the masthead light," Kate started, pulling him into the computer room.

Behind her back, she motioned wildly at Nick, who stole sideways along the photo wall and stood in front of the Yolanta sketch. He reached for it, then stopped to scan the bar once again. No one there but Arty, out for the count. So he quickly removed the frame from the wall and pushed it into his backpack. He stood still, listening to Kate dictate bulb specifications. Then he took down a second frame and stuffed it in the bag, too. Another furtive glance showed that the coast was clear. He stepped to where Kate could see him and gave her an uncertain thumbs-up. Juan's phone rang, and Kate took the opportunity to slip away.

If he'd been dragged off into a police lineup at exactly that minute, Nick figured, they would instantly single him out and declare him guilty of almost any crime. He had the downcast eyes of a sinner, and he knew it. He just wasn't cut out for this kind of thing.

"Hurry," Kate whispered.

He followed her out of the bar and a few blocks over to a tiny closet of a copy shop run by an enterprising older woman. When she was home, the copy shop was open. And she was always home.

Kate placed the first frame on the copier — the shot of Mercedes with her admirers. Nick intercepted the result as it fed out of the machine and grimaced. The flash of the copier had reflected off the glass frame, washing out the image. He turned the frame over and carefully opened it, sliding the glass off. He handed the brittle photograph to Kate, and she copied it again. There was still some glare, but the image was passable. While Kate put the photo back in its frame, he opened the framed sketch of Yolanta.

That proved a tougher nut to crack. It was old and crude, barely held together by a couple of tiny nails jammed between layers of wood and cardboard. He fiddled with it, asking himself the whole time what the hell he was doing. Finally he had it open and placed the sketch of Yolanta face down on the copy machine.

"Hey," he murmured, picking it back up. There was something scribbled across the back. He read it with a start, then angled the paper over for Kate to see.

Dear Mercedes,

Greetings from the other side. Please keep this for me until I make it back.

Yours, Carlito.

04.23.14 at 23

16-07.9 Sp 44:53

52-18.1 Sir 46:20

Kate squeezed his arm. "Carlito! Carlos — Carlito — Charlie!"

The sloping script matched that in Charlie's notebook. He and Kate exchanged looks, then hurried to copy both sides of the sketch.

Their next actions all followed in a blur: thumbing the sketch back into its flimsy frame, then scurrying back to El Diablo to return the pictures to their spots on the wall. Juan was nowhere in sight, much to Nick's relief. He and Kate waved an artificially cheery good-bye to the disinterested waitress emerging from the kitchen and raced away.

"Shit," Kate hissed, looking back.

"What?"

"Arty." She motioned. The man was slowly creaking back to life, and his bloodshot eyes blinked at the photo wall.

"Shit," Nick agreed, hurrying her along.

* * *

It was Charlie, all right. Kate knew that the minute she saw the looped handwriting. But what did the message mean?

She and Nick huddled in *Aurora's* cockpit, poring over the photocopies. "Greetings from the other side? Other side of what?"

Nick studied the writing sideways as if a secret message might be encoded between the lines. "Other side of the world? Other side of town..."

"Other side of Panama?"

"The Pacific side... It's possible."

She perked up. "Totally possible. And if so... What are the numbers?"

Both vied for a view of the note.

04.23.14 - at 23
16-07.9 Sp 44:53
52-18.1 Sir 46:20

"Why would Charlie send Mercedes a sketch of Yolanta?" Kate scratched her chin.

Nick shook his head.

What did the numbers refer to? Did they connect to the spider and coins? What did Mercedes know about Charlie's find? So many questions, so few answers.

"This note doesn't necessarily have anything to do with the coins," Nick reminded her.

"But it's all we have to go on. Let's assume for a minute it does."

"Okay then, what does it tell us?"

She had to admit to being stuck on that one.

They retrieved Charlie's letters, reading and rereading the passages about the "strange things," "much more," and "bringing it all home."

"Found." Kate tapped Charlie's letter. "He said he *found* the strange things. He didn't buy them from a collector, he *found* them. But how? And where did he find them?"

Nick shrugged. "The question is, where is it now?"

"Whatever he found could be anywhere. In Panama, or in a collection somewhere if it was discovered by someone else in between..."

Nick shook his head. "Too many variables. Let's start with what we know."

She nodded, collecting her thoughts with a deep breath. "Okay. Charlie said, 'I had to leave it all behind. How I wish to go back there.' Panama. A beautiful port. Portobelo. Or..." She trailed off.

"Or what?"

"If you found some strange, valuable things in one place, wouldn't you move them somewhere else? Hide them somewhere?"

"Like what, under my mattress?"

She made a face. "That would make for a heck of a lumpy mattress."

"So, where, then?"

She shrugged. "He'd want to get it out of here, right? Out of Portobelo, for starters, then out of Panama. But he never got it out of the country. So it really could be anywhere."

"That doesn't give us much to work on," Nick sighed. "We need more."

She shot a pointed look at the photocopy in front of them.

Nick shook his head. "I can't see any way those numbers mark a location. At least not in Panama, or anywhere near Panama. 52° is too far away either as latitude or longitude. Same with 16°."

Kate tried to picture where 52° or 16° north might be, then south, or west. Nick was right. None of the combinations would be anywhere near Panama. "But there must be something..."

"We could be barking up the wrong tree. Why would Charlie even write down the location of what he found? It's not like you'd forget where you left your... your stash," Nick challenged. Like her, he seemed to be avoiding the word *treasure*.

She had a few theories — but not a single clear one. "Maybe it was a complicated location... like in the jungle. Or maybe he needed someone else to retrieve it for him."

"What, like Mercedes and her girls?"

She gave him a look.

Nick grimaced. "I'm getting a little tired of Charlie's riddles. There must be another explanation."

At least a dozen juicy explanations clamored for attention in her mind, but they all ended up pounding against the same brick wall.

"Suppose we could actually find it. Suppose your aunt Laura sends us a handy treasure map tomorrow. What then?" She let the question sit, then continued. "What would we really do with it?"

Nick answered immediately, like he'd already thought it all through. "We get rich. We sail as far and as long as we want to."

Kate felt a smile grab her from the inside out. She liked that image, both the sailing and the "we" part. Especially with the words of Charlie's letter echoing in her mind: *a silver-lined future for us both*. She shook her head and grinned. The new Nick, ready to follow the call of adventure?

"Just listen to yourself." She meant it to be chiding, but her tone was approving.

Nick's expression went sheepish. "Okay, okay. One thing at a time. First, we figure out where it might be — if it really exists — and we take it from there. Okay?"

Kate sighed. "Okay."

"Anyway, it's time to figure out tomorrow," Nick said, turning to their *Approaches to the Panama Canal* chart. She leaned in as he ran a finger along the coastline to the deep indent of Limón Bay that funneled into the canal, then measured off the distance to the far side of the bay with brass dividers.

"It's about twenty miles to get all the way there and into the marina."

"Marina? I thought we'd anchor off Colon." She pointed to the near end of the bay.

He shook his head. "Marina."

"Anchorage."

"Marina."

"Anchorage."

"Marinas cost too much!"

Nick gave her a long look, then pulled out the guidebook. *Her* guidebook. He flipped a few pages, then quoted from the text.

"Colon is a dangerous slum, a sea of unemployment and poverty. Only the foolhardy wander the streets — by day or night. Crime is rampant, visitors targeted for anything from pickpocketing to violent assault. The knives are long and sharp, and respect for human life is small." Nick snapped the book shut with the decisive knock of a gavel.

Kate hung her head. "Marina."

"It has a pool, you know."

That sounded a little better.

He edged closer. "And a rain forest. With monkeys."

Monkeys? She liked that idea.

Nick whispered seductively in her ear. "Ruins, too."

"I guess I can suffer through that," she admitted, eyeing the promising green swath on the chart. She helped enter and double-check waypoints into the GPS, then popped back up to the cockpit for a last look at Portobelo. The yellow flicker of lights made the slumbering town look centuries younger. A flash along the walls became the glint of armor while the silhouettes of sailboats became mighty galleons with sweeping prows and tall masts. Spanish galleons full of silver and gold.

Was there really a treasure out there somewhere?

Pieces of eight shone and chimed in her mind. She caught her fingers rubbing empty air. Given the chance, would she cash in on an artifact?

Of course, the answer should be no. But what if it was small and unimportant? Just some coins, maybe? They were valuable but not unique. A little money would help stretch out this lovely sailing gig. Since both she and Nick had quit their jobs, they were free to go anywhere *Aurora* would take them — but their savings would only last so long before they had to head back to the rat race.

Unless...

She shook her head. The whole thing was probably just wild conjecture. Highly abstract. A needle in a haystack. Charlie hadn't left enough information, and she herself — well, she had a dangerous tendency to lust after grand possibilities. She forced herself to take in her surroundings instead. To appreciate Nick, *Aurora*, the here and now. What more did she really need?

She gave her surroundings one final glance before reluctantly heading below.

Good-bye, lovely Portobelo. Hello, Panama Canal.

Toro Point
June 1911

Charlie Parker languished in his private purgatory for several long, dark weeks before he managed to engineer an escape. Striving to "streamline" for "reasons of efficiency" — goals no bureaucratic higher-up could possibly contradict — he created a field office out at Toro Point. It was little more than an empty hulk of a shack with a sheet of plywood for a desk, but the corrugated iron roof kept the rain out, even if it did create a racket when it really poured. And it did pour, now that rainy season had set in with what seemed like a mission to drown all foreigners on Panamanian soil. Charlie smiled, imagining Inspector Cummings sinking away until all that remained was that ridiculous hat of his, floating on sloppy brown sludge.

"Dats aplenti fine ruff for da office!" Edgar grinned in approval. He clutched the bundle of goods Charlie had brought from the commissary — cigarettes, a couple of canned hams, and a pair of work gloves, plus a mosquito net for Edgar's newborn daughter. Like a man flush with disease, Edgar was still glowing with the joy of fatherhood. It had taken Charlie three repetitions to grasp the momentous news.

"A lufli butiful daughter!" Edgar told him, radiant as the rising sun.

Charlie took a long drag on his cigarette. "Your first?"

Edgar shook his head, swelling with pride. "Third!"

"Third child or third daughter?"

"Both!"

Charlie burst out in a fit of coughing, reeling at the thought of life in close quarters with so many females.

"Who does she look like?" he managed.

"Like ma butiful wife." Edgar beamed.

The man's joy was contagious, even in the trying conditions. Rain pelted them all morning, turning the path between Charlie's shack and the breakwater into a muddy morass, but no one seemed to take notice. Even Charlie wore a goofy smile as he worked. To think that a man could be happy with such a fate. Maybe that was a lesson he should try to digest... someday.

"Looking good, boys. Looking good," he called to the crew.

Filling out forms wasn't satisfying. But building the breakwater was. Barges arrived weekly with loads from the Portobelo quarry carrying boulders that would take the brunt of the sea's pounding forces. On the leeward side of the breakwater, a sturdy line of piles and trestles expanded into the bay. They would support rails for flatcars delivering loads of excavation spoil which acted as fill to reinforce the breakwater. He loved the symmetry: earth excavated from the canal works put to use in the dam and breakwaters. Brilliant. They weren't fighting nature, just sculpting it into a new form.

Sheets of morning rain gave way to hazy afternoons that plastered his shirt to his body like an extra hide. He'd brought in extra sheets of corrugated iron to extend his field office with a lean-to for the crew's midday break. Their singsong voices provided soothing background music. Lionel, the best reader of the gang, would read aloud from their preferred source of news, the *Colon Independent*. A hush fell over the men whenever Lionel reported the latest from Barbados.

"Price of bread goin' up agin..."

A dozen voices muttered.

"Reverend Jones of High Street Church upta his yuzzual..."

"House o' Assembly passes an act favorin'..."

Every item was met with a chorus of grunts, murmurs, or knowing nods.

"Bridgetown," someone sighed, and the rest joined in.

Charlie himself never felt homesick, but then, he was in Panama for the adventure. The Bajans, as they called themselves, came out of necessity. Charlie reflected on that for some time and decided that maybe Fortuna, fickle goddess of luck that she was, hadn't been ignoring him, after all.

He turned and looked over the white crests of waves dancing far out in the bay. In the absence of a brilliant plan for what to do with his treasure, he was brimming with ideas for everything else. His mind always seemed to work like that — the only time he could find a solution for something was when he wasn't consciously trying to do so. When his roommate in House 47 was transferred to the Central Division, Charlie used his newfound familiarity with paperwork and submitted a housing request for a fictional new employee. Within a matter of days, he welcomed a new roommate to his place in House 47 — a very quiet fellow he christened Cuthbert E. Longfellow. Charlie humored himself with a hearty inner laugh at his own ingenuity.

If only he could conjure up an equally brilliant solution for the silver.

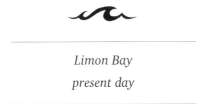

Limon Bay

present day

"Thirty-one, thirty-two, thirty-three." Nick gulped as his finger tapped the horizon. "Thirty-four, thirty-five, thirty-six."

"Thirty-seven," Kate added very quietly.

What had started as a few hulking forms on the horizon became a dozen, and the dozen multiplied until they counted thirty-seven freighters. Thirty-seven looming obstacles for *Aurora* to dodge in the approach to the Panama Canal. And thirty-seven only included freighters waiting outside the canal entrance. How many more were about to emerge from the breakwater?

Terrifying? Exhilarating? Nick wasn't sure which. There were ships weighing anchor, ships dropping anchor, and ships holding position for imminent action, smoke drifting from their exhaust stacks. It was like tiptoeing through a lava field, not knowing which caldera might erupt next.

"It makes me think of a video game with tiny sailboats dodging oncoming freighters," he said.

Kate pursed her lips. "Except in real life, you don't get three lives."

They both stood mute for a minute, scanning the scene.

They had no choice but to steer close to the ships — so close that crews high above had no way of seeing *Aurora*. To them, she was nothing more than a bobbing piece of flotsam. Ahead, the bulbous bow of a cargo ship barreled out of the canal entrance and into the Caribbean, hastening to some faraway destination. A ship among the waiting fleet simultaneously broke ranks and inched forward, making for the first locks of the canal. Nick tuned the VHF radio to channel twelve to pick up the succinct exchanges of pilots and canal authorities as they coordinated a dance of monsters. It was amazing that *Aurora* was even permitted in the same neighborhood. He had the fleeting image of hapless fans being plonked into the melee of an NBA court — that was what it was like. He wanted to call a time-out. But no — he and Kate would not only witness this awesome spectacle but actually become part of it. Soon, *Aurora* would transit the canal alongside the titans of the shipping world.

If all went well, that is.

He opted not to dwell on that as they approached the jagged form of the breakwater. Behind the low wall, another thirty-plus vessels lay at anchor — including a glimmering luxury yacht that stood out like a mirage, complete with a sleek black helicopter on the upper deck.

Kate pointed to one of two narrow gaps in the breakwater. "That one?" she asked in a tight voice.

Nick checked the chart for the hundredth time. "That one."

She altered course for the smaller and less frequented gap — a narrow blue slot where the ocean swell came to an angry halt against the breakwater. Nick let the sails out for the downwind course and spared a quick thought for Charlie. Kate clutched the wheel, staring at the smooth gap rather than at the foaming seas on either side. The noise grew to a small roar, then dissipated as they shot through the gap.

"Out of the frying pan and into the fire?" Nick couldn't help murmuring.

Aurora was now in the protected inner bay formed by the breakwater, but space there was even tighter. It would have been a huge bay if it weren't filled with anchored ships. Outside the breakwater was the Caribbean. To Nick's left, the bay funneled into the canal and the first of the locks. The roofs of Colon appeared on the close side of the bay, but the marina was located in a corner of the opposite side, across a three-mile gauntlet of more ships, not to mention the main shipping channel.

"We're sure we want the marina, right?" Kate ventured, looking at the handful of boats anchored off Colon, not far away.

Nick nodded. "We're sure. Everyone says Colon is too dangerous."

"That's what they said about Jamaica, and they were wrong."

"I'm not sure I want to find out the hard way."

"I guess not." Her voice fell.

He winched in the sheets as *Aurora* came back on a beam reach and sped on, cutting directly under the bow of an anchored freighter. Ahead lay the red and green buoys that delineated the main channel.

"Cristobal Control, Cristobal Control, this is sailing vessel *Aurora*, *Aurora*, over," Kate spoke into the handheld radio, looking at the glass-walled control tower on the Colon side of the bay.

"*Aurora*, *Aurora*, go ahead."

"Sailing vessel *Aurora* requesting permission to cross the channel, over."

"*Aurora*, you are clear to proceed," said the voice in smooth, American English.

Nick wondered how fast his heart would be beating when a similar call came for them to enter the canal. He knew he had to take it one step at a time, but it was hard not to think ahead. First, they had to get to the marina, then arrange their transit. No use worrying about the canal.

Yet.

Aurora broke through the line of green buoys marking one edge of the main channel and dashed between two passing ships. Never before had they come so close to a moving freighter. Only when they passed the line of red buoys marking the other side of the main artery could he relax slightly. Kate made directly for a sliver of land protecting the entrance to the marina. Just beside it lay the overturned hulk of a wreck like a final, ghostly warning. Nick forced his eyes away, only to meet Kate's spooked expression.

Never let that be Aurora, her face said. *Never let that be us.*

By the time they had tied up to the dock in Shelter Bay Marina, it was early afternoon. *Aurora* had sailed a mere eighteen miles that day, but it seemed to him that they had sailed to the very edge of the world — and managed not to fall off. When they finished securing and triple-checking all the dock lines, Kate caught him in a tight, excited hug. He squeezed back in an echo of her sentiment.

"We made it!" she cried.

"We made it."

"Oi!" came a familiar voice. "How about a Balboa?"

Nick turned to see Trevor waving a beer at him from the cockpit of *Free Willy*, tied in the slot opposite *Aurora*.

Yep. Everything was falling into place.

* * *

Aurora arrived in Shelter Bay Marina a day after *Free Willy*, and crews along the docks were still buzzing over the Australians' spectacular, near-miss docking maneuvers in gusty cross winds.

"It was nothing, really." Tyler shrugged as he treated his friends to a beer.

Kate couldn't tell if Tyler was toasting his relative success in getting *Free Willy* to the dock in one piece or downplaying the damage to her scarred bow.

From *Aurora's* berth on C dock, they had a view of the breakwater and the approach channel. A steady stream of cargo ships steamed in both directions, stacked impossibly high with shipping containers. Talk at the marina centered around the canal: organizing a transit, the best position for a small vessel during its transit, and last but not least, reports of freak accidents that could befall small vessels in transit. Sailboat owners worried almost as much about scratches to their vessel's paint jobs as the perils of the sea, so the six-story cement walls of the locks were a major concern.

Another hot topic was whether to organize a canal transit independently or to pay an agent to do the legwork — a debate that occupied Kate and Nick for the following days, pushing Charlie from the forefront of their minds.

"We could arrange everything on our own and save a lot of money," Kate insisted.

"But we have to go around to... how many different offices? Carrying six hundred dollars — in cash?" Nick shook his head. "Paying an agent seems safer."

Kate took a deep breath. Nick wasn't a spendthrift, but he had the annoying habit of playing everything safe. "An agent costs $300."

"Peace of mind, right?"

"And another piece of our savings gone," Kate added, making a quick calculation of the money left in her bank account. Between the two of them, they had enough savings to sail for... well, maybe a year. Two, if they stuck to inexpensive parts of the world and anchored out for free. All the more reason to stay out of marinas, right?

But there they were, in a marina, considering paying an agent. Kate scowled.

It was an old conflict, and she wondered if they would ever find some middle ground. They would need to if they wanted to stick together in the long term. Kate pressed her lips into a tight line, shooing away the doubt scratching at the edge of her conscience. Everything was going so well. Why get down about details?

Over the next three days, she and Nick skirted around the issue. They developed a new routine, starting with long morning walks through the surrounding forest, where the howler monkeys were difficult to spot but easy to hear. Underfoot, armies of ants advanced upon undefined targets across their leafy realm, and overhead, a tawny sloth drooped from a tree branch, the very apex of lethargy. By the second morning, the sloth seemed to have advanced all of six inches. Eventually, the animal completed an odyssey over to a neighboring branch and collapsed into a stupor.

Another trail led to the vine-choked ruins of WWII-era fortifications. And while they weren't exactly ancient, the remains were still fascinating to her archaeologist's mind.

"See?" Nick said.

She had to smile. He'd been right about the pluses of the marina. If only it didn't cost forty dollars a day.

They filled most of their daylight hours with repairs — jobs that took on a new urgency now that *Aurora* was facing a whole new ocean. No sooner was one job crossed off the top of the to-do list — regrounding the single sideband radio — than another appeared at the bottom. A solar panel had cut out, one of *Aurora's* two water tanks was leaking, and the anchor windlass was leaking oil — again.

Each evening, they were released from their efforts by the cheerful chime of a bell: happy hour at the marina bar. Sailors trooped over on cue, salivating like Pavlov's dogs.

It was there on the third evening that the debate over how best to organize a transit was resolved once and for all. A crowd had gathered, solemnly circling Trevor and Tyler, whose heads hung low.

"All gone, mate," Trevor moaned, "Every cent of it."

Cheryl, the Canadian sailor, whispered the news. The Australians had been robbed of over six hundred dollars on the way to paying for their canal transit. Nobody on the busy Colon street had even batted an eye at the machete-wielding thugs.

Tyler nodded sorrowfully, as if to add, *$619: That's a lot of beer, mate.*

On the plus side for Trevor and Tyler, their audience was buying the drinks that night. The crowd murmured their sympathies, patted the Aussies' backs, and quietly asked each other for the contact number of a good agent.

Kate looked at Nick.

"Okay, okay," she whispered. "An agent sounds good."

Chapter Ten

Shadow and Substance

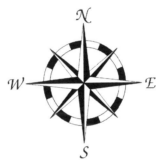

Playa Palma, west of Portobelo
January, present day

Secret hideaways have their way of attracting certain types. Connoisseurs. Criminals. The fatally curious. All of whom could be found just west of Portobelo in a small resort known as Meyer's Golden Sands, or simply Meyer's Gold to its well-heeled guests. With ten exclusive bungalows, the resort offered the best of the best in discreet, seaside holidays. Beautiful scenery and facilities, outstanding cuisine, and unrivaled services. Topping the attractions for many guests were the services of the American owner, David Meyer.

Meyer's Golden Sands didn't need to advertise. Guests came unbidden, many tipped off by wealthy friends and colleagues. A high percentage of Meyer's guests were repeat customers, many with a passion for recapturing the lost history of Central America.

Quite literally, in fact.

Few boats called at Meyer's, due in equal parts to the reef-strewn approach and the five-star docking fees. When Alejandro, the Venezuelan solo sailor, arrived aboard *Carmela*, the only other vessel gracing the dock was a massive megayacht named *Simplicity*.

Alejandro finished arranging *Carmela's* dock lines and followed a uniformed attendant up a meandering path. They stepped past a stunning infinity pool and outdoor massage tables surrounded by stacks of fluffy towels and rolled up yoga mats. Breezy walkways were flanked on each side by glass showcases that glittered in the sun. In them were objects made of gold, silver, obsidian, jade, and pearls, some hundreds of years old and exquisitely worked.

Alejandro scanned them out of the corner of his eye. Impressive as those pieces were, he knew they were mere appetizers to the main course. But that would be an exclusive menu offered only to select guests. Would he pass the test?

He propped his sunglasses back over his dark curls and smiled at his own reflection. Of course, he would.

At the reception desk, two guests were checking out — a gray-haired European accompanied by a stunning young companion in a chic, form-hugging outfit. She gave Alejandro an approving once-over, then resumed her pouty expression. Standing some distance behind both of them, a valet kept a watchful eye over a mountain of designer luggage. A scene Alejandro knew too well, having been there, done that. But a life of jet-setting with soulless beauties had quickly bored him. He needed more. After all, being born wealthy was only luck. A man still had to prove himself.

"David, thank you again." The guest shook the owner's hand with both of his own.

"Mattieu, it's always a pleasure," replied David Meyer. The sixty-something American exuded confidence and self-satisfaction. "I trust you'll take good care of your souvenir of Panama." He winked.

The guest patted his breast pocket. "Another satisfied customer." He smiled and turned toward the door. Like a trained poodle, the young woman fell in at his heels.

"I'll let you know if anything of similar quality turns up," Meyer called to the man in way of farewell then turned to greet Alejandro.

"Your collection is beautiful." Alejandro began, genuinely impressed. Maybe even a tiny bit jealous.

The resort owner waved modestly. "A small but carefully selected ensemble. I feel fortunate to combine my love of art and history here in Panama."

His eyes sparkled as he spoke: a real aficionado.

Alejandro took care to leaf through enough of his wallet in the process of checking in to provide his host with glimpses of his pilot's license, his platinum credit cards, and various memberships — just in case *Carmela* wasn't all the introduction he needed.

David Meyer tossed a second look at the graceful yacht lying alongside the dock and leaned closer. "May I offer you a tour?"

Alejandro was all ears — and eyes. He recognized a learning opportunity when he saw one. David Meyer had built himself a unique business, a thing of genius that took expertise and subtlety. The resort, he knew, was just the tip of the iceberg. What lay beneath — that's what intrigued him.

"I would be very interested in a tour, thank you."

"It's a modest collection," Meyer began, "all hand-picked."

Alejandro knew just what that meant. The items on display were just teasers, a tiny fraction of a greater collection. The choicest pieces were somewhere else. Getting to them required playing his cards just right.

He followed Meyer, admiring everything from centuries-old Mayan gold earplugs to sculpted jade jaguars and historic Spanish coins. He paused over a green blade.

"An Olmec bloodletting tool, if I'm not mistaken," he commented, throwing out a low trump.

David Meyer raised an appreciative eyebrow. "You know your art, my friend."

Alejandro faked nonchalance. "A hobby. Just a hobby. But I am looking to deepen my interests."

Meyer nodded, then proceeded to a row of exquisite gold figurines. "Very rare Cueva pieces. You can tell a true artist by his work, eh?"

"A master," he breathed, almost losing himself in his own visions.

By the end of the tour, Alejandro had slipped on a pair of mental sunglasses to mask the gleam in his eyes. "Señor Meyer—"

"Please, call me David."

"David." Alejandro smiled. "I wonder if you may help me with some... research."

"Anything for a guest."

"Perhaps there is a place where we might speak in private?" Alejandro asked, watching his host's eyes light up.

"Right this way." Meyer pointed, letting his guest step ahead. As they walked through the public areas of the resort, Meyer engaged him in subtly probing chitchat, and Alejandro parried and sidestepped each question.

His profession?

"Consultant."

The root of his interest?

"I have always admired the ancient arts."

"And you are a sailor," Meyer noted. "Have you been to Portobelo?"

"Yes, I've just come from there. So much history, there for the taking." He let his eyes slide suggestively to his host's.

Meyer's smile grew. "A beautiful city. One can imagine the scene as the treasure fleets were loaded. Like the port that preceded it, Nombre de Dios."

"Yes, I made a brief stop there also. But the anchorage there is very poor. No wonder the Spanish abandoned the port in favor of Portobelo. I can only imagine the treasures that once might have passed through both places."

That was a fib, because he had a very clear idea of what type of pieces might have passed through there thanks to the American couple he'd met recently. Fellow sailors who appeared to be on the trail of... something. But what?

"Those treasures aren't all lost, my friend," Meyer said with a wink.

He opened a door and ushered Alejandro into a magnificent sea-view office. After a theatrical pause, Meyer swept back a curtain to expose a wall of artifacts that rivaled the richest museum display — with the minor difference that the labels included price tags.

"Allow me to show you my private collection."

Shelter Bay
January, present day

"Got it?" Nick called.

"Got it," Kate echoed from overhead.

He tightened the nut, watching bedding compound ooze out around it. It was the latest item on his fix-it list: rebedding the leaking granny bars at the mast. Nick was treating it as a warm-up to some of the more ominous tasks facing them. *Take care of the boat, and the boat will take care of you.* The words had become a mantra.

"Got it?" he asked, moving on to the next bolt.

Kate was on deck, ready to secure each nut as he went, but she didn't respond.

"Got it?" he repeated.

"I said yes already!" Kate growled, more than loud enough this time.

He turned the wrench, glad for the fiberglass between them. He was keenly aware of Kate's frustration. *Aurora* had dallied on and on in the marina, awaiting the attention of a canal agent who was suddenly doing booming business. Kate had half-joked that the man might have staged the robbery of Trevor and Tyler himself to whip up business. Meanwhile, *Aurora* was accruing a hefty marina bill while Kate saw nothing new of Panama and made no progress in deciphering Charlie's notes. Nick could bide his time, but Kate? Patience had slipped out of her vocabulary — both English and Spanish.

He kept quiet, wondering what tactic he could employ to maneuver her into a dessert later on. Happy hour would be considerably happier after a piece of cheesecake perked her up. That or a chocolate sundae with extra chocolate sauce. The trick would be getting Kate past the price tag. He could hear her now. *Six dollars for a slice of cheesecake? No way.*

Footsteps sounded above, and a familiar "G'day!" carried into the cabin.

He called to the shaggy figure stepping into the cockpit. "Hey, Tyler."

"Hi," Kate called. "We're almost done."

"No worries." Tyler took a seat in the cockpit and started fiddling with the end of a line. The Australians had rebounded from the robbery and were close to scheduling a transit thanks to the pooled contributions of their fellow sailors and a special mercy deal from the agent.

Tyler's pre-happy hour visit had become another part of their routine — that, or his call for the *Auroras* to quit working and come visit *Free Willy* for a warm-up drink. As long as beer was involved, Tyler wasn't particular about location. Trevor, meanwhile, would be out strolling the docks, recruiting women to join them at the bar.

Everyone had his own notion of happy hour, it seemed. For Nick, it wasn't so much about drinking as the reassuring opportunity to hear fellow sailors' struggles with repairs. A chance to share stories with a brotherhood of grease stains and bashed knuckles. He took special satisfaction from hearing owners of much bigger, newer yachts complain about malfunctioning equipment, especially all the electronics he could never afford in the first place.

Five bolts down, one to go. They repeated the same process, then started cleaning up.

"Wild!" Tyler said, examining something he found in the cockpit.

He held up a page of Charlie's notebook where some breakwater details were sketched together with some associated calculations.

Nick glanced up as he wiped off the tools. "My great-grandfather worked on the canal."

Tyler continued flipping through the pages. "That's a funny picture!"

Nick smiled to himself at Tyler's pronunciation of the word picture: *Pick-chah*. Almost Bostonian. He peered at the page Tyler was holding up.

"Old Spanish coins," he said, then rummaged around for a beer.

"What was he, a collector or something?"

Just then Kate came up, and her eyes went wide. She snatched the notebook away and filled Tyler's surprised hands with the bottle she grabbed from Nick.

"Nick!" she barked. "Why don't you join Tyler?"

He gritted his teeth at the mistake. He and Kate had been going over Charlie's notebook earlier and left it out. Innocent enough, but having someone else see the notebook they'd agreed not to share with anyone else was guaranteed to thoroughly ruin Kate's mood. Time for damage control.

"Hey, Tyler, which lure caught you that massive bonito you were telling me about?" he asked by way of distraction.

"Aw, mate, it was a monsta!" Tyler started and continued at length.

Kate disappeared into the forward cabin with the notebook. She was still a bit red in the face when she headed out with a towel and soap, muttering something about a shower. Nick watched her go, only half listening to Tyler's rambling narrative about his lucky streak with purple — or was it pink? — octopus lures.

Chocolate cheesecake with ice cream, he concluded. That should do it.

Toro Point

November 1911

One bag of silver.

One little bag. Charlie sighed and touched the purple swelling around his right eye.

How one little bag of silver could bring him so much trouble was beyond belief. The thing was, there was a lot more where that came from. And evidently, a lot more trouble.

Always keen to experiment, he had discreetly brought one bag of coins away from his most recent trip to Portobelo and sold it to a dealer in a Colon back street. Attempted to sell it, that is, to a man claiming to be a dealer.

In retrospect, his plan might not have been as ingenious as he'd thought. The incident called to mind one of Charlie's father's many sage sayings: *experience is something you don't get until just after you need it.*

True. So painfully true.

Charlie touched his nose. He'd washed away the blood, but he could still taste it on his lips. Funny how his father seemed wiser the older Charlie got.

The dealer's salivating eyes had confirmed his hunch that the silver coins were indeed valuable. The man fingered each piece and asked casual questions about where Charlie had happened upon the loot. Charlie was circumspect, making vague references to a friend of a friend's cousin, at which point the dealer made a subtle signal to two goons waiting in the shadows. The thrashing that ensued was the worst he'd suffered since that barroom brawl back in Rapid City. Worse, maybe, if not in pints of blood leaked, then in square inches of bruising. They left him in a slumped-over heap, taking the silver with satisfied chuckles.

Charlie had lain there for a long time, groaning quietly. His hopes of cashing in on the loot were as battered and blue as his body.

Being beaten was just the start. Ever since then, the dealer's goons had been constantly stalking him as if he might lead them directly to the mother lode. Charlie admitted he could be stupid, but he wasn't *that* stupid. On the other hand, he had yet to figure out a new course of action. There was no way he could bring the silver home to Cristobal, a settlement sitting cheek by jowl with rough, tough Colon, the corruption capital of the Caribbean.

Of course, corruption could be played two ways. Maybe even three. It was all a question of creativity.

Charlie contemplated this fact while hopping from boulder to boulder along the edge of the breakwater, checking the line of trestles. Lately, Fortuna had sent him a disproportionate number of downs. Why did women — even goddesses — have to be so damn fickle? Wasn't it about time Fortuna went to bat for his team?

The salt air stung the raw spots on his face, but his ribs didn't complain as loudly as the day before. Maybe lying low was the best course of action for the time being. After all, the treasure had probably been slumbering in that tomb for a long time. Maybe even hundreds of years. It could wait another few weeks until he engineered a foolproof plan.

He sat on a boulder and looked out at the roiling sea, scowling at nothing in particular. What he really needed was a Charlie-proof plan. Because somehow, things didn't always unfold exactly as he intended.

Shelter Bay

January, present day

Kate sat several tables away from everyone else at happy hour, keeping technical conversations — and people in general — at arm's length. Right now, she preferred the company of the book Nick had given her about the building of the canal. It was the perfect distraction from the frustration of the last few days. Delays, repairs, the disagreements about the agent... Partnerships had their advantages and disadvantages, she decided as old doubts welled up.

She caught herself there. No, that wasn't fair. If it weren't for Nick, she wouldn't be in Panama. She loved Nick. She loved *Aurora*. She just hated... what?

Compromising.

There, she'd admitted it. But all work and no play didn't seem like compromise. It felt more like surrender. The bitterest pill of them all. Maybe she'd pictured herself standing on one too many a mountain or distant shore. And she'd definitely watched too many adventure movies and read too many exciting biographies: Beryl Markham in Africa, Thor Heyerdahl on the high seas, and yes, Indiana Jones. Great adventurers didn't get hung up on maintenance and repairs. They just plunged straight into their next crusade.

Unfortunately, in the real world, you had to pay your dues. She'd logged enough hours in a pool to know that. But right now, all they needed was for *Aurora* to be good enough. Nick, however, wanted perfection — a quixotic quest if she ever saw one. He would work toward it, forgetting that time could spin a web around the busiest person. Opportunities came with expiration dates. Why couldn't he see that?

She tapped her fingers on the tabletop, trying to focus on her book. As usual, she skipped around, dipping in and out of chapters and eras. Nick, of course, would have started on page one and worked his way through in an orderly fashion. Eventually, they'd both have covered every page, just in different ways.

Sometimes, their differences made her laugh. Other times, they grated. Right now, well, she couldn't quite decide. Maybe if she put in a long swim session in the morning, she'd break out of her rut.

She leafed ahead to chapter twenty, "Life and Times," and cringed at the description of the apartheid-like labor system of the American construction authorities. White American employees fell into the "gold" category, while "silver" referred to "unskilled" West Indian labor who received lower wages and fewer perks. The subject did little to lift her mood, so she jumped ahead to the picture gallery in the center, tilting the book to the light. There: a 1906 photo of Teddy Roosevelt sitting at the controls of a steam shovel during a visit to inspect progress on the canal. The next photo showed a line of dark faces, shovels slung over their shoulders. The Panama Canal, it seemed, was a joint venture of visionary minds and callused hands.

Kate imagined the immensity of it all, the setbacks overcome. A lesson for her, for sure. The frustrations of the past week — the waiting, the repairs — were all minor in comparison. She really needed to lighten up.

Another page, another photo — this one of the billiards room in a YMCA.

"Pardon me."

Kate looked up, a little irritated. A youngish, sandy-haired man stood by the table. Definitely not a sailor, she decided. His neatly trimmed hair and close shave were dead giveaways. Plus, he wore pants and shoes — with socks. When was the last time she'd worn socks?

"Have you traveled through the canal?" he asked with a slight accent.

German, she guessed, looking at the black-framed glasses. Behind them, his eyes were a brilliant blue.

"Not yet. We're still waiting." What did he want?

He looked a little disappointed but offered his hand in a warm shake. "My name is Baumann — Stefan."

Kate shook and introduced herself, secretly hoping for an opportunity to get back to her book.

"I am researching for an article about the Panama Canal for a German news magazine, *Der Spiegel*." He seemed surprised to find recognition in Kate's eyes. "You know it?"

"Sure." Kate fingered her book, wishing she could get back to it. Still, she couldn't help asking, "An article about what?"

The reporter slid into a chair opposite her, their respective sides of the glass table delineated by the six hundred pages of her book, a flickering candle, and the row of rings left by her water glass.

"I am interviewing a variety of boaters about their canal experiences. From captains of the largest tankers to cruisers on the smallest sailboats."

Small? That would be *Aurora*.

The reporter slipped into a series of questions about the application procedure for transiting the canal. Which officials had she been in contact with? What was their demeanor? Had any inspector boarded *Aurora*?

She wondered why he would be interested as she answered each question. He nodded with every word, giving the impression that her perspective was every bit as vital as the supertanker captain's. He ended questions by leaning forward like a television interviewer ready to swing a microphone and catch her reaction. When she finished a sentence, the reporter's expression kept her in the spotlight, allowing a brief silence to settle in before moving on, as if she might add some critical detail in an afterthought.

One thing was for sure, she decided. Stefan Baumann was good at getting answers.

"What exactly is the angle of your story?" she asked.

He paused, composing his answer with care. Obviously, the reporter was more accustomed to asking questions than answering them.

Well, let him practice, she decided.

"We live in the age of terrorism, yes?" he started.

Kate nodded slowly. She had felt a long way removed from that world for many months now. Quite happily so.

"Public places, trains, airports. All could be, or have been, targeted, yes?"

"Unfortunately, yes."

"I am investigating the threat of terrorism to other targets, such as..." He motioned with open hands.

"Such as the Panama Canal," Kate concluded, leaning back to consider the suggestion.

He nodded, letting her imagination work.

"One bomb and world shipping comes grinding to a halt," she finished.

Although she considered herself something of an anti-globalism tree-hugger, it was still a sobering thought. Farfetched? She supposed nothing could be ruled out. And the prospect certainly would make a good story. She began asking her own questions. What had he observed? What was his take on the canal?

The reporter's cadence varied, emphasizing important points and smoothing over others, with only the occasional incidence of reversed word order as a reminder that he wasn't using his native language. He mentioned meetings with canal officials, heads of security, and shipping CEOs. He'd even transited the canal on the bridge of a freighter.

"The Americans, of course, claim that canal security is insufficient," he said, casting out a lure.

"Maybe I'm Canadian."

"Are you?"

Kate gave in, shaking her head. "No. But sometimes I wish..."

The reporter chuckled softly. "The Americans see limitless possibilities for terrorists to stage an attack on the canal."

"There are limitless ways to stage an attack anywhere, anytime," she pointed out, folding her arms.

The reporter ceded the point with a slight inclination of his head. "They also see the canal as a drug conduit."

She snorted. "Since when have drug dealers branched out into terrorism?"

"Terrorism, perhaps not. But those who deal in drugs deal in everything that makes money. Everything. They have many connections and have their fingers in many cakes."

Fingers in pies, the back of her mind corrected quietly.

"Everything?"

"Everything."

She wondered if the reporter was right. "Did you hear about the boat that wrecked on a reef in the San Blas?"

He lit up as if recalling a wonderful event. "The *Persephone*. A boat, a body, and two hundred kilograms of cocaine." A journalist's Christmas list.

"Have they made any progress in the case? Did they find the captain?"

"No, and I doubt he will be found alive. There is a powerful cartel at work if two hundred kilos of cocaine are involved."

"I bet that would make a good story."

"Yes, but where to begin? Not all of us have boats, you know."

Kate looked out over the masts in the marina, thankful once again for Nick and *Aurora*. Some of the boats in her view qualified as fancy yachts, while others had seen better days, like the backpacker boats she'd seen passing through the San Blas.

"Did you ever think of taking one of the backpacker boats to Colombia?"

Stefan had not, so she told him about the boats that started or ended their tours in Portobelo.

"Who knows if you'd actually see anything firsthand, but you would get a taste of how small boats move along the coast. Plus, you'd get to see a little of the San Blas."

The reporter chewed on the idea, then boomeranged back to his primary subject. "What do you think about the possibility of using small boats for terrorist acts?"

Kate shrugged. "There really isn't anything to stop a lunatic, I guess. It's not much different than a person packing a van with explosives." She shifted in her seat, glancing around for some escape. The closest she ever got to criminal cartels and potential terrorists was the occasional anonymous smuggler, and she was happy to keep it that way.

"Anyway," she added with a note of finality, "you might get more information by going to the Pacific end of the canal — to Balboa. More sailboats go through in that direction, so you'd have more luck talking to sailors who've already gone through. Oh, or you could talk to Chris." She looked around for the Belgian delivery captain and pointed. "I think he's been through the canal six times. Maybe even seven."

Stefan Baumann followed her finger, a tiny hint of disappointment clouding his eyes. "Thank you for your suggestions." He stood and offered a friendly handshake. "I wish you a good time when you go."

She smiled and dove right back into her book. History was much more preferable to the uncertainties of terrorism and drug cartels.

She had barely found her place again before she was interrupted for a second time. Cheryl, the fifty-something Canadian sailor, slipped into the seat vacated by the reporter.

"Who was *that*?" Cheryl's voice dripped as her gaze slid over the German's back.

Kate shrugged. "A reporter. Doing a story on the canal."

Cheryl nodded. "Wish he'd come interview me."

Kate didn't quite know what to make of that comment, so Cheryl jabbed her finger in his direction. "Think Chippendales," Cheryl suggested and leaned in closer to whisper the rest. "Picture him without the glasses, without the shirt, the belt, the—"

"Cheryl!"

The woman put up her hands in protest. "Did you *see* him?"

Kate leaned out to sneak a peek at the man. She cocked her head, considering. "Hmmm," she mumbled, wondering when she might get back to her book. Meanwhile, Nick was approaching, back from his conversation with the taciturn Swedes they'd first met in Portobelo, probably discussing something like the compatibility of fuel filters of different makes. One of his pet topics these days.

"Ready to call it a night?" Kate asked him, giving up on her book and waving as Cheryl slipped off in the direction of the reporter.

Nick held a small menu card out like a peace offering. "How about a piece of chocolate cheesecake?"

Like metal drawn toward a magnet, Kate felt herself swaying toward the menu. But when she repositioned Nick's finger, revealing the price, she slumped back. "I don't think so."

"Come on, you deserve it."

Kate felt far from deserving anything, though looking at Nick made her break into her first real smile of the day. He was still sweet and cheerful despite her being so crabby all afternoon. Those caramel eyes smiled at her, warm and indulging, the way they always did.

"Maybe *you* deserve one," she said.

"I'll have one if you have one."

He held the menu up so that the glossy dessert images lined right up with her eyes.

Kate laughed and pushed it aside, taking Nick in instead. The man might not be perfect, but he certainly had his moments. Lots of them.

"Chocolate cheesecake for me," she said. "Strawberry for you?"

Nick flashed a smile and signaled for the waiter. "With ice cream."

Shelter Bay

present day

A week after *Aurora's* arrival in the marina, the much sought-after agent arrived to attend to paperwork at last.

"Seven hundred. Eight hundred. Nine hundred and nineteen dollars."

Nick wiped his brow and re-counted the crisp bills before handing them to the agent. Two-thirds of the sum made up the canal fee while one-third went to the agent.

Nick couldn't believe he was handing nearly a thousand dollars — cash! — to a perfect stranger. But the man proved good as his word. The next day, *Aurora* was ceremoniously measured by a canal official, with Kate and Nick in solemn attendance like parents at a baptism. After three minutes of work, the man rolled his tape measure with a snap and pronounced that the thirty-two-foot, two-inch boat to be thirty-two feet, nine inches.

Nick didn't mind as long as *Aurora* fell safely within the under-fifty-feet price class.

That's it? He watched the man tick a few boxes on a form then point for a signature. Nick scribbled his name and handed the clipboard back.

"How much do big ships pay to go through?" he asked.

The measurement officer thought a moment. "About a quarter of a million dollars, depending."

Suddenly, $619 seemed like a real bargain. Private boats must be a thorn in the side of the canal authorities, he realized. Sailboats were often rafted three abreast and squeezed in behind "small" freighters for the transit.

He looked at Kate as the agent walked away. "I wonder how small a small freighter is."

She nodded. "*Aurora* seems microscopic next to even the smallest cargo ships."

Soon after, they received confirmation of their transit date, two days hence. Nick looked on with trepidation as boats around them were plied with sets of thick, hundred-foot lines and car tires to act as bumpers. How would *Aurora* ever fit all that? A more immediate concern, now that *Aurora* had a fixed date, was finding line handlers. Every vessel was required to have four. With Nick at the wheel, they needed Kate plus three other people to handle the lines, one at each corner of the boat.

Since so many other boats were preparing to transit, the market for line handlers was tight at the moment, and Kate had been scrambling to find help. The first two line handlers she found were their Japanese neighbors in the marina, Kentaro and Mayumi. The incredibly fit, sixty-something-year-olds were all sweetness and manners. Their sailing resume included a nonstop, fifty-three-day passage from Japan to Vancouver in their forty-foot sloop. Nick had seen Mayumi around the docks and had no doubt she could scale the mast in a single bound if the occasion presented itself. So *Aurora* had two capable hands already, secured with the promise that Kate and Nick would reciprocate during Ken and Mayumi's own transit a few days later.

That left one more line handler. An enthusiastic flock of college exchange students advertised their availability on the marina notice board, though Nick hoped to find more experienced helpers. On the other hand, "available" was a characteristic highly valued by Trevor and Tyler, who recruited three North American girls for *Free Willy*. All three had pronounced the boat's name cute.

"I think the double entendre might be lost on them," Kate muttered, shaking her head at the floating bachelor pad.

Eventually, Kate's determined rounds of the marina paid off with a tip about an older man looking to crew. Pavel turned out to be a Czech engineer who hoped to fulfill a lifetime dream by seeing the canal from the inside. He seemed quiet and easygoing, so Kate signed him on immediately.

"That makes four," she said. Another minor hurdle overcome.

Nick was immensely relieved, especially when a flash of brilliant teak with a hint of gold eased smoothly into the marina. It was *Carmela*, with a perfectly coiffed Alejandro at the wheel. The man was always wearing virginal white, while Nick had taken to wild print shirts to camouflage the grease stains. Was Alejandro rubbing it in? Nick watched as the Venezuelan maneuvered his sleek yawl into a tight berth with precision and calm, as if the countercurrent didn't exist.

Nick turned his back and muttered to himself. "Thank God we don't need him as a line handler."

* * *

"Hey," Kate called the next morning. "Ready for a walk?"

He was still a little bleary-eyed, but yes, he was ready. "Where to?"

"The breakwater." She pointed. "Something different for today, I figured."

It was different, all right. And important. A pilgrimage, in a way, because that was Charlie's breakwater.

A short walk later, they reached Toro Point, and Kate motioned toward the rocky shoreline with a hopeless expression. The coast was choked with plastics: drink bottles, flip-flops, flakes of Styrofoam.

"The filth of mankind delivered back by nature," Kate murmured. An ugly truth, and the ugly side of travel.

Nick, though, remained focused on the breakwater. He eyed the gap between the boulders, then leaped. Kate quickly passed him, springing from rock to rock. He moved more slowly, as occupied with the obstacles in his mind as those lying before him.

Was it the marred scene or thoughts of Charlie that put him in such an unsettled mood? Either way, *Aurora* was going through the canal the next day. It was a big step — one that set off the same fluttering butterflies as the day he bought *Aurora*.

Butterflies? More like buffalo, Nick decided. A whole herd of them hoofing their way through his gut.

He forced his shoulders to relax, trying to let go of all thought, only to find his mind bouncing back to Charlie. Charlie and the strange trajectory of Nick's life, especially recently.

He found a flat rock and sat down, watching ocean waves crash into the unyielding wall while placid ripples lapped on the inner side. The breakwater couldn't stop the wind, blowing in at a steady force six.

He looked down the length of the structure, appreciating the scope of it all for the first time. This was just one of part of the Caribbean breakwater. Another wall, miles long, protected the Pacific end of the canal. And those were mere bookends to the engineering marvels of the canal itself. He rubbed a heel against the rough surface of the boulder. That stone had been hauled in from some distant location and sweated into place to halt the raw power of the sea. He couldn't help but wonder how that all came to be and about the characters involved, like Charlie Parker. Did he ever sit at the breakwater and look out at his future?

The ocean answered with a deafening crash. A salty mist filled the air. The waves were always moving — and they'd be crashing when the next generation of sailors came through, too. Charlie had come and gone, and now it was Nick's turn to pass through. Even if the occasion seemed momentous to him, he was just one among many, so tiny in the landscape of time. Time swallowed people up, leaving disjointed oral histories, if anything at all.

Nick studied the calluses on his hands. What would survive of his own story, generations hence? Would he be remembered for any particular achievement? Or worse, for some awful mistake? Would he be remembered at all?

God, he was starting to sound like Kate in one of her more philosophical moods.

She settled in beside him, and Nick found himself leaning into her, feeling her hair brush his shoulder as she sat lost in her own thoughts. They'd come so far together — and not just in terms of miles. Everything was going so well. Still, they'd left a lot to chance. He'd counted too much on luck, let too many chances slip by. He thought about the job offers he'd once passed up to hang on to a more secure position, as well as his first time around with Kate, when he'd foolishly let her go. It was time to be more daring.

Right on cue, his imagination presented one option that fit the bill: pursuing Charlie's treasure. The silver was out there somewhere. If he could somehow unravel the secret to its location... well, the possibilities were tempting. Even if the treasure proved to be a dead end, the effort would permanently erase the word "boring" from his profile. He would have the satisfaction of at least knowing he tried.

Charlie died in his midthirties, a little older than Nick now. By that time, though, Charlie had lived more than most people did in much longer lifetimes. What did Nick have to show for his time? *Aurora* was a good start, but he could accomplish more. Much more. Starting with what Charlie left behind.

He tried to discipline himself not to pursue wild, irrational ideas. The problem was, he'd been gaining quite a lot of practice in that dark art lately — starting with the notion to go sailing in the first place. And not just that: now he was about to enter a whole new ocean. A big one. Going through the canal was a major move. He only appreciated the scale of it now. That and the price — another thousand dollars just to backtrack wasn't in their budget. There would be no turning back once they got through.

The sentiment echoed through his mind as another wave thundered over the rocks. *No turning back once we get through.*

Chapter Eleven

The Stuff of Legends

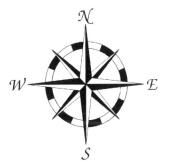

Sabanitas

January, present day

Vadz shouldered past a sidewalk vendor selling pirated phone cards and turned down a narrow hallway behind a barber shop. Every step he took put the noise of bustling traffic and the smell of hair products behind him. With every step, the ceiling seemed to get lower. The whole country was too small for his frame, like that awful bus he had to squeeze into to get here. The one with half the country and their livestock aboard.

Someday, he vowed, he'd have more fitting transportation. Someday, he'd be the one with an office — a much nicer one than this hole in the wall. But until he worked his way to the top of his own business empire, he would have to put up with a few inconveniences. Like a Spartan warrior, he would have to endure.

The office of his contact man, Cesar, was in the back, past a reception area shared with an accountant. The receptionist barely nodded when Vadz entered, so intent was she on texting. The smoked glass door to the accountant's office was firmly shut, but Cesar's was cracked open. Vadz leaned against the wall beside it, striking a casual pose while straining to hear past the clatter of an aging fan.

He made out Cesar snorting in disgust. "Sailors. Too many foreign sailors."

He could picture that weasel now, admiring the buff of his own shoes and the shine of his cuff links.

"If it wasn't for the sailors..." Cesar went on.

Vadz's jaw muscles twitched. Someday, those gold cuff links would be his.

Someone else spoke, and he recognized Arty, the drunkard with that awful American accent.

"Yeah, but where'd you be without us?" He chuckled his wheezy *har-har-har*.

The man thought everything was a joke. Well, *he* was a joke, Vadz decided. The fact that the American was even here, keeping him waiting, was an insult. Vadz had important matters to discuss with Cesar, businessman to businessman.

"Just because you provide the occasional piece of information doesn't make you critical to this organization, Arturo," Cesar said.

Arty chuckled. "I bet you wish that Frenchman who went up on the reef was half as reliable as me."

Vadz had heard about that one. Two hundred kilograms of cocaine, lost on a reef!

"Lucien will be dealt with, Arturo." Cesar's tone was icy.

Arty rambled on in a cocky tone. "I bet that police bust on the Pacific coast didn't exactly have you singing carols, did it? Did you send a Christmas card to Coronel Lopez?"

"That fool and his trigger-happy commandos mean nothing to us."

"Right," Arty chuckled. "The cartel doesn't care about losing two shipments in a row."

There was a slam and a ding. Vadz pictured Cesar hitting the desk, making the phone jump.

"Don't you call us a cartel! We are a community organization, working with and for the people," Cesar said. "Coronel Lopez's mistakes will only build support for our organization. The public despises heavy-handed government officials. They trust grassroots organizations like ours."

"Right," Arty murmured as the fan continued to scrape.

Cesar went on, undeterred. "Do you know what we do for our people? How much we contribute to the widows and orphans fund? We fill a critical role in the fabric of society!"

Vadz made a face. He'd endured more than his share of flag-waving zealots — the type who had repeated the party line so often, they believed it. But Vadz knew better. Ruling powers came and went, just like the organizations that opposed them. They all had their own propaganda. It made no difference to him. The only thing that mattered was that he came out ahead.

"And who are sailors if not another branch of the community?" Cesar concluded, buttering Arty up. Vadz could imagine the Panamanian flashing that serpentine smile. "We work together."

Every man for himself. That's what Vadz thought.

"And if what you report is true—"

"I saw it with my own eyes," Arty insisted. "I heard them talk. I saw the archaeologist take that picture."

"Then we have a new opportunity to serve our people," Cesar continued, not skipping a beat.

"Right," Arty said in a flat, disinterested tone.

Vadz was all ears. *Opportunity* was code for *profit* in his line of work.

"Perhaps not as lucrative as our regular pursuits..." Cesar said, and Vadz felt his interest wane. He started scrolling through his own phone messages while Cesar rambled on and on and on. The more reasons Cesar provided as to how the venture might help others, the more Vadz figured Cesar stood to benefit, too.

He thumbed past a message from his ex-wife without reading it. He could guess what it was about. More alimony, more child support, more money for heating. Sure, Warsaw in January was cold, but that wasn't his problem now. He glanced down the hallway and congratulated himself for the hundredth time for making his escape to the tropics.

"We can contribute to society," Cesar was saying. Shadows flickered through the smoked glass, echoing the man's sweeping gestures. "We can rescue our cultural heritage from obscurity, and funds raised from selling antiquities can go right to the people, gaining us wider appreciation. A win-win!"

"Right." Arty's voice was close to a snore.

Vadz wished they'd hurry up so he could get on to important business. He aimed a meaty finger at his phone's off switch. Nothing but junk messages on it — not just from the ex-wife but from the cousin he owed money to, plus his ex-business partner. No, he had no need to read all those expletives. Nor did he bother with more than a cursory glance at the text from his deckhand, Gregor. Vadz shook his head. That idiot was spending his day back in Portobelo helping a retired couple clean their hull — and he wasn't even getting paid! The man would never get ahead in life.

Cesar droned on until Arty piped up with something about a place called Nombre de Dios. When would they ever wrap it up?

"I have a specialist looking into that," Cesar said. "In the meantime, we can't afford to let any other leads slip away. If the Americans are on to something, it will be critical to keep track of them."

"What you need," Arty hiccuped, "is another sailor. An insider. I can find you someone, easy."

Another flicker of light showed that Cesar dismissed the suggestion. "You, Arturo, stick with finding me young travelers willing to transport small deliveries. As for a sailor, I already have one in mind," Cesar said. "Him and a backup plan, if more aggressive tactics prove necessary."

With that, it seemed, the meeting was over. Vadz slid away from the door and pretended to be engrossed in his phone. When Arty stepped out of the office, he looked at Vadz in surprise, then glanced back to Cesar with an amused expression that said, *Him? Are you kidding?* He smiled at Vadz, though, a saccharine-filled smile.

"Speak of the devil, it's my favorite Russian!"

"Pole," Vadz growled.

"Whatever." Arty turned to go, jaunty until he went stiff at the sight of two long shadows looming in the hallway.

Two thugs sauntered in, their jackets showing the telltale bulge of hidden holsters. Vadz stretched extra tall and puffed his chest out. They might scare Arty, but he had ten centimeters on the tall one, plus at least twenty kilos more on his frame. All of it muscle, pure muscle. Let them try to intimidate him!

"Ah," Cesar appeared at the door to his office, flicking a piece of lint off his sleeve. "My most reliable men." He nodded as the two thugs crowded into the reception room.

One was short but stocky, the other tall and thin with a jagged scar by his nose. Arty edged around them and slunk away like a dog with its tail tucked between his legs.

Cesar snapped his fingers at Vadz, who barely suppressed a snarl. Just because he was freelancing for the man didn't mean he wasn't his own master. He turned an unimpressed shoulder to the newcomers and brushed into the weasel's small office. Someday, he reminded himself, he would be the one snapping his fingers at the likes of Cesar.

Cesar lingered at the door, leaning out to the thugs. "You must stand by," he said in Spanish. "Be ready when called."

Vadz wondered what that was about. Well, it didn't concern him.

"We will wait and observe," came a gritty bass.

"Wait and observe," echoed the second, giving his knuckles a good crack.

Vadz scoffed and considering cracking his own, but their footsteps were already thumping away. Cesar stepped into his office, adjusting his tie in a mirror as he turned. "I have a new proposition for you, my sailor friend."

Vadz bristled. He had no friends. He didn't want or need any. He was here for business and nothing more.

"Just tell me how much it pays, my friend." He mocked Cesar's saccharine tone. "That's all that matters to me."

Limon Bay

present day

Area F, the official waiting area for small boats scheduled to transit the Panama Canal, was a forlorn little corner of a busy harbor, marked by one sad wreck of a freighter, a jumble of forest, and a skyline of cranes in the adjacent port of Cristobal. There wasn't much there to capture Nick's attention — nothing except the clock, counting down the hours to the moment *Aurora* would be summoned to weigh anchor and enter the canal.

In the west, freighters stacked high with containers steamed slowly past the setting sun, bound for the first locks of the canal. Small pilot boats and tugs zipped to and fro, their efforts coordinated by brief radio exchanges. *Aurora's* crew played cards to pass the time and stole glances at the handful of small boats anchored nearby.

"I wonder who we'll be rafted up to," Nick said.

"Four o'clock," Kate muttered. At least an hour to go.

Though the transit was scheduled for early evening, the crew was required to stand by several hours in advance. And they were more than ready. First, to enter the Gatun locks, a series of three massive steps which would lift *Aurora* eighty-five feet above sea level. Then a night anchored in Gatun Lake, a body of water created by the damming of the Chagres River, which filled both the lake and the locks. The following morning, *Aurora* would motor another fifteen miles across Gatun Lake to reach the Pedro Miguel and Miraflores Locks on the Pacific side, bringing them down to sea level and a whole new ocean.

Since the Gatun Locks would keep them busy throughout the evening, Kate was serving an early dinner to their crew — Pavel, Mayumi, and a smug-looking Alejandro.

Yes, Alejandro.

To Nick's utter dismay, Mayumi's husband, Kentaro, had fallen ill at the last minute. Just as Mayumi broke the news, Alejandro had sauntered by. Of course, the Venezuelan gallantly offered to help. Nick felt nauseous, but with almost a thousand dollars on the line, what could he do?

For lack of an alternative, he did his best to ignore the interloper. Luckily, some kinder fate had also sent Pavel, whose story captivated the small company aboard *Aurora*. The Czech had been sailing his thirty-footer in the Caribbean until it grounded on an uncharted reef off Haiti. At first, he assumed that the canoes streaming out from shore were coming to assist him, but no. Machete-wielding islanders soon looted his uninsured boat of all its contents. Pavel swam away with only the shirt on his back. To Nick, the amazing part of Pavel's story was that he showed a certain sympathy for the desperate poverty that drove his attackers to their actions. The modest, mild-mannered Czech was the antithesis of Alejandro.

"Hey." Kate tapped Nick's knee and pointed.

A fifty-foot launch approached. Aboard were canal authorities, delivering *Aurora's* advisor, whose role corresponded to that of a pilot aboard the large commercial ships. He would communicate with the control tower and neighboring boats to orchestrate a safe transit.

Or so Nick hoped.

He gulped down the last of their meal. At last, *Aurora's* turn had come.

* * *

"Wow," Kate breathed.

Nick just nodded. Simply approaching the first lock was a knee-rattling experience. Mammoth steel gates yawned before them, daring *Aurora* to enter a narrow slot hemmed in by vertical walls. Powerful spotlights threw everything into sharp relief, amplifying the effect. *Aurora's* red and green running lights were tiny fireflies in comparison.

A freighter had already taken position at the head of the lock, its lines running high above to compact locomotives known as mules. The freighter's towering stern seemed awfully close to *Aurora's* bow. Nick had to look up to read the name of the freighter so, so close to Aurora. *Clipper Mercury*, from George Town, Bahamas.

Clipper Mercury, he prayed, *please don't sink my boat.*

"Motor ahead," Carlos said in a reverent hush. The man had transited hundreds of times but still seemed awed by the magnitude of it all.

Nick took a deep breath and motored forward slowly. Very slowly.

It wasn't just the imposing size of the locks that made him nervous. He felt the pressure of three judges looking over his shoulder, too. Carlos, the sharp-eyed advisor, was one, plus impeccable Alejandro and salty old Pavel, captains of their own boats. Then there was the crew lining the aft rail of *Clipper Mercury*, peering down on *Aurora* in hopeful anticipation of some disaster, a little action in their otherwise routine day.

"Hammerhead?"

Kate shot him a doubtful look after one glance at the seventy-foot sport fishing boat they shared the rear section of the lock with.

He squinted at the Louisiana state flag flapping at the stern and caught the sound of a smooth southern drawl. Once *Hammerhead* was secured to the side wall of the lock, *Aurora* would tie up alongside like a dinghy to its mother ship. Which was fitting because he felt reduced to dinghy size as he maneuvered *Aurora* up to her big brother for the night.

Apparently, *Hammerhead's* beer-toting crew had greater priorities than the transit — namely, the Super Bowl playoff game running on the giant, flat-screen TV in the cabin. Nick was certain they would pay more attention to the hamburgers simmering on the aft barbecue than to the pesky sailboat tied at their side. The fact that they were transiting one of the man-made wonders of the world didn't seem to enter into the equation, at least not on play-off night.

He forced his eyes forward as the lock doors slid into place behind *Aurora* like prison gates closing on death row. No way out now.

"Ready to dance?" Carlos called.

Water gushed into the lock through submerged ducts, making the surface come alive with swirling currents. A cheer sounded from *Hammerhead* as a touchdown was scored in another world, light years away.

"Some dance," Kate murmured as the boats tried to spin and twist.

Nick would have called it heaving and straining. All he could do was stand back and observe the scene. *Hammerhead's* hull shielded *Aurora* from the rough walls, and it was *Hammerhead's* hired line handlers — capable and attentive despite Nick's worst fears — who managed the long lines running to the top of the lock, six stories above. As water filled the lock, the vessels inched higher and higher, and the line handlers took up the slack to keep the boats in place, just as the mules did for the freighter ahead. *Aurora* was being ushered through the lock like a baby in a stroller.

Eight minutes later, the water calmed, and *Aurora* was bobbing quietly atop the lock. Everyone took in the surrounding landscape from a curious new perspective: namely, above it. Mayumi pointed her camera in every direction, snapping away wildly. One click captured an image that Nick would long hold as one of his most intense memories: him at the wheel with Kate nearby, line in hand. Their eyes were fixed on the towering walls of the second lock, slowly revealed as the doors swung open like curtains on an opera's second act.

The mules guiding *Clipper Mercury* ascended cog rails to the higher ground of the second level, hauling their charge forward. Nick eased his boat away from *Hammerhead*, giving the larger boat space to motor ahead. It did so with an unnecessary burst of power that sent *Aurora* skittering sideways.

"Watch it!" Kate yelped.

Nick scrambled to keep *Aurora* away from the wall, then took a page from Kate's playbook and shot *Hammerhead* the evil eye.

A call came on the radio, and Carlos motioned Nick forward to repeat the process. They followed *Clipper Mercury* and *Hammerhead* forward, tied up alongside the latter, and waited. When the lock gates closed behind *Aurora*, Nick didn't let down his guard, but he wasn't quite as anxious as the first time around. He even cracked a quick smile for Mayumi's lens. Then all was serious again as the doors opened, revealing the quiet waters of Gatun Lake.

Nick sucked in a deep breath. Surely they had gotten off far too lightly. Disaster was certain to strike sometime soon. He gripped the wheel tightly as the freighter engaged its engines and steamed forward, sending a powerful backwash through the lock. But it was over in a moment, and *Aurora* sprang away from *Hammerhead*, free at last. He watched the lights of the other boats pull into the darkness ahead. The big boys would transit the entire waterway in one long night. *Aurora*, on the other hand, would anchor nearby until daybreak.

A launch came to pick up Carlos, and they were alone in the eerie nighttime world of Gatun Lake. Him, Kate, Mayumi, Pavel — and, last but not least, Alejandro.

Toro Point

June 1912

"You better see a doctor, boss," Edgar counseled. "Fixya betah."

Charlie admitted to feeling a little slouchy. Maybe the routine of work was getting to him. Maybe it was the ceaseless rain. But he shrugged off Edgar's suggestion. Doctors were in league with the devil, together with accountants and lawyers. All he really needed — badly — was a change of scenery. So when the opportunity arose to consult with engineers at the Pacific breakwater, Charlie snatched it. A week in a different setting would do him good, and the silver could wait. As things stood, Fortuna seemed in no rush to let that treasure budge. A little more thinking time to outfox that cunning goddess — that's what the doctor ordered.

Charlie boarded the morning train and waved a happy goodbye to the two thugs he left behind on the platform — the ones who had beat him up in the alley a month earlier and had been tailing him ever since. The train lurched, and they slid out of view.

Yes, this trip would do him good.

The tracks led out of town, past haunted remnants of the old days of canal construction. First came the cemetery at Monkey Hill, where row upon row of crooked crosses marked the graves of a thousand men. Most of them had expired far, far from home, falling to tiny insects bearing invisible diseases. Charlie's face grew long. He was sure that death would not agree with him. Inactivity just wasn't his thing.

You've got a while yet, he reminded himself, facing forward as the cemetery blurred past. *Just make sure you use it well.*

Outside town, the jungle closed in so tightly that the rushing train brushed branches and vines. He perked up at the sight of rusting hulks tangled in the foliage: cranes and diggers left over from the doomed French excavations under Ferdinand de Lesseps.

"Now, there was a man." Charlie nodded to himself. The man had failed miserably in the end but was still legendary for his vision.

He cast an appraising eye over the skeletons of machinery that stood half digested by a forest of weeds. If only he could emulate de Lesseps — at least the visionary part. Ideally, he'd like his own schemes to find more spectacular ends.

But which one of his many plans was the one? And when would he ever succeed?

The steaming jungle swept past in a blur of green and black, and drooping branches scraped the sides of the train. Charlie checked his watch, leaned back, and tugged his hat down to shield his eyes from the strobe effect of shadow and light. He'd taken the early morning train in order to stop over two-thirds of the way across the isthmus.

"Culebra station!" the conductor called miles later.

Charlie stepped off the train, excited to view the most spectacular of canal construction sites. No way was he going to miss that.

"Just follow the noise!" a local worker shouted over the din, pointing the way.

Breathing heavily, Charlie crested the hill at last. His jaw dropped as he took in the view.

Lush jungle spread toward every horizon in an endless green carpet. But directly below him, the earth was gashed open and smothered by a mud-covered army.

He whistled to himself and tried fanning the awe away with his hat. "The Culebra Cut."

It was a place where mortal man aspired to sculpt a waterway through the very spine of the continental divide. Even Charlie had to scrape the limits of his healthy imagination to picture great ships floating through this muddy morass. Men and machines clawed at the ground, but from the looks of it, Mother Earth was putting up a hell of a fight. A mudslide had carried away part of the opposite slope, where broken-off railroad tracks protruded from the ground at odd angles like toys in a sandbox.

Everything was in motion — even the overheated air. A maze of rail lines crisscrossed the excavation site at different levels. Cranes hefted entire sections of rails into position along the contours of the Cut. Massive Bacyrus shovels heaved alongside them, belching steam. Part dragon, part machine, their steel jaws chomped into the hillside, then swung in huge arcs to spit mouthfuls of rock onto rail cars. The groaning wagons were designed so that tons of spoil could be scraped off in a single sweep by a Lidgerwood spreader when they reached their destination.

Shoulda thought of that, Charlie thought, eyeing the system. *Brilliant.*

He let out a gasp, watching a locomotive nearly run down a man. Yanked out of the way at the last moment by a quick-acting colleague, the man simply brushed himself off, thumped his savior on the back, and got on with his work.

Panama, where life and death danced cheek to cheek. Charlie shook his head at it all. The scene was stupefying. Breathtaking. Unbelievable.

A shiver wracked his body, and he couldn't tell whether it was fever or sheer excitement — the same kind of shiver he got upon thinking about his treasure chest back in Portobelo. That loot would allow him to be his own boss someday. An entire grave full of silver coins and gold trinkets had to be worth ten years of his current salary, if not twenty — which would give him the start-up capital he needed to run his own operation. Even if his future projects didn't quite reach this scale, they would be of his own choosing and his own design. No more inspectors, no bosses, no reports. Charlie pictured the coins, the jewelry, the humanoid spider face.

With ringing ears and a mind full of dreams, he pried himself away to catch the next Pacific-bound train. For all that he had already accomplished, he figured he could do more. Much more.

The day was warm, but Charlie was still shivering when he stepped onto the next train — and he shivered even harder when he alit at the platform at Ancón. He sniffed the Pacific breeze, feeling strangely clammy from head to toe. Maybe he ought to get to bed early. That would fight off whatever it was that was pestering him.

Still, first things first. He'd wanted to get an initial impression of the Naos breakwater, but duty dictated a stop at the Office of Geographic Surveys in Ancón first. Per protocol, he'd been sending rock samples there all along. It was time to have a look at that particular ring of the bureaucratic circus.

The Office of Geographic Surveys was not what he'd been expecting, though. No owl-faced scientists chipping at stones or weighing samples. No hammering, no dissecting rock layers from various construction sites. In fact, there was hardly anyone there at all.

"We're a little low on staff," admitted the haggard young man who greeted Charlie.

The man was a musician, not a geologist, who had been pressed into service by a chronically underfunded department. Charlie glanced around the office. The window panes were covered with charts and diagrams. Sunlight projected through the glass and merged the print of overlapping sheets into a muddled mess.

"Doctor Goodwin came down with malaria last September and, well..." The young man trailed off.

Charlie eyed him warily.

"He never came back," he finished in a somber tone.

Whether Doctor Goodwin had died or simply left Panama was a detail Charlie wasn't sure he wanted to know. He studied a storeroom stacked high with dusty boxes and wiped his sweaty brow for the tenth time in an hour. Squatting next to a box, he recognized his own writing on the label. It was a sample of Portobelo rock he'd shipped months ago. The box had obviously never been touched and probably never would be. He fought down an urge to upbraid the young man. The requirement to send regular samples to this office was the geological equivalent of paper-pushing. Meaningless bureaucracy — just a little on the heavy side.

Charlie seethed all the way down the block, opening the top buttons of his shirt as he went. It felt awfully hot for this late in the day. His head ached, and his heart thumped wildly. The sooner he could quit this job and break out on his own, the better. The first thing he'd do when he got back to the Atlantic would be to find a way to turn a profit on his silver and pursue his own projects.

Pedestrians threw him peculiar looks as his boots pounded the sidewalk. What was wrong with them? Or was there something wrong with him?

A small spot on the sidewalk caught his attention. It grew and grew until it was a yawning black hole that spread and reached for him. He leaned forward to study it, and then he was falling, falling, falling a long, long way. And then everything just... faded to black.

Chapter Twelve

A Cloud of Reality

Panama Canal
January, present day

"I dreamed to be here for so many years," Pavel breathed in his choppy Czech accent, and the others all nodded.

It was ten o'clock at night when *Aurora* set her anchor in the depths of Gatun Lake, but the crew spent the next hour winding down from the adrenaline rush of the locks. Surrounding them was a disorientating landscape of mismatched views. Behind *Aurora*, powerful lights illuminated the massive locks. The gates of the top lock spit out a regular succession of ships throughout the night. Ahead was the inky peace of the lake, dotted by a few islands that had once been hilltops. On the left, a patch of artificial light marked a beehive of activity at a second set of even more gargantuan locks built parallel to the original canal.

"And I thought this canal was big," Alejandro said.

For once, Nick agreed with him.

He kept himself strategically positioned with one arm around Kate's shoulders as the crew sat in the cockpit eating carrot cake and sipping drinks. Alejandro was squeezed in beside sweaty Pavel on the opposite seat. Whenever the Venezuelan threatened to seize control of the conversation, Nick cut in to press Pavel for further details of his Haitian misfortune. It worked like a charm, every time. Still, Nick wasn't about to let down his guard.

He had initially pegged Alejandro as a braggart overoccupied with creating an impact on an admiring audience. Now, Nick decided Alejandro's charisma was genuine, and that there was another aspect to the Venezuelan. That of a son of a wealthy family who wanted for nothing. Nick knew the type. Alejandro had it all — wealth, looks, brains. Even a fancy yacht. Ambition, too, and a need to confirm his superiority over others. The only thing he lacked was a challenge. Which meant Alejandro was a man who had to seek out obstacles to overcome and even create them if necessary. The type of man who might end up seeking thrills as a race car driver, politician, or high-class jewel thief.

Nick couldn't help but eyeing him warily in the dark.

"Where are you sailing to, Alejandro?" Mayumi asked.

The Venezuelan flashed that winning smile that could have landed him a job as a cover model for a steamy pirate novel. Well, at least he had a shirt on.

"Maybe Patagonia. Maybe Antarctica. I go where the wind takes me."

Nick rolled his eyes. *Oh, please.*

"And sailing alone? Why do you like that?" Mayumi continued.

Alejandro's eyes glistened in the yellow light of *Aurora's* oil lamp. "The challenge," he answered, a little hushed.

Nick leaped in. "Pavel, tell us about your Atlantic crossing. Please!"

Eventually, Kate made up bunks for each of their guests. Mayumi took the starboard bunk in the main cabin, while Pavel insisted upon sleeping in the cockpit. Alejandro got the quarter berth — a small, coffin-like slot in the aft part of the cabin. Nick hid a smile at the mental image. He and Kate crawled into their forepeak bunk, still wired from the experience behind them and wary of what lay ahead.

"Hey, we're halfway there," she smiled, touching his cheek.

Halfway was good, but Nick wouldn't celebrate until they reached the Pacific in one piece — and once Alejandro was gone.

"Halfway." He counted the minutes ticking slowly by.

* * *

Dawn rescued him from fitful sleep. He was up brewing coffee at the earliest decent hour he thought acceptable to his guests. And a good thing, too, because shortly after, a black launch rocketed toward *Aurora* and deposited Jaime, their advisor for the second leg of their trip.

Jaime's interpretation of his role involved sitting back and texting cell phone messages to girlfriend(s), pausing only for the occasional radio exchange with canal authorities. Which was fine with Nick, who could navigate the marked channel across Gatun Lake without guidance. The lake was a paradise of green islands teeming with wildlife.

"Crocodile!" Kate cried, pointing to a ripple in the water.

Alejandro smiled at the disappearing form. "Quick, aren't they?"

Exactly why I keep an eye on you, buddy. Nick leveled his gaze at the Venezuelan.

The temperature soared as the sun climbed overhead, and the crew lapsed into a midday lethargy. Hours ticked by slowly, sleepily. Each time Alejandro ducked into the cabin for a drink or the toilet, Nick grew suspicious. What was he doing down there? Was he checking out the pictures of the places Nick and Kate had been so far? Nick's fishing book, perhaps? Or was he admiring the bikini shot of Kate under that waterfall in Jamaica?

"Alejandro!" Nick called, trying to keep the edge out of his voice. "Can you bring up the binoculars?" There. That would get the guy back where he could keep an eye on him.

When the wide reaches of the lake narrowed, everyone fidgeted with anticipation. They were approaching the Culebra Cut, where the canal — a canyon now — sliced a deep gash through the continental divide.

"This is place of most incredible canal building," Pavel said in a voice reserved for cathedrals. "They dig and dig — then mudslide cover everything!" His hand swept through the air.

"I read about that," Nick said. "Weeks of progress could be destroyed in seconds."

"Like Sisyphus," Kate commented. "The Greek guy doomed to roll a boulder up a mountain, only to watch it to roll down again."

"The difference being that the canal builders succeeded," Nick pointed out.

"And here we are," Kate agreed, smiling for Mayumi, who snapped photo after photo as if each shot would somehow help them grasp the scale of it all.

Aurora passed under the slender arch of the Centennial Bridge, a sign that they were approaching the final set of locks.

"The Pacific is very close now," Pavel said.

"So is lunchtime," Kate joked as her stomach rumbled, then ducked below to make sandwiches. "It's as if the schedulers purposely assign us lock times that coincide with meal times."

The Gatun Locks had kept them all busy throughout normal dinner hours, and now, lunch clashed with their call to enter the first of the Pacific locks. The point was reinforced when Nick saw who they were scheduled to go through the next three locks with — a sight-seeing boat filled with paying guests who viewed the action over a hearty midday meal. He watched the tourists munch on green salads and sip iced sodas in air-conditioned comfort through the wide windows of the tour boat. Meanwhile, the tourists watched the disheveled sailors maneuver alongside.

Nick took captain's prerogative and installed Alejandro at the bow while keeping Kate at the stern, a strategy that had worked well the previous day. Alejandro didn't seem to mind, perhaps because of the hundreds of photos the tourists snapped of *Aurora*. Most of them were aimed to capture the handsome Venezuelan poised for imminent action, sunglasses propped on his wave of black hair.

"I can't believe this," Kate murmured, motioning to the sight-seeing boat.

"Neither can I," Nick answered, looking at Alejandro.

Descending the locks proved to be a much quieter affair than the ascent. Instead of being forced up into the locks, water drained out, slowly lowering the boats. Nick felt rather drained himself.

"Almost there," Kate murmured.

He couldn't wait.

In no time, they had dropped through the single lock at Pedro Miguel and were on their way to the two Miraflores locks. There, *Aurora* found herself the target of even more camera lenses, aimed not only by the tourists beside them but by the crowds at the visitor's center to his left.

"Just think." Kate smiled. "*Aurora* will be in vacation albums all around the world!"

Nick liked that thought. His little sloop, come so far.

Finally came the landmark event — the last lock doors opening to reveal the Pacific. But somehow, the moment managed to sneak up on him. It was almost too much to process. So much was behind them, and there was so much to look forward to ahead.

"We're through," Mayumi said, clicking away

"And how," Kate added as a strong current ushered them out of the lock.

When *Aurora* approached the Bridge of the Americas, everything revved into fast motion. Another launch came to retrieve Jaime the advisor, who had actually fallen asleep at one point. Then *Aurora* motored under the bridge, heading for the Balboa Yacht Club, where their agent stood waving from a dock. Kate pointed Nick to a free mooring and leaned over the bow to snatch it with the boat hook. She was still fastening the line when the agent roared up in a water taxi, anxious to retrieve his lines and tires. *Aurora's* helpers jumped in the launch with him, just as eager to catch the express bus back to the Caribbean side.

Well, Pavel and Mayumi were moving fast. Alejandro seemed inclined to hang around. Nick thanked his lucky stars the man got caught up in the flurry of activity and off-loaded with the others.

Aurora practically sighed as her burden eased. Nick, too.

"Bye, and thanks!" He waved farewell, smiling warmly at a cheery Mayumi and the indefatigable Pavel. Looking in the direction of Alejandro's back, his face went slack. *Good-bye and good riddance.*

Alejandro turned to wave one more time.

"Ciao!" Kate called merrily.

The Venezuelan flashed a winning smile. "Until we meet again!"

Nick winced. God, he hoped not.

Balboa
January, present day

Aurora's mooring at the Balboa Yacht Club offered million-dollar views of an international parade of ships, three dollar beers in the shade of the club's cabana, and free launch service to the dock. A bargain in every respect. The location was relatively quiet, a leafy neighborhood on the outskirts of high-rise Panama City. Thanks to the long Amador Causeway — the breakwater for the Pacific end of the canal — *Aurora* was safely sheltered. To Kate, it seemed the perfect place to gear up for Pacific adventures, literally and figuratively.

With the stress of the transit behind them, Kate and Nick did little but sleep for two days. The past weeks had seen them constantly preoccupied with either Charlie or the canal. Now, their minds simply let go for a time. Before she knew it, it was time to relive the experience aboard Ken and Mayumi's boat.

"Funny how much easier it feels to go through the canal on someone else's boat," Nick noted afterward.

Kate smiled and looked around *Aurora's* snug cabin. "Feels good to be home."

But as Nick's eyes roamed the cabin, she caught him lingering on all the imperfections. Why did he do that? Sure, *Aurora* wasn't quite a big or as nice as some other boats. But she was theirs.

"Hey." She nudged, catching his eye. "You need to give yourself a break."

She held up the cookie tin with a tempting rattle. If only sweets had the same positive effect on Nick as they did on her. Nick shook his head but accepted the beer she held up next.

When she finally sat down with her diary, she didn't quite know where to start. In fact, it took several days and nights to digest the canal experience. Hard to believe they were still in the same, small country. Each station in their journey along Panama's shores had been a world unto itself, from the blissful peace of Kuna Yala to the ghost-filled town of Portobelo. Charlie Parker had become a part of their Panama experience, too, although more difficult to define. There was the period of limbo at Shelter Bay, the manmade marvels of the canal, and now, the urban jungle of Panama City. And the Pacific promised an equally varied smorgasbord of adventures, great and small.

Except that once again, Kate was pumping the gas pedal while Nick slammed on the brakes.

"Ready to get to work?"

To her utter dismay, Nick insisted that they begin their Pacific cruising with a thorough maintenance program for *Aurora*. Rumors had gripped the cruising community of a small sailboat lost with all hands en route from Mexico, and Nick set about examining every inch of his boat, searching for a ticking time bomb. His efforts revealed an entire catalog of issues that had to be resolved before Nick would even consider further plans.

"Boy, we really have to fix this. And that. And..."

Kate stood perfectly still, watching her grand plans fade and disappear.

Offshore islands like Taboga and Contadora beckoned — new corners of the map to lay claim to, so tantalizingly close. Swimming! Snorkeling! Exploring! And those islands were just stepping stones to the wonders of the South Pacific. At least, that's how she saw it.

"But... but..."

She rapidly reached the conclusion that the work-play ratio aboard *Aurora* was badly out of proportion. The giddy feeling of having entered a new ocean had drained away, and a cloud of reality settled over the boat in the form of a leaky hatch, blocked plumbing, and, of course, the temperamental anchor windlass. By this time in her mental planning, she and Nick should have been kicking back in secluded Las Perlas anchorages. Instead, they were still sweating over repairs and Charlie's illegible notes.

What happened to "If it ain't broke...?" Why did Nick have to be so practical? So stubborn? So... right?

Kate held her tongue. *Compromise, remember?* She should be happy Nick agreed to transit the canal at all.

She tried working off her itchy feet through a series of errands around Panama City, hunting down essentials: rubber seals, gearbox oil, and brownie mix. She couldn't resist buying a small leather-bound notebook that resembled Charlie's and immediately filled it with shopping, job lists, and notes on distances and future destinations. Unfortunately, her attempt to unclog the kitchen sink led to inadvertently snapping off the rusty connector, setting off a three-day search for a replacement part.

At least she could pick up other parts for Nick during her search, and the fact that her scavenger hunts taught her several new Spanish terms such as *impulsor* (impeller) or *empaquetadura* (gasket) was of some solace.

"Want to know how to say epoxy in Spanish?" she asked Nick. But he was elbows-deep into a project and didn't hear.

She sighed.

One good thing that came of Kate's battle with the sink was meeting Lopta, a vivacious, fifty-five-year-old taxi driver and enthusiastic ambassador for her country. Lopta took Kate under her wing, chauffeuring her charge around the city like a rotund Sancho Panza to Kate's Don Quixote. Lopta would furiously honk slower vehicles out of her way, then bat her eyelashes at their male drivers.

"Qué idiota," she murmured under her breath.

Hands waving, eyes more or less on the road, Lopta kept up a steady commentary and provided Kate with a thorough primer on Panama's current issues, from politics to the economy and race relations. Kate could just about get the gist of all but Lopta's fiercest, fastest outbursts.

Lopta seemed particularly excited about a recent drug bust sloppily executed by Panamanian security forces. The director of the armed unit was accused of overzealous use of force in his crackdown.

"Este Coronel Lopez! Loco!" Lopta whirled her finger around her ear.

A van braked abruptly in front of them. Lopta hit the horn, swerved, then checked her hair in the rearview mirror, all in one smooth, practiced motion.

With Lopta, every ride was an adventure, every journey's end a relief.

Balboa
January, present day

Nick was secretly relieved when Kate declared enough to be enough and announced a trip to the chart shop — her form of retail therapy.

"Besides, you need a break, too," she added.

Nick rolled his shoulders and heard them crack and pop. Yeah, maybe he did.

"And you can get a nautical almanac while we're at it."

She was laying it on thick now, but she had a point. He still didn't have an almanac for the new year. Without one, he couldn't calculate any of his fledgling star sights.

The chart shop was just close enough to walk to, but only just. By the time they crossed a busy Balboa intersection, they were sweating buckets, and the cool, air-conditioned air of the chart shop felt like the elixir of life. Nick spent a full minute savoring the feel of it on his skin before turning to the shelves. He found an extremely tempting volume on outboard engine repair as well as a current nautical almanac. He held it open, feeling like the Sorcerer's Apprentice holding a book of forbidden spells.

In the meantime, Kate was eyeing charts the way she eyed sweets in a bakery, salivating at the prospect of new horizons.

"Charts of Las Perlas archipelago," he heard the clerk say. "Anything else?"

Kate looked at Nick from across the store. "Pacific crossing charts?"

He took a moment to phrase his answer carefully. So far, their longest passage had been eight hundred miles. The Pacific was seven thousand miles across, dotted with tiny, isolated specks of land. The Galapagos Islands were nearly a thousand miles from

Panama, and after that came a three-thousand-mile stretch of open ocean before the Marquesas. Then another couple of hundred to Tahiti — and that was only halfway across.

"How about we come back for those?" Seeing Kate's face fall, he added a hasty, "Shall we get an ice cream on the way back?"

She flashed him a look but didn't complain. When they paid and left the store, they instantly broke into a sweat. Nick fanned himself with his book, waiting for the streetlight.

"Hey!" Kate grabbed his arm and pointed to a large building taking up the entire road front across the way. Vines choked the imposing facade, covering windows and scrambling over the wide roof line. "It's the YMCA!"

Nick could just make out the words etched into the pediment of the century-old building: *Young Men's Christian Association*.

"I was reading about this!" she said. "The Ys came in during canal construction days. Maybe Charlie went to one!"

Nick let Kate pull him up the wide stairway and through the entrance, where a disinterested security guard reclined. The man lowered one corner of his newspaper for a brief, annoyed look, then snapped the sheet back up. No comment, no motion other than shifting the position of his propped-up feet.

Nick could smell the decades. He could practically hear them in the slow creak of the ceiling fans. The workmanship of the door frames and moldings reflected the grand visions of the building's era. These days, the YMCA was an office block.

Kate ran her finger down the directory posted on the wall and laughed quietly.

"Look, Diablo Enterprises. It's the import business Juan runs with his cousin Juanito."

Footsteps echoed in the hallway on the right, and Nick caught the sound of a voice calling good-bye. It sounded familiar somehow.

With a jerk, he knew why. Alejandro. Wasn't the Venezuelan supposed to be back in Shelter Bay? Nick grabbed Kate's arm and hastened her up the stairs to the second floor, mumbling something about finding a toilet. Why the evasive action, he wasn't sure. Only that the Venezuelan was the last person he wanted to deal with on this day — or any day, for that matter. As they reached the upper landing, he leaned over the banister to see Alejandro dart past with a cell phone at his ear, giving the guard a quick wave good-bye.

Whew. Kate hadn't noticed. The coast was clear, but he continued down one wing of the upper story. Now that he had mentioned a toilet, it didn't seem like such a bad idea. Surprisingly, there really was a door marked *Caballeros*. But when he reemerged into the hallway, he looked around, puzzled. Kate was gone.

"Kate?" His voice echoed down the empty hall.

Nothing.

"Kate?"

"In here."

He traced the sound the length of the dim corridor. The last door in long, regular row was ajar, and sunlight streamed through like a beacon. He strode down the hall, feeling as if he might be caught at any moment. Caught at what, he couldn't say — it just felt a little strange to be wandering around here. Who knew what incarnation of trouble might be lurking around the next corner?

He leaned into the doorway, finding Kate in a large space three times the width of the small offices she had passed in the hallway. The walls were lined with floor-to-ceiling bookshelves and the center occupied by broad tables with bronze reading lamps. It looked all the world like a public library. Sunlight blazed through the tall windows, branding the room in stripes of light and shade.

"This was the reading room for canal employees from the early days of the American administration," Kate said, pointing to a small sign. The room was the last part of the YMCA building to retain its original form, a quiet nod to its origins.

Somehow, though, Nick couldn't picture a man like Charlie — what he knew of him, anyway — spending much time in a place like this.

Kate skimmed the bookshelves while he explored the shelf with old nautical almanacs. Hefty, hardbound volumes with dark linen covers and gold lettering — the kind they didn't make any more. Nick glanced around like a thief at a jewelry counter, then slid one of the almanacs out. He checked the spine — 1921 — and laid it gingerly on a table. Then he pulled out his newly purchased nautical almanac and opened the books side by side.

In essence, the pages in each provided the same information. Their differences were largely in presentation. He flipped to March 23 in both the 1921 volume and the one he'd just bought. Narrow vertical columns were devoted to Venus, Mars, Jupiter, and Saturn. Another section was dedicated to figures pertaining to the sun and the moon so that the angle measured on a mariner's sextant could be converted into a line of position.

Looking at this script of an ancient art so rarely practiced nowadays, Nick felt more determined than ever to work out a decent sight. His early attempts had only produced very rough positions, none better than eight miles off his true location as reported by *Aurora's* smug GPS display. Not good enough.

"Ready?" Kate called from the doorway.

He slid the 1921 almanac back into its slot on the shelf and tucked his volume back into his backpack. He followed Kate down the hallway, remembering what had brought him here. Alejandro. He felt a little silly for avoiding the man now. His dislike for the man was largely irrational and probably unfair to both Kate and the Venezuelan. All very childish, Nick's reason told him. Maybe he should give the guy a chance.

Or maybe not, his gut replied.

By the time they got back to *Aurora* after a quick internet check in the clubhouse, he was drenched with sweat, and his mind kept bouncing from subject to subject.

"Want a drink?" Kate called from the galley.

Boy, did he.

They sat quietly, taking in the view from *Aurora's* cockpit — a view that carried his thoughts from Alejandro to Charlie. The Pacific breakwater, now covered by the treelined Amador Causeway, had become a pleasant recreational area frequented by lovebirds seeking a private escape. The causeway leapfrogged from the mainland to the islets of Naos, Culebra, Perico, and Flamenco: a scenic, three-mile-long bridge to nowhere. Had Charlie been here, too?

Nick made a face and watched the mud-colored current swirl past. Somehow, transiting the canal had tipped his mood. Try as he might, he couldn't quite shake it off. Each night, he went to sleep frustrated with the constant hurdles *Aurora* threw at him. Each morning, he woke annoyed with Charlie's vague hints. Was there a pot of gold at the end of the rainbow, or did it just fizzle to a dead end, like the causeway?

His hopes had been riding on Aunt Laura, who had finally replied to his email with all that she knew of Charlie.

Charles Edward Parker, she wrote, *born April 1, 1883 in Ohio.*

Charlie had traveled widely, involved in various (mis)adventures before heading to Panama to work on the canal. Afterward, he joined a silver mining venture in Nevada, then moved on to expansion work on New York's Erie Canal. That's when he met Rosie.

Nick's email had asked Laura about a possible Peru connection. *No hint of Peru*, she answered. *Why do you ask?*

He exchanged glances with Kate and skipped to the next part.

Charlie volunteered for the Army Corps of Engineers and departed for the First World War, probably imagining a few weeks of glory and a hero's homecoming. His task was supposed to be safe enough, building a few bridges and helping the latest battle weapon — armored tanks — to roll onto battlefields.

But it didn't work out that way, Laura wrote.

His unit saw unexpected action in Cambrai, France, where he was killed on November 30, 1917. Apparently, the letter Rosie sent to say she was pregnant never made it into Charlie's hands.

Nick and Kate had stared at the screen for a long, quiet moment when they got to that part.

The baby was a girl, who went on to tell her own daughters — Nick's mother and his aunt Laura — everything that Rosie told them about Charlie. He was an adventurer, an engineer, and a bit of a fortune-seeker. A father who never met his only child. All that remained of Charlie's earthly possessions were the keepsakes in the cigar box.

Nick had to gulp away a lump in his throat by the time they finished reading, while Kate sniffled quietly. But on reading it all a second time back on *Aurora*, Nick felt like throwing up his hands.

"It's all interesting. But none of it sheds any light on Charlie's extracurricular activities in Panama."

"Such as an enigmatic woman named Mercedes or a boat called Yolanta," Kate added, propping her head on one hand.

Nothing on Peruvian spiders or Spanish silver. Nothing on the indecipherable maps sketched in his notebook. Nick muttered to himself, scratching at a mosquito bite. He really was taking the whole crazy thing too seriously.

Kate sighed and looked toward the bar. "You want to go out for a drink tonight?"

Yeah, he could use a drink, all right.

The phone rang first, though, and Nick watched Kate's face tighten as she listened to the caller. She hesitated, then handed the phone to him with a grave expression that said there wouldn't be any going out for drinks that night.

Ancón, Panama City
June 1912

Charlie Parker was ready, even eager, to die. Fortuna was calling his number. If only these women would leave him in peace.

He faded in and out, registering snippets of strange surroundings and urgent whispers. His body felt glued to a bed that was definitely not in House 47. Wild dreams that jumped between a pensive Mercedes and swarms of angry spiders with talking heads exhausted him, as did the voices that surrounded him and called him Bed Eight.

Peace, that's what Charlie wanted. To rest in peace.

At one point, Charlie bobbed a little closer to the edge of consciousness and heard the voices again. Nurses. He was in a hospital. Why? Malaria? Is that what they said? Charlie tried sitting up but felt hands pushing him down.

He didn't have malaria. He knew — he'd contracted malaria in Rhodesia, and this was not it. No, those nurses couldn't pull that one over on Charlie Parker. They were probably trying to fill a quota. So many patients trapped for so many days. He was perfectly fine!

"I don't have malaria," he groaned.

"No one said you have malaria, Bed Eight."

"My name is Charlie. Stop calling me Bed Eight!"

Women!

A thin but surprisingly strong arm pushed him back into the mattress, saying something that only registered in his dull ears much later.

He drifted in and out for what felt like decades before finally waking in a slightly more lucid state. A murky, aching sort of awake. It was quiet and warm in the screened ward that echoed with the muted click of footsteps on a well-scrubbed floor. Jovial bird songs filtered in from outside.

Ancón hospital. He heard someone whisper it. Then another nurse whisked by.

"I don't have malaria," he protested.

"No," she agreed. "You don't."

It was typhoid fever. A malady, Charlie could state with authority, that was no fun at all.

Mornings melted into humid afternoons. Evenings slid into nighttime before he even noticed. Then it would be morning again — and pouring rain. He barely noticed when the rain started — only when it ended. When the sun came out afterward, shafts of light pierced the mosquito netting and filled the ward with a soft glow. Everything was soft in the hospital — the sounds, the sights, the sheets. Everything but that bitter quinine he was forced to choke down every two hours, even at night.

"If you're good, Bed Eight," a nurse clucked, "we'll let you have some whiskey."

"Blackmail," Charlie grunted, fading out again. One of those despicable female battle tactics.

Eventually, he was granted the dignity of pajamas and the pleasure of a sip of milk. Then he moved on to eggnog and — thank Fortuna — whiskey, at last. The booze he didn't object to — other than the measly rations — but he hated eggnog. He hated being in bed. He hated being fussed over and being useless.

The nurses were perplexed that he had come down with typhoid at all. An aide from Doctor Gorgas' disease control team came to interview Charlie. Where had he been? When? With whom? Doing what?

It felt like the second coming of Inspector Cummings. The man was determined to hunt down the guilty mosquito, no matter how much of Panama he had to comb in the process.

When Charlie mentioned Portobelo, the medical inspector grimaced.

"A haven for diseases." The man nodded. "Especially in the rainy season."

Especially in the graveyard, Charlie thought. But he opted to omit that particular detail.

The doctor made another note on his report and took his leave of Charlie at last.

* * *

After two and a half weeks in the hospital, Charlie was transferred to the sanatorium on the island of Taboga, a three-hour boat trip across Panama Bay.

At first, he didn't like the sound of it. Sanatorium. A place for sick people, not Charlie Parker. But considering he could barely feed himself, let alone walk, he gave in. He even fell asleep twice — okay, maybe three times — on the ferry trip across. Charlie only stirred when the boat docked at Taboga.

"Sanatorium," he muttered. It looked like a prison to him.

But the wide, screened verandas of the place soon won him over. He could eat things like porridge and gloriously firm slices of bread with the prospect of graduating to real meals soon. He even managed a few wobbly steps with the help of an orderly. He spent the better part of each day ensconced on the veranda, overlooking the broad bay. If it weren't for loyalty to his crew, he'd feel no particular rush to head back to work.

"Thirty days." A fellow patient winked. "You know our contracts specify thirty days of paid sick leave a year?"

Charlie knew about the thirty days, but his thoughts were on his crew. Even with Edgar overseeing things, he felt obliged to do his part. And who would protect them from that evil Inspector whatshisname — Cunningham?

"Gotta get back to work," he murmured.

"Work? Work is the crabgrass in the lawn of life," the other fellow quipped.

Everybody laughed.

Charlie thought about walking away but couldn't quite manage. He sighed and resigned himself to a few more days.

From the veranda, he could see Ancón Hill over on the mainland. When the light was just right, he could make out the glint of machinery in the foreground of the hill, where engineers still struggled with the Pacific breakwater. The islands that would someday be connected by a three-mile-long causeway were high enough to make out: Naos, Culebra, Perico, and Flamenco. If the engineers ever solved the problem of soft sediment, that is. Charlie wanted to give the problem some thought, but even that seemed to take a lot of energy. So he simply observed boat traffic crisscrossing the bay, from local ferries to large steamers heading for California.

California, he thought dreamily. *Gold fields*. He drifted in and out throughout the day, barely registering the difference between sleep and awake.

Dusk found Charlie still ensconced in the same comfortable spot, his eyes open and a little less glazed.

"There they are again, right on time," another inmate — er, patient — observed, pointing to the blue fishing boat rounding a corner of the bay.

Charlie watched. It was the little vessel that set off early and returned late, with a pair of men he imagined to be brothers working the wine-colored sails. He couldn't help but admire the elegance of sailing.

"Harness the wind and off you go," he murmured to no one in particular.

He didn't have much experience with wind power, but the concept intrigued him. Maybe when he cashed in on his treasure and started his own enterprise, he would spend some time playing with wind.

Of course, he'd have to cash in on the loot first. Charlie made a face. Unfortunately, that problem was turning out to be a tough nut to crack. The problem had lost its urgency, though. He watched the setting sun cast the hills of the mainland in ever-changing, magical light, accentuated by the few twinkling lights of the city, and he let out a sudden chuckle. He'd wanted a change in scenery — he certainly got it.

A man should be more careful what he wished for.

The night passed, then another day, and a whole second week. And like all his best ideas, the solution to the treasure problem came to him when he wasn't focused on it. He was thinking about how delicious toast and jam could be and how he might win back the two dollars he lost in a card game the night before when the solution popped into his mind.

The silver-filled grave in Portobelo.

The barges, shuttling boulders to the breakwater.

His shack at Toro Point.

The Office of Geographic Surveys with its neglected boxes of rock samples.

The fishing boat. All those steamers, chugging over the placid sea to California.

Charlie could practically hear the click of dominoes as everything fell into place. When it did, he was gripped with a new urgency to get back to work — on his own private project, that is.

"I got it!" he exclaimed.

"You got what?" another patient asked.

But Charlie was already off for a pencil and paper, moving with renewed energy.

Chapter Thirteen

A Change in Plan

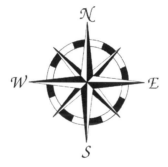

Somewhere over the Atlantic
February, present day

A continent slipped silently past, 30,000 feet below.

Nick watched the steel gray ocean with a strange feeling of detachment. After so many months of slow, quiet progress across the ocean, a jet trip in the reverse direction felt like traveling at the speed of light. He figured it would take weeks to catch up with all the time and space screaming away from him now.

His sister met him at the airport and took him straight to the hospital. His father was recovering from the heart attack, but the unexpected event had put fear in every family member's mind. After months of feeling so independent of home, Nick suddenly had a strong sense of connection, how fragile it all was.

"I'm fine!" his father insisted. "It wasn't that serious."

His mother's tightly set mouth said the opposite.

"Well, it's great to see you anyway," Nick said to break the awkward pause.

"You didn't have to come all the way from Panama."

Oh, but he did. For his own conscience, he did.

During the stilted drive home with his mother and older sister Nora, Nick struggled to find something — anything — to say.

"How's Kate?" Nora offered.

"She's good."

"Good," said Nora.

"Good," his mother said with less enthusiasm.

A pained silence settled over the car. Every subject seemed taboo: the recent holidays which Nick failed to celebrate with family. *Aurora*, the whim that he had given up a perfectly good job for. Panama, the playground where he'd been frivolously squandering time. It all emphasized his absence, his failure to be a good son.

He certainly couldn't talk about the thrill of the canal transit, much less Charlie Parker.

"How are the girls?" Nick tried. Asking about his nieces usually lubricated conversation. And it did, for a little while. Once they got home, however, things took a downturn.

"So, what are your plans?" His mother's eyes probed mercilessly.

"Uh... I'll be here for ten days."

"And then?"

"Back to Panama."

His mother and sister exchanged looks, lips set tight. Nick squirmed in his chair, recalling the time he had been interrogated about the mysterious breakage of a vase when he was nine. He wished his younger sister were around to smooth things over, but Nancy had already come and gone — back to law school, as his mother noted, stressing how productively occupied the woman was.

Finally, he retreated into his old bedroom, where he sat and studied the model planes still suspended from the ceiling, flying in rings of dusty neglect. He spent a long time staring at the biplane his father helped him assemble once upon a time, and he wondered about all the pressing things the man must have put aside to help fit part 19a into 19b and 19c. When he did go to sleep, his dreams were peppered with visions of a dying, confused father asking after his absent son.

Nick jolted awake, surprised to find the bed so stable, so empty, the air so cold. It was still dark, though the clock said six a.m. In Panama, dawn would be poised to break over the horizon, but in Massachusetts, the sun was still in the throes of a lazy winter sleep-in.

"Shh!" Nick padded down the stairs bundled in thick layers of flannel and fleece, urging the bouncing dog to keep quiet.

He brewed a cup of coffee and wandered silently through a house that was essentially unchanged from his middle school days, taking everything in. The house, like his parents, seemed to have grown smaller. The rooms were worn but well-loved and seething with memories. The same sand-colored couch he'd once built forts out of, the same piece of banister missing from the stairway since who knows when. Even the dog was another floppy-eared pointer, the fourth incarnation of his beloved Teddy — if less well behaved, since his parents seemed to tolerate a lot more misbehavior since they had become empty nesters.

It wasn't the caffeine in the coffee that launched Nick into a flurry of activity. He just didn't admit it to himself as he scrubbed all the pots in the sink, then took out the garbage. A burned-out lightbulb hung like an unvoiced accusation, and he promptly replaced it. He took the dog on a frigid walk down the block to buy fresh bagels and a newspaper before settling into a quiet breakfast. Even then his mind spun with resolutions, like getting to the jammed storm windows next.

The following days passed with him in perpetual motion, trying to make up for his long absence. His mother positively glowed, only stiffening at any reference to another home, another place. One that seemed more cramped and inadequate with every passing day.

Everything was so familiar and easy. Water came gurgling out of the tap in unlimited quantities — clean, fresh water, soft to the touch and safe to swallow. Mountains of groceries lay waiting to be purchased just five minutes away, and there was almost no physical effort involved in getting it back home. No long walks, no heaving from dinghy to swaying deck. The toilet flushed with a touch of a lever — no tedious pump, pump, pumping away. Sure, it was freezing in the wintry Northeast, but heat could be summoned at the turn of a knob.

All so comfortable, so effortless.

It had taken him four months to get used to living on a boat. It took him less than two days to slip right back into old habits, almost like *Aurora* had never come into his life. He felt himself squeezing back into a skin he thought he had shed long before. It was familiar, if a little tight, like a suit he hadn't worn in a long time. But it was his, all right. If it wasn't for the proof of his copper-toned skin, he might have wondered if he had ever been away.

Between hospital visits, he made the obligatory rounds to aging relatives who were relieved to have him back from his perilous, disconnected existence in some faraway place. They clutched at him with dry, worried hands.

"So, you're finally back."

"So good to see you home again."

Somehow they imagined he was back to stay. Which, of course, he wasn't. Was he?

Four days into his visit, Nick helped his father settle back in at home. He brought his father drinks and pills, fetched books, and discussed current events. They sorted photo albums, played chess, and even made their way into the basement where Nick reorganized the workbench according to his father's instructions. It was the most time they had spent together in years. Maybe even ever.

He saw the workbench with new eyes, eyeing all the tools he could use on *Aurora*. Boating supply catalogs attracted him in the same way. Every conceivable part was there, available with a quick phone call. No need for endless trips across a dusty city to mime his wishes to uncomprehending salespeople. Still, the descriptions of new hoses, pumps, and closed cell batteries came with an ominous subtext. Those were just parts. He would have to sweat them into place in impossibly cramped corners of the boat. Not that he didn't want to do any boat work. It was just that he wished some end was in sight. But on *Aurora*, no sooner was one task accomplished than another item would fail, once again extending the repair list. Guaranteed.

"Nick — telephone!" It rang and rang.

"Hey, Nick! You're back in town!"

"Hi, Nick! Meet us tonight?"

"Nick! What are you doing back?"

He wasn't so sure any more. And although he spent hours catching up with friends and former colleagues, no one had anything much to report.

"Damned Carpel Tunnel Syndrome — can you believe it? Too much time at a keyboard."

"You've got to see the new kitchen. It's great!"

Bill's new kitchen was great — and cost more than all Nick's expenses for the past six months, canal transit included. Still, the kitchen boasted four burners, a working fridge, and a dishwasher. Not that he was jealous or anything.

The phone rang again. "Nick! Bud! Gotta meet!" It was Mark, eager to catch up.

Nick entered the smoky bar at the appointed time and found his stocky friend.

"Nick!" Mark pumped his hand. "You look great!"

He slid into the seat opposite Mark. "You, too," he replied, trying to ignore his friend's potbelly and dark, ringed eyes. Still, Mark had the same wild energy that had him shooting spitballs across their classroom back in sixth grade. And eighth grade. Maybe even tenth...

Mark thumped him on the shoulder and launched into a breathless report about his personal life — which was to say, his work life, because Mark's job eclipsed everything else. What started as a backroom web design business had somehow blossomed into a runaway video game company. The very company Nick had turned down an offer to join three years earlier in favor of sticking to his position at a consulting giant with its promise of steady paychecks, health insurance, and an appealing stock scheme. Playing it safe had been a big mistake, not to mention a personal disappointment.

He smiled on the outside while giving himself a mental whipping about opportunities missed.

Meanwhile, Mark was brimming with news.

Mark's divorce was finally settled.

Mark had quit smoking. Again.

Mark wanted to pursue a promising new project but didn't have the time.

Mark was up to fourteen employees and was desperate for more.

Mark had an offer Nick couldn't refuse.

Boston

February, present day

"You'd be perfect!" Mark thumped his glass down for emphasis.

Nick blinked uncertainly.

Mark popped a nicotine gum into his mouth, the last from a badly savaged silver foil. "You would be! Just think!"

Nick did think. Leading a network security team for Mark's video game company would be a stretch, but the challenge had a certain appeal. If it weren't for *Aurora*...

"I don't think it would work," he mumbled.

"Sure it could! You'd be close to your parents, too."

Nick could picture the relief on his mother's face. Still, he held up a hand in a "stop" signal.

"Kate would never go for it..."

Mark waved the notion away like an unpleasant odor. "This is the thing! Our games need authenticity! She could be our historical consultant!"

"I don't think it's her thing..."

"Our new game needs world building. It has to have details. It has to have pop!" Mark waved his hands and rolled his gum from cheek to cheek. "She could do that for this new Maya game. She could even go over our medieval game. You can't believe the flak we get from people. You use the wrong kind of armor, and you get hate mail!"

"I'm not sure medieval times are her field," Nick mumbled, losing steam. He remembered Kate's enthusiasm for everything Maya on their trip to Mexico. She'd dragged him up every pyramid in the Yucatán. Some of them twice.

"She could research!"

In any other circumstance, he figured Kate might indeed be interested. But he knew how much she loved the sailing life. The travel, the freedom, the simplicity.

The uncertainty, the repairs.

"You could work together! Set your own hours. You could come in for long days, then take a couple off. Anything! We just need to launch this thing before the competition beats us out." Mark leaned in even closer, squeezing his arms onto the table. "Look, I have a couple of new guys, but they're young and green. I need someone to break them in and take this thing to the next level. I need someone I can trust. I need you, Nick."

Then Mark got into money, and Nick inhaled a long, sucking breath.

Apparently, Mark's company was doing very well, indeed. The position offered what he earned at his last job, plus an attractive equity stake.

He couldn't stop the gears in his mind from doing the math. He and Kate could live in a small apartment and save thousands on rent. Even a shoe box would seem palatial after *Aurora*. They could still enjoy the feeling of sharing a joint project. After, say, three years on the job, they could walk away with enough money for a long sailing trip — in a bigger, nicer boat. One that didn't break all the time. A safer boat. The image stuck in his mind. A perfect boat for crossing the Pacific. Hell, they could even sail around the world! In the meantime, he could placate his family and spend a little time closer to home.

It was perfect.

* * *

When he exited customs at Panama City's Tocumen International Airport three days later, he immediately spotted Kate, who wore her favorite T-shirt — "Save the Sea Turtles" — and a huge, goofy grin. They collided in a long, tight hug, then squeezed together on one end of Lopta's back seat for the drive to Balboa. He hardly noticed when the taxi reached the yacht club, where they decided on a celebratory drink.

"So, I met with Mark," he started, once they had caught up on immediate matters.

Kate leaned forward, encouraging him to go on.

"He has a lot of great ideas."

Kate nodded enthusiastically.

Nick outlined Mark's business successes and added, "Actually, Mark is desperate for help."

Kate's happy flush paled.

"He made me an offer."

Kate retracted her feet from their embrace of Nick's and set them flat on the floor.

"What do you mean, an offer?"

He filled her in on the details, including a position for her. In the silence that ensued, he could hear her heels scraping across the layer of sand covering the cement floor of the yacht club. Back and forth, back and forth.

"Why would I want some computer job back in Boston when we have *Aurora*?"

"Because... Well..." It began to dawn on him that he had perhaps miscalculated.

"Why would you want some computer job in Boston when we have *Aurora*?"

Nick tried to explain the logic that had seemed crystal-clear to him. "Just think — after a couple of years, we'll have a load of money."

Kate didn't look impressed.

"We could get a bigger boat," he urged. "A nicer boat."

"I like *Aurora*. We don't need another boat." Her heels grated over bare cement, but still she ground on.

Somehow, he wasn't getting through. He tried again. "A safer boat we could cross the Pacific in."

"We can cross the Pacific on *Aurora*."

"Bigger would be safer."

"*Aurora* is safe."

"A really nice boat," he started, ready to detail the specifics. "It would be perfect..."

He trailed off when Kate brushed a hand against her face, too slow to catch the first frustrated tears.

The conversation didn't go well from there.

Less than forty-eight brittle hours later, Nick was on another flight back to Boston.

Alone.

Isla Taboga

July 1912

Bit by bit, Charlie's solution took on the shape of a plan. Like most of his plans, it was logical but a little light in detail. The important thing was vision. So what if many aspects were left to chance and a hundred things could go wrong? That was a deliberate decision. Why? Because Charlie recognized the one critical fact that many inferior engineers failed to honor — that no amount of careful planning would ever replace dumb luck. Experience had taught him as much.

So Charlie plotted in bold brush strokes, leaving the specifics to work themselves out. They always did.

Well, most of the time.

Much of the plan was formulated by the time he was released from the sanatorium. The nurses had declared that a patient who could spend half the night in rambunctious card games was fit enough to fend for himself. Especially now that the patient was demanding too much whiskey.

"Too much is just enough!" Charlie protested. Alas, to no avail.

That was another one of his father's sayings which often slipped off his tongue these days.

"All good things must come to an end," he murmured upon his departure from Taboga.

He watched the green bump of the island deepen to a distant blue as the ferry carried him back to the mainland. Then, steaming north to the Caribbean in the first-class section of the train, Charlie leaned back and nodded off with his hat pulled over his eyes. The landscape was no longer important to him, only his plan.

When Charlie appeared at the breakwater the next morning, the crew greeted him with a hearty cheer, filling his face with a little color. The sight of their breakwater had a similar effect on him. Good old Edgar and the boys had kept up an impressive pace in his absence.

A good thing, too, since he'd be rather busy from then on.

Charlie nodded as he shook Edgar's hand, hoping his grip communicated more than his words. Where would he be without Edgar?

"Yous a little thin, boss," the foreman commented.

"An' pale, too!" Lionel noted, making Charlie and all the Bajans crack up. "I mean paler dan usual times!"

Charlie realized how much he'd missed this place, this crew. Their lilting accents and cheery faces, the special taste of the salt-tinged air on this side of the isthmus. It was the closest he'd come to a feeling of home in a long, long time.

The thought slapped Charlie like a cold wave smashing over the shore. Whoa. Maybe he was getting old.

"I bought you a few things," he announced at break time.

They cheered when he presented ten pies, fresh from the commissary bakery. Monday was apple pie day, and everyone declared it their favorite. Next, he passed around a box of goods from the commissary: tobacco, canned peaches, bars of soap. All normal purchases for a person on the gold pay scale but luxuries for silver employees like the Bajans. As it was, Charlie felt closer to the silver class.

In fact, he'd soon be calling himself a silver member — Spanish silver, that is.

Soon, everything was back to normal. Almost everything.

"D'you hear about that guy?" said a neighbor in House 47.

"What guy?"

"You know, *that* guy!" The man mimicked the unforgettable leer of the dealer who stole Charlie's bag of coins. "Killed by a prostitute, knifed in the night."

Charlie blessed the woman's vengeful soul. That sure would clear up one complication in his treasure supply chain.

Another change was Charlie's newfound dedication to the advancement of science. In fact, his efforts in collecting and sending rock samples to the Office of Geographic Surveys over on the Pacific coast was nothing less than exemplary. On each trip to Portobelo,

Charlie filled empty dynamite boxes with "rock samples," all carefully labeled, then loaded onto the barges — his personal treasure pipeline — that shuttled between Portobelo and Toro Point. The tricky part was making sure his efficient crew didn't end up lining the breakwater with Spanish silver.

"Watch it! Watch it!"

Lionel shot him a surprised look.

"The samples go over here," Charlie motioned to his field office. It was the perfect place to keep a few old boxes, right where everyone could see them. Until he could get them to the train, that is.

"What address, please?" asked the shipping agent at the Cristobal station when Charlie piled up four heavy boxes.

"Office of Geographic Surveys, Ancón," he said. "For the attention of Cuthbert E. Longfellow," he added, making sure to keep a straight face.

Off went the first boxes, straight to his secure storage facility on the Pacific coast: the chronically understaffed Office of Geographic Surveys.

But like every endeavor in the tropics, the silver-transport business slowed to a trickle during wet season. Charlie could be a slow learner when it came to pushing his luck, but he'd learned his lesson about frequenting mosquito-infested graveyards during rainy season. Instead, he put his energy into a little amateur sleuthing. A fellow inmate at Bachelor Quarters had given Charlie a book called *On the Spanish Main* which chronicled the exploits of privateers like Sir Francis Drake and Henry Morgan. In the languid Caribbean evenings, when the air was almost too thick to breathe, Charlie turned the pages as treasure hunters pillaged and looted their way across the isthmus. He spent a long time on Chapter Ten, *The Sack of Porto Bello*. Townspeople had dropped whole stashes of gold and silver into wells and other hiding places as they fled. Coins, jewelry, everything of value, like the silver spider. Maybe his treasure cache was the result of one such raid. The graveyard fit the bill as a hiding place — except that particular deposit had never been retrieved.

Until now.

The tricky part was slipping by Mercedes. She knew he was up to something, all right. Late at night, when her customers had either retired or lay slumped over the tables, she'd sit with Charlie at a corner table. It was a routine they developed — two friends ending each weary day with a drink, soaking in the humid Portobelo night, trying to read each other's thoughts.

"You look like a cat who catched a fat rat, Carlito," Mercedes murmured in her Spanish purr.

Charlie considered this long and hard. How to tell her without telling her? "What would you do if you caught a fat rat?"

Mercedes raised her curved eyebrows. "How fat dis rat?"

Charlie thought it over, then used his hands to mark the length of a good, fat rat.

Mercedes looked impressed. "I make big beezniss," she replied without hesitation. "More rooms for touristas and big restaurant — on roof! Maybe *una tienda* — a shop. Big beezniss, big money." Her eyes sparkled as her hands sculpted the future.

Charlie grinned. Now there was a woman after his own heart — a businesswoman.

Then he distracted her — and himself — by taking out his notebook and asking what he should bring back from Colon on his next trip. Mercedes leaned forward and began dictating, her eyes warm and approving.

"Cinco — no, seis! Six parasols. Vino — wine. Twenty bottles, if good price..."

* * *

After months of shipping rock samples across the isthmus, Charlie decided he'd better check his depository over in Ancón. He invented a pressing need to consult with the engineers of the Pacific Division and headed across the fledgling nation of Panama once more.

After a day at the Naos breakwater, where sediment was still agonizing the engineers by oozing away under the fill, he headed to Ancón Hospital, straightening his collar and slicking his hair back as he went. He sheepishly presented the nurses with flowers and several bottles of wine, then visited Ward 22, where one of his men was recovering from a bout of malaria. As Charlie commiserated with the man, his eyes darted around the room. This "silver" ward was very much like the "gold" wing he'd been in, yet subtly different. The beds and sheets were similar, and the ward was just as clean as he remembered his to be, but everything was worn around the edges, and twice the number of patients crowded the space.

Charlie sighed, puckering in the same expression he wore after swallowing a dose of quinine. The gold/silver division was an ugly reality that repeated itself in every facet of Canal Zone life. He left the sick man with a new pair of pajamas and a small flask of whiskey — for medicinal purposes, of course.

He had just enough time to check on his deposits at the Office of Geographic Survey, stacked in a neglected heap behind so many others. Charlie smiled in satisfaction and spent a moment studying the window. The one bursting with overlapping papers, backlit by the sun. Something about them fascinated him.

"Keep up the good work," he nodded to the startled staffer on the way out.

Reassured that he could get the treasure to the Pacific and store it there indefinitely, he decided to start shipping the special pieces, like the silver spider. He pictured the strange face and pondered for the thousandth time where it came from and what it signified.

Never mind. It was time to head back to his Balboa boarding house for the night. The place was about to collapse from decay, but it had character. He'd just settled in when he heard a knock.

"Coming."

He opened the door and let a squat Englishman in — Simon, whom he'd met down by the docks.

"Ready?" Simon asked.

Charlie eased his newest purchase out of its protective case and held it up for inspection.

The Englishman took it and nodded in approval. Then he stepped to the balcony with its sea view, where the lesson commenced. "You hold it like this."

Charlie lifted the heavy sextant, admiring it. With that elegant, curved apparatus and a timepiece, he would be able to calculate his position anywhere in the world. And he'd be needing it on his upcoming trip.

He followed Simon's instructions, step by step.

"Now put the shade in front of the mirror... Set the index to zero... Point it at the sun. No, no — like this. Now swing the index arm to bring the sun's lower limb down to kiss the horizon..."

A new vocabulary — in a foreign language Charlie could comprehend. He loved it already.

"You take star sights the same way but without the shade. Do it at twilight, when the horizon is still visible."

He thrilled in his power to move the sun, the stars. All those heavenly bodies at his beck and call. After a few practice tries, Simon talked him through the calculations using the thick almanac he'd brought. A bottle of rum and an hour of practice later, Charlie wore the grin of a cat who caught a fat rat. Soon, he'd be able to stow the sextant where it belonged and put the final stages of his plan into motion.

It was all coming together. Lady Luck was on his side once more. He could practically smell California, feel the greenbacks in his hand when he traded his trinkets for hard American cash. Everything about his plan was progressing perfectly.

That was why he should have known there would be a catch. There was always a catch.

Balboa

February, present day

Kate felt strangely lopsided, waking up alone on *Aurora*. Like a ship with poorly loaded cargo, listing to one side. She sat in the cockpit feeding herself mechanically, eyes on nothing in particular. Her ankle was bent in an uncomfortable position but she left it there, martyred to her cause.

How could Nick even think about going back to Boston? She let a spoonful of cereal clatter back into her bowl, untouched. Had she only been imagining that things had been going so well? Her legs stretched out under the table and met... emptiness.

How could he?

Last night, Nick had left for Boston for the second time. To his new job. Her mind could have kicked each of those four words. He was completely swept up in the ridiculous idea of earning more money to finance some vague future trip.

You already have a boat! she'd insisted. She said it to him and repeated it to herself now. *We don't need anything! Stay...*

She felt like a character in a horror movie, trying to warn the unsuspecting victim entering a dark house without turning the lights on. *Watch out! It's a trap!* But her warning went unheard, leaving her screaming mutely as Nick marched off to his fate.

Of course, he had scrambled to find a compromise, promising that he would just complete the first phase of the project and then return to discuss their next step. That would only take three months, and they could visit in between. Seeing the look on her face, he'd hastily curtailed that to "maybe two months."

Kate wasn't fooled. She knew Nick too well. He would go back to Boston and fall prey to the seductions of working life — something so suited to his organized nature, his need for structure. He would get started on the programming project, then start tweaking the details, always seeking a more perfect product. Three months would become six. Six months would become a year. And who would shake him out of his self-induced hypnosis? Certainly not an employer, nor friends who led the same blinkered existence.

Nick. The sweetest guy on earth, but sorely lacking in vision. It was a miracle he had embarked on his sailing venture at all.

Her cereal spoon rattled against the ceramic bowl, a staccato SOS.

Yes, Nick would come back in three months. He promised he would. But he would ricochet straight back to Boston like a dog on a retractable leash. Then it would be over. *Aurora*. Blue horizons.

Them.

The wake of a passing boat slapped the hull — a bitter, brusque sound. She could kill Mark! She could kill Nick!

She stopped just a little short of resenting Nick's father and went back to cursing Mark. And computers. And Boston. Even the Red Sox, damn it!

The wind rattled the halyard running along *Aurora's* mast, provoking it into an angry tantrum until she retreated into the cabin, pacing around on some vague errand that kept slipping her mind.

Not now, Charlie, she snapped, glaring at his brown notebook on the shelf.

She snatched up the phone instead, resolving to call Nick and knock some sense into him. But her fingers fumbled over the keypad and registered a false PIN code. A second try. A growling third. The phone beeped and flashed a curt message.

LOCKED.

She hurled the device across the cabin, then winced as it smashed into pieces against the wall. Then she stared at the wreckage, wondering what else she could break to feel a little release.

In the end, she spent two days fuming, then two days moping in Balboa. Each night, she promised herself she would do better the next day. She'd take a walk along the causeway, maybe even rent a bike. Or maybe she'd get around to topping up *Aurora's* water supply. But slow, stubborn mornings stretched into uninspired afternoons and despondent evenings.

A steady succession of small sailboats trickled past, their crews exuberant upon entering a new ocean, ready to explore the world. Kate took to sitting inside *Aurora's* cabin rather than out on deck where she'd have to watch them. She avoided the yacht club for the same reason, ignoring those happy sailors out of existence.

She did listen to the radio nets, though.

"More news on that advisor's strike..." the net coordinator started.

She leaned closer to the radio. Apparently, an advisor's strike had put a complete hold on canal transits for private yachts.

"Dozens of boats are trapped on the Caribbean coast," he continued.

"I guess we squeaked through just in time," said the captain of a boat that had come through shortly after *Aurora*.

Kate snorted. Just in time for disaster to strike.

She even considered various twisted forms of revenge. Maybe she could enter into some kind of revenge pact with Mark's ex-wife. Of course, that wasn't likely to knock any sense into Nick. She sighed.

So many places waiting to be discovered, just over the horizon. But without Nick, she was stuck. Without him, all she could do was wait. Without him—

Without him, baloney.

She gave herself a good scolding. Instead of pining for Nick, she ought to be studying charts. She could damn well do things herself and get a move on. Somewhere. Anywhere!

She had her own life to live, dreams to pursue, and enough money in her account to hold out another couple of months. Hadn't she learned more than one bitter lesson in independence from her mother, grandmother — heck, from practically every woman in her family? Immigrants, all of them, their lives marked by loss, sacrifice, new starts. She was the one born in the land of the free, so she would make up for all they had forsaken. She had to, for their sake as much as her own. That's the way it had always been. She had to get an education, guard her independence, and see the world. And never, ever compromise. The generations that preceded her had done enough of that, amassing catalogs of regrets.

So, no. She would not wait around. And she would not give up on the hunt for Charlie's treasure.

But where to begin?

She pondered as she took to the water, scrubbing *Aurora's* hull. A lackluster effort, but it was a start. After an hour of work, it was time for a reward. A drink might get her into a more positive frame of mind.

Better yet, an ice cream. A big one with whipped cream. She knew the yacht club had them because she'd been pretending not to notice the full-color promotional cards for days now. Well, tonight she was going to treat herself to exactly what she wanted.

She headed ashore at sunset and scanned the yacht club, relieved not to find any familiar faces. The last thing she needed was to explain to someone where Nick was — or where Nick wasn't.

Her eyes wandered from an insect on the thatched ceiling to the muted news program on the overhead television, then to the canal. How many more freighters would pass before she accomplished anything? How long before Nick came back? And how many more seventies disco hits was the sound system going to torture her with tonight?

The television flickered with a change of scene, drawing her attention. An on-the-spot reporter in a tangled jungle setting thrust a microphone before an excited local man who jabbered away. With the sound was turned off, she couldn't make out a word, no matter how hard she strained to read lips. Behind the reporter, onlookers preened and posed, making the most of their moment of television glory. Kate was about to turn away when the camera panned to a trampled expanse pocked by small craters.

"Wait a minute..."

She caught her breath, glued to the screen. She recognized those scars. In Turkey, in Peru: she'd seen it with her own eyes. The handiwork of tomb robbers looked the same everywhere.

She strained to make sense of the visual cues. Where was it? Could be anywhere in Panama. Anywhere in Central America, really.

Someone stepped past, blocking her view of the screen. Jesus, the man was slow. Some lumbering, black-haired sailor. One of those preying fifty-year-olds who reeked of cigarettes and shady deals. The kind she avoided like the plague. She leaned hard a-starboard to keep the television in sight.

Ticker-tape letters marched across the bottom of the screen: *Nombre de Dios*. The Caribbean port used as a jumping off point for Spanish treasure fleets until Portobelo superseded it, way back when.

She put the pieces of the mute puzzle together with a jolt. Tomb robbers at work, here in Panama. Searching for treasure. Her right eyelid started to twitch.

Between the scenes on the television and a hasty internet search, she pieced more of the story together. Modern-day treasure hunters had ripped an area of the historic port to shreds. Rumor said they'd found nothing, and no new artifacts were reported to be trickling on to the antiquities scene.

Not yet, anyway.

But that was only a minor consolation, because someone out there was looking for Spanish treasure. Probably someone inspired by the sensationalist author, Richard Brewster Lewis, a crook posing as a historian if she ever saw one. Maybe the tomb robbers went home empty-handed this time, but they would try again. It was only a matter of time before they hit the bull's-eye.

Kate took a deep breath and clenched her teeth. No way was she going to let that happen. Not to Charlie's treasure.

No way.

Chapter Fourteen

Hunger Drives the Wolf

Balboa

February, present day

Lucien Dubois ambled toward the bar at Balboa Yacht Club, shaking a cigarette out of a crumpled box as he went. His eyes darted about warily. He preferred staying out of public places, but he had little choice. It was like that old saying.

La faim chasse le loup hors du bois, he thought. *Hunger drives the wolf out of the woods.*

He was down to the second to last of his Gauloises and his last hundred dollars. Slicking his hair back, he let his lips curl in a bitter smile. Yes, he was hungry — hungry for a new chance, ever since he'd lost his boat on a reef in the San Blas, along with the most lucrative deal of his life. Two hundred kilos of cocaine left behind on *Persephone*, along with the body of the ex-partner who had tried to double-cross him.

Killing hadn't been the hard part. Abandoning *Persephone* was. She had been his entire existence, his future. The two-hundred-kilo deal would have earned enough for him to sail easy for a long time. He could have sailed to Tahiti, then hung a hammock among the palms and lived the good life.

Watching that dream crumble away — that had been rock bottom. He'd never lost a boat before. In fact, he'd lost everything — everything but his patience. Years on the sea had taught him that.

Lucien ordered a mojito, eyeing a spider in the eves. A sign of good luck, and just in time for a man creating a new plan. He just needed to suffer through these shoals, as it were, and then he'd be on his way — far away from Panama and the cartel men who would kill him on sight.

He toyed with his cigarette box, trying to reassure himself. He had a new identity now. A new look. And he was on a new coast.

He had a plan for getting out of Panama soon. He had already secured a new vessel. That part was easy. There were a dozen abandoned boats on the moorings here in Balboa, and the yacht club was all too willing to believe that he really had appeared on the owner's behalf. No one would ask questions when the hulk named *Island Dreams* sailed away.

Yes, somebody's broken dream was his new beginning. It would be a week before anyone noticed that boat was missing, which was long enough to get out of Panama. He'd sail for Mexico, where there was always work to be found. Soon enough, he'd find another promising deal — one he'd execute alone, this time — and then he could head to Tahiti at last.

That was his plan. But a good plan, like a good wine, had to mature.

The drink came, and he took it to a corner table. He kept one eye on the door, as always, while the other scanned the scenery — the female kind — while his mind ticked over his options.

His new boat was no *Persephone*, but she would have to do. For now. Lucien squeezed lime into his drink to fend off the image of his lovely sloop agape on a reef back in the San Blas. So much work he'd put into her, and now he had to start all over with a new boat — one with an inch of bird shit cemented over the deck.

He shifted his focus to the cruising boats moored below and thought it all through. Perhaps he ought to modify his plan. Why toil on a near-wreck when there were other boats? Good ones, ready to sail away. One candidate was already there, ripe for the picking. The Valiant 32 near his mooring. An unobtrusive design with a deep keel full of hidden crannies he could take advantage of. He could take that boat and sail away.

It even came with a woman — the one sitting over there. The one with the long legs and eyes glued to the television. He'd seen her climb out of the water earlier, dripping like a sea nymph after cleaning the hull. Clearly, she knew how to maintain a boat. Who knows what else she might be willing to do for him?

He could take her boat. And if she didn't cooperate, it would be easy enough to pop her over the head and toss the body into the sea. Wouldn't be the first American to wash up dead in Panama. Wouldn't be the last.

She was alone. What could be easier?

It was certainly an option. He could strip down *Island Dreams* and get some cash. Radar, GPS, autopilot. Lines, anchor chain. Everything. That would bring him a few hundred dollars, perhaps even a thousand. Then he'd take that thirty-two footer, with or without the girl, and head to Mexico. Eventually, he could trade it in for something else and get back to business.

An option. A tempting one.

But Lucien knew well enough not to rush into any plan. He would weigh it all up and leave his options open for now. For now, he'd study the woman and the boat. The sea had taught him patience. He could wait for the right opportunity to come along.

He settled back in his chair, puffed out a cloud of smoke, and studied his target.

Balboa
February, present day

Grave robbers.

Nombre de Dios.

Illicit digs for ancient artifacts.

The news did nothing to lift Kate's mood. On the contrary, that was just one more thing out of her control. She knew she had to act fast if she was going to save Charlie's treasure. But where to look? She could do nothing but fret and curse, exactly as she did over Nick.

She tossed her book across the cabin and let out a heavy sigh. What she needed was a change of scenery.

She slid into the seat at the chart table and studied the possibilities. She would damn well sail *Aurora* somewhere, even if she had to do it alone.

"Taboga," she said, trying to sound resolute.

The small island lay just ten miles away, beyond the city's noise and grit. A sleepy little beach town that swelled with weekend visitors but otherwise lapsed into a languid stupor, that's what she heard. It would do for starters. She resolved to head out and do what she was in Panama for — to sail, to explore, to have fun. She'd force herself to have fun. And with a clearer mind, she might finally crack Charlie's riddles.

She spent an entire day preparing for the trip as if it were a perilous passage instead of a mere jaunt. But it would be her first time handling *Aurora* alone, not to mention navigating a hulking fleet of cargo ships. Suddenly, her mind rebelled with a slew of doubts. What if something happened? What if a ship didn't see her? What if the weather turned?

Tomorrow, she resolved. She'd depart for Taboga tomorrow.

Four days later, she finally did it, waking up early and waging an inner battle against a wimpy voice that urged her not to leave. *Not today. Some other time...*

She fought it back with a mantra she repeated over and over. *Easy as pie. Easy as pie.*

And it was, in principle. But everything was rushed, and a feeling of impending doom shadowed her every move. She dropped the mooring at *Aurora's* bow, then raced back to the wheel to gun the engine before the current pushed the boat into one of her neighbors. Then she motored out of the narrow channel, eyes darting everywhere: forward, backward, up to the wind arrow on the mast top. Once in the open Bay of Panama, she raised the mainsail. *Aurora's* boom seemed to dislike the sailing arrangement as much as she did and demonstrated its displeasure by bashing more violently than usual. The mast seemed especially tall, the sail leaden. It didn't help that the boat was waked by a passing ferry at exactly that moment, too.

Sweating and cursing, she scurried back to the cockpit and sheeted in the mainsail. Then she unfurled the genoa in the light morning breeze, stretching her arms wide between the wheel and the line. Okay, so she overtrimmed it. Those were minor details, especially in light of the thirty-plus freighters blocking her path. *Aurora* made the first of many zigs and zags as her sole crew eyed the bay. Had it always been this packed?

The breeze was fair, the sea relatively quiet, yet Kate clutched the wheel in anticipation of some major disaster. Was that cargo ship about to weigh anchor, or was it just waiting? The yellow buoy off the port bow was a special marker that could mean almost anything. She eyed it suspiciously. A wreck? A no-anchor zone?

The ten most stressful sailing miles of her life crawled by like the sloth she'd seen back in the jungle. Three long hours later, she dropped the sails and circled Taboga's wide bay under engine, wavering between moorings. Which to take? The simple choice took on epic proportions, a thousand possible outcomes hanging on this one decision. Finally, she maneuvered up to a mooring ball and raced forward to snag it with the boat hook, wishing once again for Nick. Where was he when she needed him?

"Shit," she muttered.

She was too late — the mooring ball was already slipping out of reach. She stubbed her toe on the way back to the wheel, cursing the whole way. On the second try, she hooked the line, pulled it up on deck and dropped the loop over the cleat. And briefly, her spirits soared. She had done it! Her first solo sail and *Aurora's* first foray into the Pacific. She'd just proven she could do it: go anywhere, do anything...

Alone.

She found herself drooping at the bow, listening to her wildly thumping heart. There was no swell of pride, no triumph. All she felt was relief — and incomplete relief, at that. More like a void. If this is how Nick felt when he was sailing alone, she couldn't blame him for nearly giving up.

Shelter Bay
February, present day

In Shelter Bay Marina on the Caribbean side of Panama, the booze was flowing generously. Happy hour had come and gone, as had dinner, dessert, and most of the patrons. But a tipsy trio of sailors was still at it when the bartender made his last call.

"Two more rums," Alejandro called, prodding Tyler into polishing off his last one.

Tyler looked more than happy to oblige. After all, his new best friend from South America was paying. He and Trevor were surrounded by at least a dozen glasses. Alejandro, on the other hand, had only one.

"Yeah, mate. Two more!" Trevor called to the bartender, holding up three fingers.

Alejandro nodded Tyler back into continuing his tale. "You said something about his father?"

Tyler hiccupped. "His grandfather."

Trevor poked his friend, nearly knocking over his glass in doing so. "Gr-great-grandfather."

A bird screeched in the jungle, just beyond the marina lights. Tyler pointed back at Trevor, and the two nodded sagely at each other.

"Precisely," Tyler slurred. "His great-grandfather."

Alejandro kept his voice low. "Nick's great-grandfather worked on the Panama Canal... and what else?"

"On the canal, mate." Tyler exchanged a look with Trevor that said, *What a wanker!*

Alejandro ignored them, staying focused on his goal. "Nothing else?"

The night air was humid. Thin clouds swept over the face of the gibbous moon.

"I had a great-grandfather who fought in Gallipoli," Trevor began and would have continued at length if Alejandro hadn't butted in.

Yes, he knew a thing or two about accomplished family members. He'd come from a long line of greats in his country's history. Pioneers, presidents, business moguls. But pride alone was a hollow claim to fame. The trick was to exceed your forefather's deeds with your own — something he doubted these two Australians understood.

He steered them back to the subject. "Nothing about... something of great value?"

Both men gave Alejandro blank looks. Tyler leaned heavily to port. Trevor's eyes were at half-mast.

Alejandro tried again. "A lot of money?"

Trevor pepped up. "Where?"

"Maybe silver?"

Trevor chortled. "That man's almost as broke as we are, mate!" He nudged Tyler for approval, only to find his friend staring vaguely at the forest of masts crowding the bay, their halyards slapping in the wind. "Man, you are so pissed!" he giggled.

"So pissed," Trevor echoed.

Alejandro sighed. The men were stone drunk. It was an easy enough matter to wheedle information out of an unsuspecting fool or a drunk, but unsuspecting fools who were also drunk did not make the best informants.

He gave it one last try. "Gold?"

Trevor rubbed his head with two heavy hands, then aimed for his rum glass. Alejandro sat back, lips pursed.

"I'll tell you one thing," Trevor confided suddenly.

Alejandro leaned forward in anticipation.

"That bloke," Trevor said, stabbing his finger at each word, "is a genius at wiring," he concluded, nodding solemnly. "Nick grounded the radio to the bloody water tank in one day. One day!" The Australian folded his arms and sat back, giving the remark the gravity it deserved.

Not exactly what Alejandro was hoping to learn. He sighed as Tyler toppled into his shoulder, eyes glazed. "Maybe I should take you two back to your boat."

Trevor giggled and finished off his drink, then fell into a coughing fit while Alejandro helped Tyler up. He saw the two men down to their dock, where they stumbled past, then looped uncertainly back to *Free Willy*.

"Ladies first," Tylor mumbled to Trevor.

"That's you, mate."

"Age before beauty."

"Shit before the shovel," Trevor retorted, and they both folded into giggles again.

Alejandro watched them clamber over the lifelines with the fascination of a circus audience watching a trapeze artist taking a death-defying leap. Somehow, the duo made it on board, if not into the cabin. Tyler passed out on the cockpit floor. Trevor slumped beside him, singing a song about wenches and wrenches.

Alejandro turned and walked back to B dock. He paused to admire *Carmela's* sleek hull and custom awnings. She was beautiful, a slumbering siren — nothing like the plastic toys around her. *Carmela* had style.

He wiped his dock shoes carefully before stepping aboard. They were made for one other, he and *Carmela*. They were the samba stars who dazzled the dance floor, while sailors like Trevor and Tyler were the line dancers — loud and fun, but lacking any grace.

Would he call his evening a success? Partial, at best. But that was the nature of the hunt. Like a fox, he knew when to wait, when to plan, and when to pounce. Step by step, he would inch closer to his goal.

No, it wouldn't be easy. But easy didn't make things fun.

Chapter Fifteen

New Acquaintances

Isla Taboga
February, present day

The wind shifted slightly, and Kate's quiet Taboga anchorage became a roller coaster. Going on deck after a one-pot spaghetti dinner, she found the wind was coming straight into the bay, and what began as an uncomfortable nodding motion soon turned into violent bucking. It was too late to move, too, so she opted for wishing it away, though her efforts were as effective as wishing for Nick back. Soon, the horizon was heaving up and down. Kate burrowed deeper into a novel, pretending she wasn't worried.

She spent the night popping in and out of bed, chasing rattling ghosts from the cupboards. Each time she wedged herself back into the bunk, a new onslaught of worries descended. Had she tied the snubber line properly? What about chafe? A midnight trip to the bow, clutching at the lifelines, assured her that the line was fine. But no sooner was she back in bed than her imagination got to work again, conjuring new disasters in every corner of the boat. It struck her for the first time that Nick might have been plagued by this very phenomenon all those nights while she slept soundly. Not that she'd never checked the anchor before — it was just that Nick always seemed to beat her to it, the same way he hijacked so many of the repair jobs. That was the problem with living with a compulsive worrywart.

She pulled the bedsheets closer, wondering if she was being too hard on Nick or too easy on herself. Maybe being with Nick was making her soft. Maybe it was good to be on her own, to toughen up again.

The night dragged by in restless hours punctuated by jolts that proved she had indeed fallen into fitful handfuls of sleep. The fifth or sixth time she woke up, it was daylight, and the jerking motion had ceased. She ventured into the cockpit and blinked at the green of Taboga. The wind had shifted away, shepherding the whitecaps in some other direction. The morning sky was a bold sweep of blue. *Aurora's* white deck glittered with dew.

It was beautiful.

Her relief was short-lived, however, because she discovered soon after that the toilet pump had jammed. She managed to disassemble it without any screaming or curses, feeling too drained to put up a fight. A dozen plastic parts spread before her, none showing any similarity to the diagram in the manual. But if the goddess of love was playing tricks on her, the god of plumbing took a kinder view. Two hours later, she treated herself to not three but four cookies as she admired the reassembled toilet pump. Her first solo sail on *Aurora*, and now, her first solo repair.

Somehow, though, she couldn't quite summon any enthusiasm for her feat. Just the opposite, in fact.

A nap, that's what she needed.

When she stirred again hours later, Taboga called with alluring, innocent sounds. The swish of waves on the sand, the song of laughter along the beach, the cries of teenagers daring each other to dive from a dock. She forced herself ashore to ramble the pretty village with its crooked lanes and whitewashed church, a startling white against the brilliant sky. A hike to the top of the green hills opened wide views of the modern city to the east. To the west lay the low, brown bumps of more islands — the Las Perlas archipelago. This was the perfect place to plan her next steps...

...if only she had any idea what they might be.

It was a novel dilemma. She usually suffered from the reverse — too many plans, too many things to see or accomplish in a single lifetime. Adventures and an unconventional, independent lifestyle. That's what she had always wanted.

Independence? She laughed bitterly at herself. *Be careful what you wish for.*

It was Arizona, all over again. She'd left Nick for a promising new horizon, only to find herself unable to enjoy it without him. Just like now. She could sail *Aurora* without Nick, but she didn't want to.

Love. Sometimes the games it played weren't all that fun.

She gradually ceased cursing Nick and widened the search for perpetrators. Was it her fault? Had she driven him away? Or was it *Aurora*'s constant need for attention?

Nick. *Aurora*. Charlie. He was part of this journey, too. The covert excavations at Nombre de Dios meant that someone else was after treasure — maybe even Charlie's treasure. If only she could make sense of his incomplete clues. What exactly had Charlie found? How valuable was it?

She slammed the thought shut. If she somehow managed to find Charlie's coins — not to mention something as precious as a Sipán-style spider — there was no way she could sell them. She was no grave robber. She was an archaeologist. A piece like the spider would be a major find, a revelation. It would make an archaeologist's career.

Her career?

She paused, digesting the thought.

Far below, the steel blue of the sea teased her with endless possibilities. Should she trade the treasure and the sailing lifestyle for Nick and a humdrum existence? Or take up the chase, even if she had to do it alone?

Down in the bay, *Aurora* rested quietly on her mooring, refusing to take sides.

Her eyes shifted, looking for something to clear her mind. She found it in a splotch of color, far below. A red-hulled boat was taking the mooring next to *Aurora*. It was the Dutch ketch, *ANNA*, with Anneliese, Nils, and their children, Nya and Adam. They'd briefly crossed paths in Portobelo. When she rowed over later to welcome them to Taboga, the couple promptly invited her to dinner. They were warm, funny, and easygoing, and immediately took Kate under their wing.

"Want to come to the beach?" Anneliese called the next morning.

Kate hopped in the *ANNA*'s dinghy, thankful for the good company and the distraction. The kids played in the sand while the adults chatted and admired sand castles on cue. Kate was fascinated by the interplay between Nils, Anneliese, and the children. So many cruisers were retired couples. Others were happy-go-lucky youngsters like Trevor and Tyler — people she could laugh with but not really connect to. Here, at last, was a thirty-something pair that fit into her own age bracket. They were out on the adventure of their lives, kids included, and evidently delighting in it.

She and Anneliese hit it off immediately. Finally — finally! — a woman sailor her own age! And from the looks of it, a very capable one, too.

"Wow. You're taking three years off work." Kate tried not to sigh as she said it. "That's great. What do you do?"

"I'm a teacher," Anneliese said, "English for high school students."

It figured. The woman's English was perfect.

"Nils is an accountant. We can just manage this trip, but then we have to get back to work."

Nils leaned in with a smile. "We'll be poor again by then."

Anneliese shook her head. "No, we'll be rich. Rich in memories."

Kate nodded in hearty agreement, wishing Nick were there to hear someone other than herself preach the gospel of a life well lived.

"Where's Nic—" Nils asked, then grimaced when Anneliese elbowed his ribs. At least one of them had noticed something missing aboard *Aurora*. "I mean, where are you sailing next?"

Kate debated whether to go for the blunt truth — *I wish I knew* — or blatant lie: *Las Perlas, then Ecuador, then the Galapagos Islands. Watch out, world, here I come!*

Five years ago, she might even have convinced herself of that. Now, she wasn't so sure.

"I'm kind of limbo right now." She kept it to that, although the dialogue continued inside.

I'm sort of waiting. Waiting until... She struggled to finish the sentence.

Until what?
Until Nick comes back.
What if he doesn't come back? What then?
I can do it. I made it here, right?
Here is only ten miles off the coast.
One step at a time.

You're really going to take off alone?
Why not?
Why?

That one had her stumped. The joy of sailing hadn't stemmed from the boat so much as sailing with Nick.

Her shoulders sagged. A good thing the children came over just then in search of a referee for their latest disagreement. Nya wanted to decorate the sand castle with seashells, but Adam wanted to build higher. Anneliese was quick to offer a solution which seemed to placate them both, and Nils hopped into action, bringing back the children's laughter by digging like a dog.

Kate observed the family quietly, admiring Anneliese's vivacity and calm. She wondered if she could ever pull off such an adventure — not just having kids in the first place, but sailing with kids. Her mouth hardened at the intimidating thought and its logical pursuant. Nick. So far away.

Anneliese must have caught her at it, because she rooted around in her beach bag and pulled out a phone. "Would you like to use it?" she offered. "We can call anywhere for five cents a minute."

Kate reached for the phone, then pulled her hand back. "Oh, it's okay."

"Really, feel free."

"Oh, I couldn't."

"Of course, you could. Call anyone you like."

Yep, Anneliese had figured her out. But the stubborn side of her made her wave it away casually. "I'll wait. But thanks." She didn't need to call anyone. She was fine here on Taboga with her new friends.

Anneliese, however, still held out the phone. Kate held back for one short moment before snatching it right out of her hand and punching in Nick's number.

"Hello?" his voice answered. Two thousand miles away, but undeniably Nick, warm and sincere.

She struggled to get words past the strange twist in her throat. Nick was so far away. The connection wasn't very clear, and suddenly she couldn't piece together a sequence of coherent thoughts.

All she managed was a little mumbling about weather and Taboga. Then a long, empty silence.

"Kate!" Nils called from a few steps away. "We're going to lunch," he said, pointing at a restaurant with a *we'll-meet-there* motion. She nodded and turned her attention back to Nick, telling him about her new friends. If only the connection weren't so choppy.

"I miss you," she sniffed, hating the weakness in her voice.

With a crackle, the connection broke. She grimaced and squeezed the phone hard before remembering it wasn't hers to break. She turned to gaze at *Aurora* bobbing sadly in the bay.

Balboa

September 1913

As far as Charlie was concerned, she was a perfect ten. Curves in all the right places. Tall, well-built. The frame of an athlete with a touch of feminine grace. Just beautiful.

Yolanta lay in the placid waters of Panama Bay, calling to him like a siren. Just $160 and the little cutter would be his. A hard-bargained $158 and one bottle of rum later, she really was his, all twenty-seven feet of her.

Yolanta came with the name and a warning that changing it would bring bad luck.

"No problem!" he chirped, signing off on the paperwork.

He bustled aboard with his sextant, a clock, and a mind full of dreams. He set immediately to work, exploring the small cabin with the excitement of a child in a new tree house. His cabin! All his! There was even a small chart table with a bench and an equally small galley. Built into the center of the cabin was a narrow bunk and a table that could be raised out of the way. He flipped it up and got on his knees to remove the floorboards. There was enough space down there to stash his silver. The dynamite boxes would just fit, and the load would stay out of sight plus serve a double function as ballast.

"Perfect." Charlie congratulated himself on his brilliant plan and stood, smashing his head on the low ceiling.

Good thing he had a hard head.

He took out his notebook and jotted a few words. He needed creosote to keep the boxes watertight. Charts, too. Then he took out the silver spider and hooked it on a protruding nail over the chart table. The face leered at him, but Charlie was too stubborn to hide the piece away. It was his ticket to a silver-lined future, together with the boat.

He sniffed the air. Wait. Was that wood rot?

A seagull called, promising him it was just the salt air, the sea.

He shook his head. What he needed was a test run. That would teach him how to handle the boat, right?

He went on deck and tried to make sense of all the lines while imagining himself gliding in and out of anchorages all the way up the coast, just the way he'd seen the fishermen in Taboga do. That he had no sailing experience whatsoever didn't particularly strike him as a handicap. It would all be very straightforward. He would learn by doing, the best way.

A light breeze wafted over the deck, and for a second, Charlie wondered if he'd heard a mocking laugh in it.

He pulled up the heavy, gaff-rigged mainsail, and it flapped in confusion. Then he threw off the mooring line and shuffled back to the stern, ducking when the unsecured boom took a swipe at him. Standing at the wheel waiting for something to happen, Charlie felt very nautical. He looked around expectantly as the sail filled and *Yolanta* eased away from the mooring.

"Nothing to it." He grinned to himself.

The heavy timber hull rapidly gained momentum. He relished the sensation of cantering over the ocean with the wind in his hair. And those strange rattling noises from below? Well, he'd see to that later.

When he spotted Taboga on the horizon, he decided to steer toward the birthplace of his brilliant plan — Taboga. *Yolanta* sliced through the water, throwing up a froth at her bow. It was beautiful. Charlie stood like a goat on a hill, one leg straight, the other bent, counteracting the boat's angle of heel.

"Charlie the sailor," he called out to the wind.

Overcome with sudden inspiration, he lashed the wheel, went forward to raise the jib, and succeeded on the third try. Now they were really romping along. He could already picture sweeping into San Francisco Bay, his pretty cutter turning heads that marveled at how far she and her intrepid captain had come.

"Let's put you through your paces, old girl."

Twirling the wheel to the left with a flourish, he watched *Yolanta's* upswept bow swing around slowly, then faster. The sail flapped uncertainly before filling from the other side with an audible snap, and the boom followed. There was a crash and the sound of splintering wood, but his eyes were locked on the sea, now gushing over the side of the deck in frothy green furrows. The wind was pulling the boat over....over....

"Whoa."

He spun the wheel like an amusement park spinner to see what might come of it. The boat righted, wavered, and sped off in the opposite direction. A wave slapped the stern, soaking him as he fiddled with the bewildering tangle of lines crowding the cockpit like a nest of snakes. *Yolanta* had the bit in her teeth by then and was careening wildly toward the rocks off Flamenco Island. He gazed down the twenty-seven-foot deck wondering what to try next, but nothing he did seemed to placate her temper.

"No wonder boats are female," he muttered under his breath.

Eventually, he spun the wheel until he found a point of balance more to his liking and glanced around for his mooring. Maybe that was enough for one day. A few crashing gybes and stalled tacks later, and he was almost home free. But he overshot the mooring and missed the line. That is to say, *he* missed. *Yolanta* caught the line with her rudder. With the sails still pulling the boat ahead, it became a tug-of-war between wind and water, *Yolanta* straining to get free.

He untied lines at random until the gaff came smashing down and an acre of flapping canvas swamped the deck.

When everything finally settled down, Charlie plopped down in the small, wet cockpit. Maybe, just maybe, his brilliant plan was going to be a little harder to realize than he had imagined.

Boston

February, present day

I miss you, too, Nick was about to mumble when the phone connection broke. A man's voice had called Kate away, and she mumbled something about friends. What friends?

He put the phone down and stared at it. Kate was in some place called... Tabago? With friends. A friend?

"Thanks," he nodded as a colleague put a printout on his desk and made some comment about the time. But his focus was several thousand miles away. Two thousand three hundred sixty-two miles, to be precise. He'd looked it up on Google.

Twice.

What friend?

He fought the thought away with his most effective countermeasure: work. Online multiplayer gaming posed a minefield of issues for network security, and he was only now getting to the crux of the old system's weaknesses. In fact, he tunneled so deeply into work that he barely heard a voice calling.

"Uh, Nick, would it be okay to wrap up now?"

That was Ralf, the new guy in the group Nick headed up.

He looked at the clock. Nine o'clock already? The rest of the office was dim.

"Do you want to check?" Ralf turned his screen around.

They went over the latest updates to the code, and Nick nodded, impressed. The kid was a quick study and a hard worker.

"Want a ride?" Ralf asked as he pulled on his jacket.

Nick glanced outside. He shook his head and stood. "No thanks, I'll walk."

Ralf gave him a look like the only thing crazier would be to hitch up a team of dogs and sled home.

"See you tomorrow."

Nick ducked his head into his collar, locked the office door, and stepped outside. It was mild for a February evening but still frigid by Panama standards, with a penetrating dampness that trickled from his toes to his body. He walked along, tipping his head back to study the sky. All he caught was a brief glimpse of a planet before a cloud obscured the view. It was definitely a planet: too big and too bright to be anything else. But which? Saturn? Jupiter? He ached for a nautical almanac to look it up.

"Damn," he murmured, looking around.

The moon was hiding, too. Apparently, all his old friends were avoiding him these days. Was it nearing the quarter, or had that been last week? Somehow, he had lost track. Land life had showers, microwaves, and commuter lanes but no sense of what phase the moon was in.

And, damn. What friend?

He hung his head. There were goof-ups, there were mistakes, and there was... this. He'd managed to orchestrate no less than a first-class disaster. He'd utterly failed to show Kate the logic of his plan. He'd completely antagonized her, letting things end badly.

But surely she would come to appreciate the beauty of the idea. Lucky breaks like his new job didn't come often. He'd been in the right place at the right time. He could save money, and time would whiz by. Three months — even three years — would pass in a flash, and he would have a nice new boat to show for it. Surely Kate could buy in to that idea.

And anyway, he'd let enough promising opportunities slip by. This programming job was his chance to leave his mark on something. Hadn't Charlie done the same thing? The man rambled around the world, always seeking a chance — *the* chance. And what about Cory, the childhood classmate whose death had sparked his entire sailing caper. The fear of dying young and leaving nothing behind was gradually giving way to a fear of growing old without ever having accomplished anything to truly take pride in.

And as for Charlie's treasure — purported treasure, that is — even if it existed, finding it would be like a needle in a haystack. A needle in the jungle, actually. Charlie's treasure wasn't Nick's big chance. This job was. He would be stupid to let it go.

Ralf pulled over and rolled down the window of his Honda. "You sure you don't want a ride home?"

Nick shook his head and waved good-bye, pondering the meaning of home. He'd bought some work clothes, joined a gym, and moved into the one-room unit over Mark's garage in Somerville. His decorating efforts consisted of one small photo — the one Mayumi had taken of him and Kate going through the canal. Did that make it home?

"God, this is even smaller than my place in Manhattan," his sister Nancy had said when she first saw it.

He'd just shrugged. "Reminds me of *Aurora*." Sort of.

"I thought you were earning good money again."

"I'm saving for a bigger boat."

Nancy had given him the same look everyone else did. *Sure. Right.*

"It's not forever. Pretty soon, I'll visit Panama and see Kate. And by then she'll..."

"She'll what?"

"She'll see what I mean."

Nancy rolled her eyes and muttered something about the density of male brain matter.

"We're going sailing again," he insisted. "Just a little later. In a better, bigger boat."

"Right."

Of course he would. Wouldn't he?

He walked through nighttime Cambridge, weighing up life on shore versus life on a boat. On land, he could drink water straight out of any tap. Everyone spoke English, so he could order a sandwich for lunch and get exactly what he wanted. He could sleep all night without waking up to check the anchor. In theory, at least. In practice, he still found himself waking to check nothing in particular.

Overall, though, he was back in his world — and here, he knew how things worked. No weather worries or equipment failures. Days unfolded with a comforting predictability, especially since the news was full of issues that seemed to have grown to epic proportions since the last time he looked. Suddenly he felt very glad to have a job, insurance, and a savings plan. You never knew.

It was a world in which ideas of sailing away and pursuing lost treasures seemed like reckless fantasy. Letting things settle down would be a good thing. Kate would see the light and join him in Boston soon. Two or three years from now would be a better time to play sailor. In a nice forty-footer. Maybe even a ketch. In the meantime, he could set new standards with his security program and make a name for himself and the small group he led. It would all work out.

Or would it?

He made a face. For all the positives, there were things he missed, too — and not just Kate. He was slowly losing track of important things, like the phase of the moon or the current weather synopsis. He had vowed to keep an eye on the weather in Panama — after all, Kate was down there, alone on *Aurora*. She could handle anything, but he wanted to stay attuned to her world. But that was proving difficult. Even the local weather in Boston was hard to keep up with. How far was the low pressure system that would bring the next snowfall? Where was the following high?

He walked faster, telling himself it didn't matter. In this world, he was cocooned safely behind layers of brick and mortar, polypropylene and Gore-Tex.

Cocooned. That was the only problem he had these days. It felt like his mind was wrapped in thick layers of gauze. Cozy, yet disorienting, like lying in bed half awake in the early hours of the morning. Sometimes he felt as if he might never drag himself out.

A car beeped, and he jerked out of his reverie. His shoes scraped the brick sidewalk as an expanse of mud and grass opened to his left. Cambridge Common was empty and gray with late winter, but he remembered it freshly mowed in spring, when his buddy Eli had first dragged him there.

"You're coming," Eli had insisted.

"I have work to do!"

"You're coming whether you like it or not."

"I have a deadline…"

Eli tugged harder. "You'll like it. You need it."

"I need to work."

Nick liked Ultimate Frisbee, he really did. It's just that he didn't have the time. That is, until he made the acquaintance of an animated archaeologist at left wing. After that, he had attended the sessions regularly, even religiously. Kate played hard and fast, cutting and faking, grinning wildly except when she was concentrating on a pass. He remembered her face, flush not with the exertion but with the thrill of the competition. The same expression she wore so often as *Aurora* cantered through the ocean.

He blinked; the field was dead and empty. Winter again.

A bus drove past, sending a frigid splash across him and into the muddy void. It was a long, wet walk to the apartment.

Funny how he still couldn't think of it as home.

Isla Taboga

February, present day

"Wow, there are a lot of people here today," Anneliese said to Kate as they looked at the crowd that had grown around them on the beach.

Weekends brought scores of day-trippers to Taboga, where Kate and the *ANNAs* had started to consider a patch of the beach their own. She watched the kids cavorting in the shallows and remembered summer days when she and her siblings had engaged in the same Jekyll-Hyde blend of bickering and play as the children she saw now.

The thought summoned an image of Nick visiting his family, and suddenly she felt wistful for her own. Maybe she could afford a quick visit home? She shook the thought off immediately. No, she was in Panama and enjoying every minute of it. Yes, she was. And even if she could afford a ticket home, her family was not tidily packaged into one central location. Not like Nick's, who were all happily settled within spitting distance of the nest. No, it wouldn't be that easy. Her mother was on one coast, her sister on another, her brother in between, each of them following their own once-in-a-lifetime opportunities, just as it should be. And Kate was down here in sunny Panama, doing what she wanted, when she wanted.

She gave herself a firm nod. Yes, everything was as it should be.

Anneliese must have been half psychic, because she pulled out her phone again and handed it over before stepping away to splash with Nils and the kids. Kate hesitated over the touch pad for a good minute before deciding which of two numbers to dial. Boston or New York? When her finger started, it followed a pattern she'd known for all her life.

Her mother, bless her, was not at all concerned about Nick's absence. And why should she be? The woman had stood on her own two feet for decades and trusted Kate to do the same. She breezed right over that subject and started her usual barrage of questions about the sights, sounds, textures of everything Kate was seeing and doing. The woman was busy as a bee, though, and couldn't talk for long.

See? Kate told herself. Her mother was fine on her own. Her own person. And Kate would be the same.

Anneliese took the phone back with a smile. "Everything good at home?"

Kate nodded. "Everything great. My mom is retiling her bathroom as we speak."

Anneliese settled back down on her towel and waited a beat before continuing. "How's Nick? How's the job?"

Kate kept her eyes firmly on the bay. "Good. I guess. I don't know. I only called my mom."

Nya was kicking and calling from the shallows, and Anneliese waved back. "You miss him?" she asked without turning her head.

Kate sucked in a long, slow breath. "Sure, I miss him. A little. But it won't be long, I guess."

The words sounded meek, even to her own ears. She started tunneling her feet into the sand and decided to go with honesty, even if she could only manage that in a whisper. "I have to keep reminding myself that I don't actually need him."

"We all need someone," Anneliese replied just as quietly. She held the phone in clear view — an open invitation to make a second call.

Kate wrapped her arms around her knees and rolled out a kink in her neck. Having choices in life could be an agonizing luxury. Deciding what to do — or what not to do.

She lifted her face to the sky and sniffed once, twice.

"Wind's shifting, wouldn't you say?"

* * *

The wind did shift, making the anchorage turn bumpy overnight. Kate slipped the mooring lines in the morning and followed the red-hulled *ANNA* back to Balboa. It was good to have friends to follow like a beacon, and not just in the nautical sense. Without them, she would have wallowed indecisively at a hundred daily junctures.

Getting back to the city proved as straightforward, yet as taxing as getting out had been. When she secured the mooring line at Balboa Yacht Club to *Aurora's* bow, she wondered if she would ever find the nerve to go through another solo sailing exercise. At the very least, her first singlehanded voyage — modest though it might be — deserved the reward of a cold drink. She hailed the water taxi and made her way to land, then sat alone in a corner of the open-air clubhouse, watching her soda glass leave a succession of wet rings on the Formica. She vaguely registered the rising moon. It would trim down to a slender crescent over the coming days. A wispy cloud passed over it, proof that the scheming wind was up to something.

Her Panama guidebook lay open before her, but her eyes rested on some vague point above it. She tapped her fingers in a staccato pattern that said, *Nick, Nick, Nick.*

God, she remembered how tough she used to feel. Dammit, she'd backpacked all over South America alone. Turkey, too. What had happened to her?

Pretty obvious, she decided. She'd gotten a taste of greener pastures, that's what. Good times with Nick. Sharing the load, through thick and through thin. Sharing the views, the laughs, the worries. She let her head drop to one hand, propped up by an elbow and went back to studying charts, looking for some omen or sign of what to do.

"Hello again," came a voice.

She raised her head, pulling the small world of Balboa Yacht Club back into focus.

The face was familiar, somehow. A youngish, sandy-haired man. Slight accent. Heavy-rimmed glasses. Shirt tucked neatly into pants.

Definitely not a sailor.

The reporter from Shelter Bay.

"S...Stefan," she recalled.

He seemed pleased that she recognized him. "You are... Kate." He remembered, too. "Do you perhaps have a moment?"

She motioned to the seat across from her. She happened to have many moments.

He sat down. "I must thank you. You made me an excellent suggestion, to take a small boat to Colombia."

"Did you go?"

Did I ever, his face radiated as he plunged into a report on his trip. "No two-hundred-kilo drug deals to witness, of course. No wrecks, like the *Persephone*. But many interesting encounters."

Stefan looked supremely satisfied, brimming with news. It was an aspect of the reporter she wouldn't have guessed at during their first meeting: the excited little boy, eager to share an amazing new discovery.

He spun a tale that had her alternatively agape, amazed, and in stitches of laughter. The drug world seemed to be in upheaval after losing not only two hundred kilos of cocaine in the *Persephone* wreck, but also in a recent bust near Panama City.

"Seriously?" she gaped. Man, had she missed a lot of news.

He wrapped the story up and turned things back over to her. "So, it seems you have transited the canal."

Her mouth went dry. Yes, she'd transited the canal. A million years ago, it felt like.

"And what was it like?" His hands motioned impatiently, an old friend waiting for her to fill him in on everything he missed.

Kate groped awkwardly through her memory, trying to separate interesting facts from sensitive thoughts, like the satisfaction she had shared with Nick upon entering the Pacific. Gradually, though, she warmed up to the topic and the glow of the experience rekindled.

The reporter pressed her for more details, using the opportunity to follow up for his terror threat story. Was there a freighter in the locks at the same time as her boat? What security measures did she observe? Had anyone inspected *Aurora* prior to her transit?

Yes, a big freighter. No, not too many security measures. And no, no inspection. Kate answered each question, studying his face. Did he think that the terrorist threat was high?

She pushed the thought away and countered with an inquiry of her own. "Tell me how this works," she started. "Does the magazine assign you topics, or do you freelance?"

"Both."

She cocked her head.

"Sometimes, I am assigned. Sometimes, I follow my own ideas. For example, there was an incident in Turkey when a German tourist was arrested at the airport." Stefan's mouth quivered with a smile. "His young daughter had taken a small stone from a historic site, and the father was jailed for smuggling antiques. I was sent there to research a story — not about the man, but about the antique trade... No, the anqu- the ant-"

"Antiquities," she said.

"Antiquities — the antiquities trade." Stefan found his momentum again. "In that case, I was given that assignment. Here, I have also been assigned the subject of the canal. But if the opportunity permits, I may also collect material for other stories. For example, the boat trip to Colombia. Who knows?" He opened his hands wide. "Maybe I will write about the antiquities trade in Central America."

Kate leaned forward, all ears. "And what have you found there?"

He seemed surprised at her interest until she divulged her line of work.

"An archaeologist?" Stefan raised his eyebrows.

She had to smile. Hers was a great profession for catching people's attention, even if the reality was more mundane than people realized.

"Antiquities have long been a business in Central America," Stefan said. "Have you heard about the plundering at Nombre de Dios?"

Kate nodded.

"It seems someone is searching for something."

She leaned closer.

"My investigation is only starting, but I have several interviews scheduled this week."

She wished he would add more, but it seemed he'd only just started gathering information. Anyway, why dwell on frustrating thoughts when the evening was just starting to pep up?

"So..." She worked up the nerve to ask the question that had been on her mind all night. "Just how established a reporter are you? I always picture reporters as wearing vests with lots of pockets. Old guys with beards."

Stefan laughed, and she joined in. "Well, I have had some successes, but I'm still waiting for... *die Hammergeschichte.*"

She nodded. "The big one."

Stefan was taken aback. "And where did you learn German?" he asked in his native tongue.

"I spent a semester at the archeology program at the University of Tübingen."

He raised an eyebrow. *"Na dann, reden wir Deutsch." So let's use German.*

Kate squeezed her lips together. The problem would be, as it was with nearly all Germans, that her German was merely good, while his English was essentially flawless. Still, he indulged her in a few more sentences before slipping back into English.

A waitress paused at the table, and the reporter seemed to struggle briefly, casting an eye around the bar, considering something. Then his eyes landed back on her, and he nodded for another drink. Apparently, he was in no hurry to move on to other interviews tonight. And Kate, well, she didn't have any pressing appointments, either.

And for the first time since Nick's departure, time flew. It had been a long time since she could talk archaeology with anyone. As the night wore on, she found herself spending more time focused on the reporter's eyes than her drink or the view. The man was fascinating: a footloose globetrotter, a person who let himself dream. And he had stepped foot on more continents than she had — seven to five.

"Even Antarctica?" she asked.

"Antarctica, too."

To her surprise, she found that investigative reporters had a lot in common with archaeologists. Both conducted their own form of detective work. Stefan seemed to have the same inquisitive nature — and the same stubborn streak — she did. Except reporters, she decided, had better social skills than many of her academic-minded colleagues. When Stefan spoke, a vibrant personality peeked through his veiled exterior. When he listened, he did so intensely, almost coaxing words out of her mouth.

He shared an encounter he had with an American expat living in Panama. "David Meyer calls himself an art collector. He runs a small tourist resort near Portobelo. Did you go there?"

She shook her head. "We heard about the place, but there are too many reefs. And the price!" She rolled her eyes.

"It's incredible. The man is living comfortably here in Panama, yet he was only released recently from prison in the United States. Two years for the illegal sale of pre-Colombian artworks. All originating from Central America."

"What?" She nearly spat out her drink.

Stefan nodded. "He has quite a collection in his resort. It seemed unusual, so I researched the man. He was arrested in Texas for attempting to sell a Maya figurine for two hundred thousand US dollars."

She shook her head. "A piece that was probably found by some grave robber. A piece taken out of context. Nothing but a souvenir."

Stefan took off his glasses to rub a spot clean, and she momentarily lost track of the conversation. What was it that Cheryl had said about him?

She looked a little closer then leaned back. Okay, maybe the man was... somewhat gorgeous.

Stefan nodded. "When I asked Meyer about the collection, he seemed proud. He truly believes that his work preserves valuable art. Incredible, no? I am sure he also dabbles in — how do you say? Sales and acquisitions."

It was the perfect cue for her to bring up Charlie Parker and his treasure, but she kept the thought to herself. Stefan seemed honest and passionate about the subject, but Charlie's story wasn't hers to share.

She tapped her fingers on the table again. Nick, Nick, Nick. Could she count on him to see their *Aurora* adventures through? The answer seemed obvious enough.

She hid a scowl. Nick was thousands of miles away. At work.

Someone's watch beeped, and she glanced at the clock. Whoa. It was later than she'd intended to stay out. She looked at Stefan, about to excuse herself and leave.

But then again... Maybe she'd talk just a little longer. Why rush off?

Chapter Sixteen

A Game of Chess

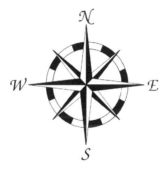

Balboa

February, present day

Lucien's patience had paid off, as it always did. His future boat was back in Balboa — the thirty-two-foot Valiant with his mermaid on board. Now that he'd raised some cash by stripping equipment from *Island Dreams*, he was ready to put the next step of his plan into motion.

She was alone. It would be easy. The minute he'd seen her head to the bar, he'd slicked back his hair, put on a clean shirt, and followed. How could she resist a rugged Frenchman with adventurous tales of the sea? The young American looked like the type who would like that — all dreamy-eyed and naïve. Not that he would approach her yet, not where they might be seen together. No, he'd position himself so she would take notice and make his move later.

Everything was ready and planned. All he had to do was wait for her to return to the boat. Then he would head over on the pretext of borrowing a tool and stay for a drink as darkness crept in. If she wouldn't allow herself to be charmed, well, Lucien would be prepared for that, too. He'd bring along a heavy wrench and dispose of it afterward, along with the body. No one would ever know.

Though that would be a pity. Things would be better for both of them if she cooperated. Lucien was enjoying just watching her.

At least, he had been until that man came along. The mismatched one with the heavy-rimmed glasses of an intellectual and the corded frame of an athlete. Apparently, he was just her type. Lucien could already see the sparks fly.

Merde. A man complicated everything. She was bound to invite him to the boat. He'd start spending nights, and that would ruin

Lucien's plan.

He shook out a new cigarette, pinched it between his lips, and struck a match with a gritty flick. A man was definitely an obstacle. Even if Lucien could get the woman alone, her new acquaintance might report her disappearance. Lucien had been counting on stealing a boat that wouldn't be missed and getting out of the country unnoticed. With the cartel already after him, he couldn't afford to have the police involved, too.

No good.

He steadied himself with a long drag on his Gauloise. This man would ruin everything. Everything.

Lucien held the smoke in his mouth and lungs for a count of five then exhaled it in a slow, controlled plume.

He'd have to wait to see what developed. With any luck, those two would burn through each other rapidly, and the man would move on. Lucien would observe unobtrusively — not just the woman, but the whole anchorage. If her boat wasn't his best choice, another opportunity would present itself. In the meantime, he could raise more cash from pawning the last bits of gear off *Island Dreams*. It would all work out as long as he planned carefully.

If life was a gamble, patience was his trump card, and Lucien couldn't wait to get back in the game.

Boston

February, present day

"Zero point four percent interest? I said, you've got to be kidding!"

"So my accountant said I should shift part of my 401(k)..."

"Lousy mileage, but it's a good, safe car."

Another night, another get-together. The kind Nick was increasingly tempted to avoid. His friends were having kids, taking out mortgages, and losing hair. They had stopped traveling and started putting on weight. Real news had quickly been exhausted — nowadays, conversation looped around the same topics like a record that skipped.

"If I think what those stocks were worth six months ago..."

"I keep meaning to get to the gym, but..."

"We're planning to refinance the house..."

He kept silent on the sidelines, nursing the unsettling feeling that he was window-shopping among major life choices, none of which appealed.

"Nice tan, Janine."

"Yeah, I went to Tahiti—"

He perked up.

"Tahiti Sun Studio, off Porter Square."

Nick heaved an internal sigh. The appeal of having a long list of crossed-off addresses, like Charlie, was growing on him. Nick Holmberg: Boston. Jamaica. Panama. Tahiti, even. It didn't sound bad now that he thought about it.

Calmer, slower places seemed more appealing every day. Because at home, everyone was in a rush, all the time. It was just like Kate said: luxury came from having time, not money. On *Aurora*, the hours felt full and rich instead of rushing by in a neverending countdown to the next appointment or deadline. Here, time was always slipping away, and the future was a source of concern, rather than something to get excited about.

"Nick, how do you like the new job?"

He found himself shrugging. "Pretty good."

"You don't sound too enthusiastic."

"I like it, but..."

"But?"

"It's just...kind of abstract." The word had come to him recently as he considered the very topic. Every step was just a precursor to the next and the next. "It's not like I'm ever going to play these video games."

"So? A job's a job."

Didn't use to be that way, he nearly said but settled for mopping up the rings around his glass instead.

"On *Aurora*, at least things were more immediate. When I had to fix something, I could see a result. You ground the radio — you get better reception. Clean the bottom, and the boat moves faster."

"I thought you were sick of all the work on that boat."

Funny, he'd thought so, too. Now, scratched knuckles and an aching back didn't sound half bad. A little boat work might cure this weary listlessness that refused to be shaken away.

He blinked a few times. Soon, he'd get to go back to that world. His job would finance a better boat, and he could escape again to fresh air and open space. The promise of a little adventure.

Nick sat a little straighter. Maybe he did have a little of his great-grandfather in him, after all.

Someone yelped, and everyone swiveled to the TV screen behind the bar. The Red Sox had just blown a double play in the first game of spring training. Groans sounded all around, along with jeers at the umpire.

Nick tuned it all out. A bigger, newer boat. The words had taken on a hollow ring, even to him. Still, it was his ticket to good times with Kate.

But what if Kate wouldn't wait? He couldn't shake the thought of someone like Alejandro elbowing his way in. Surely Kate had better taste than that. Granted, she had left him once before, but that hadn't been for another guy. Just for a more enticing lifestyle. And since he was working toward financing more sailing

— a lifestyle that held the elements of freedom and unpredictability she so craved — she wouldn't lose faith in him.

Would she?

He recalled their best moments together, exploring new places and engaging in hobbies, like the pursuit of Charlie Parker's clues. It was a fun diversion, to be sure. But Nick had surreptitiously asked his mother about Charlie, working his way through the entire family tree first so as not to arouse suspicion. And she was adamant: his great-grandfather was a listless wanderer. A hopeless dreamer. Rosie was the one to admire, his mother insisted — a woman who ran a local tavern in the days of building the New York State Barge Canal. A woman who could hold her own. Why would she need tall-tale Charlie?

It was a wild-goose chase. Nick doubted there was a treasure out there. But Kate... Kate was a dangerous cross between a bloodhound and a... what was it? A pit bull? The kind of dog that bit deep and refused to let go. But sooner or later, even Kate would come around to his plan. The new boat would bring back all the good times — and more.

Friday night rolled around, along with another chess game with his father. Part of his mind focused on strategy, while another part wandered. If only the neatly delineated blocks of black and white of the board could be applied to real life. If only he knew which course of action to follow, the way the pieces on the board did. So many steps forward, back, sideways, diagonally.

He studied the board, wondering which piece he could identify with. A pawn? He grimaced. A castle, always moving in a straight line? Not much more inspiring. Worse yet, the king, trapped and lonely behind a wall? A figure who waited for fate to come to him instead of riding out to meet it?

"Your move," his father prompted, giving him a strange look.

He made the move he already had planned, bishop to B5. His father had seen it coming and countered with rook to B1. Nick took a long time responding, his thoughts still on matching people with chess pieces. Kate entered his mind, her face a portrait of concentration as she puzzled over Spanish coins and... what did she call it? Anthro... anthromorphic spiders? Given a choice, Kate would surely pick the knight for herself. Something about horses and romantic visions of knighthood, no doubt. That and the ability to move in unexpected directions.

As if on cue, he executed a rogue move — knight to D4 — without thinking it over first. A step completely out of concert with the rest of his plan.

His father looked at him, suspicious. Was the move complete folly or a brilliant new strategy?

Nick wasn't sure either. He leaned in to study the board and found himself unexpectedly satisfied with that one, outrageous move. While his father deliberated his next step, he analyzed his own options. Had he just thrown the game?

No, he decided. The move eliminated several possibilities but opened another set of options.

Huh. He considered that novelty until his mother called from the adjoining room.

"Nick, telephone. It's your aunt Laura."

Nick took the phone in the kitchen. "Hello?"

"Hello, sweetheart!" He couldn't help but smile at the sound of his aunt's spritely voice. "How are you?"

"Fine, and you? How are things in Colorado?"

His eyes drifted over the pantry door as he spoke. The frame was marked with lines. There he was at age four. Nine. Thirteen. And now? He drew an imaginary line from the top of his head and recalled a line from a song. *What a long, strange trip...*

"Tell me all about the canal and that boat of yours. Not all of us get to live adventures like that, you know!" Laura gushed.

Nick loved that his aunt was not only a good talker, but a good listener, too. He walked to the very end of the phone cord and described the locks, the scale of it all, the swirling waters. He started quietly, though the excitement quickly crept in. For a moment, he was Nick, the adventurer, instead of Nick, the dutiful son. He could hear the wind in the rigging, smell the sea.

Laura interjected with questions. Was it scary? Thrilling? What about other ships? She was the first person back home to press him for real details. Everyone else was content to hear that his trip was simply "good" and left it at that. Finally, he got to relive the excitement of the canal transit all over again.

Glancing back through the doorway, he caught a glimpse of his father, listening with a rapt expression.

"And how is Kate?" Laura asked.

The walls closed in around Nick, slapping him back into reality.

"She's fine," he said after a tick too long.

"When are you going back?" Laura's voice sounded sharper.

"Actually, I took a job here," he mumbled. He could sense his mother standing prouder, even a room away.

A long, disappointed silence fell over the other end of the line.

Balboa

February, present day

Kate left her meeting with Stefan with his business card, complete with his local cell number neatly penned on the back and a memory stick with pictures of his trip to Colombia. For a moment, she fumbled with it.

"You can give it back when I see you next," he said, reading her thoughts.

She had to admit to liking that idea. A lot.

"Maybe on Thursday?" he suggested. "I have several interviews scheduled with government officials in the next few days, but it would be good to see you again." He added quickly, "I mean, it would give me a chance to bounce ideas against someone."

She smiled and decided not to correct his nearly perfect English. "Thursday would be great."

Of course, to meet him she would have to beg her way out of an excursion with Anneliese, Nils, and the kids, but they would understand, right?

When she woke up the next morning, she spent a long time in the cockpit, watching canal-bound ships glide silently by. Her mind, though, was preoccupied with Stefan's story of David Meyer, the so-called art collector. The pieces in that illegal collection would never be properly studied. They would never complement others to create a richer picture of a gone-by culture. They'd never feature in exhibits that could be enjoyed and marveled at by the public.

Those thoughts were bad enough, but when she imaged a man like David Meyer getting his hands on Charlie's treasure, she scowled outright. But what could she really do to prevent that?

Find it first. The words popped into her mind.

She shook her head. Pursuing the treasure was a gamble. A Pandora's box. She ought to leave it alone.

But when she pictured Charlie sketching the spider, she knew she couldn't just drop the idea. If a grave robber got to Charlie's treasure, all those pieces would be lost to history forever. The coins would glitter in the display case of a private collector. Which was a pity but not a huge loss to the world's knowledge. By their very definition, coins represented a monetary value. The spider, on the other hand, was art. A masterpiece. A piece of cultural heritage, despite having lost its archaeological context. She thumped her hand against Aurora's smooth deck. How could a piece like that be denied to science and the public?

She spent the next hour poring over Charlie's notebook and letters. There had to be a clue in there somewhere. Maybe the scribbles in the margins? She searched and searched, then rejected each with a discouraged huff. If only she could lay out all those hints and exchange ideas with someone. Someone like Stefan, for example. He had insight, imagination, and a perspective that could complement her archaeologist's point of view.

She stood and paced to the extent that Aurora's tiny cabin allowed then decided on a distraction — scrolling through Stefan's Colombia trip photos.

"Nice," she murmured, pausing over the sunset shot Stefan had called his *Hammerfoto* — the mother of all photos. The colors were stunning, the view gorgeous.

And that wasn't the only one. He'd taken some great shots: crisp, detailed, quality stuff. There were several nice shots taken in Portobelo, including one of a small group, probably his fellow travelers, assembled in El Diablo. Ruddy faces in front, photo wall behind. Kate imagined the adventure she might have had if she'd done the trip, too.

The photo wall — the homage to Mercedes — brought a grin to her face, and her eyes ran over the rows of photos like a jogger over a familiar path. There was Mercedes, alone. There she was with her girls. Over there was the shot of Mercedes with the canal workers. And next to that...

An empty space.

Kate squinted and leaned closer to the screen then zoomed in on the spot. Stefan's photos were incredibly sharp. His camera had captured the whiter section of wall once covered by the framed sketch of *Yolanta*.

It was gone.

She worked her jaw in unspoken words as she scrutinized the screen. The other pictures were all there. Only *Yolanta* was missing. Who would have taken that picture? Why?

Her heart skipped a few beats, then stumbled on. Did someone know about Charlie? About what she and Nick had learned thus far? She tried to remember the scene at El Diablo that quiet New Year's Day when she and Nick had borrowed the pictures to copy.

No one! No one could know.

She caught herself at midbreath as possibilities filtered through her mind like staccato beats of a drum. Arty, the worn-out sailor in Portobelo, cracking a joke about a treasure hunt. Alejandro came to mind, too. Hell, the whole bar would have heard Arty's wisecrack. She hadn't thought much of it at the time, but now...

She wanted to reject the thought of Arty being involved in some way. The man was such a washup, she could scarcely imagine him pursuing anything with conviction. And Alejandro? He was much too nice.

But crap, she'd been announcing her profession in casual gatherings all the way from the San Blas to Balboa. If someone thought she was secretly searching for antiquities, then...

She halted the thought, but it tumbled through her mind all the same.

Then she might just have opened Pandora's box.

She tapped her fingers on the chart table. Someone else was on to Charlie's trail. Did that person know what Charlie had found? No one else had seen his letters or notebook—

Except Tyler, that day in Shelter Bay. Kate let out a sudden puff of air. Tyler could have blabbed about the notebook to anyone.

Who? The person or people who took the *Yolanta* sketch from El Diablo? Had they already discovered the message on the back? Could they make any sense of it?

She stared at the photocopy and decided to assume the worst. Black market traders were on the trail of Charlie's treasure. If they found it, Charlie's treasure would be lost forever.

Her fingers strummed the notebook — once, twice — and she muttered out loud.

"Not if I find it first."

Chapter Seventeen

Gentlemen and Thieves

Shelter Bay
February, present day

The plan was brilliant, and he knew it.

It had everything: intelligence, insight, cunning, and of course, flair. Alejandro liked the latter best of all. He stopped polishing *Carmela's* brass long enough to admire his reflection in it.

The Americans were intelligent, but they weren't astute. Nice people, in fact. A pity they got mixed up in this business at all.

He grinned, and the face in the brass grinned back. Of course, this was all about destiny, and destiny had her favorites. Like himself. Other people won some, lost some. Some only lost.

Alejandro won. Always.

He could see it all play out already. Like the mechanized mules that guided freighters through the canal, the Americans would lead him straight to what he sought. And when he had the treasure, he would deftly cast off the lines. Of course, he needed an extra pair of hands. That's why he'd decided to bring in the Poles. They were the brawn — men motivated solely by money and, therefore, easy to manipulate. Money was all-powerful for simple folk. They rushed for it like insects to a hot, white light. He'd have to keep an eye on the big one, though. Brawny, but headstrong.

He — Alejandro Cavillo de Gutierrez Luís— was the brains. A man of sophistication with more than a profit on his agenda.

Slowly, he considered the other players in the game and discarded them one by one. The American collector, David Meyer, was of less concern to him than the Poles. He and Meyer had a gentleman's agreement that would be honored — and besides, they needed each other. Meyer knew the market and had contacts to rich customers eager to expand their private collections with authentic, untraceable Spanish silver. Alejandro would take over the supply end and therefore maintain control. He would procure the treasure that Meyer would convert into a tidy profit for them both. He'd briefly considered going straight to the market himself to turn an even bigger profit, but that wasn't his style.

He went back to polishing the brass, making sure not to soil his white shirt. His plan was perfect. He'd let others transport the pieces over international borders and tango with the law. Not him. No, his role was simply to unite historic treasures with people who appreciated them — and were willing to demonstrate that appreciation with hard cash.

Of course, the bounty offered on valuable treasures would attract other parties. Maybe even a criminal element — men whose hearts didn't pump blood so much as suspicion and jealousy. Which meant he had to be cautious, too.

A second later, he chuckled. Yes, this little project of his promised challenges on several levels.

Criminals could only think in two dimensions. The very best of them, perhaps three. He, on the other hand, was an artist, a visionary. First, he would cast his nascent drama with the right characters. Then everything would unfold the way he scripted it, ending with a tidy profit for himself. He'd let Meyer dispose of the coins — except, of course, for the fraction secreted away for Alejandro's own budding collection. He imagined the moment when he showed it to friends back home. While they had been playing at the country club and warming seats in their fathers' firms, Alejandro had been busy engineering a masterpiece.

He would let the others cross the lines of legality. He'd keep his hands clean. It would be tricky, but if anyone could pull it off, he could.

Could? Alejandro chuckled. He knew he would.

He would be the one to claim a long-lost treasure. He'd snatch the prize from under the nose of a worthy adversary. He would be the one to outfox them all and live to tell the tale.

He flicked his cloth over the brass one last time. And yes, he'd do it all with style.

Boston

March, present day

In the office, Nick took a sip of the herbal tea that Mark called a cure-all and promptly grimaced. He checked his watch then his email for the fifth try in two hours.

Nothing. Nothing from Kate, anyway. Was it the spotty connection in Panama, or was she losing faith in him? Or worse — was he the one losing faith?

Maybe it was just the cold that set in after his long, wet slog from the office a few nights back. He forced down another sip of tea, stretched his legs out under his desk, and immediately pulled them back from the empty space. There was nothing there but his backpack with his new book in it.

He had arrived at the steps to his apartment the night before to find a small brown package amidst the junk mail jutting out of his mailbox. When he took the package inside and ripped along the zip tab, two books slipped out. The title of one leaped out at him.

Pirate Gold!

Something about it rang a bell. Nick turned it over and found a tweed-clad academic pointing at a globe with a pipe. *Richard Brewster Lewis, best-selling author and award-winning academic...*

He scowled. Who sent him this?

The second book was thicker, the cover art subdued.

Captain James Cook: The Journals.

He skimmed the back cover. *In three extraordinary expeditions, Captain Cook voyaged over thousands of miles of the Pacific Ocean...*

A printed note in imitation script fell out of the book. *This book is a gift from Aunt Laura.* That was followed by a quote by Mark Twain.

Twenty years from now you will be more disappointed by the things you didn't do than by the ones you did do. So throw off the bowlines. Sail away from the safe harbor. Explore. Dream. Discover.

Nick spent a long time that evening sitting on his orange, third-hand sofa, holding the Captain Cook book in both hands. His wiggling toes wished for a little sand as his eyes roamed over the spartan room, lingering on the photo of *Aurora* in the canal.

Subtle hint, Laura.

The Captain Cook book was in his backpack now, under his desk. He nudged the lump with his foot. He didn't know whether to hug it to his chest or kick it into a corner. *Aurora* called to him, whispering about possibilities. Charlie, too, who seemed to be a kindred spirit of Mark Twain. Nick bet the two of them would have hit if off well.

Throw off the bowlines...

But life didn't always let you live by catchy quotes. Nick knew that all too well. There were bills to pay, family responsibilities. With everything his parents had done for him, how could he leave now? There was that to consider, along with the uncertainties of life. Just the other day Mark had related the story of a friend who had lost everything in a bad real estate deal. He was insolvent: no savings, no insurance, no retirement plan. What did Mark Twain have to say about that?

Nick walked to the office kitchenette to dump the tea, knowing exactly what Kate would say if she were there.

There is no such thing as a secure future, she'd insist. *Everything could come crashing down in an instant.* She knew; she'd seen it happen to the people closest to her. She had a mile-long list of what there was to lose in life — and it wasn't money or real estate or investments.

He ducked under the sink, half on autopilot, checking a dripping sound.

Life was for living, not putting off for a someday that might never come. That's what she'd say.

Which was all fine, but life could also be good. Stable. There was a lot to be said about knowing where your next paycheck was coming from and that you might still be at the same address when it arrived. He pictured Kate in the discussion they'd had many times. The woman wanted to tick off countries like other people ticked books off a reading list. Sometimes, he wondered who she was doing her adventuring for.

The two sides of him wrestled, and an ugly thought shot out of the sandstorm in his mind.

Maybe he and Kate weren't made for each other, after all.

"Uh, Nick?" came Mark's distant voice.

"Coming." He backed out of the small space under the office sink.

"What are you doing?"

"The sink was leaking."

Mark looked at him strangely. "We have plumbers for that."

Nick ran the taps and checked the connection he'd tightened. "Just takes two minutes."

"Since when are you a plumber?"

He shrugged. Since *Aurora*, he supposed. He settled back at his desk and promptly caught himself looking out the window instead of at his screen. God, the office was stuffy. What he wouldn't give for a fresh sea breeze! Then a phone rang somewhere, jolting him like an alarm clock. A reminder to keep plowing ahead with work — especially today, when he had to leave the office early to meet his mother at the bank.

His father's heart attack had incited his parents to organize their affairs — dusting off insurance policies, assigning beneficiaries, checking their wills. A bit macabre, all of it. Today, his mother wanted to copy the house deed that lay in their safety deposit box and insisted that Nick accompany her.

"See you tomorrow," he called and headed to the bank.

He jerked a smile into place when he stepped up to the building. His mother was already waiting outside, fifteen minutes early as always. She kissed his cheek and led him inside. It reminded him of a trip to the bank vault when he was little. He felt the same way right now — out of place and twitchy, especially with his mother pointedly including him in every exchange with the bank employee.

"My son and I are here to open our safety deposit box," she said.

"My son has the key," came next, as she handed Nick the key under the table.

"My son will let you know when we're done," she announced.

Obviously, she was doing her best to shift the mantle of "man of the family" onto his shoulders.

He squirmed under the weight. Why not his older sister? Nora was good at that kind of thing. Why try to fit a round peg into a square hole?

A second later, he laughed. Kate was the round peg. He was the square one. But it seemed that *Aurora* had filed off the sharp corners of his personality. He no longer fit into this cookie-cutter world.

The bank official removed a long, thin safety deposit box from its slot with an unnecessary flourish and showed them into a curtained alcove with two chairs and a narrow shelf.

His mother let him slide it open with a faint metallic scrape — a sound he remembered, too. She reached over and picked out several small pouches — some cloth, others velvet. She lingered over each while Nick pulled a sheaf of envelopes from the bottom of the box.

"My grandmother's wedding ring!" his mother exclaimed, pulling the piece out of the first pouch.

Nick leafed through the papers. Fire insurance... old passports... There — the house deed. He held it up for his mother, but she remained focused on the jewelry spread before her. She beamed as she introduced him to the characters playing recurring roles in their family history.

"This is the cross every child in my family has worn at their christening for the past four generations..."

"Oh my goodness! This is the butterfly pin my great aunt wore that Thanksgiving dinner when the table collapsed..."

"This pocket watch belonged to my father's father..."

It was a trove of memories rather than riches, and his mother treasured each piece. Except for the signatures on the documents, Nick realized, there was very little evidence of male influence in this thin metal box. Plus or minus a few items, the same collection would someday belong to one of his sisters, then her daughter, and her daughter's daughter. It was just like Kate once said. *Women are the custodians of family history, not men.*

It was the same with Aunt Laura and Charlie's box. Except now, Nick was custodian of that particular memory — which he'd left behind in Panama, along with Kate.

He coughed in the stuffy air of the alcove. Damn, did his throat ache.

He looked around, wondering what his safety deposit box might contain if he ever got one. Insurance documents? Property deeds? One thing was for sure, he was back on track for that kind of existence.

He could hear Kate's voice as if she were sitting next to him. *Rich experiences don't need a vault.*

Charlie chimed in, too, saying something about the open road and wide horizons. Nick scratched his chest and winced. His sore throat rasped. Funny how everyone was so worried about his safety on *Aurora*, yet he'd never gotten sick while sailing.

"This was Rosie's," his mother said softly, reaching for a plain cloth bag.

All of Nick's fuzzy senses snapped into focus as she pulled out an oval watch on a thin leather band, then a tangle of necklaces. She handed him the necklaces, murmured something about old-fashioned tastes, and went on to explore the contents of a different pouch.

Nick poked Rosie's necklaces, wrapped around one another like strands of spaghetti. The thin straps caught on pendants and stones, any of which he could picture on Aunt Laura. He picked through the shapes and extracted one at a time, wondering what the pieces might have meant to their owner once upon a time.

One of the necklaces didn't fit in among the others. It had a simple leather strap that neither glittered nor sang in audible metallic clinks. He traced the line to the oversized pendant tied into the loop and pulled it free.

His mother glanced over and dismissed it with a wave. "Some foolish old souvenir from Charlie. You'd think a man could find a more suitable piece of jewelry for his sweetheart." Her voice softened to a whisper. "Grandma Rosie never took it off."

He gaped at the piece. A thin hole had been drilled through a coin to string it on the thong, but the rough inscription and the lines subdividing the coin into fourths were unmistakable. They were all a little blurry, like the crudely minted coins Kate had lectured him on. His heart thumped, knowing exactly what it was.

A Spanish piece of eight, tarnished with time and too much wistful rubbing.

He stared at it while his mother gathered up the house deed and her grandmother's bracelets, then repacked the box. In a stealthy move that made his face flush, Nick pocketed Rosie's necklace.

His mother would never understand.

Balboa

March, present day

Kate scrambled into action, nearly late for her meeting with Stefan. He would be the perfect person to help her uncover Charlie's secrets. She just knew it. The man had imagination, vision. He would have some new insights to share if she confided in him.

But should she? Could she?

She thought it over. Surely she could trust him. What was wrong with confiding in a friend? She was early to their meeting point in the restaurant of his hotel, not far from the yacht club. Stefan was early, too, sitting over a cup of coffee, watching a ship steam toward the locks. Kate stopped at the doorway for a moment, suddenly wishing she had worn something more presentable than just a plain T-shirt. Then Stefan looked up and smiled, spurring her legs into action.

"*Morgen!*" His eyes were bright as she sat down.

"*Morgen,*" she replied.

They grinned at each other for half a second. "So, how did it go?" she asked, fumbling a little with her words.

As usual, Stefan had a great story to tell. As Kate listened to his experiences at the National Institute of Culture, she marveled at the way he could put a spark into every report. A gifted reporter, no doubt about it.

He reported a "mixed-up bag" of impressions. The head archaeologist, Doctor Carlos Ruiz, seemed genuine enough, but the man was a little long in the tooth and an idealist who refused to address illegal trade in antiquities. His assistant, the lovely Doctor Sofia Hidalgo — Stefan's generous hand motions suggested exactly how lovely she was — on the other hand...

"A woman of, let us say, mixed motives," he said.

"How mixed?"

Stefan considered for a moment. "Off the record?"

Kate nodded eagerly.

"I think she may be open to... dealing and wheeling."

Her eyes widened. "She works for the cultural ministry, and she's dishonest?"

"Naturally, I can't be sure," he replied, though his expression suggested otherwise. "But it would not surprise me to discover that she might have her price. I imagine — let me say that I only imagine — that such a person, should she discover ten items of value, would perhaps bring nine to the cultural ministry. And the tenth, well.... Oops." Stefan mimicked looking around as if he had misplaced something — quite by accident, of course.

"And whatever it was would end up on the black market..."

"Never to swim to the surface."

Kate broke into a smile. "Never to resurface."

"Never to resurface," he echoed, correcting himself.

Kate was about to bring up Charlie when Stefan went on. "There's another man, there, however. The junior of those three. Doctor Rodrigo Ortiz. He appears very dedicated and honest. He is very passionate about fighting the trade in antiquities. But I believe frustrated, also."

"Who wouldn't be?"

"Especially with Doctor Hidalgo virtually controlling the department. She monitors all calls, all press contacts."

Kate shook her head in disgust.

"And the work is dangerous sometimes," he added. "The cartel is rumored to be active in the antiquities trade, too."

She blinked. "The cartel is interested in antiquities?"

"They have lost two hundred kilos of cocaine. They are under some pressure now," Stefan said with a hint of satisfaction. "So naturally they will try to increase profits in other areas."

"But antiquities?"

"In many cases, what started as drug organizations have evolved into sophisticated international organizations with various interests. They already control key corridors and transportation networks. They can use these to move other valuables, no?"

Kate was about to erupt in a barrage of questions when a loud clatter of dishes pulled her attention away.

"I think they're setting up for brunch," Stefan said, looking at his watch.

She leaned over and grasped his wrist, turning it to see the face herself. "Wow. Time flies."

"I have another appointment," he sighed, giving her a wistful look.

She tried not to sound too disappointed. "Who next?"

"I change my hat. Back to terrorism. I have an interview with Coronel Juan Rodrigo Lopez." He gave a mock salute. "The deputy director of... I think you would call it a kind of SWAT team for anti-terror missions." Stefan said it casually, as if Kate, too, were about to rush off to a similar appointment. "He has the reputation of being something of a cowboy, ready to... How do you say it? Kill a sparrow with a cannon ball."

Stefan's speech was fast, but he remained seated, his expression pensive. He looked out over the canal, then back at her with intense eyes. Then he leaned away and pulled out his phone.

Kate found herself holding her breath, even if she wasn't sure why. She let it out when his face lit up at something in his messages.

"Good news!" he said, working the keys in a reply. "They agree to move the interview to tomorrow."

She grinned a mile wide. "So there's no rush?" She'd be happy for more of his company, especially now that she knew a drug cartel might share her interest in Charlie Parker's extracurricular activities. Was the whole thing bigger than she thought?

"No rush," he echoed, looking very happy indeed. His eyes slid to the buffet area. "Can I invite you for brunch?"

She was all smiles, especially when he leaned back and declared it a day off. Suddenly, the morning was full of possibilities, and none of them involved moping around the boat. She immediately decided to give herself a day off from Charlie, lost treasures, and black marketeers.

A day off from a lot of things, as it turned out.

Brunch was delicious, the conversation riveting.

".. but there were no Sherpas available, so we had to..."

"...except the project ran out of funds while we were still in Ankara..."

"...and then the driver said, you owe me one hundred rupees!"

They sat on the hotel patio overlooking the Bridge of the Americas and lingered over their empty plates long after the other guests had gone. It was a grandiose setting for small talk between two people getting to know each other better and better. Morning stretched to noon, but neither wanted to break their momentum. They remained seated in lively conversation even when waiters started cleaning up around them. When they finally took notice, Stefan suggested moving a level lower to the outdoor pool.

Kate snuck a wistful glance at the clear water.

"Tempted?" Stefan's eyebrows curved.

She hesitated, suddenly unsure of his meaning.

"You want to have a swim?" he asked.

She deliberated. "Is it okay? It won't take me long to get my suit..."

He put his hands up. "My day off, remember? I have time."

She raced over to *Aurora* for her swimsuit and returned in record time. She hopped in the pool and swam endless, glorious laps. At the end of each lap, she flipped and pushed off the wall, gliding just above the tiled floor like a bird skimming a wave. Flip, push, glide, stroke. On and on, smooth and easy. Her arms barely raised a splash with their measured motions. The fresh water felt light and clean against her skin, clear and blue at the same time. She'd devoted thousands of hours to swimming in her racing days, a slave to the clock. Now, she was mesmerized by the sunlight catching in the fluid layers of the pool. Thoughts of the morning slid over her in the same way. A perfect day, all of it. The conversation, the company, and now this. A chance to let go of her worries for a while.

Finally, she pushed herself out of the pool and found her way back to Stefan, taking off her goggles as she walked. Gravity guided tiny rivers along the length of her body. Her wet hair was slicked back, her breathing quick but controlled. The trail of liquid footprints she left vanished almost instantly in the midday heat. When she spotted Stefan, she couldn't help but lock in on the blue of his eyes.

He appeared to have read very little of the book he had been holding for the past half hour. Leaning out from his lounge chair to hand her a fluffy white hotel towel in silence, he looked more intense than usual. When she took the towel, his hand hung empty in the air before he remembered to pull it back. His eyes zoomed in on hers, peripheral vision obviously registering the rest.

She had just started drying her shoulders when Stefan cleared his throat and asked — ever so quietly and politely — if she would like to come up to his room. And this time, his meaning was perfectly clear.

Chapter Eighteen

Time to Say Good-bye

Toro Point

January 1914

Good-byes were always the hardest part. Especially when they were forever. Charlie knew from vast personal experience — a wealth he had just expanded.

Sometimes, the pain of good-bye came from leaving a special place, like the way the boundless Yukon had taken a piece of his heart away when he'd left those northern climes. Other times, it was leaving a building, like his rustic lean-to on the edge of the endless African savanna. In Panama, it was saying good-bye to people that added a few more scars to his collection.

It started with his parting from Mercedes. Her backbone was rigid as she wished him well.

"*Qué te vaya bien, Carlito.*"

Her soft words carried as much undertone as the few wavering syllables he mumbled in return. Would that he might ever find her equal!

When he finally broke away from those dark, searching eyes, he turned quickly and let his long legs carry him down the hill from El Diablo for the very last time. He nearly turned around for a second look but forced himself to carry on. No sense in that. He just wished...

Well, a man could wish a lot of things.

He brightened up afterward, imagining the look on Mercedes' face when she discovered the five boxes of silver he had left her in plain view, covered with a tablecloth and a note in the room he'd rented.

Gracias. Yours, Charlie.

That's all he wrote, but he figured it was enough. He'd left a sack there for Angelina, too. After all, he would never have explored that graveyard if it hadn't been for her.

He thought that would be all there was to it. One painful goodbye and he would quietly slip away. But making the break from his crew proved almost as hard. The men stood in a somber line, hats off, hands extended. Edgar's grip was tight, and the two men shook for a long time, letting motion make up for a lack of words.

"You're a good man," Charlie said, then finally pulled away.

Good men, all of them. He looked back from the small launch that carried him across the bay for the last time. The crew was spread out along the breakwater, waving hats and hands for all they were worth.

He took an extra deep breath at the sight. The breakwater — their breakwater — was almost complete. Maybe not the most elegant or innovative structure but one that would withstand the strength of the sea and the test of time. He imagined sailors transiting the canal in decades and even centuries to come. Would they spare a thought for the modest men who toiled there?

He gripped his hat tighter. Another few months and he could witness the canal opening with his crew. A historic moment they'd all contributed to. Maybe he should...

But, no. He shook his head. He wasn't one for pomp, ceremony, or the festival of form-filling that invariably marked the end of every project. No, he had to look to his own future, and it was a bright one.

Bright and silvery.

The crew moved back to work, leaping from boulder to boulder. He smiled at the thought of them divvying up the odds and ends he left, knowing they would put everything to good use — his last commissary coupons, train passes, and a few personal bits and pieces. He'd also left canned milk and a bolt of cloth for Edgar's newest family member — a fourth daughter — together with a canvas sack plump with Spanish coins.

He took a last, long look at the breakwater then turned away, forcing his face into an emotionless expression.

Get on with it, Charlie. Get on with it already.

* * *

His trip to the Pacific coast was a blur that passed beyond the brim of the hat he pulled low over his eyes. The train whistled into the station where a young Panamanian with a mule buggy waited for him. Mercedes had arranged it, assuring him that although the young man — a nephew of her sister's friend's cousin — was a little slow thinking, he was strong, silent, and reliable.

Charlie counted the mules' hooves clip-clopping along the street all the way to the Office of Geographic Surveys. His "rock samples" were just where they should be, faithfully awaiting Dr. Cuthbert E. Longfellow. Charlie hid his glee with an indignant comment about having to take care of everything himself then started transferring the loot to the buggy. There were twenty-six boxes in all — solid, weighty things. His helper expressed no interest in whether it was rock samples or other mineral deposits they were transporting across the city to his boat. No interest whatsoever, as long as he was paid. And he would be — handsomely.

The toothless old man at the rickety dock in Balboa was paid handsomely, too — both for keeping an eye on *Yolanta* for the past few weeks and for looking the other way as Charlie and his helper loaded up the vessel.

The old man knew full well they were up to something. Charlie could read it in his eyes. But since he probably imagined something along the lines of embezzling materials from Americans, the man raised no objection. All he cared about were the generous tips he received from this crazy gringo.

Charlie was so busy with his work that he barely noticed a street artist approach — the type who catered to tourists with scenes of Panama. He was about to brush the man away when he saw the black-and-white sketch of *Yolanta*. Using his imagination, the artist had drawn the little craft reaching through the sea, her sails billowing in a stiff breeze. Charlie paid without even bothering to bargain and admired it for a long minute before tucking it away.

When at last he had sweated the last box into place under the floorboards, Charlie sat back on his heels and surveyed his handiwork. Moving the treasure across the isthmus was a logistical feat nearly on par with the building of the canal as far as he was concerned. Too bad he had no one to boast about it to.

The boat seemed a little low on her waterline, but buoyant nonetheless. He set sail that very afternoon, easing *Yolanta* away from the shore in a light breeze that carried the scent of so many memories. The salt water made him think of the breakwater at Toro Point. The dank smell of trash burning made him think of Portobelo. He pictured Mercedes and then Edgar — the closest he'd come to making real friends in Panama. He supposed that spoke volumes about his character and maybe theirs, too.

He closed his eyes and pictured them both. Edgar with his sunny, good nature. Mercedes with her indomitable aura. Their lives would go on without him, and his would go on, too. Not in parallel but in diverging lines, never again to meet. He steeled himself to look ahead to a shiny new future of his own.

"A new adventure," he murmured to the horizon, searching Yolanta's compass for more than just cardinal directions. He eyed the ocean ahead, reminding himself the first step was always the hardest.

A good, stiff breeze, that's what he needed to carry him forward. A good, stiff breeze.

Boston

March, present day

It wasn't a wild-goose chase.

Charlie really did find a treasure.

Nick sat contemplating the Spanish coin under the only decent lamp in his apartment. He'd called off chess night with his father, claiming a sore throat, which was true — technically. He'd simply chosen to leave out the part about a five-hundred-year-old coin.

He pinched Rosie's necklace and tried to herd his stampeding thoughts in one logical direction. Charlie found a treasure in Panama but had to leave it behind. He'd never made it back to reclaim the loot.

Nick paced the tiny apartment. How many more coins lay hidden on the isthmus? He wrestled with the clues he and Kate had discovered again and again. The letters to Rosie. The sketch of Yolanta. Charlie's notebook with its map of Portobelo. And the most cryptic piece of the puzzle — the note to Mercedes with its series of numbers.

Charlie really had discovered a treasure. Kate was right about being on a real trail, not an illusion.

If I hadn't already enlisted when I met you, I never would have left.

That's what Charlie had written to Rosie from the war. Nick had to wonder if Charlie wasn't the scoundrel his mother made him out to be. Maybe he was just a man juggling obligations, opportunities, and regrets.

Just like Nick.

He dialed the phone on *Aurora* again and again. Nothing. Had Kate forgotten to charge the battery? He was burning to talk to her, unrushed and in person. And about much more than just pieces of eight. The Captain Cook book practically glowed beside him on the lumpy orange couch.

But what about his job? His commitment to Mark? His big chance?

For all the uncertainties, a few things had suddenly become clearer. The moment Nick completed the skeleton of the operating system, Mark would beg for the muscles to move it. His mother would bring him another piece of furniture while his older sister delivered an entire lecture on responsibility with a single cutting glance. He'd fall back into a cycle of work, uneasy rest, and work again. And all the while, Kate would drift away.

He already had what he needed in Panama. The job wasn't his big chance. Sailing with Kate was.

Sooner or later, he would have to come back to work — but not right away. *Aurora* was small, but she didn't cost much to maintain. She was old but sturdy, and he and Kate had enough savings to last for another year — possibly two, if Mark would accept a compromise with Nick doing some part-time work remotely. The new guy, Ralf, was good enough — more than good enough — to assume greater responsibility.

And when the money ran out, he and Kate would find a way to balance work with doing what they enjoyed. Together.

His mind wandered to Cory, the classmate whose death had sparked this whole crazy phase. Because of him, Nick had bought *Aurora*, and *Aurora* had brought Kate back into his life. Then he imagined Charlie, waiting for a chance to get back to Panama. Waiting to get back to Rosie.

Wait too long, and it will be too late.

He wasn't sure where he'd heard that, but it sounded ominously true.

The phone rang and he snatched it up, only to deflate upon seeing Nora's number on the display. His sister was probably checking whether he really was committed to attending his parents' upcoming anniversary party or to check his symptoms on their mother's suggestion. She was a doctor, after all. He assured her he was all right, relieved when she spared him from chatting to each of his nieces in turn. They were great kids, but he was not in the mood to discuss the adventures of Dora the Explorer just now. He was even more relieved that the anniversary party never came up.

"Thanks for calling. Bye." He took the first opportunity to sign off. Whew. He'd gotten off lightly.

And the second he looked around, Captain Cook peered out resolutely from the cover of the book.

Therein lay the problem. Adventuring was all well and good, but Cook had just sailed off and left his family behind. Shunning work was one thing. Family was another. He couldn't just abandon them.

He squeezed Charlie's — Rosie's — coin tightly. Wasn't Charlie family? Wasn't Kate, too?

The clock advanced one minute with a heavy tick, and he sighed, tired of the inner debate. It was only seven. He could still get over to his parents' house for that game of chess.

* * *

Somewhere between positioning his rook and losing his knight, Nick faded out of the game and let his eyes wander around the room. He decided he knew why his parents hadn't changed anything in fifteen years. Because familiar was comforting. Safe. Easy. But the warm embrace the house delivered each time he stepped over the threshold was starting to feel a little too tight. Possessive, almost. The hallway alone spoke volumes — especially the way it was lined with pictures of him and his sisters as kids. His parents were invested in the house the way he was invested in *Aurora*. With blood, sweat, and tears.

"Nick."

He caught his father saying his name and looked up with some delay. Why was his dad wearing that strange look again?

"Remind me when you were planning to go back to Panama."

He had to remind himself. June seemed an awfully long time away. Too long.

"Lots of last-minute flight deals these days," his father said in an offhand way.

Nick stared, then looked at the pictures on the walls again.

His father, though, pointed to the oversized, first-generation laptop set up in one corner of the room. "Just have a look." His eyes sparkled, his head tilted toward the computer.

A few minutes later, Nick sat staring at the screen.

Boston to Panama. One way. One seat.

Tomorrow.

He blinked at the offer. His father stood next to him, quietly appraising the quote. It was amazing how quick he was for someone recovering from a heart attack.

"Not a bad price," his dad commented.

Behind them, the house seemed to hold its breath.

Nick didn't dare look up. "Mom will kill me."

His father rolled his head from side to side. "Only a little," he said, pointing to the "Book Now" box at the bottom of the screen.

Colon

March, present day

Vadz scratched his clean-shaven scalp and pondered his predicament as his eyes swept over the streets of Colon from his vantage point at a sidewalk cafe. There was a solution. There was always a solution. He would just have to give it more thought.

Unfortunately, action came more easily than thought to a man of his ilk.

He began the search for a solution by congratulating himself on his various successes. That always helped. He had an innate instinct for business, that was certain. On his own initiative, he had organized backpacker runs to and from Colombia, turning a tidy profit each time. The young travelers he dealt with were like sheep: stupid, unsuspecting, easy to herd. A little like Gregor, his assistant. Or apprentice was more like it — a student learning from a master.

One good thing had led to another, bringing Vadz into contact with other businessmen — big interests who obviously admired his talent. They, in turn, expanded his horizons with the offer to transport more than just people over the border. It was all so easy.

He rewarded himself with a hard swig of vodka. He was on a roll. More and more offers had come along, including this latest one, which was so laughably simple. All he was required to do was keep tabs on those two Americans. He doubted that those ordinary-looking sailors could be up to anything much, let alone be on the trail of something valuable, but you never know. And anyway, the money was good.

The big boss needed Vadz, Cesar had said, because he was special. He was a sailor, with a boat of his own.

Yacht, Vadz had corrected the man.

He puffed out his chest a little more. At this very moment, the ladies at the next table would be admiring him. A shame he didn't have more time for such frivolous pursuits. But he was a busy man. He had a boat, muscles, and charm. He had it all! Even the cartel needed him. Soon they'd be giving him more responsibility, and he'd climb the ladder. Eventually, he would set up his own organization. From humble beginnings to such heady successes! He could practically feel the gold cuff links now. Real gold. Or maybe diamond...

All he had to do was stay close to the Americans without arousing suspicion and keep Cesar, his contact man, informed of developments. All very easy.

Except that things got complicated fast. Soon after Vadz accepted that offer, the Venezuelan came along with a similar idea. Alejandro needed Vadz's help when the time came to relieve the Americans of their prize. It would be three against two with Vadz, Gregor, and Alejandro. More like four against one, since Vadz had the strength of two men, and one of the Americans was only a woman. Easy.

Alejandro had been secretive, as had Cesar, but Vadz figured they were after the same thing. Something old and very valuable. Some kind of ancient relics. He couldn't care less about some old pieces of junk, but other people did, which meant there was money in it. Alejandro's offer exceeded that of the cartel — which meant more profit for Vadz, thanks to his hard bargaining.

So now, he was working for two parties both pursuing the same thing. His tasks, though, were different for both, so his participation was completely legit.

The difficulty was in keeping the two sides ignorant of each other. Early on, he'd toyed with the idea of a double-cross. Why not jump the Americans himself once something valuable turned up? Why did he need the Venezuelan or the cartel? He could keep the entire profit. But he quickly realized he was no historian. He'd need expert consultation once he had the artifacts anyway, so he decided to work with the others. For now, at least.

The problem was that the Americans were proving more slippery than he had imagined — always making impulsive decisions and unpredictable moves, damn it. One was back in America now, probably meeting with prospective clients. Who knew what they'd do next?

Vadz cursed. His work was already complicated enough, what with him shuttling between two coasts. His cheeks heated just at the thought. *Odysseus* had been denied a canal date thus far, as had Alejandro's *Carmela*. Something about an advisor's shortage causing a backlog of small boat transits. At least, that's what the authorities wanted him to believe. Vadz, however, smelled a conspiracy. And he should know: he had a nose for such things.

In the meantime, Cesar was growing jumpy. Something was amiss; a deal somewhere had gone wrong. The man was suddenly overcautious, moving very slowly. Maybe that was a good thing, given Vadz's lack of success in bullying canal authorities. No matter what he tried, they just wouldn't let *Odysseus* through. Who knew how long it might take?

Well, he'd allow things to slow down for now. It would give him time to think.

He checked his imitation Rolex. It was almost time for his appointment with the weapons dealer. After all, the right equipment was critical for this new business venture. He pictured himself not too far in the future, a sort of Polish cross between Rambo and James Bond. Big guns, diamond cuff links, fancy cars. BMWs. Porsches. Maybe even a Hummer...

He paid his tab, tossed a paltry tip to the waitress, and strutted down the road without waiting to see her grateful expression. Yes, he would find a way to make things work soon. He'd make a huge profit and sail off into the sunset with a woman on each arm.

Yes, a solution to this minor dilemma would come to him soon. Very soon.

Balboa

March, present day

Kate stood in front of Stefan, still but for the lazy droplets of pool water sliding down her skin. His eyes drew her in, warm and inviting.

She understood exactly what Stefan was suggesting, and her reaction was not a curt *No*. On the contrary, she could imagine it perfectly. Comfortably. Her mind moved into the building with him. Into the elevator and up to his room, inching closer to each other each step of the way. A brush, a touch, then more. The door would shut the world away behind them, and they would be alone.

She lost herself in the boundless blue of Stefan's eyes. Such an interesting man, such a compelling offer. Someone she had so much in common with. A person she could spend time with, pursuing new adventures and new horizons.

She watched it happen in his eyes the same way it unfolded in her mind. Slowly, sweetly. Imagined him just the way Cheryl suggested: without the glasses. Without the shirt. Without the belt...

Like a person mesmerized atop a skyscraper, she leaned farther and farther out toward the heady view. And like the person standing perilously close to the edge, she realized with sudden clarity and a sharp intake of breath how very, very long the fall would be. The thought was like an arrow, notched by her better conscience and aimed with merciless accuracy.

She blinked.

If things had been different, she might have taken Stefan up on his offer. A different time, a different place. But even in a different time or place, she realized, Stefan still wouldn't be Nick. He would never be Nick — sweet, smart, sensitive. Dogged with the most difficult challenges, like repairs that kept *Aurora* afloat and headed for the next adventure, his scraped knuckles forging the way for both their dreams.

Nick. He was indulgent of her crazy interests. Encouraging, even. Occasionally, he put on the brakes, too, keeping her from going a little too far.

Like now, maybe.

She wrapped her towel firmly across her shoulders, tight enough to answer Stefan's question.

No. Thank you.

Nick was the best thing that had ever happened to her, and she'd nearly blown her chance with him once. She wouldn't do it again.

Stefan's eyes fell, and the two of them stood quietly for a long time, eyes averted. When their eyes met again, his look was rueful.

Worth a try, he seemed to say.

Kate slowed her breathing as her mind fished for something tactful to say. She gathered up her things, thanked Stefan for a lovely morning, and headed back to *Aurora*. Alone.

Which wasn't to say she would avoid meeting with Stefan again or that she would turn down an offer of another discussion hour. But an unspoken agreement fell over them: make like it never happened and stick to safe topics, like terrorism, the canal, and illegal trade of antiquities. They'd keep it professional, like a couple of colleagues.

Because it didn't happen. Because he wasn't Nick.

"Home sweet home," she murmured as she stepped into *Aurora's* cabin.

She reached right past Charlie's notebook and found her diary instead. Hugging a pillow to her stomach, she hunched over the pages. Flipping over the past months, she found a sudden fascination with her own life as if reading about someone else. She thumbed through memories and the ebb and tide of her moods. Excited. Content. Frustrated. Sad.

Lonely.

She skimmed from the beginning in New Jersey onward, wondering if it had been *Aurora* or Nick that kept her happy.

One thing was clear — she was still on *Aurora*, yet thoroughly unhappy.

October 20, Intracoastal Waterway, somewhere in the Carolinas...

November 2. Port Antonio, Jamaica...

December 6. San Blas Islands...

She found an entry detailing one of the sweaty projects she and Nick had toiled over together. She'd cursed his obsession with repairs at the time but chided herself now. The delays and those pesky details were a small price for freedom and adventure with a good man at her side.

The afternoon breeze ruffled the pages, bringing her to a breathless entry — the day she discovered that sections of the Camino Real still survived out in the Panamanian wilderness. She had been in the midst of plotting a day trip there when that phone call had come, calling Nick to Boston. Back when she'd been living her life, instead of clinging to principles.

What other adventures, great and small, had she missed living with Nick?

* * *

She was standing by the curb the next morning, staring into space when Anneliese came by, sending Nils and the kids ahead to play along the causeway.

"Hey. We're renting bikes," Annalise said. "You want to come along?"

Kate cleared her throat, feeling it go dry. She'd spent much too much time with Stefan lately and not enough with her friend.

"Sounds great, but I'm taking a little day trip."

"No problem. How about a quick drink?"

She hesitated. Right now, she needed time alone to think. But Anneliese was always good company, and a cold drink while she was waiting — that would feel good, too.

Anneliese chuckled once they sat down with their drinks. "Can you tell I'm feeling wild? Ginger ale with ice." She held up her glass in a toast.

Kate met her glass halfway and let them clink. "Fanta and ice. But what's my excuse? I don't even have kids."

"Oh, but you're the solo sailor. Much more work."

Solo sailor. Somehow the title didn't feel so enviable any more. She managed a weak smile. "More work than two kids? I doubt it."

"Three kids," Anneliese corrected her, waving toward her family. "Nils is in the same category."

Kate laughed but sobered quickly. "I don't know how you do it."

"Do what?"

"The kids, the boat... The partnership thing." She found herself emphasizing the latter.

"Sometimes I ask myself that," Anneliese laughed a little, then grew more contemplative, keeping her eyes on the kids cavorting outside. Nya was twirling, Adam hopping along. "I'm lucky. Nils wanted to do it all, too — the kids and the trip. I'm lucky to have him."

"Maybe he's lucky to have you."

Anneliese nodded. "That, too."

Kate found herself studying the rings her glass made on the Formica table, wondering about luck. Wondering about Nick.

"Do you ever..." she started, then caught herself. Maybe it wasn't a polite question to ask.

Anneliese cocked her head.

"Do you ever think about the things you gave up to be together?"

"You always give something up." Anneliese shrugged. "Being alone, being together. Either way, you lose something, you win something else."

"That's the problem, though. Deciding between them."

Anneliese was studying her, and Kate felt caught between aching to ask for advice and desperately wanting to joke the topic away.

"It's like this," Anneliese offered at last. "What did you give up to sail?"

She couldn't hold back a dry laugh. "Nothing much."

"List it," Anneliese insisted.

"Easy. A job. An apartment. Stress." She ticked them off on her fingers. "A couple of flowerpots and a car."

"Exactly. And what did you gain?"

"What did I gain?" Kate struggled to find the words and ended up just waving her hand at the view over the mooring field. "This. All this."

"Can you say it? Count it?" Anneliese prodded.

Kate opened her mouth to answer, then closed it. Where would she begin?

Anneliese pointed at her, nodding. "That's it. Much harder to say, right? But where would you rather be?"

"Here!"

"That's what it's like, being with a partner. The things you give up are easy to count and to name. But the things you gain are bigger. Better." Annalise's eyes wandered over the water. "I read a good line somewhere: loneliness is a terrible price to pay for freedom."

Kate was about to protest that she wasn't lonely, she was just... Just, um...

She reached for her glass and took a long swig of her drink. *A terrible price to pay for freedom.* The words echoed through her mind like ripples over water.

Beep! Beep!

She looked up to see Lopta screech through a tight U-turn that brought her cab hard against the curb.

"Hola, amiga!"

Kate waved to Lopta, drained the remainder of her Fanta, and stood. "Gotta go. See you later?"

"See you later," Anneliese said softly, rising to join her family.

Kate stepped toward the cab, then turned back to her friend. "Thanks."

Annalise smiled and waved good-bye. And Kate... She stood there a while. Funny how her legs felt a little shaky, as if she'd just made landfall after a long passage at sea.

Lopta met her with a disapproving look. *Still no Nick?*

Kate hopped into the cab and pulled out her map.

The outing proved to be a welcome break — whether from Balboa or from her own thoughts, Kate decided not to explore. To keep Lopta from dispensing unsolicited love advice as they drove into the brushy outskirts of Panama City, Kate pressed her for information on the Camino Real. But Lopta had never even heard of the historic trail. She did, however, know every gruesome story of horrible fates suffered by other people along this very road. A crocodile attack here, a car crash there. She was a lot like Nick's mother — full of warnings of spectacular ways to go.

The trailhead was easy enough to spot: a wide space on the side of the road with an information board and a couple of rusty old cannons. Kate set off for a solitary walk, leaving Lopta and her warnings of bandits behind. The taxi driver posted herself in the parking lot with her chin jutting and a trigger finger on her cell phone.

Let anyone try to get past me! her fierce expression said.

Within minutes, Kate was swallowed up by the thick vegetation and transported to a primal world where chirping insects and singing birds called out from concealed niches. Howler monkeys growled their low, guttural calls, and an owl hoo-hooed. The footpath itself was unremarkable — just another dirt track scratched through a world of meandering tree roots and dangling vines.

Then her sandaled foot registered a hard surface, different from the cushioned forest floor. She nudged aside the leafy debris blanketing the ground, and there it was: the paved Camino of colonial times. Rounded cobblestones lay like a clutch of dinosaur eggs, packed tightly into the ground. She paced over them, concentrating on each step like a person trying out a new pair of shoes. The undulating surface was warped but astonishingly solid.

Was it minutes, hours, or centuries that passed as she stood there? A tiny figure dwarfed by magnificent trees, dwarfed by time. On impulse, she turned to crack a joke to Nick. *In Boston, road crews patch the streets every two years, and they're still a mess. This road had survived for centuries.*

Then she frowned, remembering she was alone. Alone but for the spirits of the Camino.

Nick. The man had no faith in anything. Not the weather. Not *Aurora*. Not the economy. Nothing — except his unshakable faith in her.

Nick, so very far away.

The owl hooted, and the forest rustled. Spirits? Maroons? She'd read about escaped slaves in her book. Maroons — the term came from *simaran*, the flight of an arrow. She whispered the word out loud.

Simaran.

If only she could fly like an arrow and find her mark. If only she knew where to aim.

She looked up into the canopy as if the answer to her deliberations might be encoded in the foliage. It wasn't. But she reached her conclusion anyway. With a deep, sucking breath, she nodded and made up her mind.

With a last, lingering look at the historic pavement fading into the jungle floor, she headed back to Lopta. Her mind sifted images of Nick, *Aurora*, and Stefan into their proper places as she walked. A plan was already forming in her mind.

"Did you find much?" Lopta asked in Spanish.

Kate didn't know quite what to say. In Lopta's terms, she probably hadn't found much. But in her own terms...

"Yes. Just what I was looking for," she replied.

Chapter Nineteen

Into the Maelstrom

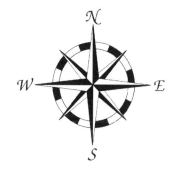

Bay of Panama
January 1914

Yolanta was zipping along beautifully.

"We'll make California in no time." Charlie chuckled out loud.

He loved the symmetry of this trip already. He'd start with a night anchored off Taboga, the very place he'd hatched this brilliant plan back in the sanatorium. And this morning, he'd gotten underway in earnest. In a couple of weeks, he'd be back in the good old U.S. of A. He smiled at *Yolanta's* broad, hardwood decks.

It was only when he cast a good-bye look at the mainland that he noticed anvil-shaped clouds creeping ominously over the hills. Now where did they come from?

He looked around and registered something else. The bay was devoid of seabirds and boats. The space they'd vacated was already filling with something far less friendly.

A storm.

He turned forward, blinking at Taboga. Plenty of time to sail back and get an anchor, right?

When he peeked back again, the clouds were gushing his way. He pursed his lips, thinking back to the previous day when he had cast off. Might there have been a whisper on the wind? Fortuna, calling a warning?

Be careful what you wish for...

He risked another peek over his shoulder. And hell, the entire horizon was black and blue and the clouds surging like waves. The hills had already surrendered to a thick wall of gray.

His mind spun. Back to the mooring?

Too late. Wisps of black were already slinking over the water like scouts creeping ahead of an army.

He remembered something about running for the open sea. Isn't that what old salts did? But taking on the storm in its own element didn't seem like a good idea. Taboga wasn't too far. Even if he had to sit out a squall in that bay, it was better than the open sea.

He glanced over his shoulder, urging *Yolanta* on. Even the capricious boat seemed to take the threat seriously because she ran for all she was worth.

In a matter of minutes, the wind backed from the north through the west and into the southwest, and his comfortable downwind run became a hammering windward beat. *Yolanta* leaned heavily to port until the entire rail was under water. A green furrow of foam hissed over the deck and chilled his feet. When the wind howled with new intensity, *Yolanta* was forced even harder into the wind and heeled over so far, he thought she would flip.

He fought the rudder with all his might, but it was only when he hit on the idea of letting the boom out that the rudder responded. He coaxed *Yolanta* back to port and regained a measure of control. Behind him, multistory monsters hissed and coiled, hungrily eyeing their prey.

Okay, scratch Taboga.

His mind whirled, seeking an alternative escape route. But where? How?

He made up his mind to run east, keeping the wind behind him and the boat balanced. But the wind howled, and each new gust threatened to spin *Yolanta* around. He felt like a mouse dodging the claws of a cruel cat that liked to toy with its prey.

Maybe the squall would blow itself out.

Another look behind his shoulder crushed that fragile hope. The mainland was already obliterated from view. The leading edge of the maelstrom was an eagle with two swept-back wings on either side, stretching its talons forward to scoop *Yolanta* up. Charlie wondered what would happen when it struck.

Whatever it was, it wouldn't be good.

Balboa

March, present day

What was it Mark Twain said?

Nick breathed in the humid night air and ducked his head for a view of Venus. He could just spot it through a corner of the taxi's windshield. The planet shone like a beacon — one that was about to be swallowed by the rumbling thunderstorm roiling over Panama City.

Throw off the bowlines.

Part of his mind was back in Boston. When his mother threatened to throw a fit at his sudden departure, his father had quietly intervened.

"The boy's got an adventure ahead of him. Let him live it."

The way he said it made Nick wonder if his father had any regrets of his own, any missed opportunities.

Sail away from the safe harbor.

He was grateful for the taxi driver's silence. Lopta's incessant chattering wasn't what he was in the mood for. This driver was decidedly quieter, singing softly along to the tunes on his radio while Nick fiddled with the straps of his backpack. If only he had been able to get in touch with Kate before boarding his flight. He was coming in on a wing and a prayer — literally. Under his shirt, his skin was cool and heavy with the weight of Charlie's silver coin. He touched it through the fabric. What would Kate say when she saw it? What would she say to everything they needed to discuss?

His eyes scanned the black-on-black sky. The air crackled, and Venus was gone.

With a clap of thunder, the storm broke. And just like that, it was raining. Pouring. The taxi's wipers flew across the windshield in jerky swipes, unable to keep up with the deluge. The headlights illuminated the cascade of rain immediately in front of the vehicle, but nothing beyond.

"Whoa," he muttered as a car swerved, missing them by a foot.

He wondered if the driver was very skilled or simply insane. He was leaning toward the latter until they splashed to a halt in front of a low, isolated building.

"Balboa Yacht Club."

"Gracias," he murmured, handing over the fare, then timing his exit.

The short sprint from the curb to the bar drenched him. The huddle of people peering out from the doorway parted to let him dash in, and someone cracked a comment that made everyone chuckle.

Nick didn't catch the words. He didn't care. He stood shedding his own raincloud in the entrance for a long minute before registering the scene. So familiar, yet somehow unreal. He really was back.

Back in Panama. Back home?

He looked around. How to find Kate? She was probably hunkered down in *Aurora's* cabin. Was the water taxi even running in this deluge?

The rain was a low roar, battering the thatched roof. His eyes swept through the club until they landed on the profile of a solitary figure at the far edge of the restaurant.

It was Kate, leaning intently over the screen of a laptop as if willing it to do her bidding. Looking bronzed as ever, but with a shadow of anxiety shrouding her frame. He took three steps across the restaurant then paused, suddenly unsure. What would he say?

Water flowed off his short sleeves, dripped onto his bag, and continued to the floor.

What would she say?

"One step at a time," he uttered the words he'd been repeating ever since he left Boston.

He forced his legs to cover the remaining distance. The pounding rain drowned out voices, footfalls, music. The brightly lit space narrowed to just the path before him. Beyond it, everything ceased to exist.

He slipped wordlessly into an empty chair beside Kate, focused on her profile the whole time.

"Hi," he said, a little hoarse.

She turned from her laptop screen with a look of annoyance, then sheer surprise. He wanted to smile, to grab her arm, to do something, but he was frozen, a statue awash in raindrops.

Her mouth fell ajar, then shut. She bit her lip. He desperately wished she would say something, but she only stared, following the water running down his face and clothes. Separate drops slid and joined in tiny streams then miniature rivers, forming a human landscape in liquid form. He could sense the puddle spreading under his feet.

Kate yelped and jerked back to the computer. "Wait!"

Her eyes and fingers searched frantically until she jabbed a key. She studied the screen an instant longer, her finger poised to strike again if necessary. His eyes followed hers to a boxed text on the screen.

Transaction canceled.

When he scanned the rest of the screen, his eyes went wide.

Panama to Boston. One way. One seat.

She stared at him. "Hi," she whispered.

For one second, neither of them moved. The next, she was pressed up against him.

Panama to Boston, he marveled when he could think again. *Transaction canceled.*

Balboa

March, present day

Nick slipped out of bed early and watched the sky model an entire wardrobe of color. He'd been alternating between bed and *Aurora's* cockpit all night, assuring himself that he really was back. It even smelled like Panama — or more precisely, like Balboa: lush jungle with a hint of metropolitan decay.

A freighter steamed through the shipping channel, and he watched it glide past, delighted to be back to this view. The sky was clear blue, the storm blown away by its own intensity. Kate came up and sat, too, leaning into him, taking in the same panorama.

He closed his eyes, feeling warm inside and out. Kate. *Aurora*. Home.

They didn't speak much. They didn't have to. After the most delicious breakfast of tasteless cereal he'd ever enjoyed, he felt the inevitable energy crash when it all caught up to him. He dozed off in the forepeak with Kate curled up next to him. Soft morning light filled the cabin as the sun rose higher in the sky. When they eventually roused themselves enough to indulge in a cool drink at the bar, he found familiar faces all around. A breeze of possibility carried snippets of conversation through the air.

"Can you even believe the backlog in the canal?"

"Thank God they cleared up the advisor's strike. I thought we'd never get through."

"Where are you headed next?"

"Galapagos."

"Marquesas."

"Easter Island."

"Straight through to Tahiti."

There were people they had met back in the San Blas, the Christmas party at El Diablo, and happy hour at Shelter Bay. There was even one crew they had been leapfrogging with ever since the Chesapeake Bay. Now, they all felt like brothers-in-arms.

The *ANNAs* greeted Nick like a long-lost friend, and Nils got to chatting about the time they'd recently spent in Las Perlas, the island group forty miles southwest of Panama City. Anneliese described a wonderful discovery.

"We found a beautiful, uncharted cove off a larger bay. It seemed impossible to enter, but we managed to navigate our way in."

"And the best thing is" — Nils winked — "it has internet! There's an eco-resort on a nearby island with a signal powerful enough to pick up from there."

Anneliese laughed. "Captain Nils is completely independent — as long as he has an internet connection."

Once again, Nick's world was full of laughs and possibilities. Everyone seemed soaked in contentment. Their faces were ruddy and their eyes bright as if the tropical sun radiated more than just warmth and light. Conversations focused on new places, solutions to equipment problems, and uproarious stories — all the more so since Trevor and Tyler had appeared in Balboa on *Free Willy*. Everyone seemed to be enjoying the present and optimistic about the future. It was a different world.

Even in the small subuniverse of *Aurora*, things were different over the ensuing days. Both he and Kate were exceedingly sensitive, determined to banish any hint of discord. He slipped on a pair of well-worn surf shorts with a contented sigh and took an inventory of fishing equipment rather than spare parts. His only repair job was to resurrect the cell phone to reach his enthusiastic father and dry-toned mother. Kate, for her part, appeared to have called a moratorium on plotting ambitious itineraries — at least, temporarily.

Both of them were brimming with ideas for making the most of their time on *Aurora*.

"We could cut costs and eke out our savings to sail as long as possible," he said.

Kate nodded eagerly. "Less eating out, more time in the five-star galley aboard *Aurora*."

"I might even be able to earn a little money while we go."

Mark had grudgingly agreed to let the new guy, Ralf, take over Nick's job — provided Nick called in as remote support from time to time and made a couple of week-long trips to Boston over the next few months.

Kate was full of ideas, too. "I can probably continue my old job, writing grant proposals for the professors I'm still in touch with."

When they put their minds to it, they found lots of ways to top up the cruising kitty. They could spend months enjoying Panama's Pacific islands — and who knew? Maybe even venture beyond.

Everything was falling into place.

Everything but the insistent specter of Charlie Parker. When Nick first took out Rosie's necklace, Kate simply nodded as if it was what she was expecting all along.

"It proves that Charlie really found a treasure. But get this." She told him about the sketch taken from El Diablo and the illegal dig at Nombre de Dios.

"What?" Nick practically yelled.

Was someone else on the trail of Charlie's treasure? If so, who? And did they know *Aurora's* crew shared their interest in the matter?

Not quite ready to face those riddles, he and Kate decided on an excursion to the canal visitor's center at the Miraflores locks. Lopta greeted him like an old friend, brushing his cheek with her hand and shooting Kate an approving wink.

Seeing the massive locks rekindled the excitement of *Aurora's* transit, just as displays on the making of the canal raised more questions about Charlie Parker. Nick found his gut tightening and his resolve growing. The canal builders hadn't given up, in spite of overwhelming setbacks. The least he could do was try to finish what Charlie started. Even if there was no pot of gold — or silver — at the end of the rainbow, he would have made peace with Charlie's ghost.

He stole a glance at Kate and found her eyes shining back, a tinge of green around the summer blue. They exited the visitor's center in a tight, happy squeeze that only cracked when they saw the anguished expression on Lopta's face.

"Lopta, what's wrong?"

"What happened?"

Lopta grabbed Kate by both her forearms and fixed her with a probing expression.

"*Qué haces, chica?*"

Kate shook her head, bewildered, and Nick did, too.

"*Estos hombres!*" Lopta's voice was breathless. Her eyes darted around the parking lot.

He touched Kate's arm as he followed the taxista's worried eyes. "What's going on?"

Lopta chattered and gestured away at Kate, whose face went from perplexed pink to a chalky white. When she finally found the words to reply, he could only catch phrases like *"No sé!"* and *"Nada!"*

He put his hand up, butting in. "What's she saying?"

Lopta stopped speaking and scanned the parking lot, holding up her keys like a weapon.

"Two men came up to her while we were inside," Kate said, rushing the words. "Asking about us. Asking what we're doing, what we're after—"

"What men?"

"I don't know! Two men." Kate asked Lopta for clarification, then translated. "Local men, Panamanians."

Lopta's body language was clear. They were this tall and this big. This rough. One had something on his nose, according to Lopta's pantomime. The other man seemed to lurch more than he walked.

When Nick caught the word "cartel," he froze, looking at Lopta. "Are you sure?"

"*Seguro!*" Lopta insisted, hands on hips.

They stood beside Lopta's battered old Toyota like two muddled sheep before a hysterically barking dog. The taxista plunged on, barely giving Kate a chance to summarize.

"I said, this girl is a good girl! You're all mixed up, I said! I don't drive any bad tourists in my taxi!"

Lopta's speech grew faster and faster, sassier and sassier. Her finger jabbed the air as she reenacted the face-off. Nick felt himself melting under her glare. He could imagine the effect she must have had on the men. Charlatans who thought they could get away with strong-arming her!

She went on and on. Idiots! Criminals! Soulless devils who dared call themselves Panamanians!

Kate tried reassuring Lopta that she wasn't mixed up in any bad business. No drugs. No shady deals.

"*Nada!*" she insisted.

"*Nada?*" Lopta asked, studying her closely.

Kate looked like she'd been slapped. "Nada!"

Nick shifted his weight from foot to foot and looked around. Were they being watched? Followed? Where were the men now?

Lopta gradually modulated to a calmer form of rage and hugged Kate, squeezing the air out of her while murmuring in a motherly voice. Then she motioned both of them into the taxi, squeezed behind the wheel, and slammed her door with a bang. She gunned the engine to life. From the back seat, Kate leaned forward to take something from Lopta, then showed it to Nick.

He stared at the numbers scribbled on a scrap of paper. A phone number?

Lopta started narrating again while revving the engine to a high whine. He felt like they were fleeing down a highway even though the vehicle remained in neutral.

Kate relayed for him. "They gave her this number. Told her to call them to say where we go, who we see."

"Why?"

Kate and Lopta shrugged simultaneously.

"What did she tell them?"

Lopta's look didn't need translating, but Kate did all the same. "She told them to go to hell!"

He shot her a grateful look in the rearview mirror. "Go, Lopta."

She rewarded him with a brief smile before going back to her no-nonsense expression. Then she wrestled the aging clutch into gear with two hands and hit the accelerator. Nick lurched into the backrest as the taxi sped out of the parking lot. The tires screamed through a turn, and they hurtled down the road in silence. Lopta spent more time scanning the rearview mirror than the road ahead.

"*Malo, malo,*" she kept muttering. *"Malo, malo."*

Bad. Really bad. Nick couldn't help but agree.

When they reached the boat club, Lopta begged them to be careful. Kate emphasized her ignorance of any wrongdoing, and Nick brooded. When Lopta sped off, they sank onto a bench. Kate's mouth opened and closed like a suffocating fish. He sat beside her, equally numb. When he leaned against Kate, she lost the last strand of her nerves and buried her face in her hands, hiding a torrent of tears. There was little he could do but wrap himself around her slumped shoulders, feeling neither comforting nor comforted.

Malo, malo.

Bay of Panama
January 1914

Charlie could see the wall of wind before it hit. The powerful gust flattened the waves like a steamroller. *Yolanta* briefly sat upright, a moment's reprieve as the storm inhaled. He tightened his grip on the wheel and glanced back, looking for the exhale.

"Hey!" he yelled as the wind yanked his hat off and blew it into the sea.

A first sacrifice to Poseidon. He hoped it would be the last.

In the next instant, the leading edge of the storm struck — literally. *Yolanta* was knocked on her side for a long, dangerous minute, then slowly creaked back a few degrees. Hanging on to the wheel more than steering, Charlie could feel, see, even taste the wind.

He held a hand to his eyes. Was that rain or sea spray? Whatever it was, it pummeled every inch of exposed skin. He clawed his way over a slanted deck to the mast, then fumbled with the halyard to drop the mainsail. It fell with a crash, allowing the boat to pop upright. He used his body weight to wrestle the sail as the thrashing canvas fought back with wild slaps. A cowboy in a wild blue rodeo, that's what he was.

The leading edge of the storm had swept overhead, followed by a series of hissing waves determined to pick a fight. The horizon was a relative thing, an uncertainty — all fluid mountains and deep valleys. Looking back was terrifying, so he kept his eyes over the bow.

Ahead. There was no way out but through.

The canvas of the jib strained at every seam. How long would it hold?

The plaintive cry of battered wood sounded below decks. Charlie struggled with the temptation to wish the noise away, lest he discover an ugly truth he wasn't ready to face. But no, he had to check. He lashed the wheel and pulled himself to the companionway, hoping for some reprieve.

Inside, the boat moaned like a tortured ghost. Cabinets rattled and clanged. Pots erupted from a cupboard, and he ducked. Then the door of the cupboard slammed against its frame in panic. A wave lifted then dropped Yolanta, producing another heart-stopping crash from beneath the floorboards.

"Whoa."

He froze for a moment, then fell to his knees to yank up one of the floorboards.

"Idiot," he cursed himself.

He'd left spaces between the boxes of silver. What a fool! Every wave sent them hammering into the hull's ribs. The letters stenciled on the wood blurred, but he knew just what they said.

Dynamite. Warning.

God, the irony. He might as well have left the dynamite in those boxes for all the damage they wrought now. He grabbed anything that came to hand — a spare shirt, a shoe, a towel — and rammed them into the spaces between the boxes, trying to lock them in place.

By the time he came back up on deck, *Yolanta* had rounded into the wind. He could barely see the bow, let alone what lay beyond. The compass identified north, west, south, and east, yet nothing pointed to safety. All he could do was bowl along, a puppet to the screaming wind.

Yolanta teetered from crest to trough and crest again, surrounded by foam. One stumble and she would be lost. His hands clamped around the wheel and forced *Yolanta* downwind. Was it hours or minutes that were ticking by?

He shivered and tried bolstering himself with images of all the close calls he'd survived. An angry mama bear in the Yukon. That bar brawl in Rapid City. The slip that nearly sent him tumbling down the face of a waterfall, somewhere in the back of beyond. He counted through all the fingers of one hand and part of the way through the other. At most, he had used seven of his nine lives. No

— eight, including the time he surprised a very pointy rhino. But that was it. He had at least one more life, damn it.

And hell, it sure looked like he'd be needing it.

Each wave heaved *Yolanta* to a lofty lookout point, then dropped her into a dungeon with a deafening crash. Charlie learned to anticipate the highs and systematically survey his surroundings, trying to stitch brief glimpses into a cohesive whole. Mostly, the view served to impress him with the severity of his situation. The wind might have abated a notch, but the stone-gray seas were more confused than ever.

California never felt farther away.

He scanned the tossing seascape, straining to make out a dark smudge as *Yolanta* crested the next liquid peak. Land?

He spotted an island. No, several islands. Charlie was elated for the briefest of moments before he realized the ugly truth. Those rocky shores harbored death. A glance behind revealed several more islands. That *Yolanta* had missed them in the whiteout of the storm seemed a small miracle.

Fortuna, are you with or against me? His knuckles clutched the wheel in silent prayer.

The boat's motion seemed quieter, and at first, he took that to be a good sign. Then he reconsidered. The motion was more sluggish than quiet. He could feel it in the way *Yolanta* slid off the waves. No longer skipping through the sea, *Yolanta* was lurching like a drunk. He couldn't for the life of him understand what caused that. Only that it didn't bode well.

He made for the cabin once more, toeing for one step at a time in the dim light. One, two, three: his ankle splashed into shockingly cold water. He looked around the dim cabin in disbelief. Inches of seawater sloshed over the floorboards, sweeping back and forth with each foundering roll of the vessel. The boat was taking on water — and fast. Every lurch added more to the pool weighing down *Yolanta*. The engineer in him wondered if she would break apart or sink with an unnoticed blub.

Either way, she couldn't last.

He slumped on the second step, gripping the handholds, staring at his destiny. Wondering what it felt like to drown.

All that silver, going to the bottom, along with him. Would anyone ever know or care what had become of him?

His Panama acquaintances would imagine him living a new life in a new place, not dead in the bowels of the ocean. Family back home would think he had run off or had finally been killed in one of his crazy schemes. Which wouldn't be far from the truth.

He looked around the moaning cabin that was supposed to be his future. The silver spider still hung on its nail, mocking him.

Eight down, one to go.

Charlie straightened with the thought. He had at least one life left, damn it!

Balboa

March, present day

A misunderstanding? Lopta didn't seem to think so.

A mix-up? Kate couldn't imagine how.

"A mystery," was all Nick could contribute.

There was no making sense of it.

"Who would want to know what we're up to?" Nick shook his head.

Kate hung her head and cracked her jaw, wanting to protest to the world. She and Nick were just a couple of sailors who had nothing on their minds but a peaceful reconciliation under the sun. Unless, of course, they had stumbled into something more dangerous than fun.

"How about we do a quick email check at the club, then head home?" Nick asked.

She cast an eye on the rapidly sinking sun. Yes, home sounded awfully good right now, especially a home — *Aurora* — that came with a protective moat around it.

She sat in stunned silence, taking in the spectacularly brief sunset while Nick checked his email. In the sky, the colors deepened then faded as nighttime rushed in to claim the earth. Kate closed her eyes and tried to buy into the pleasant optimism of the cool night. Cheerful crickets, familiar faces — anything to get her mind off two thugs in a parking lot asking about her.

Nick rooted around in the backpack for something. The movement allowed Charlie's coin necklace to swing free of his shirt. He held it at the end of its strap, and they both leaned in to contemplate it for the hundredth time. Somehow, the clumsy, off-center design made the coin all the more fascinating. She raised a finger to trace the lines quartering the coin, wondering if the luck it brought was good or bad.

"If only Charlie were at the bar," she murmured. "We could call him over and drag the details out of him over a drink or two."

Nick nodded. "The whole story. Not just the story of the treasure but about him, too."

That coaxed a smile out of her. What would Charlie think of the modern sailing scene? The far end of the bar was filled with boisterous young Panamanians celebrating the weekend. The near end was occupied by sailors, most of them glued to laptops to check the usual: weather reports, email, online catalogs. Trevor and Tyler were there, too, surrounded by beer bottles and flirty backpackers, one of whom was hand-feeding Trevor greasy fries.

She imagined Charlie walking toward her table with a drink in his hand and a tale at the tip of his tongue. Nick seemed lost in similar thought, scrutinizing the necklace.

"Long time no see." A smooth voice in slightly accented English jarred their reverie.

She whirled to find Alejandro leaning casually over the waist-high railing that served as the outer perimeter of the open-air bar. In a strange counterpart to Nick, the open collar of his pink polo shirt revealed a small cross hanging from a gold chain.

She jerked her arm up to Nick's shoulder, blocking the view as he tucked the coin out of sight. Too late?

With a wolfish grin, Alejandro ducked under the rail, crossing the boundary into the premises. The subtle scent of oaky cologne followed him.

Kate flicked her eyes to Nick's in an uncertain exchange. Had Alejandro seen the coin?

"Hi." She only had to utter one syllable, but her voice was cracked and dry.

"May I join you?" Alejandro asked, already reaching for a chair.

She fumbled for a response, but Nick beat her to it. "We were just about to Skype my parents."

Alejandro raised one dark eyebrow and scanned the noisy bar. It was a Friday night, and the place was filling fast. Not exactly the best time or place for a phone call. He turned back to Nick with an expression that said, *I doubt it.* But Alejandro only pursed his lips and released the chair.

"I'll leave you alone, then." He nodded politely, turned, and walked away.

"He's keeping good company," Nick muttered.

Kate followed his glare. The Venezuelan was joining Vadz and Gregor — the Polish sailors from *Odysseus*. They had cleaned up since the last time their paths had crossed in the San Blas, but she still let out a huff of disgust. Vadz's massive shaved head and crooked, once-broken nose still reminded her of a neo-Nazi, and Gregor, well, she just couldn't forgive herself for misjudging the man. He and Vadz cheated those backpackers she'd met in Portobelo. Who were they planning to cheat next?

The patchy lighting in the bar imparted the duo — no, trio, because even Alejandro looked suspicious now — with calculating expressions.

"Do you think he saw Charlie's coin?" she whispered, keeping the threesome in the corner of her eye.

Nick made an indecisive face and pushed a palm against his shirt. "Hard to tell."

Gregor turned in their direction, escaping the conversation around him. His goatee was impeccably trimmed, his shirt neat. All in all, he looked more like the neatly groomed deckhand of a megayacht than a criminal. But still, Kate was suspicious. Criminals came in all flavors, so you never really could tell.

Gregor raised his beer glass in a friendly toast then turned back to Vadz and Alejandro. All three leaned in toward each other, and Kate couldn't shake the image of vultures back in Portobelo, huddled in conspiring groups. What were they up to?

"Let's go," Nick murmured.

"Way ahead of you." She nodded, rising. She glanced at the laptop, where a message from Nick's aunt Laura ended in a smiley face. All she could make out was the postscript.

PS — Keep having fun on that sailboat of yours!

Right. Kate grimaced as Nick clicked the screen shut.

* * *

Given the creeping pace of *Aurora's* dinghy, Kate always found it thrilling to ride the powerful water taxi through the mooring field, especially at night, when the black-tinted seawater seemed more solid than liquid. She was glad, too, for the comforting distance it put between them and the club's latest arrivals.

The water taxi swung alongside *Aurora's* sturdy hull and hovered there as she and Nick clambered aboard. She paused on deck, giving the surroundings a goodnight glance. The graceful Bridge of the Americas and a fully loaded container ship were both lit up like small cities. The long finger of the causeway stretched into the night, dotted with a chain of yellow lights.

Nick, she saw, was casting an appraising eye along the height of *Aurora's* mast.

"You know," he said, "even with all the work a boat takes, it's worth it."

She hugged him. Finally, the man was coming around.

"*Aurora* is perfect. We can feel at home anywhere we travel. We can lock the outside world away and hide inside our private universe. Safe and cozy, right?"

But Nick tensed and abruptly pulled away. He stared at *Aurora's* locked companionway, choking on some comment. She turned to see, one arm still on his shoulder, and gasped.

The companionway was half open, the lock twisted and limp.

A break-in. *Aurora* had been robbed.

A long, shocked minute stretched by, marked by the hammering of her heart. Too late, Kate turned to call back the water taxi. Maybe she and Nick could go away, come back, and find everything all right. But no: the evidence was in a long scratch at the companionway, the carcass of the lock, the useless key dangling from Nick's fingers. The wake of a passing ship hit *Aurora,* rolling her from side to side, making her rigging groan.

"Oh, my God," she whispered.

She clutched his arm as they peered into the cabin. Even in the darkness, they could see the disarray. It was a long time before either of them dared cross the threshold. Then Nick broke the spell, descending the steps and flipping a light switch to reveal chaos. Everything shaken and stirred — by human hands, not the sea.

No longer an impenetrable castle surrounded by a moat, *Aurora* felt like a ruin, exposed and cowering.

"Oh, God," she murmured, looking around as if in a trance.

Nick ran a finger over all the electronics at the chart table, but they looked untouched.

"GPS, radio, radar..." He checked one after another.

Every valuable instrument was in its place, undisturbed.

She inched past him, staring at a heap of books that had been thrown to the floor. She leaned over to pick up one that was fanned out and bent as if it had been stepped upon. Next to it lay the packet of Charlie's letters to Rosie.

"Jesus, what a mess," Nick said, peering into their forepeak cabin.

She cradled the letters, shivering despite the warm air. Settees had been pulled up to reveal the storage areas underneath. Cabinet doors swung back and forth with the rocking of the boat, drumming the walls in an irregular rhythm.

"Look." Nick leafed through the wallet that had been left in full view on the chart table. "Cash, credit card, ID — all untouched."

As were their passports, the toolbox, and camera. All those valuables laid out for the taking, yet ignored. Slowly, the gears in her shell-shocked mind ground back into motion.

Aurora had been searched, not robbed.

An hour later, they'd patched *Aurora's* interior back into order, which was more than could be said of Kate's frayed nerves. She questioned the water taxi driver, but he hadn't seen anything.

"*Nada?*" she tried, trying not to sound too shrill.

"*Nada.*" He shrugged and rambled a vague commentary. Balboa wasn't the safe neighborhood it used to be, he noted through tobacco-stained teeth. But anyway, nothing was missing, right?

Nothing but the small, leather-bound notebook Kate had bought when they first arrived in Balboa. The look-alike to Charlie's notebook, which was safely tucked inside the backpack Nick had carried all day. He took it out and turned it over in his hands.

Coincidence?

Nick's dry look said, *hardly.*

"Whoever broke in to *Aurora* was looking for Charlie's notebook."

"Why? Who?" She searched his face for reassurance, but he still wore the same grim look.

She didn't voice her next question. She just shook. What would the intruders do when they discovered they had the wrong notebook?

Chapter Twenty

Burial at Sea

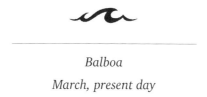

Balboa

March, present day

Lucien extracted himself from his unobtrusive vantage point and made for the seaside promenade where he could watch his mermaid leave.

Merde! Another opportunity lost to the night. The girl had a man now — a different one. One who looked very much at home, like he wouldn't be leaving anytime soon.

He kicked the earth and cursed again. That meant his choices were rapidly narrowing. He sighed, took a deep drag of his cigarette, and contemplated the mooring field.

He had to get moving soon. To spread his wings, as it were, and migrate to new territory. Safer territory, away from his enemies in the cartel.

Unfortunately, the fresh flow of boat traffic through the canal had failed to provide the expected flood of new opportunities. Any of the private yachts would have suited his purpose, but they only made short stops in Balboa before heading out into the Pacific. Moving targets, so to speak, and thus difficult to trap.

His eyes slid to one of the bigger boats among the new arrivals. Maybe that would do. Maybe it was an even better prospect.

Odysseus — that was the name of the sloop. Fifty feet of aluminum. Sleek. Strong. Fast.

Within a few minutes, he couldn't even remember why he'd been considering that inadequate little thirty-two-footer. Because *Odysseus* was better. Maybe even perfect. Sure, the hull was little weathered, but it was a solid vessel with plenty of space for cargo. With it, he could make longer runs in less time and earn more money, fast. Then he'd sail away to Tahiti and live the good life.

It was perfect. Once he had *Odysseus* to himself, his future would be assured.

He would have to get rid of the Poles, of course. The ones he'd bumped into doing Colombia-Panama runs. One was big and stupid. The other was completely harmless and naïve. Still, two were more than one. He'd have to talk them into some scheme and lure them offshore where he could dispose of them one at a time. All it would take was a dark night: a sharp knife stuck into one and a shove overboard for the other. He'd eliminate the big one first. The other one — Gregor — would be easy. And *Odysseus* would be his.

Lucien laced his fingers behind his head and leaned back, satisfied.

He had already made his overtures and enticed the Poles with hints of a hugely profitable smuggling scheme. He'd made sure to mention that he had contacts all the way from Nicaragua to Mexico.

"Rich, important men. Businessmen," he'd assured his prey.

The big Pole's eyes had glittered in response.

"Trust me," he'd said. And fools that they were, they had.

He grinned into the night. It took a master thief to rob a thief, didn't it?

"Just as soon as we finish this next job, we'll be ready to go." Vadz had said over a late-night vodka. His beady eyes seemed busy imagining an easy fortune.

The "next job" was what caught Lucien's attention. Vadz had played coy after that slip, but Lucien was certain something was stirring. Something involving gold and silver — vast quantities of it. It sounded farfetched at first, but he'd overheard Vadz — amateur that the man was — whispering about it on the phone. He could practically see precious metal glowing in the man's eyes.

Something was brewing, and it called to him like the sea.

So once again, he decided he could risk watching and waiting. Just a little longer. He would shadow his new associates and keep the booze flowing. More information was guaranteed to slip out of their stupid mouths. Whatever plan those amateurs harbored, it was bound to be full of gaps. There was another man involved, as well — a South American of some kind. An unknown quantity thus far. The three of them were plotting away in the bar at that very moment.

Lucien lit a cigarette and took a long, hard drag, watching them.

When the time came, he would act fast. They'd never see the hand of the master thief coming.

He let out a long plume of smoke and nodded to himself. Yes, he'd make it to Tahiti, after all. Soon. Very soon.

Balboa

present day

Sleep was impossible. Night, a welcome conspirator.

Kate peered through the darkness, took a deep breath, and dropped the mooring line.

Go, she signaled to Nick, who stood at the wheel, ready to make their escape in the frothy wake of a freighter.

"Running lights?" she asked quietly.

Nick shook his head. They only flicked on the running lights when the narrow channel opened into the breadth of the Pacific. Even then, it seemed *Aurora* approved of stealth, because the masthead lights refused to come on. She shot Nick a look — another repair for the list — and settled for the deck-level lights.

Where could they go? What would they do?

Her mind ran over the rough plan they'd agreed on as they cleaned up the cabin, still half in shock. They'd decided to head for the secret anchorage Annalise and Nils had discovered among the islands of Las Perlas, fifty miles to the southeast. Away from the city, away from the yacht club. Away from whoever it was who had broken in to *Aurora*.

"It'll be fine," Nick whispered, not too convincingly.

"Fine," she echoed in a thin tone.

They communicated in brief, quiet exchanges, raising the sail once they were clear of the channel. As if glad for a cooperative wind, *Aurora* rushed southeast for all she was worth.

Gradually, the glare of lights and tight knot of ships thinned as they raced into the night. Kate kept glancing back toward the city glow and adjusting the sheets. This was one of those rare times when optimal sail trim was paramount in her mind.

"Who would break in to *Aurora*?" Nick asked. "Why?"

Stefan's words ran through her memory like a river of ice. *The cartel was involved in everything.*

Everything?

Everything.

She clutched the wheel and glanced around. How far would the cartel go to get what they wanted? The two men who approached Lopta hadn't made any direct threats, but they didn't need to. Now that they had gone so far as to break in... The thought was so disturbing, she let it trail off.

"You think it was the two men who approached Lopta?"

"Could be." Nick shrugged. "Could be someone else."

"It had to be them. Who else is out there?"

The look on Nick's face said he didn't want to guess.

She shook her head, thinking of other possibilities. A cartel was the worst possibility, but not the only enemy.

But wait. Since when did *Aurora* have enemies?

Since this treasure hunt of theirs, she decided. God, she'd been playing with matches, and she might just have set off a blaze.

Nick avoided meeting her eyes even when their paths crossed during constant, sweeping inspections of the horizon. Dawn's golden light revealed the low-lying islands of Las Perlas and with them, a crumb of hope. Kate tried to gather some resolve as the sun warmed *Aurora's* deck. The archipelago had served as a pirate's den centuries ago. It would serve equally well as a refuge now.

She fell asleep slumped in the cockpit while Nick steered. When she woke, his expression was just as hard-set, and *Aurora* was gliding past the northernmost outliers of the islands. She took a turn at the wheel, constantly referring to the chart beside her to track reefs and submerged rocks while Nick sat in a half-daze beside her, unable or unwilling to sleep.

"Getting there," she murmured, trying to reassure herself.

Unlike the crowded San Blas, Las Perlas seemed virtually devoid of people — not only of cruisers but also of a local population, except for a few dots on the map. A village here, a small resort there. The anchorage penciled in by Nils was wedged between a maze of fractured islets in the northern portion of the archipelago and the southern half, where islands spread into hilly chunks. By midday, *Aurora* was swinging into the lee of uninhabited Isla Viveros, where a huge bay and sandy beach came into view.

"Not a boat in sight," she noted with relief. She turned *Aurora's* bow into the wind, ready for Nick to strike the mainsail.

"This bay would make a great anchorage, but..." Nick trailed off.

She nodded. If anyone sailed past, they'd spot *Aurora* immediately.

So they pushed on. They needed more than a good anchorage — they needed a hideout.

"Slow ahead," Nick called, waving her forward from the bow as she powered up *Aurora's* engine.

She nosed the sloop toward a narrow, rock-lined gap between Viveros and a neighboring islet, a slot no sane sailor would approach. God, why did the *ANNAs* ever decide to venture this way?

"What if it's the wrong entrance?" Doubts gnawed at her gut.

Nick shook his head. "That has to be it."

She checked the chart for the hundredth time as if the details might have changed in her favor. The chart showed a mere three feet of water ahead — much too little for *Aurora's* five-foot draft. According to Nils' description, however, there ought to be enough water for *Aurora* to slip over the shallow bar now that it was half tide.

"Ought to?" she murmured, wondering who she should have more faith in — Nils or the chart maker.

"Eight feet," she called, watching the depth sounder. "Seven... six... still six." She held the wheel tighter, half expecting the grinding sound of the keel against rock.

"Six feet... back to seven." She held her breath.

The waterway ahead was so narrow, so shallow-green, it seemed impossible that *Aurora* could get through. Ahead, land squeezed in, rock looming to sheer walls.

"This is crazy," she called, about to frantically spin the boat around.

"Slow ahead," Nick insisted, waving her into a sharp left turn from his lookout position on the bow.

She held her breath through a tight turn to port, another turn to starboard, and then—

"Wow," Nick breathed.

They were through.

"Wow," she echoed as *Aurora* glided into a wide, placid lagoon where depths dropped off into double digits.

She guided *Aurora* in one tight loop, then hovered in the center as Nick let the anchor drop to the muddy bottom. She backed down hard to set it, then eased and cut the motor.

Peace descended over the scene, cushioning the new arrivals. Curious birds regarded the strange, new animal in their midst. Her eyes met Nick's for the first time that morning. Then she sat down with a dull thud.

"We made it. We're safe." She exhaled.

"For now, we are," Nick murmured.

* * *

They collapsed into sleep for the remainder of the afternoon, huddled close in the forepeak. When Kate emerged from the cabin in the late afternoon, the beauty of *Aurora's* surroundings struck her for the first time. The secret cove was essentially a lagoon, all but cut off from the ocean. Inside was space enough for a solitary boat to swing in a full circle.

Nick came up beside her and nodded in quiet approval. "Looks good."

They launched the inflatable kayak and rowed ashore, then bushwhacked to the top of the nearest hill, where she emerged upon a cluster of boulders and looked out.

"Perfect," she decided after a good look around.

Uninhabited Viveros was small and low, but the hills were just high enough to conceal *Aurora's* mast. She scrutinized the beaches visible from this vantage point: not a single boat, and the sand looked undisturbed. They were well and truly alone. Hidden. Safe. The sun was slowly setting, casting a soft glow over the view.

She looked down at *Aurora*, resting so peacefully in her private boat basin. Safe for how long?

With a loud rustling of leaves and vines, Nick emerged from the bushes and clambered up beside her. He turned in a slow circle to reconnoiter the area.

"Nice, huh?" she said, trying to sound upbeat.

Nick pointed silently at a rugged hill to the east. A metal frame protruded from the undergrowth there — the antenna Nils had mentioned, with an internet connection they could tap into.

Satisfied with their hideaway, they headed back to Aurora and soaked in the scene. It was such a contrast to the cacophony of Balboa. Aside from isolated bird calls, only a choir of crickets brought the lagoon to life, tuning up for their evening performance. Night brought sweet silence, with sparkling bioluminescence imitating the stars above, all the clearer without a city's dimming effects.

How long would the peace last? she wondered as she lay half asleep in the first dark hours of the night.

Never long enough, she concluded, nudging closer to Nick and pulling her head under the sheet.

Balboa

present day

"Idiots." Alejandro cursed into the pink of dawn.

Gone. *Aurora* was gone.

He pushed his hair back, flipped open his cell phone, and dialed.

"What?" a sleepy Vadz grunted into the other end of the line.

"They're gone," Alejandro said in an even tone. He left out the second part: *you were supposed to be keeping an eye on them.*

Damn it. He couldn't afford to lose track of the Americans. They were the key.

He scanned the water once more then fixed his eyes on *Odysseus*, where Vadz was just heaving his bare-chested mass up on deck. Angry huffs came across the phone as the man stamped in fury. But stamping and swearing wouldn't change anything.

"Meet me on land in thirty minutes," Alejandro ordered, snapping the phone shut.

In spite of everything, he took his time with his morning routine, brewing a latte on the high-tech espresso machine in his roomy galley and sipping it in the cockpit. Only afterward did he hail a water taxi and question the driver. Yes, there was something unusual last night, the man said. The American boat was broken in to.

"A real shame. Nice people."

"Nice people," Alejandro agreed, eyes darting around the mooring field.

He stepped ashore, outwardly calm even though he was seething inside. He brightened upon spotting the Dutch family already out and about. Surely Kate's friends would know where *Aurora* had gone. They were outside the club, letting the children run off their morning energy. He ambled over and made a few polite inquiries before asking about *Aurora* on the pretense of having a USB stick to return.

Anneliese looked surprised. "They left? Why?"

That's what he wanted to know, but neither Anneliese nor her husband had any idea where their friends might have gone.

"No problem." He smiled. "I'm sure they'll turn up."

It was clear what must have happened. Last night, the Americans were in normal spirits when he'd seen them. A little jumpy, possibly, but no more. They must have gone back to their boat to discover the break-in, which spooked them into leaving in the dead of night.

The issue was the break-in. Since the Americans were clearly not rich, he immediately suspected what the robbers were after.

He tapped his fingers against his belt. Yes, he'd guessed there might be other interested parties. Now he had proof. Someone had just butted in on his poker game, damn it.

His grimace stretched into a smile. That simply upped the ante. A new challenge would make this game that much juicier, and the end result more rewarding.

Vadz came lumbering over, seething, and Alejandro excused himself from Anneliese before the Pole startled the children with those murderous eyes of his. He motioned the beefy man over to the clubhouse wall. The building was closed, and the windows were expressionless, reflecting the morning sun.

"They got away," Vadz growled.

Alejandro raised an eyebrow and waited for more.

"It was Gregor's fault," the idiot insisted.

Right. "And what about this break-in?"

"What break-in?"

His nose twitched as he observed Vadz. Something in his demeanor wasn't quite innocent. Of course, there wasn't an innocent bone in that hulk of a body. But still, there was something — a flicker of recognition in the man's dull mind. Not enough to incriminate him in the burglary, but enough to show that he wasn't surprised.

He knew Vadz ran a few low-level jobs for criminal organizations. That was a given, considering his enthusiasm for quick round trips to Colombia. But what other ventures was he involved in?

Alejandro smoothed his collar, making sure it was properly folded, and continued to scrutinize Vadz. Obviously, the man had already immersed himself in the degenerate criminal world. He could easily picture the Pole making covert calls to some weasel of a contact man in the cartel. What a fool.

He hid a sigh. It was too late to bemoan his choice of help in the muscle department. He had to keep things running, maintain control.

"This job needs a soft touch," he said in a tone that was both scolding and soothing. "Finesse."

Vadz nodded, although Alejandro doubted he knew what finesse meant, even in his native tongue.

"I'll take care of it." Vadz scowled.

"No!" Alejandro barked. "I'll take care of it."

All he needed Vadz for was his muscle. If he let the man get too close to his quarry beforehand, they'd be scared off again. No, that wouldn't do. Alejandro didn't need the Pole to find *Aurora*. He knew just the man for the job — a man named Jorge.

"I'll handle everything," he said, stressing that point again. "Then the prize will be ours."

Or rather, mine.

"You're sure?" Vadz growled.

He adjusted his designer sunglasses just so. "Leave it to me." He caught his own reflection in the glass and smiled.

Leave it to me.

Las Perlas archipelago
March, present day

The secret cove was a magical, serene place. The only disturbance to the calm water were ripples radiating from surfacing fish. It was a soothing oasis in which high anxiety could give way to cooler, calmer thoughts.

Nick caught Kate's eye as they sat over the remnants of breakfast, still spread across the cockpit table. *So what do we do now?*

Running away wouldn't do forever. Or would it? Should they leave Panama? Leave *Aurora*?

He should have known the very suggestion would make Kate bristle.

"I am not leaving Panama on account of some bullies!"

"How about criminals? Lopta said cartel." The word swung between them like a punching bag. "What would a cartel want with us?"

Kate took a long time answering. "I think they want Charlie's treasure."

"How would they know about Charlie?"

Her hands churned the air. "I don't know! But what else could they be after?"

"Since when are cartels into archeology?"

"Artifacts, not archeology. There's a big difference." She made a face. "Apparently, the cartel does everything that makes money."

"Everything?"

"Everything," she murmured, staring at the table. "Remember what I told you about Richard Brewster Lewis, the guy who wrote the book about treasure in the Caribbean?"

He nodded, deciding not to mention that he now owned a copy of *Pirate Gold!*, courtesy of Aunt Laura. Kate would flip out if she knew.

"There's always been a market for antiquities, but there's even more interest now that this book is out. There are rumors of rewards — big ones — on the black market for a good find." Kate turned her wrath on a fly sampling the milk at the bottom of her cereal bowl. "Charlie!" she muttered, splashing it away. "If he left us some half-decent information, we might actually have something to go on."

Nick was more forgiving of his great-grandfather. He imagined Charlie arriving in Panama for a taste of adventure and getting a lot more than he bargained for. A little like him right now.

"He probably wasn't thinking it would take a hundred years to get back on the case."

Kate's drooping shoulders admitted he was right.

Would it take another hundred years to sort things out? Nick leaned forward, searching for an oracle in his coffee mug. Disappointed, he settled for another sip.

"Why would a cartel be involved in the black market?"

"Apparently, they'll do anything that turns a profit. Think about it — they already know about smuggling drugs. Why not branch out into smuggling other things?"

"And how would they know about us?"

Kate's eyes met his, then dropped away.

"What?" When no answer came, he leaned closer. "What?"

Slowly, carefully, she spoke. "An archaeologist and the great-grandson of a canal engineer showing an interest in pieces of eight..."

His first reaction was, *So what?* But then it hit him. Not only had they mentioned these innocuous facts to several people, they had been seen researching pieces of eight. He winced at the memory of Tyler seeing Charlie's notebook back in Shelter Bay and of their indiscretion back in El Diablo.

"Alejandro! Arty! They knew we were interested in old coins!"

"Them and who knows who else. But none of them seem like cartel types to me."

He reluctantly had to agree. Much as he disliked Alejandro, the Venezuelan didn't seem the criminal type. And Arty seemed too washed-up to be up to anything sinister.

"Anyway, someone figured out we know something."

"Too bad we don't actually know anything," he muttered.

Kate plowed on. "That's why they took the *Yolanta* drawing from El Diablo. That's why they approached Lopta."

"Somehow, we need to get them off us."

Kate looked like she wanted nothing better.

"Are they after us or the notebook?" he wondered out loud.

"Same thing."

"Maybe not," he said, toying with a spoon.

"What do you mean?"

He took a long time answering. "Theoretically — just theoretically — if they had the notebook, they might leave us alone."

"What?" Kate screeched. "We call them up and say, it's all yours? Here's the notebook. Please leave us alone now?" She let the words sink in before punching on. "We can't just give up on Charlie!"

He replied a little too fiercely. "I don't want to give up on Charlie! But we need to figure out what to do!"

Kate sucked in a long breath of air and pushed into the seat rest behind her, backing away from him.

He closed his eyes and concentrated on deep breaths. Another long silence ensued, marked only by the distant splash of a pelican. Finally, he stretched his legs out until they found Kate's. After a stiff pause, she wrapped her ankles around his.

"Even that wouldn't necessarily stop them from coming after us again." She played with the spoon in her bowl, then abruptly broke into action, stepping down into the galley.

"Can we report them? Or the treasure?" he asked, handing down the rest of the dishes.

"No good. Stefan said there's a corrupt official in the cultural ministry."

"Who's Stefan?"

The dishes clattered into the sink. Kate kept her back to him for a long minute before she turned.

"Remember the reporter in Shelter Bay? I met him again in Balboa and..." she stuttered, then finished in a rush. "He told me about that."

He eyed her closely, sitting very still while his heart beat faster. Harder.

She spread her hands in the air. "We spent some time together..."

His eyes narrowed as she rushed to finish.

"Not that kind of time!"

Another staring contest ensued, in which Kate's eyes pleaded innocent while he took close stock of her unconscious cues. She was nervous, unhappy with a memory. What else? Silence pulled at the air around him, alternatively squeezing and sucking him dry. *Aurora* shuffled restlessly, twisting her anchor line, then paused as if holding her breath.

An image of Kate hunched over a laptop as rain pounded a thatch roof came to his mind. *Panama to Boston, one way*. She'd been on her way to him, leaving *Aurora* and her sailing dream behind to be with him. So there was no need to get all uptight, right? Still, he had to work his jaw before he could force out a few words.

"What's with the cultural ministry?"

She came back up into the cockpit and slid in next to him instead of across the table. He felt her stroking his arm, but the stiffness refused to dissipate.

After a long, quiet minute, she summarized the situation at the National Institute of Culture. One junior archaeologist, Doctor Ortiz, was honest, but his female superior, Doctor Hidalgo, was probably corrupt. And she essentially controlled the department. If Kate reported Charlie's clues to them, there would be no telling where the treasure might end up. An impossible situation.

"Great," Nick huffed.

"What do you do when you can't trust anyone?" Kate wondered out loud, staring at her feet.

He watched a pelican circle, then fold its wings and hurtle into the water.

"Just like repairing the boat, I guess. You do it yourself." Even his voice sounded weary, uncertain.

With a loud splash, the pelican broke the surface, struggled, then popped up empty. A miss.

He refocused to find Kate fixing him with a penetrating gaze. He started to backpedal, realizing what he had just said. Do it yourself?

"That doesn't necessarily apply to this situation!"

"Why not? We know more than anyone else about what Charlie found. If we find the treasure and bring it in to an honest member of the cultural ministry..." She stressed the word *honest* then plowed on. "If we make sure it's public enough that nothing can disappear — then it's all taken care of, and whoever is after us will leave us alone. They'd have to."

He looked at Kate. The flashing, defiant look in her eyes told him she meant it. Was she nuts or brilliant? Then he remembered the chess game with his father, the unplanned move with his knight. But was real life anything like chess? His gaze shifted from the boundaries of the cockpit to the limitless sky.

"But what about...?" he started then trailed off. Even if they managed to find Charlie's treasure, he couldn't swallow the thought of just giving it away. Maybe they couldn't cash in on a rarity like the spider — but what about some of the coins? Wasn't that what Charlie would have wanted?

"What about what?" Kate asked.

He brushed over the thought. "It's all a moot point if we can't find where Charlie hid it."

"We need to find it," she said, frighteningly resolute.

He nodded slowly. It was true. They needed that treasure.

Taking that as her cue, Kate stepped below and came back with Charlie's notebook, the note to Mercedes, and Rosie's letters. He added a notepad to the collection and placed the coin necklace beside it. Then he started scribbling notes, more to spur ideas than to record any information.

"This time, I swear we'll figure it out," Kate murmured, echoing his thoughts.

But an hour later, they were still staring at Charlie's notebook with blank eyes. Nick rattled his pencil on the paper then leaned back to study the sky for new inspiration, having used up the meager supply at deck level. His peripheral vision caught the masthead, a reminder of the light that didn't work. That, at least, was something he could solve. Even though he'd have to do it without his trusty Red Sox hat to shield his eyes from the sun. Somehow, in the craziness of the last twenty-four hours, he'd managed to lose it.

Trading Charlie's mementos for a harness and tool belt, he slapped on his backup hat and tied into the halyard. He started pulling himself up the mast, aided by Kate on the winch at deck level.

"One of these days," he puffed, "we're getting mast steps."

Pausing halfway up to take in the view of *Aurora* and the lagoon beneath, he couldn't help cataloging all the tasks that lay ahead of him. First, he'd fix the contacts on the masthead light. Then the iffy anchor windlass. After that, they'd have to figure out a way to get a cartel off their backs. And eventually, they might just take *Aurora* across the Pacific.

Simple, right?

He half laughed, half cursed and resumed his climb.

Bay of Panama
January 1914

Charlie sat hopelessly in the din of the storm, his ankles awash in cold water, contemplating death.

Imminent death.

The silver spider over *Yolanta's* chart table swung with each lurch of the boat. Those beady eyes remained fixed on his, mocking him as always.

And that's what did it in the end. Charlie found himself sneering back. He refused to die. This was not his day to go. Not here, not now, and certainly not with that ghost of a spider eyeballing him like that.

"No, siree," he said aloud, if only to spite that damn spider.

He struggled to his feet and clawed his way back to the wheel with new determination. One chance was all he needed. Any chance, no matter how slim. With or without Fortuna's help, he would find a way out of this mess. True, he was desperate, but desperation brought inspiration.

He cast about for some starting point to build an escape plan around. The flailing mainsail? The little launch lashed to the coach roof? The nearest island? Somehow, he had to save himself.

Yolanta was rapidly closing with the north shore of a long hump of land. What if he drove her aground? The boat would be lost, but he might just survive. He squinted through the spray for a closer look and promptly shook his head. Too many rocks, too much power in the waves. Even if he weren't crushed along with *Yolanta*, he wouldn't make it to shore alive. Not in those waves.

What else? He might just clear the east end of the island. Turn the corner, get in the lee.

His mind whirred, calculating. It was worth a shot. His last shot?

The idea tantalized and terrified him. If he could reach the lee of the island, he might just survive. He might be able to beach the boat or even just float ashore on a scrap of wood. Anything was better than open water in a foundering boat.

Turn the corner, get in the lee.

The words rang over and over in his mind as *Yolanta* clawed her way closer to her goal. Esperanza Island, he dubbed it, remembering the name of one of Mercedes' girls. Esperanza. Hope.

And damn, did he need hope.

Yolanta labored up from the bottom of a wave, telling him his time was running out. The seams of the little jib were holding on by the skin of their teeth, pulling *Yolanta* onward. His mouth stung with the taste of salt. His eyes felt scrubbed raw but refused to stop staring at the island. *Yolanta* was nearly at the corner where a field of partially submerged rocks gnashed their teeth at him. A second island jutted out behind Esperanza. A narrow strait separated the two. Smack in the middle of that strait, a reef exploded with waves.

He shielded his eyes with a hand. Was that a navigable streak of water on the north side, or was it death?

Yolanta waddled on, and the rain-streaked view opened up. He saw a line of yellow-gold — a strip of sand on the south shore of Esperanza Island.

"That's it," he said to no one in particular.

That was his chance. His one, slim chance. If he could sneak past the reef, he might just find himself alive at the end of the day. And if not, well, at least his body stood a chance of washing ashore.

He sucked in a deep breath and eased the wheel over, stiffening as the boat heeled in the teeth of the wind. The howl increased to a roar, augmented by the frantic flapping of the doused mainsail. He muttered to *Yolanta* to hang on. Just a boat length ahead, the sea seemed marginally less frothy. The lee of the island lay just there. *Yolanta* was inching into something akin to shelter.

He didn't dare look as they slid past the roaring reef. His teeth were clamped against the crash he expected, but somehow, *Yolanta* stumbled clear. She was past the reef, but would she make the beach?

His hopes lifted, then sagged. The little craft was being swept sideways by a current. She wouldn't make the beach, not in her bloated state. His eyes drifted farther left, where a rocky ledge descended into the sea. They would ground there.

Between a rock and a hard place. He didn't smile at his own joke. It was that or nothing. Even if the boat was smashed to smithereens, he might have a chance to get ashore.

Might.

They were closer now, much closer. The water went green. With a sickening grind, *Yolanta* slid up a rock ledge, and her timbers screeched. The wheel jolted and writhed, fighting his grip with a deafening hiss. It was like looking straight up into the mouth of a sea dragon. He could feel the beast slide its claws under *Yolanta's* hull, ready to lift, flip, and destroy.

That wave would either kill him or drive the boat ashore. His hopes were on the latter. His money, though, was on the former. He braced himself for the wall of green just as the cold fist of it exploded over the stern, burying both man and boat.

Chapter Twenty-one

Light-years Away

Las Perlas archipelago
March, present day

Nick slept surprisingly well that first night in the secret anchorage and woke the next morning wondering if it was exhaustion or the magic of the location that did it. Either way, he felt refreshed, if none the wiser regarding the adventures of Charlie Parker.

Kate was already up, tidying the last of the break-in mess — a pile of papers that had been scattered across the floor and hastily put aside in the rush to flee Balboa. Many of them were photocopies and sketches from fellow sailors detailing lesser-known anchorages of Panama's Pacific coast. At one time, they all seemed so promising. So many possibilities, so many places to explore.

Nick sighed. Now, all he wanted to do was hide.

He watched her hold a page to the light. Sunlight radiated through it, projecting the lines from one side of the double-sided sheet through to the other. The result was a jumble, at least from his perspective. Which was fitting. A jumble — that's what his life had become.

"Crap," she murmured, lowering the sheet.

He nodded, wishing for the thousandth time that Charlie had left a clue half as clear as these rough sketches. Their treasure hunt was becoming more of an obsession than an innocent diversion, and all he wanted was to put the whole escapade behind him, along with any shady characters.

"There has to be something here," she murmured, leafing through the pages yet again.

"Maybe there isn't." He sighed.

Kate didn't reply except for whispering, "Talk to me, Charlie. Talk to me."

"How about a break?"

She dropped the notebook and scowled at it. "A break would be nice."

"How about we tackle the Enchanted Garden?"

She smiled at the joke. The Enchanted Garden was their name for the thick layer of growth blooming around the hull after too many weeks at rest.

"Sounds good to me."

He was half a step ahead of her — pulling on his mask, gulping a deep breath, and diving down under the hull. Rays of sunlight filtered through the cold water, wavering around him, and soon, he had a rhythm going. Dive, scrub, surface. Suck in air, repeat. That's how he would describe this sloppy duet of splashing fins and whisking cloths.

An eternity later, with nine-tenths of the tedious job complete, Kate kicked violently past him in a rush to the surface. What was wrong? He shot up and found her sputtering a string of rushed syllables. Something about getting hit or bit.

A jellyfish? Shark? He glanced wildly around. "You got bit?"

"I got it!" Her voice was strangely jubilant.

"You got what?"

She was already reaching for the swim ladder, yanking off her fins and clambering up. He followed her out.

What had gotten into her? "What is it?"

He followed, watching her drip all over the cockpit and swipe the salt water away with a towel without bothering with a freshwater rinse. Tossing the towel to him, she ducked below then emerged with something in her hands.

"I got it!" Her hands shook open one of Charlie's love letters.

"Watch out." He rubbed the towel over her hair before it could drip onto the letters. "What are you doing?"

She dried her head clumsily before throwing the towel over her shoulder. "Look!"

She folded and unfolded the last letter from Charlie to Rosie. All he saw were the words they had read and reread countless times, wandering erratically through the air.

"See?"

She folded the letter again and held it up to the sun. With the backlight, the words from each fold blended into an illegible tangle of ink.

"Here!"

She pointed at the margin, where several scribbles overlapped to form a single unit, and all of a sudden, he saw it, too. That curve indicated a coastline. That M-shaped mark, a boulder. A drooping, forked form was a tree. There was a bold X and near it, a faint W-shaped scrawl. Lining up in the corner of each of the folds were L-shaped marks with which to align the sketch.

Charlie had left a treasure map — not in his notebook but in a letter to Rosie. They had it! Now they knew! Now they could follow it and—

Follow it where? He deflated as quickly as he'd soared. They had nothing.

Yes, the three sections of the letter folded together to form a reasonably clear map that showed a section of coastline and a pair of landmarks. If the size of the T — a tree? — was any indication of scale, the area in question was a few hundred meters across. But where was it drawn? They couldn't comb over every inch of the Panamanian coastline — both oceans of it — searching for a match.

Kate threw Nick an exasperated look.

"The other letters?" he suggested, setting off another flurry of folding, unfolding, and scorching of retinas. Eventually, they set the letters aside, rinsed in fresh water, and tried from the beginning, studying the letters and Charlie's notebook for veiled notes.

"A specific region would be good. A coast even," Kate muttered.

"Coordinates would be even better," he added, pushing himself back from the table with both hands.

They were one tantalizing step closer to solving Charlie's riddle, but still light-years away.

He decided to search for inspiration in the minutia of the anchor windlass. Two hours later, he stretched his back and looked around with a sigh. As far as boat work was concerned, they were making excellent progress. As far as Charlie's treasure went, however...

When he eventually reinstalled the windlass in its tight bow compartment, it was with a silent prayer that he would never, ever, have to contort himself into that particular corner of the boat again. He crossed that task off the list with especially bold strokes of the pen. If only he could do the same with Charlie's treasure. Done. Dusted. Move on.

As long as they were hidden in Viveros, he felt safe, but his brightened mood tiptoed across a tenuous foundation. What was going on in Balboa? Was the cartel on their trail? Would they come after *Aurora*?

One thought was paramount in his mind. *Find the treasure before they find us.*

Within a few days, however, a new problem arose. They couldn't hide away forever, and their rushed departure from Balboa had left no time to provision, so supplies were running low. Kate's perusal of their cruising guide described a small settlement on Contadora, an island at the northernmost end of the archipelago. Being closest to the mainland, there was more development there than any other of these sparsely populated islands.

"Maybe we can reprovision there," she suggested.

When they slowly piloted *Aurora* out of the lagoon, Nick felt like a hermit crab cautiously emerging from its shell. Luckily, there was no one in sight there nor anywhere along the four-hour sail to Isla Contadora, where they anchored behind a handful of other boats. The outgoing tide exposed a wide beach with rocky caves at the foot of steep bluffs.

"The perfect place to hide treasure," Kate murmured.

He looked around, remembering her comment about pirates frequenting this archipelago. He was beginning to suspect that buccaneers spent more time tarring the rigging and repairing torn sails than counting their treasure, though.

Charlie, where did you hide yours?

There was no answer except for the gentle lap of water on the beach.

Contadora turned out to have a smattering of beach hotels and posh weekend residences, but no supplies despite the fact that single-engine airplanes buzzed overhead in hourly flights. Just being in view of other people made Nick jittery. Kate walked unusually close to him, too. Frustrated, they rowed back to *Aurora* and agreed to make a late afternoon dash to a less conspicuous place. Just four miles around the corner from Contadora was the uninhabited island of Chapera.

"We can anchor out of sight there," Kate noted, looking up from the chart. "Then we can figure out what to do next."

The slanting rays of a rapidly drooping sun ushered *Aurora* into the deserted anchorage on the south side of the island, which seemed like child's play after the twisting entrance to the secret anchorage farther south.

"Hey," he called from the bow once he was sure the anchor had a firm bite on the bottom. "Look." He motioned Kate forward and gestured wordlessly at the gold-hued beach backed by knots of vegetation.

"Pretty," she whispered.

The beautiful view and a tight hug were mildly reassuring. He took the feeling with him back to the cockpit and watched the reds and oranges of sunset give way to the first stars. Tracing constellations, he remembered all the resolutions he had made on the plane ride from Boston to Panama. He'd vowed to take full advantage of the cruising lifestyle and appreciate all the little things, including having someone he cared about to spend peaceful days with.

Right. Peaceful.

What else was on his list? Become a better weatherman. Finally master celestial navigation.

The stars winked at him from above. *What are you waiting for?*

He stirred. If he was quick, he could get in a few star sights — a perfect distraction. That would allow him to put his new almanac to use and check out of the real world for a while longer.

Kate joined him on the coach roof, taking in the darkened silhouette of an island alive with bird calls and insect chirps. He scanned the sky and decided on a couple of promising stars. Orion was over there, so he zeroed in on Rigel at the foot of the constellation and pulled it down to the horizon in the split frame of the antique sextant he'd picked up in Jamaica — a gift from an ancient mariner he'd never forget.

"Mark," he murmured, prompting Kate to jot down the time as he lined the star up with the horizon. He lowered the sextant and read off the angle. "70°43.5."

Getting a good fix wasn't hard on a stationary boat. The real challenge would be to get a reliable measurement from a rocking boat in the rolling sea. But he'd take it one step at a time. He took a backup sight and then turned to the east, repeating the process on Procyon. Check the reading, reset to zero. Try again. Each time, the process narrowed the world to one small, bright point in a vast universe, insisting that the world slow down for him.

Was it working? Well, he pretended it did.

Kate took a turn with Rigel, then slipped away to resurrect the previous day's leftovers into a whole new meal. Dinner conversation was stilted, though. It had been a long day, and it was time to face the facts. Sooner or later, they would be spotted. And sooner, rather than later, they needed to reprovision.

They regarded each other hopelessly for a long time until Kate used an artificially bold tone to propose a plan.

"So, how about this. We make a quick run back to Panama City tomorrow. Avoid Balboa. We can head to Las Brisas anchorage, instead. There are so many boats there..."

She trailed off, but he knew what she meant. There were enough boats there to hide *Aurora* behind.

"If we leave at about... eleven? We'd make it in close to sunset. We don't want to leave too early and arrive in broad daylight."

He checked the chart. "Forty plus miles. The forecast says northeast fifteen knots. We don't want to cut it too close."

"Okay, we'll leave at ten. We'll do our shopping the next morning and get out of Dodge."

He nodded and let his eyes wander back to the night sky, where the stars arced steadily overhead. Eventually, he headed to the chart table with his almanac and notes to work out his sights. When Kate finished washing the dishes, she came to squeeze in next to him, settling her chin into the space between his cheek and shoulder. She tarried just long enough to distract him with a soft hint of a kiss.

"Boy, it's late," she commented casually. "I'm turning in."

Nick recognized the hint. For a very, very brief moment, he hesitated. Then he snapped the nautical almanac shut and headed straight for bed. The star sights could wait.

Bay of Panama
January 1914

Charlie sat in the sand with his head in his hands, ignoring the wreckage of his boat. Minutes dragged by in silent condemnation as waves gossiped over the wreck in the shallows.

What a failure. And a spectacular one at that.

The storm had taken a day and a night to blow itself out. He'd spent the whole time huddling in the lee of a boulder, wondering when he had last felt so cold or wet.

When the tempest finally cleared, it left a swath of brilliant blue sky and a pulsing swell that harassed *Yolanta's* tattered wreck. The salty crust of his shirt rubbed his skin, but he let it be in quiet martyrdom. He shooed a fly away absently and contemplated the sand.

Something ventured, nothing gained. Yet another of his grand plans — one of so many — had come to a disappointing end.

He sighed and tossed a pebble across the beach. Sometimes, he had to wonder if he was actually moving forward in his life. If he had drowned, would anyone have cared? What would they remember about him? Which of his accomplishments?

Had he ever really accomplished anything?

He dug his heels into the sand then tilted his head back and looked at the sky. Blue. Boundless. Beautiful. He squinted at the sun, feeling very small and terribly empty. What was it all for?

He looked for inspiration in the sand and found...shattered seashells, worn down by time and the elements. Just like him.

He could hear the faint echo of his father's voice, lecturing him on the challenges of canal construction. Tropical diseases, mudslides, difficulties with the breakwaters on both coasts. All those setbacks were being overcome through sheer willpower. Yeah, he knew the moral of the story. But did he have it in him? Thirty-plus years of life on this Earth and all he had to show for it were a few scars and a wrecked sailboat. Wrecked like so many of the dreams that preceded it.

A hermit crab peeked out of its shell, deemed him harmless, and scuttled along the sand.

He took a deep breath. He had picked up the pieces before. He could do it again. He would get over this loss and eventually pin his hopes on some new undertaking. And if that, too, crashed and burned, oh well. At least he tried. Life was full of ups and downs.

If only the downs weren't quite so down.

He sat quietly, trying to rally himself as minutes ticked by. He was alive and only slightly wrecked. *Yolanta* was a total loss, but the hull still harbored his belongings, including the treasure, just a few steps away in knee-deep water. And damn it, he could practically see the silver spider sneering at him through the thick boards. He felt no particular rush to retrieve it just now.

What to do next? Which step would be the first of many, leading to some unknown destination? He glanced at the crushed remnants of *Yolanta*. A wave was toying with a broken piece of the coach roof. Wait, that wasn't the roof. It was the little tender, still there. Somewhere in a locker were the oars.

A tiny flicker of light kindled in his soul.

He still had his hands, most of his heart, and maybe, deep down, a tiny measure of hope.

"Time to get back to work, Charlie," he murmured to himself. "Time to get back to work."

Las Perlas archipelago
March, present day

The sun seemed hesitant to peek over the horizon, as if it, too, had reservations about the day. Nick tried losing himself in his morning ritual — brewing coffee while tuning in to the morning weather forecast. At least it was an improvement over mornings in Boston. Back then, mornings consisted of brewing coffee while tuning in to the traffic report. He allowed himself a half smile at the one positive among the issues crowding his mind — such as a lost treasure, a great-grandfather with the habit of leaving incomplete notes, and a dangerous cartel.

How dangerous? He asked himself the question over and over. How sound was the idea of finding the treasure and turning it in?

A conundrum, at best. Especially the latter point. He stirred and restirred his coffee, not quite ready to swallow the idea. Charlie intended to use the treasure for a silver-lined future, not a museum collection. But Kate had a point, too, and he absolutely, positively didn't want trouble with the law — or the cartel and with Kate, who would never accept selling the treasure for profit.

Not even just the coins? The thought just wouldn't go away.

He and Kate fiddled with a thousand unnecessary things, ready to weigh anchor more than an hour ahead of time. But sailing was a game of patience if nothing else, so they waited in edgy silence.

And waited. And waited.

At 9:52, they ceded victory to impatience and started the engine. The windlass hummed without complaint, prompting him to shoot a triumphant look to Kate at the helm. She rewarded him with a congratulatory thump on the back when he stepped back into the cockpit.

"Nice job, Captain."

He grinned at the horizon, which looked a tiny bit brighter than it had a second before.

Soon they had the sails up and engine off, making good speed to the northwest. As the first hour ticked by, Isla Chapera slid out of view behind Contadora. Eventually, Contadora began to shrink behind them, too, the low green shell of it resembling a turtle in a slow dive under the horizon. The good news was that the windlass wasn't the only thing in working order on the boat. The hull was keeping the water out, and the sails were pulling *Aurora* along on a nice close reach. The freshly cleaned hull cut through the water with ease, and he smiled. It felt good to have *Aurora* back in shape and out in her element. Cavorting dolphins further lightened his mood, while seabirds swooped overhead.

"Wow!" Kate pointed. A whale breached straight out of the water in the distance.

He felt a short thrill with each startlingly beautiful occasion, then lapsed right back into brooding. What would they find in Panama City? Answers at last? More questions?

Or maybe just trouble. It was all well and good to make bold declarations from a hidden anchorage, but quite another to face a dangerous foe who loomed closer with every passing moment.

Gradually, the silhouettes of skyscrapers came into view, followed by the hulks of container ships waiting to transit the canal. Weaving through massive freighters seemed like old hat to him now, and Kate stood at the wheel, munching their last carrot casually. He supposed that's what happened when a new threat arose — old worries seem trivial in comparison.

"Last chance to head for Balboa," he murmured, pointing toward their old spot.

Kate dismissed the idea with a terse shake of the head, and he was secretly relieved.

"Las Brisas," she said, steering for the other anchorage.

The sun was rapidly sinking toward the horizon, and he checked his watch. Slowly, his worries about what might await them in the city gave way to anxiety about a night arrival. Slipping a mooring and sailing away in the dark was easy, but anchoring in an unknown bay in the dark was an exercise he hoped they wouldn't have to resort to.

Kate threw him a tight look. *Maybe we did cut it too close.*

Aurora raced the setting sun and won by a whisker. Just as the anchor dug into the bottom, the last gasp of color drained from the sky. Nick looked around, not quite ready to let his guard down. The anchorage, although uncomfortably exposed to wind and waves, harbored enough boats to allow *Aurora* to hang inconspicuously at the back of the pack.

Or so he hoped.

"We made it," he said quietly.

Kate nodded and looked around. "We made it. Step one."

* * *

In contrast to low and leafy Balboa, Las Brisas offered an incredible panorama of downtown Panama City, where skyscrapers vied to reach ever more ambitious — or foolish — heights. Kate chewed her dinner in the cockpit alongside Nick, taking in the familiar city from a new angle.

What are you thinking about? she nearly asked, then thought better of it.

She cleared the plates away and folded back the sun awning, inviting a universe of stars into *Aurora's* small cockpit. Like magic, they all fit. She stretched out on her back, watching for shooting stars. The stars weren't quite as bright as out in Las Perlas, but nice all the same.

"Sometimes, feeling tiny and insignificant can be a reassuring thing."

Nick mumbled vaguely. He was sitting across from her, wearing a head lamp that gave him the look of an old-time miner. He turned on the red bulb and got to work on his star sights from the previous night. Scribbling steadily on a notepad, he referred to his nautical almanac and reduction tables between sips of an after-dinner coffee.

Nothing like evenings on Aurora. Kate sighed and caught her lip with her teeth, trying to arrest the moment. *Evenings on Aurora with Nick,* she amended, remembering her days alone. She let her eyes wander over the night sky, tracing constellations with a finger extended like a paint brush.

Nick mumbled and tapped his pencil at the numbers on his sheet.

She looked over. Had his calculations gone badly wrong and pointed to Alaska instead of Panama?

Not saying a word, Nick dashed below, reappearing a moment later with Charlie's notebook.

She sat up. "What is it?"

He raised his hand as if holding up traffic and concentrated on the notebook. Flipping through it, he pulled out a sheet of paper and fumbled to unfold it.

It was Charlie's message to Mercedes from the back of the *Yolanta* sketch. What did he want with that?

He glanced up with a disbelieving expression, then back down to the copy.

"What?" she insisted.

Drat Nick and his annoying habit of thinking before he spoke. It seemed an eternity before he shifted over beside her and spread the copy out. Even then, he stared for a long time without saying a word. She was beginning to wonder if the photocopy might speak before Nick did.

Finally, he pointed with a finger that glowed red under his head lamp.

She read, puzzled, "'Dear Mercedes, please keep this for me...'"

Nick cut in. "No — the numbers!"

04.23.14 at 23
16-07.9 Sp 44:53
52-18.1 Sir 46:20

She read the numbers to herself, then again aloud, making as little sense of them as before.

"See these?" He showed her the paper where she had jotted down his star sights the night before.

"Sure. 70°43.5 and 63°18.4."

Then it hit her. The pattern of numbers was the same as the second two lines in Charlie's note. Degrees, minutes, and a decimal?

"Charlie sent Mercedes star sights?"

Nick tapped the floor as he hesitated. "Sp....Spica?" He searched through his almanac, then tapped a page. "Spica."

"Sir..." she read the third line of Charlie's note. "Sirius?" The Dog Star, one of her favorites.

Nick nodded. "Usually, you take star sights, make some standard corrections, and then use the tables in the almanac to calculate latitude and longitude. But these could be raw sight results. The numbers straight off the sextant, before Charlie calculated them out. If he ever calculated them."

"Can you work them out? Convert into a position?"

He swung his head from side to side, neither a yes or a no. "I'd need the date and time..."

She triple-checked Charlie's note. "*04.23.14 — at 23...* The fourth of — no, the twenty-third of the fourth month — April. And 14...1914 would match some of the other dates in his book."

The red head lamp swayed from side to side. "If that's really the date the sights were taken. A big if."

"Well, it's the only thing here that could be a date. But what about 'at 23'?"

"Twenty-three... twenty-three hundred."

"Eleven o'clock at night?" Kate looked at it again.

Nick was building momentum now. "If we put that together with the second half of the numbers, we have hours, minutes, seconds. 23:44:53 and 23:46:20—"

She cut in. "But you take star sights at twilight, right? That's always somewhere around six in Panama."

"Local time," Nick corrected. "But you do star sights in—"

"Universal Time, right." She thumped the table in triumph. "So we got it! You can work them out! We have the time, the star angles—"

Nick shook his head. "We'd also need height above sea level, his assumed position..." He didn't sound so sure. "You realize this is a long shot, right?"

She nearly said, *Long shots are the ones that pay big*, but bit her tongue.

"Charlie told Mercedes 'on the other side.' That could mean the Pacific side of Panama. Does that work?"

He made a face. "Then we're making an assumption about an assumption."

"Well, we could use Balboa as an assumed starting point, right?"

"We'd need an old almanac, too." He trailed off, then sucked in a sharp breath. "The YMCA — there were old almanacs in the reading room."

Her mind flashed an image of bookshelves and sunlight streaming through glass. She struggled to keep her heart rate down as images of Spanish coins and the Sipán spider fluttered through her mind.

"And then you can do the calculations?"

Nick rubbed his chin. "Maybe."

She scrutinized his face.

"Possibly."

She sat very still.

"I think so," he ventured.

Silence fell over *Aurora* as they wondered if this could finally be it.

Chapter Twenty-two

Pandora's Box

Bay of Panama
January 1914

"Good enough for pirates is good enough for me," Charlie murmured to no one in particular.

He shoveled the last spade of earth over his treasure and leaned back to count.

"Twenty-four. Twenty-five. Twenty-six."

Twenty-six boxes, now in the bank. The Bank of Esperanza Island. It was all there, blanketed by dirt. Even the silver spider. The loathsome thing was obviously bad luck. Near his foot was a backpack full of coins that might just pay his way to... Well, wherever it was he might end up.

He looked up at the endless blue sky and wiped the sweat off his brow.

If nothing else, it felt good to have something in common with pirates. Inspirational, almost. He glanced around and identified a few landmarks, then paced them off, jotting down the position of his cache in his own special shorthand. At some point, he would find a way to camouflage the information, just in case. He didn't want any nasty surprises when he came back for his treasure.

The thought arrested him. Even if he got away from this island, how would he ever return?

"One thing at a time, Charlie," he told himself. "One thing at a time."

He kicked the dirt and nodded to himself. It might take a couple of years, but he'd be back.

Hopefully. And if not him, then someone worthy of his cause. He'd make sure of that, if he ever decided to share this little secret. Though he doubted he ever would trust anyone enough to share the information. It was best to finish the job himself when the time was right.

Right now, though, he had to figure out where he was. Just how far had the storm blown *Yolanta*?

He climbed to the high point of the island, his shoes picking up muddy soot as he went. There must have been a fire recently. All the underbrush and most of the trees were done for — except for that great granddaddy of a tree halfway up the slope. The mainland was visible across a labyrinth of shoals and islands on the northern horizon. How would he ever find his way back to this particular patch of ground?

He glared at the burning sun. "You could have made an appearance yesterday, you know."

The sun radiated warmth back at him, spotlighting a vague idea and bringing it into focus.

Sun. Horizon. Clear skies.

With the rush that came with a new idea, he took off down the slope in long-legged bounds and slogged over to the wreck of *Yolanta*. Knee-deep in cold water, he clambered aboard and groped around the dim cabin. The ribs of the hull were already half buried in the sand, and everything lay at an angle.

"Where is it?"

He cursed, searching desperately. Before setting out, he had wrapped his watch in an oilcloth pouch. Had it survived the storm?

"Gotcha!"

He pulled out the bundle, unwrapped the timepiece, and held it to his ear, holding his breath. Still ticking! He kissed the face and gave *Yolanta* a grateful tap.

Maybe he would get the chance to use his navigation skills, after all.

Holding the clock and his boxy sextant case out of reach of the waves, he waded back to the beach and scanned the sky.

The lazy afternoon heat quickly faded into a cool evening, and the blue of the sky bled into reds and oranges. Twilight — the tipping point of day and night when the stars and horizon were all so clear. Twilight on a tropical island, no less. He allowed himself to register the beauty of the plan before cracking down to business.

"Spica," he murmured, searching for the star. "There you are. Now, Sirius." He whistled for the Dog Star. "Good boy."

Not only did he have both stars, there was a good crossing angle between the two. Maybe Fortuna was smiling on him, after all. He carefully measured both angles and jotted down the results, deciding that was enough for now. The calculations could be worked out later.

He leaned back in the sand and watched the lesser stars come out as the night deepened. He had to laugh at himself, taking those star sights. That wasn't what he had in mind when he practiced with the sextant all these past months. But at least it had served some purpose. Someday, somehow, those sights would guide him back to his treasure. Back to this island of singing insects and giggling waves.

And treasure. His own private treasure island.

Charlie sighed and let the starlight lull him gradually into a deep, exhausted sleep.

Balboa

March, present day

How to hail a taxi while remaining inconspicuous?

Nick stood on the Amador Causeway, trying to look small. *Aurora* was anchored so far at the back of the pack of boats rolling off Las Brisas, she was practically invisible. Taxis were just as hard to spot, though, and the YMCA was miles away, down the causeway and well into Balboa. Beside him, Kate fidgeted with the straps of her backpack while she watched the road like a hawk.

"Taxi!" she hollered when finally — mercifully — a yellow cab appeared.

During the cab ride, Nick tried not to let his hopes climb a very rickety ladder. He was probably wrong about the star sights, right?

Maybe.

Possibly.

Maybe not...

He practically leaped out of the vehicle at the YMCA. Entering the building was a minor relief, but even there, he felt on edge. The cartel could be anywhere, everywhere.

His efforts to look casual went unappreciated by the security guard, who was glued to a soccer match on TV. The hysterical voice of the television commentator followed him up the stairs, fading away as they walked to the end of the hall. The glass door to the reading room was ajar.

"Here we go," Kate murmured.

He headed straight to the shelf lined with nautical almanacs and ran his fingers along the volumes.

"1921, 1920, 1919... 1914."

There. He left his finger on the spine for a moment. Then, with a long, slow breath, he drew it out from the shelf. He flipped through the pages, scanning words and numbers that were a kind of holy scripture for sailors.

"February... March... April."

He turned to a table and laid out everything he needed. The almanac, Charlie's note, a notepad, and calculator. Kate skimmed the bookshelves in exaggerated silence, giving him space to think.

"You know how hard it is to get a good fix with just two stars, right?" he reminded her.

She answered with one of her *You can do it* looks.

With slightly shaky fingers, he opened the almanac to April 23, 1914 and looked up the declinations and hour angles for Sirius and Spica. That was the easy part. He pushed the almanac aside and opened his sight reduction tables. The latter were modern, but the steps involved in calculating star sights had gone unchanged since Charlie's time. It was a cumbersome procedure akin to filling in a tax form, reminding him of his resolution to find a computer program for celestial navigation — or better yet, write one himself.

He completed another step and double-checked his work. It wasn't only Kate peering over his shoulder. Charlie was back there, too.

The room felt eerily silent when his pencil stopped scratching away. Kate edged in, obviously torn between patience and throttling him for an instant answer. She sat down and bit her lip. *Well?*

He circled his tense shoulders before answering. "Got it."

Kate tipped her head. "Got what, exactly?"

Funny, he was wondering the same thing.

He took a measured breath and started plotting his results on their Gulf of Panama chart. First one long line, then a second, perpendicular one. He moved the ruler and peered at the intersection.

"Las Perlas," he said in a careful monotone.

Kate leaned so far over the table, she nearly nudged it askew. "Charlie was in Las Perlas?" The lines crossed just east of an island. "Could Charlie have meant a spot under the sea?"

"In that case, we can forget it. No way are we going off on some lunatic underwater treasure hunt." He shook his head. "No, we have the sketch map of a place on land, and the closest thing—"

"What do you mean, the closest thing?"

"It's hard to get a perfect fix, especially with just two stars. Who knows what conditions Charlie took his sights in — or how exact his reading was. But even a couple miles off is still a good star sight." He placed his right hand along the line of 08°35.5 north. "The latitude is probably okay. Time error would show up in longitude, so it could be anything along here..." His finger swept left and came to stop at the island closest to Charlie's fix.

"Isla Chapera," he read in a whisper.

"We were just there!"

He nodded, studying the contours. "Looks like we're going back."

* * *

From the moment they left the YMCA reading room to the point when *Aurora* weighed anchor, everything was a blur. After a rushed shopping run, they headed out to sea, pointing the bow into a wind that had come around to the east. The only other boats underway were all heading for the mainland. Except for one freighter heading northwest, they were alone.

"God, am I glad to be out of there," Kate murmured, looking back.

Nick glanced over his shoulder. "Me, too." Then he looked forward again, wondering how crazy this whole quest was.

Aurora seemed determined to find out, too. The little sloop doggedly held a course close to the wind, while waves slapped over the deck, drenching them both. Nick found himself almost enjoying the ride in spite of the choppy motion. He rarely pushed his boat — or himself — this hard by choice, but *Aurora* shouldered each wave aside and sped on. He couldn't help thinking that maybe, just maybe, his little boat really could handle the whole Pacific. And putting thousands miles of ocean between him and a cartel had its appeal, too.

He turtle-tucked his head into the tall collar of his foul weather jacket and replayed their conversation of the previous night. The nearest match for Charlie's coordinates was Isla Chapera, but he still lacked a specific point on the island. The nautical chart didn't provide a great deal of detail for that speck of land, either.

Other than a few contour lines, it neglected to detail any features. Chapera was almost a mile long and half a mile wide — plenty of space for a wild-goose chase.

"The chances that Charlie meant the southeast side of Chapera are good," Kate said. "The only two decent anchorages are there."

"Of course, we're assuming the top of his map is north."

"We're assuming a lot already." Kate shrugged then chuckled. "Maybe we're taking this a little too seriously."

"Do you think?"

She whisked a finger under his chin. "Just don't start talking pirate to me."

"Aye-aye," he replied and dodged as Kate thumped his shoulder.

By the time *Aurora* rounded the corner of Isla Chapera, the wind had eased. They anchored and stared at the beach, alive in a blaze of afternoon gold not two hundred yards away.

"Not a soul in sight," Kate whispered.

She wanted to leap straight off *Aurora* and swim to shore, but Nick talked her into paddling over with him. With nightfall not far off, there was just enough time to kayak ashore for a quick look. The island was untamed and uninhabited with no sign of recent visitors except for the footprints from their last visit, pacing back and forth at the boundary of beach and bush.

Nick scanned the dense greenery.

"Maybe that rock?" Kate pointed.

"How about that one?" he tried.

A six-seater commuter plane flew overhead then looped around to land on the neighboring island of Contadora.

"Big loop," he observed, watching it disappear over the trees of Chapera.

Kate shrugged.

Shadows lengthened and played tricks on their eyes until they grudgingly retreated to *Aurora*. Looking back to the island, now a solid golden shape in the glare of the dying sunlight, Kate pointed out an irregularity in the silhouette.

"Do you think that could be Charlie's tree?"

He was too worn-out to judge any tree, boulder, or island this side of Mexico. "What do you think?"

She sucked on her lip. "Hard to tell. It could be big enough. Old enough..."

"Could be anything," he murmured, feeling weariness set in.

When the sun slipped behind the horizon, the moon took over, illuminating the scrubby landscape, teasing him with shadows and hints.

"A full moon surrounded by a faint halo," Kate commented, looking up. "What does that mean?"

He foraged through one his weather books to find the reference and groaned.

"What?"

He made a face. "You don't want to know."

"I don't?"

He sighed and read aloud. "A ring around the sun or moon is a sign of potential bad weather."

"Great," she muttered.

He snapped the book shut and followed her to bed. "Yep. Just what we need."

Balboa

present day

Something was about to happen. Something big.

Lucien watched city lights sparkle on the moonlit surface of the Balboa mooring field, knowing his waiting game was about to pay off. He only had to stay close to the Poles and choose the precise moment to strike. From the appearance of things, that moment was very, very close.

The Americans had disappeared a few nights before, spooked by something in the middle of the night. Somehow, they seemed connected to the Poles' scheme, though Lucien couldn't imagine how. Last night, Vadz, his Polish sidekick, and their South American accomplice had been locked deep in another conversation, plotting something with fresh excitement. Whatever net they were casting was about to be drawn.

Well, Lucien was ready, too. Ready as a cat staring down a fat rat.

He'd been awake for his four a.m. smoke — a habit from so many night watches at sea — contemplating the water and imagining his future in Tahiti, where he would soon be playing *boules* under the palms.

Then the lights flicked on aboard *Carmela* and *Odysseus* as their crews stirred in a pre-dawn flurry of activity. He caught the telltale signs of a burgeoning venture: the faint chime of a phone answered after one ring. The burly Pole grunting at his hapless assistant. Their silhouettes on deck, fumbling to assemble some gear. Then they'd gone still. Lucien could see the big Pole waiting with his phone with an air of arrested anticipation.

He knew that pause. It was the split second between the lightning strike and the thunder.

Any minute now, they'd be leaving *Odysseus*. His first instinct was to follow along, but a tantalizing thought struck him. Why not take *Odysseus* as soon as the Poles left? The wind was good, and he would be long gone before they returned from their amateur enterprise. And when they found their boat missing — what then? The Poles couldn't go rushing to the police. There'd be too many questions about their repeated runs to Colombia and their source of income. He would have all the head start he needed in that gazelle of a boat. All his, the easy way.

Tempting. Very tempting.

But who knew when the Poles had last filled the fuel and water tanks? The pantry? Amateurs like them left everything for the last minute, like they were doing now. *Odysseus* would likely offer little besides vodka and canned sardines.

He shook his head. Too many things could go wrong if he acted in haste. He should remain true to his plan and accompany the Poles offshore. He could seize the boat later, as he originally planned. And although he was loath to admit it, he was also curious about their scheme. If there really was Spanish treasure to be had — that much, he'd gleaned from Vadz's loose tongue — then he wanted a share. Better yet, he wanted it all. If he played this right, he'd end up with the boat and a bonus cargo, all ready to go.

The Poles boarded a water taxi. The South American — Alejandro was his name — stood waiting on the jetty, where a lamp cast a triangle of yellow light over the blue-black night. Lucien leaped into his dinghy without bothering to lock his boat. There was nothing left on *Island Dream* for anyone to steal, anyway. He pulled the start cord and mounted his pursuit.

The Poles were already stepping ashore, but Lucien wasn't far behind. He could see them cresting the hill to the slumbering clubhouse. A second later, he took off over the uneven wooden boards of the dock, ignoring the protests of the water taxi driver. Let him tie up *Island Dream's* tattered old dinghy.

He wheezed to the top of the hill, cursing a lifetime of chain smoking. But he still had the trio in his sights — right down the street. Vadz's bald head shone like a beacon through the rear window of a departing taxi, practically crying, *Follow me!*

Another taxi stood at the curb. A figure in the passenger seat gestured, and the driver eased forward to pull out. Lucien wrenched the door open and threw himself in the back seat as the driver slammed the brakes in surprise.

He waved his wallet and sputtered in Spanish. "Fifty dollars! I'll pay you fifty dollars! After that car!" he managed between breaths.

The Poles and their accomplice were heading in the direction of the Causeway — to one of the other marinas, perhaps?

The driver and his companion must have thought him crazy. But when one ugly face and the other stretched into greedy smiles as they twisted in their seats to look at him, it dawned on him that the men were familiar. Familiar, but hard to place.

A second later, his gut sank as he identified the faces. Faces he'd hoped never to see again.

The tall one had a scar on his nose, and his pulse beat visibly through a vein in his forehead, just like Lucien remembered. The shorter, beefy one flashed a reptilian sneer.

"Lucien," he said. "What a surprise."

"What a surprise," echoed the one at the wheel.

Cartel men. The two who took care of the dirty work. Lucien had crossed paths with them a few times before, but never like this. Never as a wanted man.

He'd managed to evade the cartel since the wreck of the *Persephone*. He thought he was in the clear. Yet somehow, he'd managed to throw himself right at their feet. How? What were they doing here? And what had possessed the tall one to wear that ridiculous American baseball cap like some kind of trophy?

Lucien was about to blurt out an explanation when the short one raised a gun and aimed it at his chest. Lucien jerked back, but there was nowhere to go but centimeters deeper into the back seat. He stared down the long, dark length of the barrel. Death was in there, he knew, unless he thought fast.

"Listen, I—" He raised his hands innocently.

"We were here for a very different fish," the Panamanian cut him off, making a slight motion toward the speeding taxi. "And we caught you instead. It must be our lucky day."

"Our lucky day," the tall one nodded, reaching past the steering wheel to crack his knuckles.

The beefy one's face went from dangerous to outright deadly as he leaned closer to Lucien, cocking the gun with a meaty thumb.

"Our lucky day, my friend. Not yours."

Isla Chapera
March, present day

Nick found little rest that night. Erratic dreams full of threats, real and imagined, jerked back and forth with images of a great treasure. Every time he woke, he cursed reality. That silver lining Charlie talked about was looking more and more like fool's gold.

Awaking to an oppressively humid, hazy day, he scanned the sky and then tapped the rapidly dropping barometer. The weather was definitely deteriorating.

"We're going to have to find a more secure anchorage soon."

Kate looked at her watch and nodded without a word.

Breakfast was rushed and quiet, with few words exchanged. When he and Kate headed ashore, they packed a crowbar, the biggest screwdriver from the toolbox, and a garden trowel Kate had picked up in Balboa. He felt a little ridiculous holding their fourth tool: his fish grappling hook, brought along as an improvised digging tool. A good thing no one was there to witness their ridiculous scheme.

"This is the first time I've worn socks in four months," Kate muttered as they stepped ashore. Having anticipated a morning of bushwhacking, they wore long pants and closed shoes.

He compared the landscape to Charlie's map for the thousandth time. "Okay, where's that tree?"

The tall tree they'd spotted the night before may have towered above the island's green canopy from afar, but it took fifteen minutes of sweaty exploring to find from ground level.

He squinted up along the weathered trunk. "What do you think?"

Kate pulled the strands of a spider web from her shirt. "That's the only one it could be."

They weren't too far from the beach — he could still make out the occasional patch of turquoise through the foliage.

"Tree: check. Boulder?" Kate murmured.

They scrambled over uneven terrain and pushed through the tangled undergrowth, calling back and forth at each possibility.

"Maybe this one?"

"How about over here?"

Then Kate called him over to the granddaddy of all rocks, covered in moss and lichens.

"That's gotta be it," he agreed.

They huddled over Charlie's map, looking from the rock to the landscape.

"Okay, there's the tree..." Kate started.

The map showed a tree, a boulder, and the letter X near the boulder, plus a faint W which might — or might not — belong with the rest.

Kate kicked at the earth. "Here?"

He shrugged and poked his hook into the earth while Kate scraped with a trowel. "Here goes nothing."

A solid hour of poking, digging, and scraping revealed nothing but bedrock within a few inches of the surface. The whole time, Nick marveled at the strange journey that had brought him from corporate America to jungle Panama. Before long, though, he grew sweaty and jaded.

"Um, quick break?" Kate suggested.

He nodded immediately, and they retreated to the beach. The shallow water, usually a stunning turquoise, had lost its brilliance under the slate-gray sky. Beyond, *Aurora* nodded at anchor, encouraging her dejected crew.

Kate unscrewed her water bottle and sighed. "Maybe X marks the spot is a little too obvious."

Nick picked up a rock and threw it across the beach.

Maybe this whole venture is insane.

Kate glared at Charlie's map. "If X doesn't mark the spot, what does it mean? And what about that W?"

They spent another half hour cursing and considering the problem while eyeing the sinking clouds.

"X is.... X-ray..." he tried.

Kate gave him a hopeless look.

"X is... excellent..."

"This is excellent," she muttered, rubbing the bloody scratches the brush had left along her arms.

"What else could X be?"

They left the question open, tensing as a fancy motor yacht with tinted windows hummed into view. It made a loop through the anchorage, then seemed to reject it and move on, out of sight. Kate went back to shoving sand with her heels, muttering about X being the location in the deepest depths of the sea where she would drop Charlie's remaining personal effects very soon.

"X is ten?" Nick tried. "Roman numeral ten..."

She looked, about to dismiss Nick's suggestion, then cocked her head at the map.

"X is ten," he continued, "and W is... Water? West?"

"West!" They both shouted and jumped to their feet, ready for another try.

They picked their way back to the boulder, then paced ten steps west, trampling undergrowth as they went.

"Okay, somewhere around here..."

Kate prodded the earth with the grappling hook. This time, it sank into loose earth.

"Well, that's better than solid rock," she said.

She poked again while he scraped with the crowbar. They worked steadily, exploring an area to the depth of a few inches around their starting point.

"Switch tools," Kate said, swapping with him. She kneeled and drilled down with the grappling hook. It wormed its way down, then stopped.

"More rock," she muttered.

He moved in with the crowbar, scratching away roots and soil to reveal a rock.

"Damn." Kate leaned back on her heels and cast her gaze around.

Not ready to give up yet, Nick scuffed the rock with the bottom of his shoe. When he pulled the crowbar across the rock, the forked tongue of the tool left a double trail.

"I dented the rock," he said, staring at the ground.

"How can you dent a rock?"

He looked up at her, then down at the rock. "Not sure, but..."

He wasn't sure what the *but* might be — only that he wasn't stopping now. He traced the hard surface with his tool until he found an edge and worked around it. Kate used the trowel to do the same on her side. The crowbar slipped away from the straight edge, and when he backtracked, the tool swerved right, revealing a corner.

A perfect, ninety-degree corner.

Kate reached the end of the edge she'd been following and found the same feature.

"Whoa."

Nick was no geologist, but he was fairly sure there were no perfectly square rocks in Panama.

As they continued to dig down along the edges, he hit another hard spot that abutted the first. Now they had two square rocks, and eventually, a third. Kate wiped the surface of the first one with her hand, scattering the last layer of dirt, then looked up at him with wide eyes.

"Not rocks. Boxes."

The tops of three wooden boxes lay exposed before them, blacked with creosote as protection against the elements.

Nick moved in with the crowbar, motioning for Kate to keep her hands clear. He was about to pry at the edge of a box when he caught the grimace on her face.

"What?"

"Treasure hunters destroy valuable evidence when they do this kind of thing. Even the best archeology is destruction, but this..."

"This isn't archeology," he said. "It's..." *It's what? Great-Grandpa's treasure chest?* He could have snorted out loud at that one. "It's Charlie's. This isn't any different than picking through your grandparents' attic."

He tried to sound sure of himself, knowing full well that jungle soil was not quite the same thing as a dusty attic.

Kate murmured something about context and grave robbers while he plunged ahead, prying at the box until the crowbar found purchase. The box creaked as nails resisted the upward pull, and the sound caused the birds in the surrounding woods to erupt into wild chatter again.

"Come on. Come on...."

He pried the lid ajar, yanked it off completely, and dropped it to one side. Inside was a dark, uneven layer that Kate poked with her trowel, revealing the rotted remains of a coarse, canvas-like material. She probed deeper.

Chink.

The sound of metal against metal. Kate made a stirring motion, and the contents gave way, grating against her tool. She raised the trowel and came up with a collection of... flattened chips?

Nick dropped to one knee as she picked one of the chips off her trowel and brushed it clean.

"Whoa."

She let out a disbelieving breath and tilted her hand to show him an oblong shape. He didn't have to look twice to guess what it was.

A silver coin. A piece of eight.

He picked another coin from the trowel as Kate cleaned the first against her pants. He rubbed until the four-section design was clear. When he caught Kate nodding at his shirt, he slipped the coin into his pocket and pulled out Rosie's necklace to compare with Kate's. Exactly the same as Charlie's coins: off-center and poorly struck, but magnificent all the same.

"Wow," she murmured with the look of a little girl who just captured her first worm.

He shook his head. "Unbelievable."

"Unbelievable," she agreed. "Charlie's treasure."

Nick looked at her, clenching his teeth together so that his jaw wouldn't go slack.

"It's our treasure now."

* * *

They uncovered a dozen wooden boxes. More lay beneath in a deeper, second layer. The first box was filled with crude Spanish coins of the pre-1700s type. That, Kate could immediately tell. The coins dated back four hundred years — coins that set the standard for world currencies that followed.

"Charlie wasn't kidding, was he?" she said, looking over the boxes poking up from the dirt like a warped floor of tiles.

Charlie's words echoed through her mind. *A silver-lined future for us both.*

A second box contained more pieces of eight, all with blurry inscriptions and rough crosses. Nick pried open a third and shoved aside the rotten canvas layer.

"Look at this." He pointed at irregular edges and twisted shapes.

Kate peered in and brushed away the remaining bits of canvas. With deliberate movements, she eased one object free and held it up.

It was a small, flattened fan shape, with a curved edge like an ax blade.

"Hammered gold." Her voice was in a museum hush.

Tiny filaments dangled off the lower edge, where her imagination placed small beads.

"Maybe an earring?" She laid it across the lid of the box then felt along the tops of the next shapes and extracted a small silver figurine no bigger than her thumb.

"Look at the detail in that," she whispered.

A stylized man stood with wide-thrust arms and legs, a gaping mouth, and two beady eyes. The expression was probably meant to terrify or deliver a horrific omen. She put it aside, rushing just a little, and wiped her hands on her pants.

"Wow," she breathed, turning quickly to the next piece.

It was a snake made of tiny, interlocking silver rings. It caught on something, so she left it in place and moved on to a different piece — a broad, silver armband with a circular crest like the face of a clock. Filling up the crest was a taloned bird of prey with a sharply hooked beak that was both fierce and beautiful.

"Look at that detail," she said, touching the golden feathers of the condor's wings.

Never in her archaeological career had she seen so many treasures in one place. Sure, there'd been a coin here, a bead there, but never such an array of precious metal worked to such perfection, all in one cache. Boxes and boxes full. Even Nick was mesmerized, leaving his camera untouched in its case.

Under the condor was a flat disc nearly as wide as her palm. She felt around the thick edges and worked it free.

"Holy..." She turned it over in her hands and choked on her own surprise.

An abstract web ringed a human face that made up the body of a spider. The delicate strands of the web contrasted with the chunky face and bulging eyes. It was round and thick, like a hockey puck.

"Charlie's spider," Nick said, hushed.

She stared into the eyes of the piece. The sound of insects and the wind rustling the trees faded all around her. Her whole world became the artifact, lying mutely in the palm of her hand.

"Is it a Sipán spider?" Nick's voice reached her from far away.

She tilted it in the dappled forest light. "Just like it... But silver, not gold."

The spider was even more beautiful in silver, she decided. Ancient craftsmanship, in her hands.

"Just like it?" Nick echoed.

She nodded. "It's essentially a twin to the Sipán spiders."

She imagined a leather-gloved Spanish soldier picking it from a religious site in Peru and thrusting it carelessly into a bag along with the other objects. Somehow, those pieces must have been bundled in a shipment with coins and other treasures. Then all of it must have been brought to Panama to cross the isthmus by the jungle path that had preceded the canal.

What then? What strange sequence of events left the treasure forgotten until centuries later, when Charlie Parker came along?

The silver glinted in a ray of sunshine, making the spider's eyes shout with fury.

It was an effort just to put it down. When Kate did, she stood beside Nick, surveying their findings. Several more boxes lay unopened. Would they contain more coins? Jewelry? Other treasures? The sheer volume of it all was incredible.

It was a treasure that could make her career. A treasure that deserved a worthy end. All of it in her care.

"How did Charlie ever move all this?" She looked at Nick. "And what are we going to do with it all?"

She knew her answer. Nick's eyes glimmered with it. *We get rich. We sail as far and as long as we want to.*

A gust of wind hurried the leaves above, making the birds screech and wheel away.

"A silver-lined future for us both," she murmured.

"First things first," he said, breaking the ensuing silence. "How are we going to move all this?"

Then they both froze as a smooth voice spoke from behind them.

"Allow me to assist."

Chapter Twenty-three

A Sly Fox

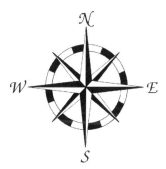

Isla Chapera
March, present day

Nick wheeled to find Alejandro standing with his arms folded in a nonchalant pose.

"What are friends for?"

Flanking him were the two Poles, Vadz and Gregor. Alejandro wore his most dazzling smile, while stocky Vadz sported a sleeveless muscle shirt and a scowl. Gregor had an apologetic look that didn't quite cut it.

And, crap. Vadz flaunted the longest rifle Nick had ever seen. At least that's what it looked like when he stared down the barrel pointed his way. Alejandro, he noticed, held a small revolver like a plaything, while Gregor seemed unarmed.

Nick stuck his hands in the air. He felt his face go hot just seeing their cocky expressions. Both Vadz and Alejandro looked as if they might have rehearsed their poses in front of a mirror. Alejandro stood proud and aloof like an artist at the presentation of his defining exhibit. Vadz was a coiled mass of muscle, his only movement the twitch of bulging veins. It was almost laughable — except for the guns.

Nick edged away from the advancing threesome, but Kate held her ground, bristling.

"Hey!" she barked. "This is ours!"

The three intruders looked unimpressed, making Kate falter slightly before regaining her composure.

"How did you get here, anyway?" she demanded, hands on her hips.

Alejandro grinned like a self-satisfied cat. "I borrowed a boat from a friend."

An image clicked in Nick's mind. The motor yacht that looped past earlier — that had been Alejandro piloting it?

"Nice friends."

"That's... That's cheating!" The foot Kate stamped sent up a tiny dust cloud. "This isn't yours to take!"

Alejandro stood steady, looking ridiculously pleased with himself. "I think it is."

Nick felt his face heat. This wasn't Alejandro's treasure. It was Charlie's — and now it was his and Kate's. He wanted to pummel the Venezuelan, but his roiling gut signaled a warning.

"What are you going to do with it?" Kate's voice rang with scorn. "Sell it to the highest bidder?"

"This is part of what I plan, yes," Alejandro agreed.

Vadz threw him a sidelong look, tinged with suspicion.

Kate glared. "And have it disappear forever into some private collection?"

"Academics aren't the only ones who can appreciate a masterpiece." Alejandro grinned.

Nick concentrated on calming Kate down. The men were armed, for one thing. Who knew what they had up their sleeves or how many others lurked behind them? He touched her back, but Kate flicked his hand away. He could see an insult poised on her lips, ready to be hurled their way.

When Vadz swung the rifle in her direction, Kate crossed her arms, unimpressed. "I bet it's not even loaded."

She even means it, Nick marveled, clutching the back of her shirt.

Vadz raised the barrel of his rifle and blasted a coconut out of the tree behind Kate. *Boom!*

Three heads ducked as the shot and its echo thundered through the woods: Nick's, Kate's, and Gregor's. Neither Vadz nor Alejandro flinched.

A coconut thumped to the ground, making roughly the sound a human body would make when it dropped dead with a bullet between the eyes.

Nick threw Kate a cutting look. *He means it!*

Vadz gloated, caressing his weapon, and an uneasy silence settled over the forest — silent but for the mutterings of thousands of leaves agitated by the rising wind. The weather was deteriorating fast.

Kate inhaled as if to protest, but she squeezed her lips together instead.

Good girl, he thought just as an engine droned overhead. Another small plane was preparing to land on Isla Contadora.

Alejandro looked up through the foliage and gave the plane a mock salute. "That would be Jorge."

"Jorge?" Nick squinted at the smug Venezuelan, and it dawned on him. The plane that circled the previous night had spotted *Aurora* and reported their position.

"How could you?" Kate admonished.

Alejandro didn't seem bothered. In fact, he seemed even more pleased with himself. Vadz spat casually. Gregor just stared at the ground.

Nick shook his head at the scene. The treasure lay at his feet — a loot that Charlie had discovered and harbored such high hopes for. All for nothing. Now it would be Alejandro's silver-lined future — not his, nor Kate's.

There was the sound of footsteps, quick and resolute, and Nick was shocked to realize they were his own.

What the hell are you doing? a voice cried in his mind.

Get him! urged another voice, propelling him over the scarred earth, right at Alejandro. All he could see was an image of Charlie — not just a face from a faded photograph but a real man. A young man. A friend. One with scratched, sweaty hands and a dirt-smeared face that regarded a great, heaping treasure that remained painfully out of reach. All that effort! False starts, false hopes. Wanting so badly to leave his mark, but falling short again and again. Getting sidetracked, making mistakes. Lonely flights, cut-off phone calls...

Wait, he was getting it all mixed up. Where did Charlie end and he begin?

Nick found himself glaring past the barrel of Alejandro's gun, fixated on those perfect white teeth, the unwavering poise.

Except now, Alejandro wavered ever so slightly. His smile was frozen, and he seemed to be holding his breath, wondering what Nick was capable of, gun or no gun. Nick wondered, too. He felt big. Bigger than Alejandro. Bigger even than Vadz. His shoulders were wide, his balled fists ready to fly.

It would all be over if he didn't act now. Alejandro would take the treasure. He would take it all away, and Nick would lose. Charlie would lose. Kate would lose, too, and...

That's when it hit him. He had so much more to lose than some coins and trinkets. They were scraps of metal, nothing more. "Cashing in on buried treasure" was about to be erased from his list of life accomplishments, but what kind of accomplishment was that? His destiny lay elsewhere, and he would go find it. Starting with something much more important.

He cast Alejandro a last, ferocious look, then stepped away, grabbing Kate's hand. He didn't have to force a defiant look. It just came. He and Kate would get out, and they'd get out ahead. Not just with their lives, but with their dignity and with each other. They didn't need silver or gold to forge a rich future.

There was a short, awkward standoff while Kate gripped his hand and the three conspirators exchanged unsteady looks. Nick found himself breathing again, almost panting.

True to form, Alejandro swiftly recovered his composure — after a reassuring look at the guns and thugs he'd brought along. He switched his self-assured smile back on and made a small sideways motion with his gun.

Nick did a double take, unsure if he interpreted correctly.

"How do you say that in English?" Alejandro mused, frowning. "Oh, yes." He brightened again. "Beat it." His voice dropped in imitation of an old gangster movie.

Nick fixed Kate with an intense look and squeezed her hand. *Don't say anything.*

They gathered their backpacks and the grappling hook then backed away. Kate cast Alejandro and Gregor a last, cutting look. Vadz, she ignored entirely. Nick gripped her shoulder and stepped away, scattering dirt with his feet.

It was Gregor who called out then, surprising everyone. Maybe even himself, judging by the look on his face.

"*Czekaj*... Wait."

He squatted over one of the boxes, holding something in his hands. Nick was sure it meant trouble, especially when Vadz started muttering. But Gregor didn't even look at his captain. His eyes were on Alejandro as he showed the Venezuelan the object in his hands while tilting his head toward Kate and Nick.

Alejandro considered then gave a curt nod. His expression was disapproving but softer than before. Gregor straightened and mimicked a tossing motion that said, *Catch*.

Kate reached out instinctively when he tossed the object with a second fluid motion. Her hands closed around it, and when she looked down, she drew a sharp breath.

Nick did, too, the second her hands opened to reveal what it was.

The silver spider.

The spider was theirs.

It took Nick a second to process the gesture. Torn between acknowledging Gregor and despising his involvement in the whole affair, he hesitated. But Vadz was glaring, and the urge to flee returned. He prodded Kate forward and fell in step behind her, propelling her ahead while covering her back — just in case. They had to get away before Vadz decided on another demonstration of his power or before Alejandro thought the better of Gregor's little gift.

Nick forced himself to look forward. Let the treasure be Alejandro's problem. He could already imagine the Venezuelan and the two Poles arguing over their spoils. A small consolation.

Neither he nor Kate spoke as they pushed the dinghy into the water and rowed to *Aurora* with vicious strokes. The view widened, revealing the motor yacht anchored in a second bay.

"Figures," Kate muttered.

Nick just scowled, mute.

They weighed anchor in record time and disappeared around the corner of the island, then the next corner, and the next. The archipelago was a labyrinth in which they could find escape. The wind was up, so speed was not a problem, though a line of approaching squalls was.

A cigarette boat emerged from behind the northern islands, its engine droning as it made a beeline for Isla Chapera. Nick turned his back, concentrating only on getting away. A minute later, *Au-*

rora turned a corner, putting the entire scene behind them. The secret lagoon anchorage beckoned from fifteen miles away.

The sky broiled with angular clouds. He figured his face must have looked about the same. He could feel it in his pinched skin. At least the robbers would be more occupied with the treasure than *Aurora*. But there would be no police, no recourse. This was Panama, and the theft in question involved historic treasures. He harbored no delusions about finding justice, however that might be defined.

It was over.

He puffed out a long breath. That's what he'd wanted, wasn't it?

He stared blackly through the maze of islets, pushing away images of Charlie and a silver-lined future. There was nothing to see along the craggy coastline ahead but dashed hopes. He spun the wheel to turn south, murmuring to himself.

"To hell with the treasure."

Kate, like him, had been watching the contours of Chapera slip out of sight. "I can see them now, the bastards."

He could imagine the scene all too easily. Alejandro would be admiring his loot with greedy eyes as Vadz rifled through fragile pieces with disregard.

"God, I blew it," she groaned.

"We blew it."

"We failed Charlie," she whispered.

God, the truth hurt.

A long, mutual silence passed. Nick kept his eyes on the horizon, not quite ready to meet Kate's gaze.

"The treasure is lost. Not only to us, but to posterity." Her shoulders slumped. "It would have been better to leave it in the ground than let it fall into the hands of those crooks." Her fingers pushed at her temples, ten points of fury and frustration.

He shook his head, thinking of the long road behind them from the first time they'd opened Charlie's notebook in the San Blas to the riddles of Portobelo. The weeks alone in Boston... He shut his eyes tight. As far as he and Kate had come together, they had still failed.

Kate thumped the deck. "That treasure is bound for the black market and somebody's private collection. Never to resurface."

A second later, Kate's bowed head snapped up with a jerk. Her eyes bored into open space. Then she leaped to her feet and dashed below, emerging a second later with the cell phone.

What was she doing? Who was she going to call?

She fumbled to turn the phone on, then swung it around, searching for a signal. "Come on... Come on..."

"What are you doing?" He'd thought it through already. There was no one to call.

"One bar..." She swung the phone again, biting her lip. "Two bars." She stabbed a number into the phone.

"Um, Kate..."

She put her hand up, listening intently. "Come on... No! Don't let the connection go now!"

Even with five bars of reception, who would she call?

Kate gripped the frame of *Aurora's* spray hood for balance and held the phone high while studying the display.

"Two bars... One... two again."

She redialed, punching the numbers. Hope was written all over her face, from the folds of her brow to the thin line of her lips.

The dial tone was loud enough for Nick to hear. Then the connection clicked, and someone picked up.

"Hello, Stefan?" Kate shouted into the receiver.

Nick bristled at the name, but Kate put up her hand in an I'll-explain-in-a-minute gesture and spoke rapidly into the phone.

"Can you hear me? I think I have your Big One — *die Hammergeschichte.* Ready?"

Las Perlas archipelago
present day

Aurora flew south, back to her secret anchorage where the lagoon locked away the worst of the weather, if not anger or fear. No one followed them, but Kate still felt like holding her breath. Once Aurora was anchored out of sight, Kate waited, watching the narrow entrance of their hideaway.

Two days passed along with the storm that broke out not long after they'd anchored. She and Nick made a dozen trips to the rocky outcrop to check for other boats and only slowly recovered their nerves.

Those two days were full of unspoken words about what might have been — if, when. Then the phone rang, breaking the uneasy silence of the post-storm calm. A bird skittered away, leaving a trail of ripples over the placid water. Kate watched as Nick picked up the phone, considering for a long minute before choosing the green button instead of the red.

"Hello?" His voice was gruff. He listened, then held the phone out to her with a hard look. "It's Stefan."

She took it gingerly. "Hello?"

"Enjoying your quiet anchorage?" Stefan asked, sounding elated yet weary. "Sorry, but I have to be brief now. I have a deadline. Are you ready for the news?"

She nodded and scooted closer to Nick, just in case.

Stefan filled her in on the many developments pulsing through the Panamanian and world press. "It's been a busy couple of days."

Stefan started by relating the effects of his anonymous phone call to Coronel Lopez, head of Panamanian security forces.

"The good colonel was very helpful. He reacted just as I hoped he would — by dispatching two helicopters, three speedboats, and fifty armed men to subdue the terrorist cell reported to be plotting an attack on the Panama Canal from their island hideaway of Chapera. Imagine the colonel's surprise to discover only three foreigners with a cache of historic artifacts."

Kate felt the creases on her forehead relax. "Beautiful!" She angled the phone so Nick could hear.

"That is to say, they discovered three people on land," Stefan continued. "There was also a power boat approaching the island when Lopez arrived. This boat was apprehended and discovered to be manned by thugs from a cartel."

Her throat went dry as she contemplated another near miss.

"Coronel Lopez declared it 'a great day for peace in our nation.' His only comment on the fact that the bust seemed to have been a false alarm was this: 'There are no false alarms in the war on terror.' A good line, no?" Stefan laughed.

Tipped off by yet another anonymous call — Kate caught an audible swell of pride in Stefan's voice — to the private number of Doctor Rodrigo Ortiz, Panama's National Institute of Culture was able to intervene in the subsequent investigation, making sure the seized artifacts were properly cataloged and the discovery site secured.

"Doctor Ortiz is already making arrangements for a full examination of the treasures by a team of international archaeologists. The research was expected to take months. But listen to this — they already have an interesting sponsor."

"Who?"

"The bestselling author, Richard Brewster Lewis," Stefan said. "You know him?"

Kate rolled her eyes. Yes, she knew him, all right.

"Brewster Lewis pledged a percentage of the profits from his latest book to build a special exhibit hall for the collection."

Nick snorted something about hypocrites while Kate sighed.

"However, I regret to report that your Venezuelan acquaintance seems to have gotten off lightly," Stefan continued.

She felt Nick's shoulder tense beside her. "What do you mean?"

"He is something of a...*a schlaue Fuchs*..." Stefan said, slipping into German. "A sly fox. He managed to convince authorities that he was rescuing the treasure from a band of North American art collectors."

"What?" she screeched. "He's calling me an art collector?"

Stefan pressed on. "He seems to have — how do you say? Hit it on well with Doctor Sofia Hidalgo. You remember her?"

Well, she clearly recalled Stefan's hands outlining her curves.

"So our Venezuelan fox seems to have evaded the law, though he may have trouble with an angry cartel. But I have to admit, this man has style."

She was about to protest, but Stefan rushed on. "The two Poles are still in custody. They may have genuine ties to the cartel."

"Serves them right. At least Vadz." She did feel a twinge of regret about Gregor, hoping he wouldn't languish in a Latin American prison.

"There is also the mystery of a dead Frenchman found near Balboa Yacht Club."

"Dead? Who?" Her blood ran cold.

"The captain of the *Persephone* — the drug boat. Remember that? It seems the cartel got their revenge. Did you ever meet him? Maybe in the San Blas?"

Not that she recalled. But still... she shivered. Had she gotten off more lightly than she imagined? She'd always thought that as an honest, careful person, she could avoid trouble. But sometimes, trouble came looking for you.

Stefan's end of the line beeped with another call. "You'll have to read the rest in my email." He finished with a curtailed good-bye.

She'd given up nail-biting years ago and yet found herself gnawing as she opened her email account. While she waited for a connection, she took one of Nick's hands and clasped it to her chest, eyes shut tight for a long moment of contemplation.

Sometimes, adventure wasn't all it was cut out to be.

The email opened at last.

Dear Kate,

I have been very busy, so I am sorry for only a short Note now. My Articles shall appear in the next issues of Der Spiegel. I will send them to you soon. Here, I attach for you, some Articles from the Press.

I don't remember if I said Thank You. Here is the first of a thousand times: Thank You for the Big One.

I will be in Panama for approximately another Week. Any chance for Brunch?
Kind regards,
Stefan
PS - That was a bad German joke. You can bring your friend to Brunch, too. I will try to be nice to him.

Kate found herself edging closer to Nick as she clicked on the attached links.

"Priceless Treasures Rescued," she translated the title of a news article from the Panamanian press.

The article featured a photo of an exultant Alejandro, standing oh-so-close to Doctor Sofia Hidalgo. Their hands and shoulders brushed as they displayed the condor figurine for the camera.

Venezuelan rescuer delighted to present artifacts to curators of the National Institute of Culture, the caption read.

Alejandro really did look delighted, squeezed in beside a grateful-looking Doctor Hidalgo. The two of them edged the owlish Doctor Rodrigo Ortiz out to the periphery of the photograph.

"I only did what any dedicated art lover would do," the Venezuelan was quoted.

She shot Nick a sour look and followed the next of Stefan's links.

Cartel's Revenge: Missing Captain Found Dead. The face in the old, grainy photo looked familiar, though she couldn't quite place it. She didn't want to, either. After summarizing the article, she breezed on to the last link.

A headline in *USA Today* jumped off the screen. *Canal Strike A Near Miss!*

The breathless account was accompanied by a dramatic rendering of an unidentified "Treasure Island" off the coast of Panama, crowded with arrows and stick-figure soldiers in a play-by-play of the terrorist bust.

"Where do they get this nonsense?" she wondered out loud.

Nick bumped her ribs with his elbow. "I don't know, but, hey. You did it."

"We did it," she corrected him. The treasure hadn't been lost to posterity, after all. "We did it."

She smiled as a glow of satisfaction spread inside.

Chapter Twenty-four

Into the Sunset

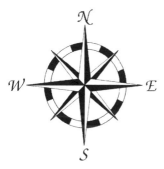

Bay of Panama
January 1914

The sun rose over the boundless Pacific, all gold, all warmth.

A new day. A new beginning.

Charlie pushed off Esperanza Island in his little rowboat, setting off across a calm and friendly sea. A mockery of its former self, if he did say so himself. Not far to the north was another island that might be inhabited. That was as good a place to start as any. He dipped the oars and put his back into it. With each stroke, his treasure slipped farther and farther away.

So much effort, such grand dreams, all dashed to pieces. What was it all for?

The sun glinted off the water, and he smiled for the first time in two days. Why? Because he'd found the answer at last. Now, he knew what it was all for.

The adventure.

It wasn't how many dollars you departed this life with; it was the stories you had to tell. That, and the way you handled the obstacles in your way. He could practically hear his father's voice speaking those words. The man was full of gems like that. And he was right.

The more Charlie rowed, the more philosophical he grew. Life wasn't about collecting riches. It was about living. Learning — sometimes, the hard way. Friendships, too, he noted — something he would treasure more conscientiously in the future.

An image of Mercedes came to him, standing proud and alone. That woman was full of dreams — a lot like himself. Then he thought of Edgar's shining face welcoming the arrival of each daughter like the greatest treasure of all.

You'd make a good father, Edgar had once said with no irony whatsoever.

Charlie had laughed him off at the time, but now he caught himself imagining the unimaginable. What would it be like to have a child? A daughter, even? Maybe if you started young, you could train a female to be only half as difficult to deal with. Keep her away from big hats and lace. Give her useful things to learn from instead, like hammers and pulleys. Properly raised, a daughter might even be brought to learn something practical. Like carpentry. Metallurgy. Maybe even architecture.

Charlie considered this alien prospect for another few oar strokes before laughing out loud. He paused just long enough to watch the image skip and scatter like sunlight bouncing off the sparkling sea.

"You, Charlie Parker, are a man of adventure, not a family man." He said it aloud then drew in a long breath of salt air, sniffing for some hint of his destiny.

Sitting up a little straighter, he drew longer, more purposeful strokes. He wasn't just rowing away from a lost cause. He was moving toward a new, as yet undefined challenge. A new adventure.

His mind was already scheming. There was more silver in the world, after all. Nevada was packed with the stuff, for starters. Then there was always Europe. South America. He could go anywhere, do anything. He could build bridges or canals. Maybe another breakwater. Of course, his future adventures would be accompanied by the requisite misadventures. The two went hand in hand, like mismatched dance partners always stepping on one another's toes.

He wasn't an oracle. He couldn't see what lay ahead. The only thing clear to him was that Fortuna didn't want the silver to leave Panama.

At least not yet.

He smiled a mischievous smile and rowed on.

"To adventure," he whispered into the wind.

Las Perlas archipelago
March, present day

Nick scanned the secret anchorage, contemplating another perfect sunset. *Aurora* nodded on a ripple in the water, agreeing with his sentiment. A pelican folded its wings in midflight and rocketed into the water with a splash. A moment later, it came up, gulping a fish as if nothing spectacular had just happened.

Nick watched the bird shake, swallow hard, and fly away. It faded into the distance, and his focus pulled back to Kate, tucked next to him in the cockpit. The squally weather had passed. A promising zephyr whispered through the lagoon, and it felt like his cue to finally ask the only question left burning his mind.

"So, where to next?"

He forced a casual tone while steeling himself for her answer. He knew what to expect. The directive to head to some uncharted territory far, far away. A new horizon, a new adventure. Well, if that's what it took, he was game.

Kate took a long time considering before leaning into him with a surprisingly fierce hug. "Right here is good," she said in a muffled voice.

He sat very quietly while something inside him followed the bird high into the sky.

"I'd be okay spending the rest of the season here in Las Perlas," she murmured.

God, did he like that plan. A modest plan, for a change. *Aurora* could zip in and out of Panama City to provision, and then they could return to these unspoiled islands.

"We'd have lots of nice, quiet time to get the boat ready for a Pacific crossing," he hinted.

But Kate just made a noncommittal gesture. "Maybe next year."

Everything was falling into place. Him. Kate. *Aurora* was just the vessel — they were the glue in their own relationship, and it seemed to be a pleasingly permanent compound.

The silver spider lay on the table in front of them, together with Charlie's necklace and the coin Nick had pocketed. They had been admiring the pieces while musing over the rest of the treasure for the past few days.

"It's not so bad that we didn't get the treasure," he said. Maybe it wasn't destined to be a boon. More of a curse. In a way, he was relieved to have it off his hands.

"It would only have brought trouble," Kate agreed with a very slight sigh, touching the spider.

They sat in silence for a moment, digesting the words. He looked at her hands, still scratched from digging and scraping, then back at the spider. It was lovely and fragile, yet ugly and powerful. Who knew what it signified?

"What are we going to do with it?" he ventured.

Kate looked at the piece, then at him. He already knew her answer. Soon, it too would join the cultural ministry's stunning new collection, an anonymous donation entrusted to the honorable Doctor Ortiz.

"Never mind," Kate said with a slight waver in her voice. "It's the journey, not the destination."

Nick nodded, figuring Charlie would agree. "The challenge, the mystery. And anyway, we still have the boat. And we have each other," he added, leaning into Kate.

She burrowed into him with a hug and a very long kiss.

He let his eyes travel the length of *Aurora* to the serenity of the cove beyond and sighed, truly content. A sigh that wasn't for the coin or the balmy temperature or even the beautiful view. It was something far more important than that.

"Lovely place, Panama," he murmured to himself. "Lovely place."

* THE END *

A Note from the Author

Thank you for reading *The Silver Spider!* I hope you enjoyed it and that you will please leave an honest review on the platform you purchased the book from.

The Silver Spider was conceived during the season my family and I spent cruising both coasts of Panama aboard our 35 foot sailboat before heading out across the Pacific. Though I wasn't consciously scouting locations for a novel at the time, our experiences in Panama eventually inspired *The Silver Spider*. Where better than the crossroads of two oceans to interweave the stories of a seventeenth century Spanish soldier, an engineer working on the Panama Canal in 1912, and modern-day sailors? I hope my love for Panama and its contrasting landscapes and cultures comes through in this book, and I hope my passion for the sailing lifestyle (with all its ups, downs, and zany characters) does, too.

While many of the characters in this story were inspired by a combination of colorful characters of the sailing world, no single character matches a real person on a one-to-one basis. Locations and sailing details, on the other hand, are all based on personal experience. Every effort has been made to remain true to the history of Panama, although fictional characters have been inserted for narrative purposes. So while the details of colonial Portobelo and canal-era Balboa are all based on carefully researched facts, some characters and story elements such as Pedro, Charlie, the silver spider, and the secret anchorage at Viveros are products of an imagination fed by many a starry night on the open ocean.

You can read the story behind *The Silver Spider* on the blog section of my author website, **nslavinski.com**. Those posts discuss locations, the real-life spider that inspired the silver spider, and the process of weaving historical fact and fiction.

About the Author

Nadine Slavinski is a sailor, author, and archaeologist turned teacher. Her travels and work experiences inspire both her fiction and non-fiction books.

Nadine Slavinski's first career as an archaeologist brought her to excavations in Peru, Costa Rica, and Germany. After discovering the rewards of teaching young visitors about these sites, she made the switch to education. She has been teaching in international schools since 1996.

A lifelong sailor, Slavinski lived aboard her 35 foot sloop, *Namani,* for four years with her husband and young son. The family sailed from the Mediterranean to Maine via the Caribbean and later, from Maine to Panama and across the Pacific. Her fiction works place memorable characters in exotic locations and vividly capture the fun, fascinating world of globe-trotting sailors.

Slavinski enjoys writing for sailing magazines and is the author of several books, including *Pacific Crossing Notes, Cruising the Caribbean with Kids, Lesson Plans Ahoy, and Lesson Plans To Go.*

Visit Nadine's website **nslavinski.com** to find interesting and informative blog posts, links, and resources. That's also where you can contact her or sign up to receive updates on new content and releases.

Made in the USA
Middletown, DE
25 June 2018